IN THE LAND OF DABBLERS

In the Land of
Babblers

by Mark Rosenfelder

YONAGU BOOKS
www.yonagu.com • Chicago • 2014

Cover illustration by Edwin Perales

© 2014 by Mark Rosenfelder.

All rights reserved, including the right to reproduce this book or portions thereof in any form whatsoever, except for review purposes.

ISBN 978-1500786342

Guide to Pronunciation

Cuêzi
c, g	always hard, as in *cash, get*
x	palatal fricative, as in German *ich*
s	never voiced (as in *rose*)
r	approximant (like English, not American r)
f, v	bilabial as in Japanese *Fuji*, Spanish *haber*
a e i o u	usually have standard Continental values
ā ē ī ō ū	high even tone, double-length
â ê î ô û	low or falling tone

Caɖinor:
	as in Cuêzi, except—
ȟ	velar fricative, as in German *Bach*
t̂, ɖ	voiceless and voiced th, as in *think* and *this*
k	uvular stop, like the Arabic q in *Iraq*
f, v	labiodental, as in English
e, o	closed (as in ¡*Olé!*) in syllables with final consonant, open (as in *pet, caught*) in all other syllables

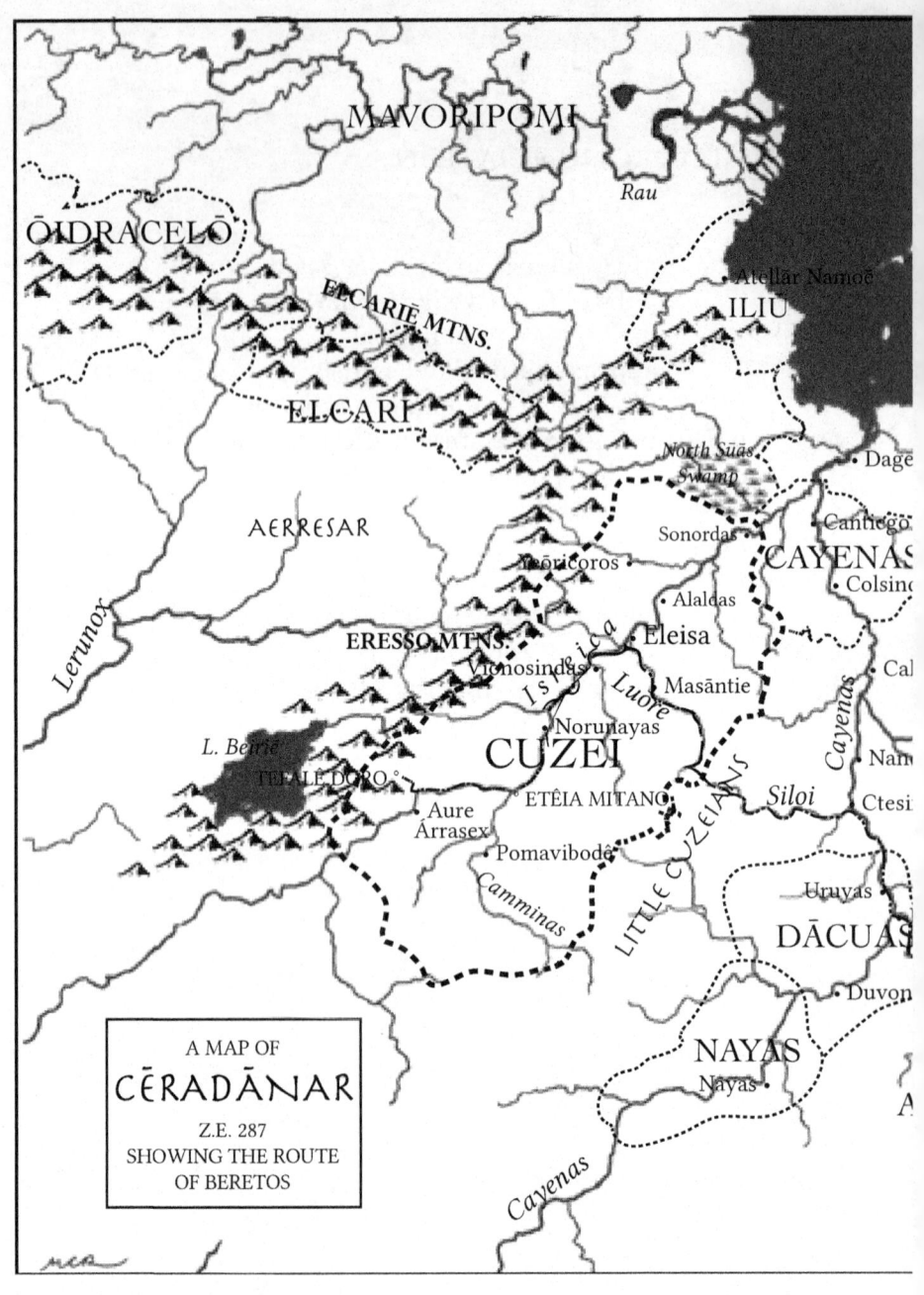

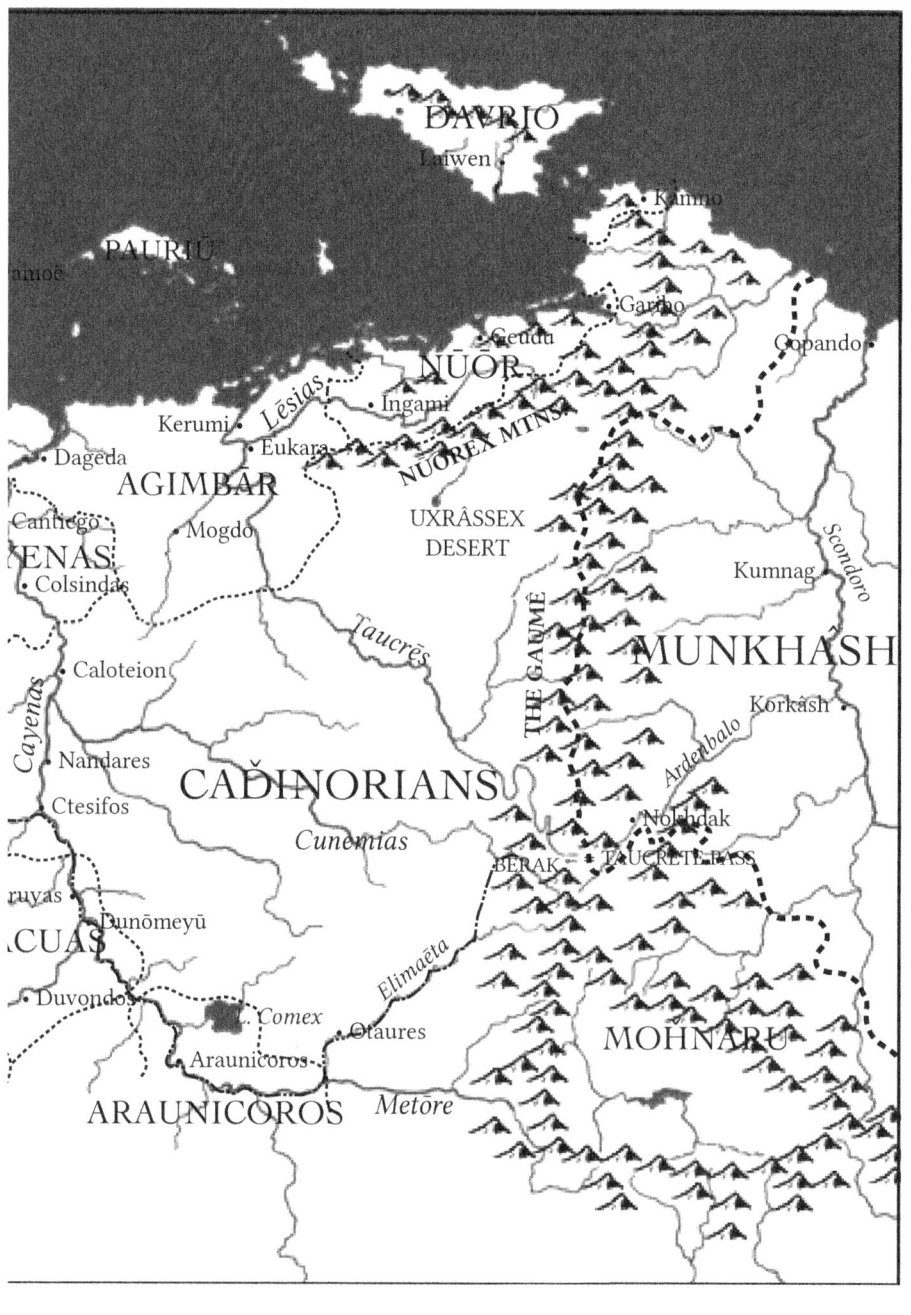

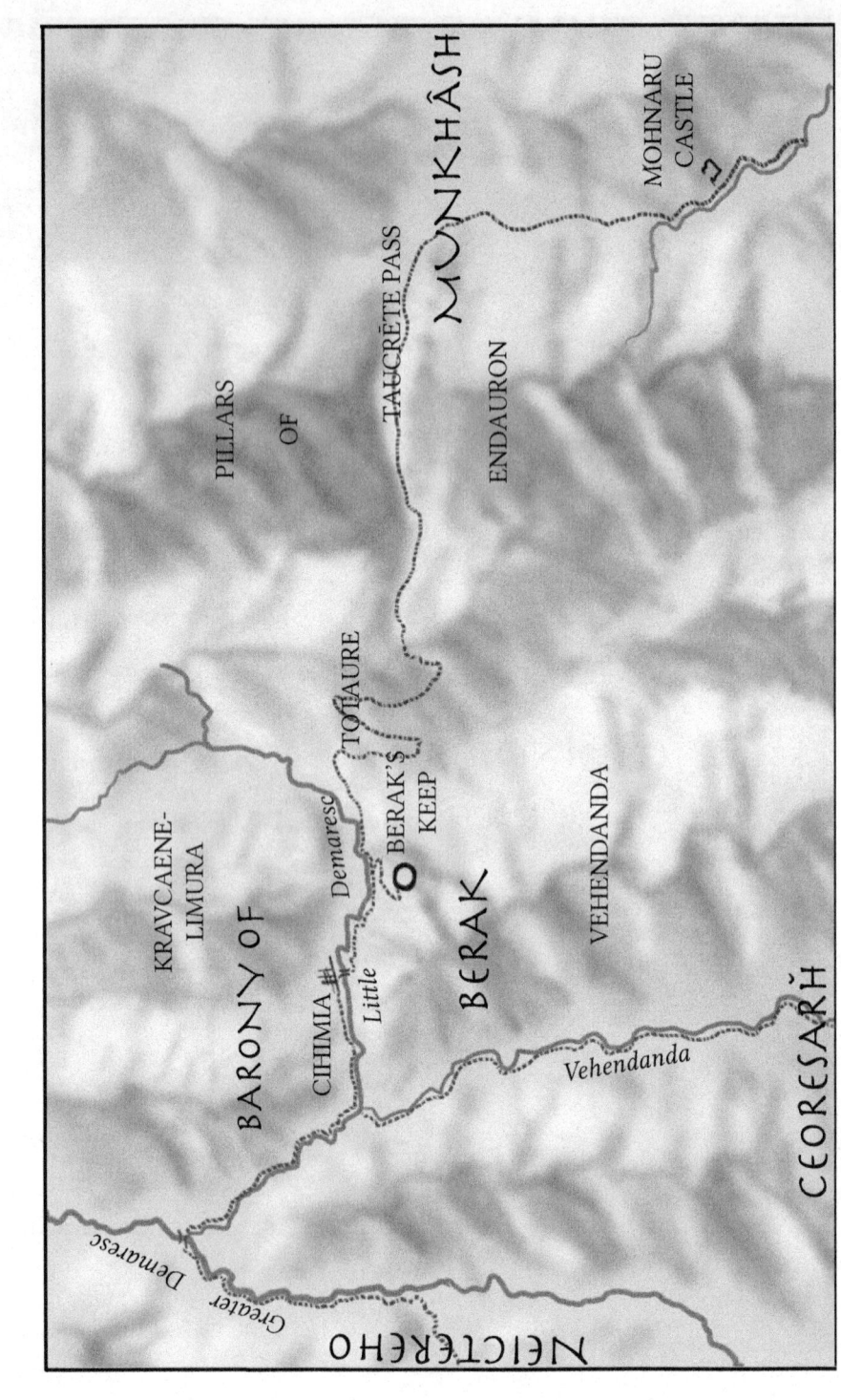

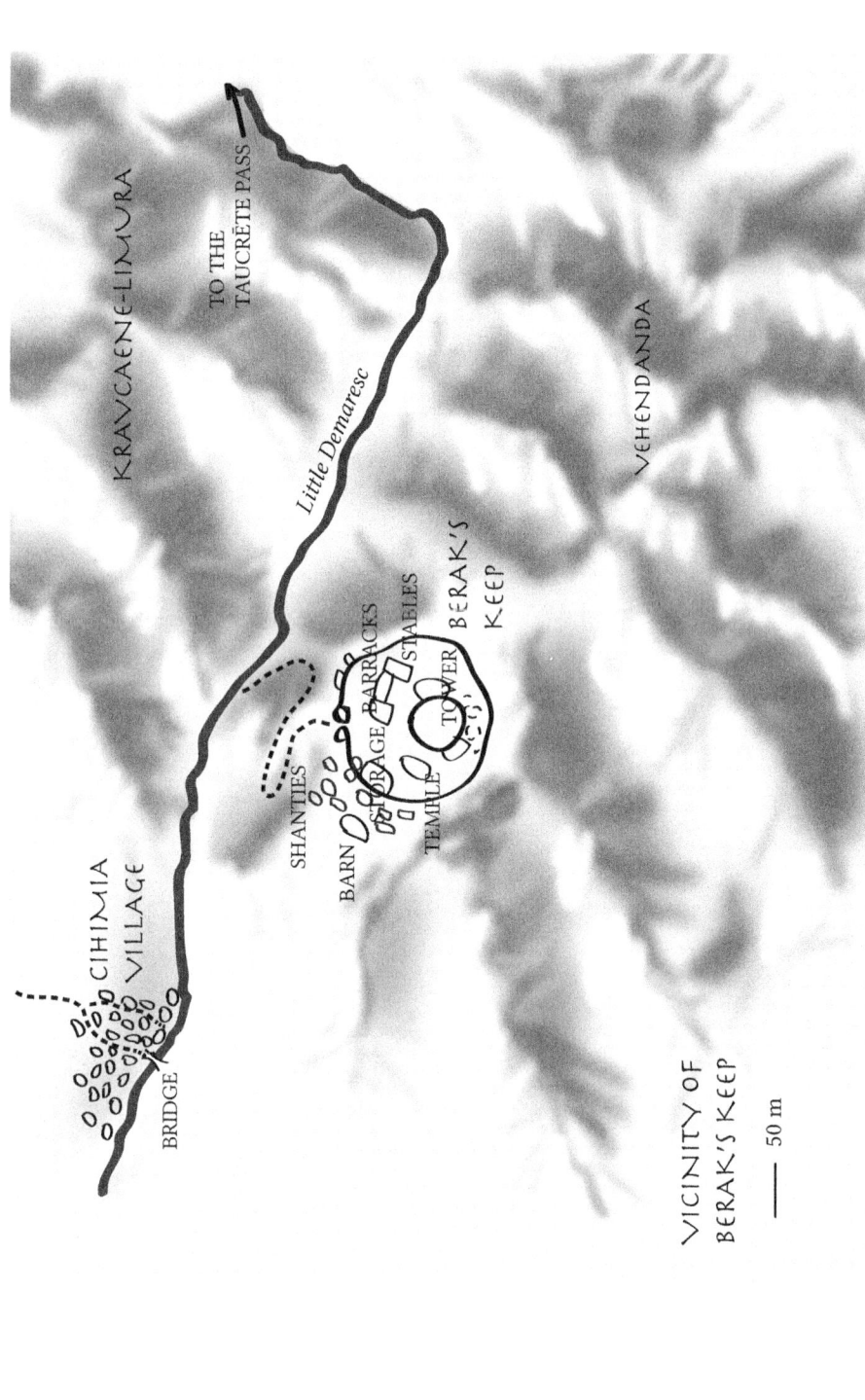

1 · T̄Z̧ḺϬZ̧ꓘXΔ · *Baezāuco*

In one of the epics the Sojourner is taken before a king, who demands of him that he tell a story; if the story pleases him he will spare his life. And he warns him that he is not easy to please.

The Sojourner asks how he ought to begin his story. "At the beginning," says the king.

"In the beginning," the Sojourner said, "Iáinos Onnamêto created the Uncounted Worlds, and hung Almea from the deep of stars."

"That's not the beginning of a story," objected the king. "That is simply the Count of Years."

"That is the beginning of all stories," replied the Sojourner.

I also have come before a ruler, and my life and more depended on what story I told. I did not avail myself of the Sojourner's stratagem, which was to tell the story of the world from the Creation onward; as the story could never end, the teller could not be executed. But I felt myself in the sandals of the Sojourner then, and I feel so now, because like him I am conscious that no story truly has a beginning, except in Creation, and I do not know where to begin.

But these words recall another of the epics. "I do not know where to begin," complained the maiden of the tower, when she was rescued by the rider in black, and asked her story. Samīrex advised her to begin by stating her name, her place of birth, and her lord. This was very much in the nature of Samīrex, who though kind was always blunt, and had no poetry in him.

But it is good advice. My name is Beretos, I was born in Tefalē Doro, and I am devoted to the service of the Lady Caumēliye of the House of Etêia Mitano.

The reader has undoubtedly heard rumors of the events I will relate here: that the household of Zeilisio lived in scandal and impiety; that I amused myself during my life among the Babblers with debauchery when I should have instructed them to know Iáinos; that Zeilisio has already sentenced me to death; that the Munkhâshi have already sent their forces into Cēradānar, the Plain; that the Munkhâshi are insignificant and nothing to disturb our councils; that Lady Caumēliye took peasants for lovers. All of these tales are lies.

In this book you will learn the truth— the full story of the trial and imprisonment, what happened to Oluon, how the Babblers see us, and whether the Taucrēte Pass truly protects us from the demons.

2 · dlΛZNĮ ÇᴬƆᴬ · *Tefalē Doro*

Tefalē Doro is in the high mountains, almost at the edge of the Cuzeian lands; there are Babblers living not far away, and they would come to our House now and again, seeking to trade the gems they found in the mountains, and the goat-hair ponchos they made, for our knives and arrow tips and fired stoneware. They know none of the arts of housed fire. I used to wander through their camps, smelling the strange foods over their open fires, and listening to their language, whose intonation I can still recall; they have many consonants, which burst in the mouth like nuts. These were not the Babblers whose tongue I learned later.

My father was in the service of the Lord Árrasos Tancī, and so we lived in the House. He was in charge of the granary. He disbursed seed grain to the peasants, watched over their crops, received the harvest, and distributed it to each household and to the Glade. He kept the granary's accounts and was responsible for them to the Steward and to Lord Tancī.

All the children of the House grew up together. My constant playmate was Caumēliye, who was the daughter of Tancī, and had the same age as myself. We were taught together, the two of us, by the old Knower: reading and writing, history, the epics, the holy Books, drawing, figuring, and the lyre. It would not be thus in Eleisa or Norunayas, I know. There, I would have been sent to a Glade school, and Caumēliye would be taught by tutors. But we were far from any large town, and Tancī was glad to have me educated. From an early age he saw intelligence in me, and he found that his daughter learned better if she had someone to compete against.

When we were not studying we played together: climbing trees, swimming in the little lake in the woods, running races, hiding from each other in the fields, watching the cows and the pigs, bothering the servants. Or we would simply find a hiding place, in the barn, in the woods, in the cellar, and talk, or play at epics.

One day, when we were both twelve years of age, we were lying together in a meadow by the woods, looking at the ants. We have a type of ant in the mountains which feeds on leaves; it ventures out of the nest, finds a young plant of a certain type, and brings the leaves, cut into little pieces, back to the anthill. We were watching the ants leaving the nest, and returning with pieces of leaf many times bigger than themselves in their jaws. It could be seen that it was an awkward job for them; they were continually dropping them and picking them up again.

"What do they need them for?" I wondered. "They don't eat the leaves."

"For decoration," she suggested. "They bring the leaves back to their wives."

"There was a marriage in the village the other day," I told her. "Two of the peasants got married. One is named Bāuros and the other is called Niōre. They were married in the Glade in the village, and everyone walked with them to their new house."

"I know Niōre," she said. "Her cousin is one of my mother's maids. She's very young, I think. The peasants marry young."

"When we grow up we'll get married," I said.

"No we won't," said Caumēliye. "I'm already going to marry someone else."

I felt utterly betrayed. "You're lying," I said.

"No I'm not," she said, unoffended. "His name is Zeilisio and he's a Lord in another House. We'll be married when I'm seventeen. It's been arranged for I don't know how many years."

"You never told me that."

"It doesn't interest me," she shrugged.

"Why should you have to marry him? You can marry me instead. If you want I can rescue you, like Antāu rescued Isiliē of the Castle Forest."

"I can't marry you, because you're a servant, and I'm a Lady," she explained.

I had known we were not equals, but this was the first time I understood what it meant.

"Where does this Zeilisio live? What does he look like?"

"I don't know. I've never seen him."

"I hate him."

"Don't say that, or Eīledan will punish you."

"I don't care. We've always been together. I don't see why you have to get married anyway."

"Do you love me, Beretos?" she asked.

"Of course I do," I said, fighting back tears.

"I love you too. I always will, no matter who I marry," she said, and gave me a kiss. And I believed her, but I knew that something irrevocable had changed; that things would not be as before, not starting with her marriage, but from this minute forward.

It was not long after this that I began my apprenticeship in swordsmanship, riding, and tracking. It was Lord Tancī's decision; he had heard much about me, no doubt, from his daughter, and decided I was worthy of a good education. From this time I saw less of Caumēliye, as she began instruction in the management of households, accounting, and statecraft. She also received instruction in riding, but from the wife of Tancī's horsebreeder, instead of from his Master of Arms. We still were taught literature, music, and theology together by the old Knower.

The first day of my training I fell off the horse five times, and it is told of me that I have scarcely improved my knack since. The sword was great excitement— holding my sword high I felt myself as one with the epic heroes— but also great frustration. Swordsmanship is a matter of strength and discipline and knowledge whose acquisition takes long years. At the start, one wants to fight battles glorious, to sweep one's blade through cursed foes. Instead I was given a wooden stick and trained to make endless figures in the air; and when I was finally allowed to spar, it was only the dance of control, in which one stops just short of the trainer's stick, and actually touching his wood rates a punishment.

This was the way our fathers were taught the sword, and if one has sufficient perseverance, and if the supply of whippings is plentiful, it is effective enough. I do not teach this way myself. I start with lunges and parries, which are precisely the strokes the beginner is longing to try, and is sure he knows already; and I allow the student to develop his own motivation to learn these skills truly, by realizing that he is spending his time being struck rather than striking.

However, I was immediately captivated by woodcraft. To wander the woods with Sūro the Master of Scouts, learning the names of plants and trees, which ones can be eaten, which are medicinal, which yield poisons or dyes; what are the messages of the animals, how they can be caught or tracked or killed; how to make shelter, how to find water, how to read time by the moons and the seasons by the stars— all this seemed effortless, like reading; it was not like schooling, but like learning the answer to a riddle, or like uncovering hidden treasure. But it was most like learning a language; as there comes a moment when the babble becomes words of speech, so the rush of signs and sensations of nature becomes an open scroll— as Sūro said, a communication from Almea itself, or from Eīledan.

It is indeed Eīledan who speaks through the earth, because the earth never lies, nor does it mislead. If you see the track of a deer, then a deer has been there; if the sky is gray and the wind is from the east, it is going to rain, while if it is from the west it will not; if there are white-shouldered eagles, then rabbits also are to be found. And Almea gives her lessons to anyone who has eyes to see. The squirrel makes her nest proof from the rain with large flat leaves; she is teaching us how to build a shelter, if we are lost in the woods. The coyote stays upwind of the beaver he is after; this is how we can capture her ourselves.

If only the tongues of men once learned were so innocent of deceit!

I tried to share this knowledge with Caumēliye, but this was ever more difficult. To begin with, her clothes were no longer suitable for walks in the woods. This did not bother her any, but the women who were in charge of her scolded her if she had ruined her clothes with mud and grass. Later they scolded her even if she had gone out with old clothes. Wandering Eīledan's earth was apparently not something a Lady did.

I must record here some of the words of Sūro.

"When I am finished with you, I will be able to leave you naked in the trackless desert, and you will get on as well as if I had left you by your hearth."

"Fear is only lack of knowledge. Learn the ways of the snake, and you will know how to live with her."

"If a man had a thousand years of age, he would still not have learned to hear all that the earth is telling him."

"As the voice of the earth is the voice of Eīledan, what you receive you take from Eīledan's hand. Do not kill an insect or bend a leaf, without necessity."

"There is no animal who is so small that he has not a lesson for your eyes."

Sūro was an old man, whose hair was feathery and his voice soft; but his back was as straight as an iron rod, and he had all his teeth. Unlike the Master of Arms, or the old Knower, he never struck me, or even raised his voice to me; in fact, I can recall only one rebuke he ever gave me— and for that reason, perhaps, it is engraved on my memory as if in steel. I had told him that I liked walking in the wood, because I could pretend I was one of the epic heroes. "Foolish boy," he said. "You deaden your mind with thoughts of stories written by men, when all about you is a story which is written by the finger of God."

There is a paradox here. When I was with the Master of Arms I felt at every moment the great weight of my ignorance, all that I did not yet know about arms and their use. Yet today I am a better swordsman than he ever was. I never felt overwhelmed by Sūro's knowledge; I felt as easy with him as with an old friend. But he is my master still; I will never possess half of his lore and skill.

I first heard about Munkhâsh and the amnigō from the old Knower. In his soft voice, hard to hear, he told how Amnās, imprisoned deep in the earth, was informed by trolls of the formation of Cuzei, and in response directed the amnigō to create Munkhâsh.

When I heard this, what stuck in my mind was the tunnels used by the trolls. Did they still exist? Would the trolls come up from the earth to attack us? The Knower said no, Eīledan protected us.

When I was older, hearing the same story, I wanted to know where the entrance was— was it nearby? I didn't want to meet Amnās, but it would be thrilling to go down and at least get a glimpse of him. The Knower's information on this, as with all the really interesting topics, was unsatisfactory.

The holy books had little more to say about the amnigō, but they reappeared in the epics— along with the Giants and Ogres, the warrior women, and the dragons. Often I played at heroes with other children. If I was alone with Caumēliye I would choose various heroes, but she was always Xetīsiē, the warrior Lady betrothed to Celōusio's brother-in-law. When there were other children, some of them would have to play amnigō, and this was never popular, because they always lost to the heroes.

Too often we are assured that if Munkhâsh comes into Cerādanār, Eīledan will protect us. But is this teaching sound?

8 · IN THE LAND OF BABBLERS

Doesn't the Count of Years record that in the last of the wars fought by the iliū and the amnigō, the whole former world was destroyed?

3 · ᏣᎢᏂᏣᏛᏣᎠ · *Zeilisio*

When she was seventeen, the Lady Caumēliye was married off to the House of Etêia Mitano; but I did not lose her; I and two of her maids went with her, as her personal retainers.

Etêia Mitano is about sixty lests from Tefalē Doro— less than two days' travel, on our good roads, but as different in climate and situation as any two Houses could be in Cuzei.

It is on the great River, the Isrēica, which is indeed more than a lest wide at this point. Ships and boats pass by at every hour, and the great city of Norunayas is only a day's journey downstream; so the House is grand and busy and prosperous where Tefalē Doro is small and isolated and sleepy.

It is also warmer, since one has descended so far from the mountains. It is very hot in the summer, and its winters are by no means severe; and it is flat, with only rolling hills rather than mountains. It is well-populated, the land a blanket of fields with only the occasional small woods, where Tefalē Doro is lonely amid thick forests and mighty mountains. Even the animals and plants are different.

I disliked the country, and longed for my old surroundings. Contemplating the endless fields of grain, only ennui moved me, while the wide river seemed to me, accustomed to chattering mountain streams, as tame and dull as a sleeping dog.

The House itself was immense. It had been built two centuries ago, and each Lord had enlarged it, till it was as big as the entire village back in Tefalē Doro. It was in built in stone, painted white, with brown tile roofs, and extended itself on a hill above the river like a cat stretched out on a ledge. Stairways and gardens spilled down the hill to the water's edge.

The House's lands extended for six lests along the river, and an even larger distance away from the river, to the east. Perhaps four thousand peasants lived on these lands, as compared to the three hundred of my native House.

Zeilisio was close to thirty years of age when he married, well-built, tall, with a prominent nose, carefully groomed moustache, and an eternal half-smile. Tancī you could meet in his old clothes, striding through the muck of the pig barn, or laughing over his dinner, with his feet on the table and a flagon of beer in his hand. Zeilisio was never seen without fine and spotless garments, made not in the House but in Eleisa; and it was as if he had likewise clothed his spirit in some fine raiment, which could not be soiled with loud laughter or strong emotion.

My first meeting with Zeilisio was not propitious.

His chief steward, Corumayas, was bustling about finding places for us. It was easily seen that we had completely upset the old man's sense of order: half the residents of the House, it seemed, had to be moved. Those who had lived in our rooms had to be moved elsewhere, respecting their rank; this meant displacing yet others, and so on. And Corumayas, it appeared, was one of those who is rendered confused, dilatory, and irritable by stress.

Cauméliye was satisfied with her rooms, but not with ours— they were too far away. She sent me to ask the steward to change them. I found him in a hallway, talking with Zeilisio.

"I tell you, my Lord, everyone has been informed where they are to go," he was saying, petulantly. "Nothing more is possible."

"But you can't put Mavoros next to Sanūr. We'll have a war. There'd be bloodshed in a week, and think of the tedium of hiring replacements."

"It is impossible, O Zeilisio. It is impossible."

"Excuse me, Corumayas," I burst in. "The Lady Cauméliye has sent me to ask you for a small change in our rooms. She wishes them to be closer to her chambers."

Corumayas stopped, stared at me, and opened his mouth several times without saying anything. Zeilisio laughed.

"I believe you are the one who is Cauméliye's favorite servant," he said, looking me over. "You look like a mountain lad. Bulky."

"I'm from the mountains," I said, stupidly.

"Where have you put them, Corumayas?"

The steward explained, not without mistakes. I learned later that he had not laid a line on paper to assist in this project, and his memory was severely taxed.

"Yes, well, use the rooms next to hers, why can't you? Who have you got there? Never mind, never mind. Tell me when you have it worked out. What do you do, lad?"

"I don't know," I said, not understanding the question.
"You don't *know*?"
"I don't know, O Lord," I corrected myself.

He laughed. "Not a favorite for your brains, are you? What are your skills? What shall we do with you?"

"My father was in charge of the granary."

"I see. Would you like to work in ours, then?"

"I don't know, my Lord."

"Do you know reading and writing?"

"Yes, my Lord."

"Hm. And figuring?"

"Yes, my Lord."

"Very good. Corumayas could use some help with the books." Corumayas looked surprised at this, and then annoyed. "Would you like that, lad?"

"I don't know, my Lord. My Lord, I can also use the sword."

"The sword? Iáinos! Well, you won't need it to cut up the numbers. Corumayas will tell you what to do, later."

And he strode off with Corumayas, who began expostulating with his master as soon as they were out of earshot; about what, I could well imagine.

One day I saw birds flying back and forth over the river— large birds, the size of hawks or eagles— and I laughed; there were no mice or rabbits to be found in the watery waste, were there? But in this thought I recognized something unfaithful to my master Sūro— nothing of Almea is without a story to tell, he would say. So I watched the birds with more attention, and saw that they dove now and again into the water. From where I stood I could not see what they found there; I walked down to the water's edge. Even here I was an arrow's flight away from the birds, far out over the water; but now I could see that they were catching fish. From this I learned that the creatures of Etêia Mitano could speak to me, if I paid them heed.

There was none with the wisdom of Sūro to explain their ways to me, but I began to ask questions, and observed as well as I could, and spent many hours walking through the fields and the woods, and alongside the river, or swimming and boating in the river. I learned the names of the animals and the plants that were new to me, and saw how they lived and grew, and what the signs of them were. And though I never knew or loved this river land as I did my homeland, I did come to love Etêia Mitano, and learned how the voice of Eīledan speaks in more ways than one.

I worked with the books of the House for something over four years. At the same time I served my Lady whenever she required me, and continued my instruction in swordsmanship, as I had found a soldier of Zeilisio's guard, Oluon, to instruct me.

It was not, at first, easy to understand the books, in part due to my own inexperience, but mostly due to Corumayas' ways. He had no ability to put things in order. If he wrote something down, he lost it. If he tried instead to commit it to memory, he forgot it. If I asked a question, he answered a different one. If I made a suggestion, he rejected it, because "that isn't the way it's done."

Mostly he relied on other people for the information needed for the present crisis. If a peasant brought in a certain amount of grain, he might write down the amount, after weighing it, or he might attempt to rely on his memory. Needless to say, when the time came for the peasant to withdraw grain for his winter bread or his spring planting, there was no record of how much he was entitled to (but Corumayas was sure it existed somewhere, and we had to waste a quarter hour searching for it); we had to rely on the peasant's own recollection. Naturally, the peasants had large memories; the result was that the granary stocks always ran low. Corumayas' solution was to buy grain from a neighboring House.

He did not see the relationship between his accounting practices and the grain purchases; he said (when I or Zeilisio asked) that he bought grain late in the winter because it had always been done that way.

The Houses along the river are so large, and have so much commerce, that it is useful to trade using a medium of exchange, usually gold, silver, sheep, or grain. In Tancī's House, by contrast, each family has a traditional task which is its responsibility and its contribution to the community. Etêia Mitano is too big for this system to be applied; instead, each family owes the House an amount of silver (the amount varies according to the size of the family, how long it has been established at Etêia Mitano, and how much land it farms). This amount can be paid by labor, by providing animals or vegetables, or out of silver the family earns by selling crafts or services to the other villagers.

Now, the great advantage of this system is that it virtually runs itself. Even in so small a House as Tancī's, there were endless disputes about whether a family had fulfilled its responsibilities, and a great fuss if additional work needed to be done and no one could be found to do it. But a House of ten times the size can be run with half the disputes, using a medium of exchange; and if there is extra work the House simply pays for the work to be done.

It is simple, that is, unless Corumayas is in charge of it. First, he neglects to keep proper records— he forgets to write down some man's labor, or pays out coins without recording it, or records it wrong, or under another man's name, or as a credit rather than a debit. The rates for various goods or types of labor are fixed in his head, and he will not change them, no matter what crises it causes, because "that's the way it's always been done." So, for instance, we pay half what our neighbors do for wagons, and the result is that none but the most desperate will build wagons for us, and the ones we get are of bad quality; while our price for oranges is too high, so that everyone wants to sell us oranges. Oranges were a luxury forty years ago, but now every House grows them, and the price should be lower.

It was hopeless, of course, to ask questions such as whether a particular peasant had discharged his debt or not, or how much the House was spending on vegetables, or whether we were making money selling olive oil to the cities; they could not be answered.

Corumayas resisted every change— he could not see the point in it. I made a book with the name of every peasant household in it, so that we could keep track of what grain was his; Corumayas refused to use it. Zeilisio made him use it, and now I repented of the idea, for every page became a nightmare of illegible scrawls, erasures, errors, corrections, corrections of corrections.

Slowly, but accompanied with reverses or quarrels which made me think each time of stalking out of the House and seeking my fortune in Norunayas, I acquired greater and greater control over the accounting. Though stubborn as a turtle, and impervious to a direct attack, Corumayas lacked persistence, as well as aggression. He would protest if he saw me doing something the way it wasn't done here; but it would not have entered his head to look into what I was doing when he was not around. He continued to deal with the peasants when he saw them, but he had other responsibilities and I did not, so I saw them more, and he soon found it easier to let me do most of the work.

The peasants themselves became my allies. They knew that with me there would be no disputes over payments, no hunting through scraps of paper for a lost memorandum, and no trouble with the weighing (Corumayas had terrible trouble with the scales). They started to avoid Corumayas and come to me— the honest ones, at least; the others had learned how exactly to take advantage of the old steward. Once this pattern became noticeable, my Lady ordered Corumayas to send all the peasants to me, on the pretext of saving the steward's time.

It was astonishing how smoothly the books could be managed, without Corumayas' help. For each peasant, I now had a page on which the grain he brought in and took out was recorded; there were no more disputes (once they learned that I was both honest and hard to fool), and no necessity for buying extra grain. Similarly, I kept records for each family, recording what labor they did for the House or the value of the goods they sold; and records also of our trade with merchants or other Houses. Once all was in order I trained several of the educated House servants in the recordkeeping, so that I could be free to accompany Zeilisio or my Lady on journeys, or to do whatever other work they asked of me.

I saved the House much silver with these changes; and Zeilisio ordered that it be used to make improvements in the peasants' villages. We built new walls and roads for them, and dug a new and deeper well, and whitewashed the walls of their houses, and bought each household a new copper pot for their cooking. We were certainly the best run House in the region; indeed, our villages were always accumulating peasants mislaid by nearby Houses.

I had not liked Zeilisio when I came to Etêia Mitano, and I could even say I had resolved to continue disliking him. But I found this difficult, and ultimately impossible. It is one of the laws of Eīledan, perhaps, that one comes to love those whom one pleases; and as I rose in Zeilisio's estimation I found him pleasant rather than condescending, amusing rather than mocking, and civilized rather than overrefined.

He also had a library, and it was impossible for me to use it without getting to know him better, for we both are great readers. Inevitably we came to talk about what we read, and sought to discover what books we had in common, delighting in our mutual likes, and arguing over our disagreements. I have always best loved the epics, and books of travels, and the holy books; from Zeilisio I learned also to appreciate books of philosophy, and works of theater, and manuals of leadership, politics, or strategy.

My only sorrow was that a true friendship did not seem to develop between Zeilisio and my Lady Caumēliye. He treated her kindly, and gave her all she asked (though she was never covetous or dainty); but they spent little time together, and conversed little.

Once a week they sat down together and discussed the affairs of the House; for he trusted her more and more with the running of the household (as he trusted myself with the running of the lands). The rest of the week they generally did not even dine together; and for that matter, he was often abroad, doing business in Norunayas or Aure Árrasex, or taking part in the Council at Eleisa, or merely visiting friends. Caumēliye was free also to travel, and we often visited Eleisa, or went home to Tefalē Doro; but she seemed to prefer to stay in Etêia Mitano.

It was therefore something of a shock when I learned, about two years after our arrival in the House, that Caumēliye was pregnant with her first child. I watched her growing belly with a naïve confusion; I was completely unable to imagine Zeilisio taking her in his arms, or laying together with her; I fancied that he had given her this child chastely, unmediated by touch.

4 · XZ ʇ7ʎιɴϹɑι · *Caumēliye*

The peasants chose the worst possible moment to come. Zeilisio was returning from Eleisa with guests, and my Lady took this as a signal to clean, fix, and rearrange everything in the House, although she had kept everything in order in the two months he was gone, and he wouldn't notice. I was rushing to and fro giving orders, prodding the lazy, soothing slights, sending boys on errands, untangling confusions. The Lord's children had to be forcibly separated from the servants' and dragged to the bath. And on top of this a flotilla of Little Cuzeian merchants had sailed up the Isrēica and besieged the House, demanding lodging, and claiming in heavy accents that Zeilisio had sent for them.

There were two dozen of them, plus their women and children, breaking flowerpots, trampling on the garden, clamoring for food, getting in the way of the servants. Corumayas, ruined, ran to me to complain: "What answer shall I give them, O Beretos? You don't know what they've done to the patio. They say the Lord asked for them!" I had food and wine given to them, on condition that they go back to their boats. If they were indeed merchants, I told them, and not bandits who had heard of Zeilisio's absence and thought to profit by it, they could return in two days.

During such crises Corumayas is well pleased to defer to young Beretos; as soon as they had gone, he went back to arguing about the arrangement of the dining room.

"That isn't the way we do it," he insisted.

"You can't have the table that way, the light will be in the Lord's eyes," I said.

"That isn't the way we do it," he repeated. "I have served this House since the day I was born, sixty years ago," he added.

I was thinking of new ways to insult age and loyalty when a boy ran in, with the news that a delegation of peasants had arrived, and wished to be received. Leaving Corumayas to have his way, I went to the front gate, where fifteen or eighteen peasants were waiting. It was easy to tell which were the aggrieved parties: two men stood well forward, arms crossed, with angry expressions. I hoped it was not the House which would receive the heat of their anger. The others stood back and watched, with an air of expectation. The Cuzeian peasant is a born spectator.

They waited, with difficulty, for me to speak. "What is it?" I asked.

"My name is Banimu, O Beretos," said one of the aggrieved parties, a young man, heavily muscled, as they say, except inside the head.

"And I am Dulāu," said another, older, weatherbeaten, with the wary eyes of a man who expects every meeting to turn into a fight.

Their seconds did not introduce themselves. They waited, patiently. "Lord Zeilisio is not yet returned," I ventured, finally.

"It's the Lady we seek," said Dulāu.

I knew that Lady Caumēliye was friendly with the peasants, but I was surprised that they would seek her out. "She's very busy," I said. "She's arranging the House for the Lord's return."

"Tell her that we have a dispute which she must settle."

I looked them over again, without learning anything. "I will ask if she will see you," I said.

"She'll see us," commented another villager, as I went into the House.

The Lady was in the young lord's room, watching as a maid cut his hair. I took in the rare sight of Vissánavos at the same time clean and sitting still, and told Caumēliye of the peasant's request. As the villager had predicted, she got up at once.

We stopped first at her dressing room. She was already dressed to receive her husband, in a simple but elegant gown, covering one breast. Over this she put on a blue and white sash (her own colors), with a purple counter-pattern (Zeilisio's), and also changed her sandals. I observed that she was dressing more formally for the peasants than she dressed for high society.

"I like peasants more," was her comment.

She stepped into the courtyard, and the peasants all went to their knees, and began talking all at once even before rising.

The Lady stopped them with an upraised hand. "Who is it who wishes judgment?"

Banimu and Dulāu stepped forward. The Lady turned toward Banimu.

"Thank you, O Lady. Know that I am Banimu, of the Near Left Glade in your Lord Zeilisio's House. I am here to plead against this man, who stole my woman, and despoiled her, although everyone knows she belongs to me."

"Ulōne strike him! He's lying!" cried the older man.

"Hold, friend," commanded the Lady. "When Banimu is finished I will hear you, and not before."

This produced a smirk on Banimu's face, which faded immediately when Cauméliye turned back to him. "There is a certain Little Cuzeian maiden who has come to the Near Left Glade, and her name is Lonae. I have given her many gifts, even a sheep of her own, and everyone in the village knows that she is mine. Yet today this man surprised her in a field, and lay with her."

He stopped, but then, seeing that the Lady's eyes were still upon him, he said, "O Lady, I am wronged by this man, who has taken what does not belong to him, like a thief. As for Lonae, she has condemned herself, because she didn't return to me."

"What do you ask of this House?" asked the Lady.

"Under Eīledan, for the chastisement of these sinners, whipping and scarring and drowning," said Banimu, hotly. "Also I should receive back my sheep." He looked fiercely at his opponent, then at the Lady, in worried beseechment, then at the ground.

The Lady turned to Dulāu, and he began to speak: "O great Lady, now you will hear the truth. I am Dulāu, and I am from the Ashwood Glade in your Lord's House. Yet I was not born in this House, but in Eusuvas in the lands of the Little Cuzeians."

"You are a Little Cuzeian then, O Dulāu?"

"No, Lady, I am Cuzeian, but my House ruled a tribe of our little brothers in Eusuvas. In that place I was a prosperous man, and I bought a slave, for outside the Houses and Cities of Cuzei it is permitted to own slaves. Her name was Lonae, and I lost her to a raid of Babblers. The remainder of my substance was lost in the drought, and I came to your Lord's House, one year ago. Only today did I learn that this same maiden was living in the Left-hand Glade, and that this man had her. If I lay with her it was my right to do so, because I purchased her lawfully, and she was taken from me."

"Do you know the laws of this country, Dulāu?" asked the Lady.

He did, and changed his argument at once: "O Lady, I was speaking in figures. I am her benefactor, who raised her like a father, and moreover I am a shaper of metal and wealthier than this other man. I left her with a necklace and a jeweled earring which are worth much more than any sheep."

"What do you ask of this House?"

"O Lady, under Eīledan, that this Little Cuzeian be returned to me, and that Banimu be whipped for his presumption."

The Lady asked a few more questions, learning that the maiden had been living in the House for four months, having escaped from her Babbler masters, and that she had seventeen years. Upon learning this fact, anger came to her cheeks; the villagers noticed this, and whispered among themselves; Dulāu and Banimu shifted from foot to foot, and looked anxious and hopeful and vindictive all at once.

When Caumēliye spoke it was not to the two of them, but to the peasants standing behind. "O Cuzeians, how shall I judge these men? So quick to ask for punishments under Eīledan's name, and so loath to learn Eīledan's commandments! Here is a woman who has escaped from slavery and barbarians, and one man takes her to bed for a sheep, and another takes her in the field, because he once owned her flesh!"

She turned to the two men, who now looked worried. "Where is the maiden?" she asked.

"She is in the Near Left Glade," said Banimu. "She fled from me when I discovered her sin, and I did not pursue her there."

"If a woman is safe only in the Glade we must make the Glade bigger," said Caumēliye. "Bring her here to me," she said to me.

I walked to the village, taking with me two of the villagers who knew her. I found her in the center of the Glade, clinging to the altar with both hands, as if she expected to be dragged from it. She was a pitiable sight: her clothes torn, one eye bruised, her face wet with tears.

"Come with me, child," I said. "The Lady sends for you. No one will hurt you."

When Caumēliye saw her, she came up to her, took her hands gently, and kissed her as she would receive a guest. Tears ran down her cheeks.

Banimu seemed to feel a need to defend himself. "I meant no harm, O Lady. I should not have hurt her, but anger from my guts overwhelmed me. I will make recompense."

The Lady rose up and faced them; again she was a judge, unmoved and mighty. Dulāu and Banimu looked at her, abashed.

"You who have come for judgment, be ye judged!" she said. "My word is this, that one of you take this maiden to be your wife, and be a husband and companion to her. And as it is written in the *Teaching of Kings* concerning despoilers of virgins, the other shall be as a father to her, and give to the other her dowry.

"Will you decide among yourselves which shall marry her, or shall I?"

Dulāu looked up. "She is very pleasing to me, and I will take her as my wife."

Banimu looked relieved. "It is just, O Lady," he remarked. "It would be like bearing a heavy weight for me."

Caumēliye turned to the maiden. "O Lonae, I will not force this judgment upon you if it is not your will. Is it pleasing to you, that you should marry Dulāu?"

"Yes, thank you, O Lady."

"Is he a kind man?"

"He's always been very kind, Lady."

Caumēliye kissed her, and gave her hand to Dulāu.

"Dulāu, you are master of Lonae no more, do you understand me? We have no slaves here. Your wife is your companion, and as you treat her, so Eīledan will treat you."

"I understand, O Lady."

"And you, Banimu, you who are glad of my decree; do not forget her dowry, and be glad that I have not asked of you what you asked of Lonae, both life and property."

"I am glad of it, O Lady."

She dismissed them, and they knelt once more before her. I marveled to see these two men, who had come to the House seeking gain and blood, and who had instead been served with rebuke and obligation, look at the Lady with something like worship in their eyes.

"How long have you been a judge over these folk?" I asked, when they had gone.

"Oh, for a couple of years," she said. The time of the drought: she had visited the peasants often, bringing food for them, laying hands on their sick. Evidently they had not forgotten her.

"They must see great wisdom in you," I suggested.

She shook her head. "No, people don't seek out a judge for wisdom, but for vindication. They never think that they may be proved wrong."

"Do you worry about making the wrong decision?"

"Of course, but if I feel great confusion, either I don't know enough about the case, or the wrong lies on both sides."

"It's an honor for you," I suggested. "Not all Ladies would be trusted so by their people."

"It's an honor I'd gladly pass by," she said. *"Those who judge, Ulōne judges."*

That was from the Wise Sentences, but I could not ask what she understood by it, for at that moment we spotted Vissánavos, the young lord, who had found his way to the garden in his clean clothes, and covered them and himself with dirt. We advanced upon him to administer cleansing once more.

5 · ⊂I⊂C-⊂IᴧZ · *Neni-nemā*

It is high time that I begin to speak of the Babblers.

There are many kinds of Babblers, but the ones I know best are those who live in the East, who call themselves Cađinorians. They are a simple people, without writing, or cities, or art, except for those who live very close to us, and have by imitation acquired some of our arts.

The Cuzeian who ventures into the land of Babblers experiences a progression of loss. The clean and well-built Houses of his homeland, the mighty cities, the lifelike sculptures, the theaters, the books, the direction stones, the schools, the prosperous and patterned fields, the full granaries, the comforting inns, the ships on the rivers, the canals, the bridges, the brick roads, the mills, the forges, the terraced hills, give way, first to poor imitations, and then to nothing at all. Glass, steel, and silk become rarer and dearer, and their place is taken by pottery, brass and iron, wool and fur.

This is well known, and the Cuzeian is saddened but not surprised by it. What surprises him is the difficulty of the Babblers' lives. There are no Houses to order the lives of the people and assure their prosperity; the Babbler lords have no duties toward their subjects. Each man raises his own crops, as he sees fit, so that one sees wheat on one half-acre, and oats on the next, and apples on a third, in a hodge-podge. A quarter of the yield is taken immediately by the lord, and another share half that size by the godspeakers; it is easy to see that what is left is barely enough to live on, especially as they have more children than we. One often sees hunger among the Cađinorians, as never among us, except in the worst years of plague or drought. And each Babbler and his family must work hard, and do all their work themselves. Unless he is very well off, he has no draft animal, so he and his wife turn the earth with a spade, or a stick; there is no House to bring by the common animals. If his house burns, or disappears in a flood, he must rebuild it himself.

Their houses are of wood, or clay, depending on the region. Stones may be embedded in the clay, but I have never seen them build entirely of stone, as the least among us does. The floors of their houses and the streets of their villages are bare earth, muddy when it rains, and dusty when dry. The resulting dirt does not seem to bother them, and it is well for the Cuzeian that the first Babblers he sees will be along the rivers, because only these wash themselves with any regularity. The smell of the villagers of mountain or forest is overpowering.

Compared with the Cuzeians, they are a short and heavy people, dark-haired like us, and about the same color, when they wash (not like the deep brown Babblers to the north, or the pale pink ones far to the south). Their children are thin and numerous, and outside the towns they run naked. In their larger towns (which are not so big as a small Cuzeian city), most of the children and many of the adults seem sick with various diseases. I have never seen so many cripples, lepers, and blind men as in Araunicoros.

Some of the blame for this I lay at our door, because they live in towns in imitation of us, but we have not taught them how a city should be built, how to pave the streets and keep them clean, how to keep the people fed. In the countryside or in the forests they are healthier and happier.

In the west, along the Cayenas, there are Caðinorian princes who live in cities, and have laws, and taxes, and hire Cuzeians to record their chronicles for them and write their poems. Deeper in their lands, however, they have only barons, who are the sole law of their little realms; and in the forests isolated Babblers live, owing allegiance to no one.

The first of the principalities one comes to, traveling from Norunayas, is called Ctesifos. It is situated on an island at the confluence of the Cayenas and the Silois. For this reason, perhaps, its prince seems to think it very secure. A single catapult on the hills overlooking his town could reduce it to sticks in half an hour. He has built a wall around the city— of wood! On our way to the Gaumê, Oluon and I dined with this prince, and told him (what we had heard from a merchant), that some of his neighboring princes were getting tired of his raids and claims against them, and were planning to come and burn his city down. The news seemed to alarm him. All the princes in this region belong to one family, which is called Scadrorion. There is not much harmony in this family, however.

Going south from Ctesifos, one comes to the very lands described in the Count of Years, when the dukes Inibē, Voricêlias, Calēsias, and Lēivio led the Cuzeians into Cēradānar, conquering it from the weak and divided Metailō. From the holy book one expects to find Dunōmeyū as a strong walled city, a city whose leader was so proud that he stood up to the four dukes assembled, and for his foolishness lost both city and kingdom. But it is a small, dirty town, filled with shabby wood houses; it is now the seat of our little brothers' kingdom of Dācuas.

To the north there is a more substantial Caḋinorian state, called Cayenas, after the name of the great river. The nobles in that land all speak Cuêzi, and they have abandoned the worship of their gods to worship Iáinos. The land of Agimbār on the sea belongs to another kind of Babbler; these are the unconquered remnant of the Metailō who once possessed all of Cēradānar.

To the east of Dācuas, now following the Metōre, is Araunicoros, the first conquest of the dukes, now ruled by a Caḋinorian prince, because of the rebellion of Inibē's lineage against Iáinos.

The Caḋinorians see nothing wrong in the sale of human flesh. They raid other Babbler tribes for slaves. They do not sell our little brothers, because we would not stand for it, but they do go to war with them, and the Little Cuzeians must ransom any prisoners which have been taken from them. Sometimes the very poor sell their own children into slavery, or a ruler with great debts will sell some of his peasants; worse yet, some men will sell their own wives to strangers to sleep with. To do the Babblers credit, one sees these shameful things only in their towns, and not in the countryside. We cannot say this of our own little brothers.

If there is one thing in which the Caḋinorian outshines us, it is in his hospitality toward the stranger. Among us the stranger, unless he is a pilgrim or on a Council's errand, is something suspect: why is he not safe within his own House? We do not like to see foreigners encamped on our fields or living among us, except perhaps in our largest cities. The Caḋinorians, by contrast, are friendly with strangers, and make it a point of honor to invite them in, and share their bread with them, and hear their stories. When I have asked about this, they say that any stranger might be a god in disguise. This is something Eīledan might truly reproach us with, I believe. In many of our Houses a traveler, even if it were the Sojourner himself, would find no welcome.

6 · ZOZ ʇCCXᴀOᴀb · *Araunicoros*

I had learned the Babbler tongue, Caðinor, from certain Babblers who came regularly to trade with us. I had no sort of schooling in the language; that is not how one learns a Babbler language. One must simply hear it spoken, ask questions, and make attempts to speak it. I used to wander among their caravans, and I made some friends among the younger Babblers, and from them I learned the language.

One day I was present at a meeting for trade, and I heard the Babblers talking among themselves— laughing at us, because they were cheating us; a new source for tin had been discovered, and the Babblers had acquired many loads for a low price, and were selling it to us at the high prices that had formerly obtained. I told Zeilisio what they were saying, and after a suitable interval he told the Babblers that we were not interested in tin after all— that we had enough.

They were troubled, as they had thought the deal as good as done; they asked if the price was the objection. "No, it is simply that we do not need the tin," said Zeilisio. "I am sorry if I had talked about buying it; my mind was wandering."

"Well, what shall we do?" asked the leader of the Babblers, clearly discomfited. They had already unloaded their wagons of the heavy metal. "We have come scores of leagues to bring you this tin; what can we do with it?"

"Ah, that is too bad," said Zeilisio, sympathetically. "Simply out of friendship, we will take it from you at half the price you have mentioned."

Zeilisio was impressed with the assistance I had rendered to him, and from this point onward he entrusted me with many of his affairs, whether at Etêia Mitano, or with other Lords, or at Eleisa; and when the Council heard word of agitations in Araunicoros, Zeilisio recommended me to look into it.

It sounds very fine to be a Council's Emissary, with plenipotentiary status; what it meant was that I was sent alone, armed only with a letter from the Council and some of Zeilisio's gold, to discover why the Cuzeian Resident, one Ambrisio, was unable to maintain peace in our relations with the Babblers.

Araunicoros is the remotest of the Cađinorian principalities, on the Metōre east of Dācuas. It is close to a city in size, with perhaps ten thousand inhabitants. In Araunicoros one sees the wealthiest of the Babblers, and also the poorest. It is a center for trade: Babblers from many lests around come here to acquire goods from Cuzei, or horses from the south, or even gold and slaves brought from the eastern mountains. I first met the Munkhâshi here— they come to trade, bringing iron and silk and slaves. There is a lake near here, called Comex, which is the earthly home of the Cađinorian gods, and Araunicoros is the center of their worship. There are parts of the town which are entirely inhabited by godspeakers. People come from afar to see them when they need to hear the words of a god.

I wondered how Ambrisio would react to my visit, which was after all something of an official rebuke; but it did not at first seem that my fears were justified. Ambrisio, a bald and fleshy man in his late forties, took me to his bosom like a son. He pressed me for news of Eleisa, asked what books I had brought with me, and devoured conversation on the epics or the latest theater. "Among the sons of Cuzei who make it to this shantytown there is an oversupply of merchants, mercenaries, runaways, and adventurers," he told me. "How marvelous it is to talk with a truly cultivated young man."

He dismissed all attempts to discuss the political situation— "a topic of infinite tedium," he assured me. The Babblers were sons of violence, he told me, yet I should take nothing that they said very seriously. And he steered the conversation back to matters of Cuzei.

I accompanied Ambrisio to the Prince's palace, to dine with the Prince and his court. The palace was made of wood, like his subject's houses, but unlike them had also a floor, so that it was appreciably clean. The Prince himself, Garđom, was a proud and handsome young man, whose most striking feature was his large black moustache. He greeted me in serviceable Cuêzi, and I responded in Cađinor, which seemed to please him.

We were shown into a large, dark hall, where several dozen men and a few women were already seated at long tables, laughing and talking noisily. Soup was put before us— a greasy broth with large chunks of vegetables and a large slab of pork on the bone in each bowl. A flagon of wine was placed between every few diners. The Babblers began to sup, noisily and without grace.

Ambrisio summoned a servant girl, and sent her off somewhere; she soon came back with a knife, a spoon, and a cup. "Can't stand to eat like savages," he confided to me.

I shrugged. In Tefalē Doro, which is on the very edge of Cuzei, we also eat without knives. I picked up my soup bowl and began to drink, quietly; and when I wanted wine I asked the nearest man, in his own language, to pass the flagon to me.

"You eat like a man," my neighbor approved, his words contrasting strikingly with his appearance: hair uncombed, clothes made of skins, face liberally smeared with grease.

"Why should I not?" I asked.

"I thought you Cuzeians all ate like him," he replied, jerking his thumb toward Ambrisio. Like a woman, I thought at first he meant; but the Babbler women ate in the same way as their men. Like an elcar or an iliu, then, perhaps— a non-human.

"How do you think it will be when we raid you? Do you think you'll fight like men?" he asked. His tone of voice, if not his message, was friendly, inquisitive.

"Are you planning to go to war with us?" I asked. "Are we not at peace?"

"It's not a war," he said, dismissively. "A raid only, to teach you the respect of us, and to see if you can fight as well as you give orders. We're tired of you. But tell me. Is it true that in your country you people sleep on beds of gold, and that your women bear their children through their mouths, instead of the *bacou?*"

But at this point Ambrisio stole away my attention. "Rescue your poor companion with civilized speech," he pleaded, peevishly. "I don't gabble this filthy language, as you do."

We had a few moments together with the Prince, after the dinner. I gave him my thanks for the dinner, which he graciously accepted.

Ambrisio seemed out of sorts, and his words to the Prince were tinged with annoyance. "Prince, you and I have to talk.

Some of our traders have been beaten in the public squares. You know that we can't stand for that."

"I have heard of the misadventures of these drunken men," the Prince replied. "Yes, let us talk. You may call tomorrow."

"I'll come by in the afternoon. Please be sure to be there. I'm not going to wait for you. Let's go, Beretos."

As soon as we were back in the street, his anguish burst forth. "Hideous time. I'm sorry you had to sit through it. You see what kind of animals they are. Did you hear the gall of that princeling? Drunken men! It's probably his own men who did it, too. They'll do what they can— what we let them. They're envious little vermin. What's needed is firmness— and force, if it comes to that. I wish I had a few more Cuzeian men of arms here— good ones, I mean. So many of our men here end up going native."

Knowing that Ambrisio would be visiting the Prince in the afternoon, I resolved to call on him in the morning. He received me in an inner room, warmed by a fire and made comfortable with cushions. A boy added a log to the fire, placed a bottle of wine between us, and a bowl of nuts and fruit, and sat off to the side in case we had need of anything.

The Prince studied me for a long time, and then spread his hands. "You," he said, in Cuêzi, "I cannot figure out. You are not unwilling to eat with your hands, and speak our language, so you are like to the merchants and mercenaries your country sends us. But you're evidently of noble blood, and not rude and greedy as they are. Yet you have not the arrogance of the Resident. I don't know what kind of Cuzeian you are."

"My prince, I am neither noble nor peasant, but a free man, and perhaps Cuzei has sent you too few such. I have been sent by the King's Council, to enquire into the relations between our realms, and right any wrongs that there may be; and if these wrongs be on our side, they will be corrected."

"These men of yours must stop making a nuisance of themselves," he said, at once.

"The drunken men?"

"As you say. They're petty traders, worthless men, who violate our laws and get into fights— with worthless ones of our own, I'll say it myself; but it's their provocations that get them into altercations, and your Resident will say nothing to them."

"Where can I find these men?"

"My master of troops will show you how to find them."

"I'll have them reminded of the laws of Eīledan," I promised.

"I'm obliged to you," he said— warily, I thought; no doubt he expected some demand to be placed upon him in turn.

"And have you no other grievances? There is nothing else which threatens the peace between us?"

The Prince now looked quite uncomfortable. "There is nothing," he said, with such a palpable air of shamefulness that I almost laughed aloud. I could see that the Prince was an honorable man; it was a humiliation for him to dissemble.

"If there is nothing, my Prince," I said, switching to his own language, "then the rumors that I have heard, that a force is being prepared to wage war against our land, must be completely unfounded."

"Where did you hear that?" he said, sharply.

"At your dinner table," I said, smiling.

He was silent for some time; his expression moved by degrees from anger, to calculation, to amusement. Finally, he filled my glass, and raised his own to me. "We are used to keeping secrets simply by speaking them out loud," he said.

I smiled, and waited.

"There are those on my council who are impetuous," he said, at last. "I am not long on the throne, and they wish to see me feared and respected. I have love for your people; that is why I have learned your tongue. But it is good, sometimes, for a younger brother to test the strength of his elder, and show him that he too is a man."

Now it was my turn to be silent, as I considered what to say. Kind words and a listening ear had enabled me to discover the truth of things here; but to put them right would take skill and action; and as I had no men with me, and only the authority the Resident and his guards allowed me, the action must be quick and sure.

It came to me how to approach the Prince, in the way that he would understand.

"My prince, there is wisdom in what you say," I said. "The elder secretly delights to see the manhood in his younger brother. Still, there are those in our own Council who would see in it a cause for war, and for the sending of armies, and I cannot foresee the outcome of it, except that many would die, and understanding between us may decrease rather than increase. Would it not be wise to attend first to the quarrels and disorderliness which shame our nations, and to take more counsel before embarking upon any rash action?"

"I am willing," said the Prince. There was relief in his voice; but then he seemed to think of something unpleasant. "Your Resident," he said. "I warn you that it is not always easy for my men to control themselves in his presence."

"I quite understand," I said.

What was necessary was, to me, as obvious as the sun: I must get rid of Ambrisio for a few weeks, or months; but I had no idea how to do it.

However, it proved easier than I thought. That very day I found Ambrisio extremely vexed, and learned that he was fretting over his upcoming interview with the Prince. For all his talk of firmness, he found no pleasure in it, or for that matter in any serious exercise of his office. His Residency offered him a life of importance and ease, though in an alien land; and substantial profit as well, through trading. He was visibly relieved when I told him that I had already talked to the Prince, and he himself offered the suggestion that there was no reason for him to go to the palace as well.

Later I suggested that he take advantage of my presence to take leave of Araunicoros for some time— heading perhaps for Dācuas, the nearest Little Cuzeian kingdom; it was not Cuzei, but there would be Cuzeians there, and books, and plays, and proper houses and food. I said nothing of the political situation in Araunicoros. To my surprise, he agreed. He organized an enormous caravan for the journey, and took two score of men with him, which makes me think that he aimed to satisfy commercial as well as cultural longings that went unfulfilled in Araunicoros.

With Ambrisio out of the way the situation could be corrected fairly simply. I had the "drunken men" disciplined, and sent some of them away. I also organized athletic competitions, and bouts of swordfighting and wrestling, in hopes of satisfying some of the Caðinorians' desire to test our strength, as well as to amuse our own soldiers, who were as much alienated by Ambrisio's refined ways as were the Babblers. And I dined frequently with the Prince, both at the palace and at the Residency, to set an example of dignified and friendly relations.

Within two months there was no more talk of raids, and no more outlandish questions about the humanity of the Cuzeians. I felt I could return safely to Cuzei.

I gave my report to the Council, which was well pleased that I had extinguished the flames of discord, but chose to dismiss my chief suggestions: that Residents be required to speak the language of the kingdom in which they would reside, and that worthless men who valued gold above Eīledan be prohibited from trading with the Babblers. Such ideas were naive, I was told, sometimes brusquely, sometimes with sadness. It was difficult enough to find men who could be entrusted with a Residency, without requiring that they gabble in foreign tongues as well; and as for worthless men, it was better that they should gravitate to the lands of the primitives, which suited them, rather than cause trouble at home, and impossible to prevent them from doing so anyway.

Only Zeilisio, and a few other Lords, listened to me with open hearts; but indeed I learned more from them than they from me, for I was not the first to have thoughts such as these. "These Babblers are more important than even Agimbār or Dācuas, because they are between us and Munkhâsh," they told me. "Yet we send them fools such as Ambrisio."

The Council did accept one of my recommendations— that another Resident be found for Araunicoros. It seems that there was no very high opinion of Ambrisio in Eleisa; he had been shipped off to Araunicoros, in a sense, to get rid of him. Now the Council simply ordered him to remain in Dācuas, as an assistant to the Resident there. I received a letter from him from that city— a perfectly friendly letter, complaining of the poor cultural life of Dācuas— "but then Araunicoros had none at all, as I'm sure you remember."

Ambrisio did have some friends in Eleisa, among them Inibē of Alaldas; and they conceived an enmity for me as a result of this incident. They already hated Zeilisio, and he them; his name for them was "the idiots."

7 · ⁊Ḷd⁊ᒐ△⁊Zb · *Mētudomas*

"What next?" asked Oluon.

"The Dance of Swords, number 26," I replied, panting. Oluon nodded and raised his sword. We paused, tensely: the prayer to Ulōne. (The swordsman does not address Iáinos or Eīledan, who are too far away; only Ulōne, who is inside us, is close enough to offer assistance in a fight.)

Then the air was filled with flashing bronze. Sword clattered on sword, we danced a nimble figure on the pavement, attacking, retreating, defending; and every movement, every jump, every stroke, was predetermined, dictated for us by our text. For we were reenacting the fight of one hundred years ago, between Eressos of Sūās and Ailuezeiles of Noxos, with one variation: by means of a rapid parry, a twist of the body, and a precisely timed counterstroke, I avoided the fate of Eressos, which was decapitation.

The noises of the world— birds in the trees, the river, voices from the house— returned.

"Ulōne! Sweat's in my eyes," said Oluon.

"If we weren't following the book, I would have run you through, you big horse," I said. "You left your stomach unprotected so long I could have carved my name on it."

"If you still had a sword, you mean. You hold it like it was a walking stick... How many times do I have to tell you to hold it like it was part of your arm?"

"I think it's the balance," I said, inspecting my sword.

"That can be your entry in the Memory of the Dead."

"All right, all right. I know you're right, but your stomach was still open. Should we try again?"

"Let's go."

We assumed the initial position; paused; and went at it again. I concentrated on the feel of the sword— Oluon was right, I had a tendency to distance myself from it. An advantage of the ritual of reenactment is that one can focus on such things; in free combat one's mind is too full of stratagems. Still, one should not think too hard about a correction, or one will make the opposite error; once or twice, indeed, I found myself overextending a stroke. Oluon, I noticed, had corrected his own error; he protected himself well. Slash, twist, strike, and the fight was over once more.

"What, no blood?" came a familiar voice.

Lord Zeilisio was leaning against one wall, watching us.

We bowed the knee. "I'm sorry if our bout was so lacking in amusement," I said.

"It's forgiven. May I drag you away from this simulated mayhem for a moment's discussion?"

I nodded to Oluon, and he discreetly withdrew. "I may be somewhat unfit for the presence of a Lord," I noted.

"Ah, yes. We Lords do not sweat; we are exempt from the decrees of Iáinos concerning the sun. Come then, we'll go to the river."

We walked down from the House to the river. Along the river there runs a long stone deck, fitted with couches and gardens, and divided by high walls, running some way into the water, into four areas: the Lord's Bench, the Women's Bench, the Men's, and the Glade's. The divisions always amused me— why is it that Lords and Ladies and their guests may see each other bathing, and also villagers of both sexes, but not free men and women? And why can these different classes not see each other? In Tefalē Doro no one cares about these things. When I asked Zeilisio one time about it he said that servants were fastidious above all other creatures.

We put our clothes on the deck of the Lord's Bench and dived into the Isrēica. The water was cool, and refreshed me. I swam back and forth for awhile, then lay floating on my back, looking up at the blue sky, until Lord Zeilisio, who had already left the water, called to me from the deck.

I clambered up the stone steps out of the river. The sun was bright; I felt hot and cool at the same time. Zeilisio was reclining on a couch; I lay down on one next to his, facing the river. The Isrēica is a lest and a quarter wide at Etêia Mitano; Lord Domānavos' wheat fields on the other side looked far away, and hazy.

"I have been with Cauměliye," announced the Lord. "We have been through such a heap of accounts, fields planted, fields planting, peasants' grievances, festivals, cheating merchants, animals, linens, servants, and barbers, that even a Little Cuzeian would think twice about getting rich."

"Is the House in order?" I asked.

"Caumēliye is very wise and prudent, for a woman, and for a mountaineer, you are— no, I won't say anything. You haven't been amusing enough this morning to deserve any compliments."

"Haven't I flattered you enough, O noble and generous master?"

"Not nearly as much as Corumayas. He's been completely tiresome today."

"He wants a favor for a cousin of his," I said.

"It's favor enough not to run his misbegotten kin off my land. But it wasn't to blather of these affairs that I interrupted your exercises, O Beretos. We have serious things to discuss."

I tried to look appropriately serious.

"We were speaking of certain unpleasant matters in the King's Council, and your name came up," continued Zeilisio. "I have an assignment for you. It will please you, I think. It will make full use of your many gifts, and it requires travel."

"I like Etêia Mitano."

"You are fond also of the mountains, I think?"

"Yes," I said, cautiously.

"Munkhâsh has many mountains."

"Lord!" I exclaimed, alarmed. "You're jesting with me. I can't go to Munkhâsh. Believe me, O Lord, my gifts are nowhere near enough for that. Let them send someone else."

"The true son of Iáinos the one God," Zeilisio said, abstractly, his eyes closed, "does not hesitate to advance into the nest of the viper, nor into the abode of stinging spiders, nor among lovers of deceit and violence, to do the will of Iáinos, for surely Ulōne is in him. You do not doubt this doctrine?"

"No, Lord, but I'm not suited to be a spy. I am aware of its good effect on the soul, yet I have no stomach for torture."

"Are not the Munkhâshi men of a like nature with ourselves?"

"Yes, but they are ruled by demons."

"We must make a distinction in logic," the Lord informed me, "between a people ruled by demons, and a people composed of demons. The amnigō live in the swamps far to the east: the western domains of Munkhâsh are nearer to Eleisa than to them. I doubt very much that you will have the pleasure of the acquaintance of any demon."

"I am pleased. What is the assignment? With what sort of death exactly will I glorify Iáinos?"

"The mission is military in nature."

"I'm a steward, not a warlord."

"But you've served as a soldier, and as a diplomat, and moreover you are fluent in the speech of the Babblers, if that isn't a contradiction in terms."

A cloud had passed in front of the sun; I suddenly felt cold and naked, though not only because of this. I got up to fetch my robe, and wrapped it round myself. I inspected Zeilisio's face; it told me nothing, as usual.

"This isn't some scheme of the idiots, is it?" I asked.

"It's a scheme against the idiots. I volunteered you myself."

"Oh, thank you," I said, miserably.

"You're welcome. Of course I need not insult your integrity with the mention of gold, of presents, of Knowers of Eīledan scrambling to do you honor."

"You really intend to send me to Munkhâsh?"

"Close enough," said Zeilisio. "To the land of the Babblers, in the Gaumê."

I felt relief wash over me, and then anger and shame, at having been taken in, and then I smiled, weakly. "You are a natural diplomat yourself," I said. "Why not save the wagonloads of silver you're going to pay me, and go in my place?"

"I'd love to," he said, with perfect hypocrisy, "but I don't know the language, and you do. You have heard of the Taucrēte Pass, I suppose. You know its strategic importance; there is no way into the plain of Cēradānar but this, for a hundred lests north and south. If the Munkhâshi commanded it they would be— well, they'd be three hundred lests closer. There's a little Babbler baron, named Berac or Borac or something— I can't reproduce these pagan eructations— who holds a fortress at one end of the Pass. It is your glory to be the first Cuzeian Resident at the court of this worthy— a position which combines the functions, though not the salaries, of ambassador, military counselor, tutor in Cuêzi, and Knower of Eīledan."

I recalled the map of Cēradānar; this fortress must be four hundred lests away or more. I would think Araunicoros the height of civilization, after venturing so far into savagery— and within hailing distance of the empire of Munkhâsh.

"How is it that this Borac maintains the Pass against the Munkhâshi? Is he so strong?"

"It isn't Borac but the Pass itself which accomplishes this feat. Two dozen men can hold the Taucrēte Pass, if they are well positioned within it. It's not invasion we fear, but subversion. The fortress that defies a thousand generals opens readily to a friend."

"This little chieflet might go over to the Munkhâshi? But we have an alliance with the Babblers."

"With which Babblers?" asked Zeilisio. "A wise man has written, when two Babblers live together, they form three tribes. Berac is very far from those of the Babblers who are our friends, and very close to Munkhâsh. I trust you see the wisdom of establishing a Cuzeian presence in this place."

"When do I leave?"

"Oh, not before three weeks have passed, at least. And Oluon will go with you."

I could have turned the assignment down, I think. It was not a mission one could fulfill unwillingly. But I understood well enough both our situation in Cēradānar, and in Eleisa. There were not many who could be trusted with such a task; and it would be a disaster if one of Inibē's party were appointed to it. It was a large thing for Zeilisio to ask of me; but it would be a large thing also to refuse.

After a time Zeilisio rose, and strode over to the bench where his clothes lay, with that particular, careless refinement which proclaimed him to be a Cuzeian Lord, though a naked one.

"We will talk further, O Beretos," he said, pleasantly.

"It is well, O Zeilisio," I replied, without enthusiasm.

He walked up the stairs to the House; I stayed on the bench, watching the river run by, and thinking of the thousand things that I would miss.

For myself, one of the most pleasant journeys that can be conceived is by boat to the most beautiful of human cities, Eleisa. As it lies some hundred lests north of Etêia Mitano, the journey takes a week— a week of lazy days watching the boatmen work, standing at the rails watching cities and Houses pass slowly by, or reading, reclining on a couch by the bow, listening to the gentle plash of the water, or talking with Lady Cauméliye over a cup of sherbet in the cool twilight.

We see with the eyes Eīledan gives us, of course. There is plenty of toil for the boatmen— keeping the boat moving, worrying about ropes, hoisting the sail when there is wind, driving the mules when there is not. But for me the journey is a blessed interregnum, without the responsibility of the House, or the intrigue of Eleisa, and without the adversities of travel among Babblers.

Zeilisio has no patience for river journeys. He feels truly alive only in the capital, dining with friends, sparring with enemies, attending plays, confronting diplomatic problems. He hates transportation. Therefore he rides to Eleisa, a journey which takes three days only, and offers some of the worst discomforts which Cuzei can offer.

At night the boat rests, and the water rocks its passengers to sleep. But Cauméliye takes me by the hand, and leads me ashore, and we walk along the river bank under the light of two moons, hand in hand, as if we were children again.

We walk past some fields, toward a line of trees; and then we are in a little wood, which comes right down to the towing path. And here there is a bridge, crossing a quiet little inlet. We look at each other and climb down to the water, seeking to find where this little backwater goes. The bank is slanted and muddy, and we have to step carefully, and climb over boulders and tree roots. I keep turning to Cauméliye to help her, because she is a Lady; but she only laughs; she is as surefooted as she was when she was a girl, exploring the woods and mountain streams of Tefalē Doro with me.

The woods grow thicker as we walk; we would be in darkness except that we can see the sky, and one moon, between the trees on either side of the creek.

After about half an hour of walking, the water opens out into a wide pond, quiet and almost still, bright with moonlight, as welcoming as a fire amid the dark shapes of trees surrounding it. Caumēliye sighs with the beauty of it.

And now she begins to remove her clothes. Belt, shawl, under-dress, sandals, are arranged neatly on the bank; I recognize the same carefulness, and even the same gestures, from our childhood. But it is not a child but a woman who now stands naked before me, the moonlight coloring her smooth soft skin in blues and silvers, and making her black hair gleam like glass. Her face is lovely, with her large eyes and smiling lips; her breasts are round and high; her back and hips are long and finely shaped; her feet are small and graceful, though already dark with mud. The hair at the center of her is a triangle of midnight.

I have already removed my own clothes. She smiles at me, and enters the water. Only a few feet from the bank it is deep enough to swim. The water is cool; but the rivers in the mountains are colder yet. She has not forgotten how to swim, either. It was not till I had thirteen years that I could swim faster than she.

We swim for a long time in the pond. With the moons looking down on us, it feels as if we were swimming in light. We swim across to the other bank; we have a race, which I win; later still, we play in the water, or float on our backs, looking up at the stars.

When we have had enough we climb out, and Caumēliye says she is cold.

"If we walk along the shore you'll feel warm," I suggest.

She laughs, and turns in a circle, displaying her body. "Maybe you simply want to keep looking at me, Beretos."

"You're the most beautiful woman I know."

She looks at me, for a long time, hands on hips. In the dark it is hard to read her expression. "Do you think so, Beretos? I don't think I'm so pretty any more, now that I've borne children. Don't you think my breasts are too big?"

"Ulōne, no," I say, surprised. "What makes you say such a thing?"

She turns away from me, and sits down on a fallen log. I sit at her feet. "Zeilisio," she says, sadly. "I ask him how he likes me, and that's what he says."

"Really? Is he that direct?"

"Oh, it's not exactly what he said, but it's what I felt. I was complaining about how my breasts looked, and he said that I had to expect them to get bigger after bearing a baby."

"Maybe he's teasing you," I suggest. "He's always told me that he's very proud of you."

"If you keep talking like a courtier, Beretos, I'll throw your clothes in the water," she says. "Don't you think I know how he feels about me? He hardly looks at me."

I do not contradict this time, for I cannot gainsay the truth. There is every amity between my Lord and Lady; but little affection, little conversation, and certainly no adoration. Zeilisio talks of his wife, when he refers to her at all, as he talks of Corumayas— as a fact of life, as a fact of the house. He does say that he is proud of her; he means that he appreciates her skill in administering the House, and the adornment she lends to his position in society.

She is shivering with the cold. Our clothes are across the pond, but I come close and put my arms around her. She moves against me, holding close to me. I try to warm her lovely bare body, still wet from the water, with mine.

"I'm dreading this trip," she confides.

"Why's that? Don't you enjoy being in Eleisa?"

"There's so many people, and they all want something. I can never relax. But this time is worse. Zeilisio's campaign... it's like learning a part for a play, but there are no lines. I'm afraid I won't know what to say."

"You're very wise... you will find the right words."

She laughs. "And don't the *Ten Prophets* say that Eleisa cannot bear wisdom?"

"I'm not looking forward to meeting with the idiots. Or living among Babblers. But there's nothing we can do about that now, so I'd rather not think about it."

"You're right... just be here with me. *Ulōne talks loudest when we are silent.*"

We hold each other for a long time, and keep the chill at bay with kisses.

She gently strokes my face. "When you marry, Beretos, promise me that you will hold your wife in this same way."

"Because you ask, I will promise; but no woman can ever hold my heart the way you do, O Lady."

"Don't be foolish, Beretos," she replies. "I could not marry for love, but what need do you have to imitate the nobles in their folly? I wish you would marry, and have the happiness of man and wife, for my sake."

There was no use arguing; but it seemed to me that with no other woman could I feel the happiness I felt merely sitting at my Lady's feet.

On my first visit to the Garden House, Zeilisio's residence in Eleisa, I was full of thoughts of Samīrex, visiting his Lady in the Quarter of Fountains in that city, making love to the sound of splashing water. This trip, the beauty of the city passed me by. I was thinking of the idiots. Zeilisio had warned me that Inibē and his party were opposed to my mission among the Babblers. I would have to do some hard arguing to be allowed to undertake this trip I didn't want to make.

I had been foolish enough to suppose that the matter would be argued in Council, and that the decision would be the King's; but this is not how it is done in Eleisa. Dissension and disputation would offend the dignity of the Council; it is a place for consensus, for concord, for grave and stately ceremonies of state, such as the one which actually saw me on my way, about a month after our arrival. I was taken before the forty assembled Lords and Ladies, gaudy in gold and scarlet, the old King sitting worn and silent in the center, the music of stringed instruments charming our ears. My ambassadorship was proposed (by Zeilisio's friend Feroicolê); speeches extolling my virtue and predicting great glory for the Kingdom were declaimed (by Inibē and Ximāuro). One speaker gave reasons to pursue an opposite course (Inibē's associate Murgêde): the fiction of debate must be maintained. The King intoned the usual formula, in a voice so low only those of us very near the throne could hear him: "The course of Feroicolê will be adopted. Friends, I thank you for your counsel, and may Iáinos smile upon this venture." Then the Ruler of the Council informed me of the Council's decision, admonished me to do honor to the King, to the Council and to Iáinos, and gave me the chain and key which were the signs of my office. I gave my thanks and my promises, and kissed the hand of the King. "O Ambassador, the Council asks no more of you, save that you faithfully execute its will," the Ruler said, and I retreated to take my place.

Perhaps decisions of state were once debated in Council, as we read in the epics, and even in modern romances. I will now tell how such affairs are truly managed.

Zeilisio began his campaign with a dinner party, on the night of our arrival in Eleisa; not only his supporters, such as Feroicolê and Ximāuro, but also Inibē and the idiots were invited.

"You must be graceful and solicitous," Zeilisio instructed me. "Witty, if you can manage it. No, cancel that; I shudder to think what you'd produce if you attempted wit. Don't display any knowledge of the Babblers whatever, and on your life, don't think of giving an *opinion* about them."

He asked Caumēliye to stay away from certain Lords and Ladies, and to cultivate others. I knew the names better than she, and could see what he was doing. Caumēliye can talk for hours to the peasants, but she has no talent for the small talk of the nobility— servant problems, marriages, liaisons, the theater— and Zeilisio was steering her toward those who could either value the signs of her intelligence and simplicity, or enjoy them as charming provincialisms.

I had met Inibē before, after my assignment in Araunicoros. He is an older man, almost bald, rather large, with an expression of permanent indignation. He greeted me gravely but courteously, and asked after affairs in Etêia Mitano and in Tefalē Doro. I was surprised that he remembered my natal House; but of course it was my Lady's, as well.

"In some days you will be a guest at my own table," he informed me.

"I will be honored, O Inibē."

"Perhaps we will discuss the expedition which your Lord is proposing you lead. You are something of a traveler, are you not? Dācuas. Araunicoros."

Remembering Zeilisio's warnings, I said, "My travels have only made me fonder of Cuzei, O Inibē."

"*Who wanders from home wanders from Eīledan,*" Inibē quoted. "That is, if the home is dedicated to Eīledan. If not, one would be wise to get out."

"I suppose so," I said, not understanding what he meant, though his sternness showed that he meant it very strongly.

"I will go to compliment Lady Caumēliye on her kitchen. The hors-d'œuvres. The ices. All very well made," he added, in the same serious tone, as if he were approving the adornments at a funeral.

I had no other conversations that touched even so close as this on my mission. Instead I talked with Lords and Ladies about their Houses, about what plays I should see and what poets I should hear, about the dust and heat of Eleisa (an obligatory topic, in this city which dances with fountains and flowers), about crops and orchards (a passion for some Lords), about the excellences of Lady Caumēliye's cook.

Zeilisio explained it to me later in the evening. "Most of them know nothing about Babblers and even less about the passes of the Gaumê. But they know how an educated upper servant is supposed to talk and act, and if you didn't, we'd have lost before we'd begun."

"How can they be offering counsel, then?" I asked.

"They won't be," explained Zeilisio. "But if they didn't like you, you couldn't be chosen. Everybody talks to everybody else in Eleisa. But from now on we'll concentrate on the people who know what they're talking about."

Whatever it is to the native, Eleisa seems to the outsider to be dedicated chiefly to intrigue and to the arts. In the afternoon you conduct a heated dispute with an enemy, accusing each other of betraying the King or disgracing Iáinos; in the evening the two of you attend a play or a concert together, and politely ask after each other's wives and Houses.

It is the city of passion, as well; almost every Lord is devoted to some Lady, who is generally, of course, the wife of another. Even if he has no other business to conduct, a Lord will arrange to come for some months of the year to Eleisa, in order to spend time with the woman of his heart.

Eleisa seems a different world from the Houses of Cuzei; and yet subtle threads connect them. It is the richness and prosperity of his House which gives a Lord influence in Eleisa. But a House of only medium extent in the north, near to Eleisa, is the equal of a huge estate in the south; this is why Feroicolê is the leader of Zeilisio's faction in the Council, although Zeilisio's House is actually the larger. On the other hand Zeilisio multiplies his own influence through intelligence and skill; in the same way Inibē dominates Murgêde, though he has only half the land the other does.

Many Lords have enriched their Houses by skillful management of their affairs in Eleisa, bringing trade or knowledge, hiring servants, or arranging alliances with other Houses. Foolish Lords have bankrupted or isolated their Houses by spendthrift or maladroit conduct in Eleisa; others have gone so far as to neglect their Houses, leaving them to evil stewards or incompetent brothers, while they give themselves to the attractions of the capital.

There are also, so to speak, the Lords who are not here, such as Tancī, my father's Lord. Tancī has never visited Eleisa, or even Norunayas; he has never seen the need of it. Such a policy saves him enormous trouble; but also leaves him at the mercy of chance in many things. He must rely on local rumor if he wishes to hire a Knower or a Master of Troops; he has no voice when grave matters, a war or a drought, are decided by the Council; his daughter married well only because a connection of his, the Lady Alaldillê, could arrange it in Eleisa with the father of Zeilisio.

My own favorite occupation in Eleisa is to spend an afternoon in the great Mansion of Learning, browsing the poets and the practical manuals, reading epics or philosophy, or conversing with other readers. If there were three things I chiefly missed in the land of Babblers, they were the music of my Lady's voice, the mountains of Tefalē Doro, and the scriptorium of Eleisa.

I also paid a visit to the Glade of Eleisa. Eleisa's Glade, for all that it was founded by Lerīmanio himself, is entirely the work of man; its floor is of tile, in designs which suggest a meadow or a forest glen; its trees are marble columns; its flowers are made of silver and of gold. Iáinos lives there in a very different way than in a village Glade. There, in a sense, one goes to Iáinos; for the Glade is the work of Eīledan, and thus Iáinos already dwells there. Here, Iáinos comes to us, because we have constructed a beautiful mansion to entice Iáinos to come.

I asked Iáinos to give me the virtues I would need to accomplish my journey; I was sure I would not be able to manufacture them by myself.

In the Glade I saw Murgêde, who is a fat and very rich old man, full of false joviality. He was talking to one of the Knowers— giving him counsel, rather than the reverse, by the look of it. As I rose from my prayer, he noticed me. He seemed surprised to see me; but immediately broke off his conversation and strode toward me, with an expression on his face that was the announcement of some ready mockery. But I felt I had no need to hear it; I rose and smiled at him, then took my leave of the Glade, as if I had no idea that Murgêde might wish to speak to me. There was some triumph in this, but I had lost the feeling of the presence of Iáinos, and would have to return another day to recapture it.

9 · ɩNɩCbZ · *Eleisa*

Inibē's mansion is well suited to him; it is one of the oldest houses in Eleisa, and it is furnished richly and without a hint of frivolity. We dined on a verandah overlooking the Isrēica, and before the servants had finished clearing away the fruits and ices, our host had begun to attack Zeilisio's proposal.

"It's utter foolishness to send a Resident and staff to such a crack in the mountains," he said. "Never been done. But if you insist on it— and with all respect to your honor, O Beretos— a Knower of Eīledan should be sent instead, so these savages can be instructed in the worship of Iáinos."

"A Knower is part of the entourage," Zeilisio reminded him. "But you understand that the chief purpose of the Residency is military rather than cultural, and requires the delicacy of a diplomat. Beretos is the best man for the job."

"Delicacy! With barbarians!"

"Are you proposing we show them contempt instead? That will surely cement our alliance."

"You twist my words. I said nothing about contempt, but we can't treat them like civilized men— we'd only lose their respect."

"Beretos left Araunicoros with the full respect of the Prince."

There was no reason that this would make an impression on Inibē, who after all was a friend and protector of Ambrisio. "I don't know what reasonable men are to make of it," he lamented. "Four dozen men. Two horses each. Barrels of gifts. All to benefit some Babbler chieftain and to address a threat which has been kept at bay for hundreds of years without any such aid."

"Munkhâsh is getting stronger. With respect, Inibē, you are like a man who ignores a tumor, because he has always lived with it so far."

"They have six hundred lests—"

"Four hundred," Zeilisio corrected him.

"Four hundred lests to travel before they reach us. Fighting their way through Babblers all the way. What do you think would be left of them if they got this far? And if they did, you don't think they could defeat us as they can defeat the barbarians, do you? No, there's something else going on."

"What's that?" asked Zeilisio, innocently

"It's as striking as the sun!" exclaimed Inibē. "Interest. Interest. A Residency for a favorite servant. Levy on the Houses. Influence in Council, prestige, perhaps an elevation."

"*To the evil-minded man, all men are evil,*" said Zeilisio, for once making no attempt to show his disdain for the chief of the "idiots." "Do you think I am so starved for honor that I scheme to invent Residencies at the end of the earth? Or if I had turned my heart to corruption, do you think I couldn't find a position of greater influence for Beretos here in Eleisa, and without the tribulation of losing my best steward?"

Inibē assumed a crafty expression. "If it is as you say, you'd be pleased to allow another to lead this mission, would you not? The man isn't more important than the mission, is he?"

"Name the man."

I think Inibē did not expect this. He made as if to speak, once or twice, without saying anything; when he began to pronounce a name, Zeilisio interrupted, "Who speaks Caḋinor," and that shut him up again. But then he recovered himself, and stuttered, "That's not the point—"

"I believe it *was* your point," said Zeilisio.

"It's not the point. Let us say we have someone—"

"I propose yourself. Wise, honest, tactful, devoted to Iáinos— there couldn't be a better choice."

Inibē looked apoplectic. "You overreach yourself, O Zeilisio. Your pride and arrogance have made their impression. Fortunately there still exist men in this land who believe in Cuzeian civilization; who yearn for holiness and trust in Iáinos to protect our land. Whatever the motives behind this scheme of yours, Zeilisio, be assured that we will be watching you, and by Ulōne, any misconduct will be punished."

"Inibē will never support us," I complained to Zeilisio later. "Why did we even visit his house? It seemed only to increase his anger."

"To know what his approach will be," he answered, immediately. "Then we can take counter-measures."

"What's the counter-measure for all his talk of *interest*? As if I'll be living in luxury in the Babbler lands..."

"Bring a long book with you," he suggested. But then, more seriously, "It's an offense to your honor, Beretos, and I'm sorry to put you through it. But they talk about interest because it's how they are themselves. One of their allies, through an aquaintance, offered to support your Residency, if they were allowed to have their own Resident in Nūōr. With the same titles and numbers of men and expenses paid by the Council, but with the charming proviso that this Resident would not actually travel to take up his post."

I shook my head. "That's completely brazen. I hope you rejected his offer?"

He shrugged. "The corrupt are the easiest to deal with. Our difficulty is the ones that *can't* be bribed to do the right thing."

We rode the next day to Aēti Fulauto, thirty lests out of Eleisa, where we were guests of Feroicolê for two days and nights.

Feroicolê is plump, fond of wine, and somewhat slow; but he is perhaps the most important of Zeilisio's allies, due to the antiquity and riches of his House, and to his influence in the capital, among both Lords and Knowers. There is also more than one marital link between our two Houses; notably, between Zeilisio's cousin and Feroicolê's grandson.

We brought with us from Eleisa the Lord Ximāuro and the Lady Alaldillê. I had met Ximāuro before, in connection with my mission to Araunicoros; I remembered him as pedantic and argumentative. He was a little younger than Zeilisio. I had never made Alaldillê's acquaintance. She was ancient, with a high, penetrating voice, that I heard raised in anger more than once in the few hours I had known her.

We sat down to take counsel together.

"Ximāuro, no Cuzeian knows more about Munkhâsh than you," Zeilisio began. "Why don't you let Beretos know what's in store for him?"

"Yes," said Ximāuro, and sat thinking for some time. At last he began: "You know that Eīledan, following the will of Iáinos, created out of the substance of Ulōne the nation of the Eīnalandāuē; and out of matter four thinking Kinds: the giants and the iliū, who are free of evil; then the elcari and ourselves, who are of mixed virtue."

"Yes, we had heard that rumor," admitted Zeilisio.

"The creator of the amnigō is Amnās, who is as evil as they," continued Ximāuro, ignoring him. "Amnās is the Master of Arms for Ecaîas, who is the Opposite, the principle of death and absence, the enemy of Iáinos. The amnigō live in swamps, and their food is rotting flesh. There were once amnigō in Cēradānar, in the swamps north of Sūas; but they were driven from there by the iliū more than ten thousand years ago, in the first great War of the Kinds, in which the giants also perished.

"Now they live far to the east, in the swamps at the head of the River that is nameless, by the sea which is forbidden. And they have brought men under their sway, and made them their slaves, and made a great empire for themselves; and the name of their kingdom is Munkhâsh.

"For many centuries the shadow of Munkhâsh has been growing. In the days of the Calēsiōri it was unknown to any man of Cēradānar. A hundred years ago it was more than a week's journey from the Gaumê to the darkened realm. Today their banners fly above the mountains, and their agents venture with boldness into Cēradānar. The wise of Cuzei have watched their advance with apprehension, and have attempted to build unity and strength among the peoples, in preparation for the trial by fire which is to come.

"It is your task, O Beretos, to temper the steel of the Babblers who face them, and if it is the will of Iáinos, to avert that trial for a time."

We sat some time in gloom; and then I fairly exploded with questions.

"How many amnigō are there? Legions?"

"We do not know; but surely tens of thousands."

"And how many men in Munkhâsh?"

"Many millions."

"And the amnigō, do they breathe fire, or possess a skin of iron?"

"The books of the iliū say nothing of such things. They are compared with frogs and reptiles."

"Haven't you ever seen an amnigo?" I pursued, incredulously. "I thought you'd been in Munkhâsh yourself."

"Through Ulōne's protection, no. But I have read every book and scroll on the subject, and talked to every Cuzeian who has ventured there. Few have seen the amnigō. They only rarely leave their marshes; but if they do, it is only the grace of Ulōne that will save the man who sees them."

"Well, this doesn't hold together," I complained. "How can a handful of demons rule over millions of men, without even moving from their swamps? Why don't the men rise up against them?"

"They do not because they never have!" he exploded. "They are evil men, worshippers of Amnās since the last War of the Kinds, governed by the very creations of Amnās! This is what the holy books say, and it is the teaching of the iliū, who do not lie. There is no rebellion, because there is too much fear. Do not ask why it is so; it is the power of Ecaîas."

"Then send someone else," I retorted. "I'm not willing to fight against Ecaîas."

Ximāuro did not reply; he simply looked away, with an injured expression. Feroicolê looked at him worriedly, and then admonished me: "O Beretos, it is unseemly to speak against an elder and a scholar. You yourself don't know more about this evil realm than Lord Ximāuro, do you? Then be silent and receive instruction."

"I'm not speaking against Ximāuro, I'm asking questions," I said. "Besides, I have met Munkhâshi myself, in Araunicoros, and I didn't see that they had the powers of demons."

"I have no doubts concerning your knowledge of Babblers," said Ximāuro, in a voice that suggested the opposite, "but these are not Babblers. Do you not know, the threat from Munkhâsh is not one of armies, but of gods!"

"Gods who are held back by the power of one Babbler baron?"

Ximāuro turned to Zeilisio. "O Zeilisio..." he said; and what he left unsaid was eloquent.

"It's most unseemly," said Feroicolê, shaking his head. "Most unseemly."

Alaldillê spoke. Her eyes promised words of scorn, and I felt fear; but to my relief her words were not directed at me: "Leave him be, you old crows! He's the one who's going, not you. And I like him. He listens with more than his ears."

Ximāuro turned bright red at this, and Feroicolê huffed to himself but said nothing intelligible.

"Now, go ahead, Beretos," Alaldillê told me. "You have something to say. Take a deep breath and try to say it clearly."

I did take a deep breath, and then I said, "O Lords, I don't mean to give offense. But I believe that we must leave this talk of demons aside, and speak of armies instead. There's a freedom in the immensity of the threat of demons, my Lords: because we are utterly powerless before it, we must leave it in the hands of Iáinos, and concern ourselves with what is human. Tell me instead where the forts of Munkhâsh are; how many are their soldiers; how strong are their swords."

"Yes, those are good questions," said Feroicolê, with an air of surprise.

Ximāuro still wanted to talk about demons; but the sense of the meeting was now against him. We should perhaps have let him discourse on demonology, because he was completely unable to address my questions. He did not know how large was Munkhâsh's army— in fact, no one had really seen any armies, though they had seen many soldiers. The advance to the Gaumê, which he made so much of, had occurred half a century ago. He did not know if they had iron or steel weapons. He thought they might have horses, but "authorities disagreed." He drew a map, and carefully indicated the swamps of the amnigō, but could only place one city on it— Gopando, at the mouth of the Scondoro, almost as far from the Taucrēte Pass as it is from Eleisa.

I am afraid I complained bitterly to Zeilisio about Ximāuro, when we were alone. "That pious fool is an embarrassment to our side," I said. "He's never gone farther than Araunicoros himself, and if he's talked to anyone who made it to Munkhâsh, he's forgotten everything they said."

"He's extremely valuable to us," said Zeilisio, simply. "He's absolutely stunning on the subject of demons. And that's exactly what most of our audience wants to hear. Slavery and idols and creeping shadows— by the time he's done with them they'll want to go themselves."

"Well, what do we know about Munkhâsh on the human level?"

"Not much," he admitted, cheerfully. "You'll talk to Sauōros, who's the man who negotiated your Residency with the Babblers. An excellent man. He arranged it with a cousin of your man Borac's."

"Oh, is he the culprit? I don't know if I want to see him."

"You've got to— he's the only one who knows how to find the place."

I did talk to Sauōros, when he arrived from Masāntie a week later. I liked him immediately; he was direct and courteous, and very knowledgeable about the wilderness of eastern Cerādanār. He not only provided a route, but advised on what supplies to bring, what gifts would be appreciated, what weather to expect. "Avoid my greatest mistake, which was to bring only a few sheets of paper," he suggested. "Anything else you can buy or make or steal— and I'll show you how to make your own ink— but nothing's more frustrating than to run out of paper."

He was testing me as well: he insisted on conducting our conversation in Caḑinor. He said that I had an accent— that of the middle Cayenas— but that I would be understood. He demonstrated the mountain dialect, which I found nearly impenetrable. "By the time you get there, you'll understand it," he assured me.

Sauōros had visited Munkhâsh— he had accompanied a group of Caḑinorian traders to the city of Korkâsh. They were given an escort of Munkhâshi soldiers, which greatly limited his scouting ability. But at least he could report on their armament. Their swords and shields were iron, but the officers carried steel; their armor was padded leather. He thought they would not be the equal of a Cuzeian man of arms, but they were more numerous.

By his account, the finer men of Korkâsh dress in snakeskin, alligator hide, and bird feathers, and wear crowns that imitated the tentacles of the amnigō.

Zeilisio's strategy was simple and effective. He let Inibē blanket Eleisa with denunciations of "this exaggerated and extravagant plan," while he and Ximāuro spoke of the Munkhâshi threat and our duty as the people of Iáinos to steward Cēradānar. The Council wavered between us like a dog between two bones. There was even some preference for Zeilisio's plan, perhaps because Inibē (a man who is never indirect) made his malice too evident. About two weeks after our arrival in Eleisa we were discussing the alarming possibility of a majority of the Council approving the expedition.

I do not know who it was— it was certainly not one of us— who considered both points of view, and derived the reasonable, inevitable compromise: to send an Emissary, but not an entourage. Oluon and I alone would travel to the Gaumê, sent by the Council, but paid by Zeilisio. The Council seized gratefully upon the idea.

"Shortsighted fools!" said Zeilisio, cheerfully. "Full of virtue, always eager to embrace grand missions, so long as it can be done cheaply. I'd be cursing them if we hadn't planned it this way. And the best part of it is that Inibē thinks he's won."

But Inibē's final warning should have been a warning to us. He who thinks his enemy a fool has put his mind to sleep.

10 · ᛌᚾᚋᛌᛐ · *Oluon*

As we traveled into the Babbler lands, I taught Oluon Caḓinor. While we moved slowly up the river, pulled by a Babbler's mule on the footpath, or as we walked the dusty trails that are the roads of these parts, it was as good a way as any to pass the time. I had tried to begin the instruction back in Etêia Mitano, but Oluon, being a highly practical person, was incapable of grasping a concept he could not immediately use. Now that he could not ask for a drink or greet a pretty girl without it, however, he was eager to learn the language.

Caḓinor has some resemblances to Cuêzi. It also has male and female nouns and those which are neither. It has only five roles of noun, and its times and styles of verbs are not as eloquent or precise as ours. It has four sounds we do not make, and if you fail to learn them, the Caḓinorians will not rest till they have taught you. Their t̂ and d̂ are like a lisped s and z; they have two x's, one harsher than ours [h̆], one simply the sound of the breath [h]; and their k must be made far back in the throat, different from a c.

It is not simply babbling; there are many words which resemble the same word in Cuêzi. For instance:

creget – he eats [creye]
rugites – red [ruyise]
prenet – he takes [brine]
caer – port [coros]
meis – water [meyu]
ueronos – eagle [araunas]
adures – blue [adāure]
aestas – summer [āetas]

This matching has been noticed before. It used to be explained that all men once spoke Cuêzi, but that on Babbler lips the language has become corrupted. However, this cannot be so if what the iliū remember is true, that we ourselves were once barbarians, and that the first men spoke differently. Moreover, not all Babbler tongues are so similar to ours; those of the Babblers who live to the north or west of us, for instance, are completely unlike Cuêzi.

It is more likely, perhaps, that the Caẑinorians originally spoke a different language, but in the course of many centuries of living beside us, back to the time of Lerīmanio and before, they have come more and more to approximate their language to ours. The Babblers in the West have less contact with us, so their language has not changed; while the people in the north, those of Agimbār, have retained their language out of pride, because they ruled Cēradānar until we conquered them.

In Araunicoros Oluon and I called upon the new Cuzeian Resident, who received us cordially enough, and on the Prince, who received us very warmly, remembering me very well from my former mission, when I had taken care of Ambrisio.

By the time we left Araunicoros, Oluon's Caẑinor was good enough to get us dragged into a Babbler rite of god-possession.

Our adventure started with a girl, as it usually does with Oluon. We wanted a boat to take us upriver, and Oluon found her among those who had boats for hire. There is no mule-path along the river from this point on; instead one must paddle, in long, thin boats called *murinet*. Oluon suggested that we take her boat, and as the price was acceptable, I agreed.

We placed our baggage in the boat, and climbed in. The Babbler girl took the bow, Oluon the middle, and I the stern; we started paddling. Much more work than being pulled by mules!

Oluon talked with the girl, as best he could. As she did not turn around to talk, it was difficult for him to make out her words, and all the more so due to his weak grasp of Caẑinor. Their conversation would go something like this:

    Oluon: What is your name?
    Girl: Ariȟmiera.
    Oluon: What?
    Girl: Ariȟmiera.
    Oluon: What— how— what years do you have?
    Girl: Eighteen.
    Oluon: Are you alive near this place?

Girl: What?

Oluon: Do you have your— (to me, in Cuêzi) Damn it, Beretos, how do you say House?

Me: *Kesuile.*

Oluon: Is your *kesuile* near here?

Girl: I live half a day's paddling up the river.

Oluon: You are very— very— good to look to you, Ariňmiera.

Girl: (Laughs.)

Oluon: Do you have brothers and— (damn, what's the word)— Do your father and mother have others plus you?

Oluon has the patience to talk such drivel for hours, in a language he barely knows, and with a barbarian, just to see where it may lead. It is why Zeilisio, speaking of our trip, said that it would be a holiday for the female servants.

The sun rose in the sky, and the day became hot; with our steady paddling, we became hot and sweaty. I took off my tunic. Somewhat to my surprise, Ariňmiera pulled her robe off her shoulder, so that as we proceeded we could watch her naked back. Bravely despising heat and fatigue, Oluon persevered with his jokes and questions, hoping no doubt that she would turn around; but she had an admirable discipline, and paddled away without a stop. She had thick arms, as thick as many men's.

We did have a glimpse of her when we stopped at noontime to eat the bread and cheese we had brought; but she chose to cover herself again while we ate. Babbler maidens are more bashful than ours are. When we began our journey again there was a breeze, and it was no longer hot.

Anyone listening to the two of them would have concluded that the Babbler girl was the more serious and intelligent. She smiled at Oluon's weak jokes, but made none of her own. She was working with the boats because making them was her father's craft, and he did not make enough with it to feed her younger brothers and sisters; her mother was dead. She could not think of marrying till the younger ones were older, and were able to support themselves. She was a pretty girl, but already she looked older than her years, and her eyes were tired.

She pointed out, as we passed, the little village where her father lived— a collection of hovels nestled on a patch of mud on the riverside.

We paddled on till nightfall, and camped on a hillside above the water, sheltered by some trees. Oluon suggested that we take a swim, to cool ourselves off. Ariȟmiera said she was not hot, and I laughed. Oluon was thinking like a Cuzeian; Caḓinorians do not much care how clean they are.

"Well, we are going into the river," I said. "Come join us if you want."

And she did join us. The water was cool, refreshing; we let it carry away the aches of our muscles and the dirt and sweat of the day. Oluon splashed water on Ariȟmiera; she laughed and splashed him back. After a time I climbed out and sat on the bank watching them— or, to be honest, watching her. She was beautiful, as all young women are, but she was not to my taste. None of the Babbler women are. They are short, they do not know how to hold in their stomachs, and their breasts are too large and too low.

Before we ate she prayed, and threw a piece of her bread in the water. This seemed to me to be unusual for a Caḓinorian, and I asked her about it. She said she had made a vow to share her food with Aelilea, the goddess of water, so that the goddess would help her father with an illness he had, which sometimes left him for a week unable to work, or even to rise.

"You should not pray to these gods of yours," Oluon told her. (The reader will forgive me if I do not reproduce the hesitations and errors of his actual speech.) "Your gods are not as strong as ours. I will pray for you."

She shook her head. "I have made a vow, and I cannot break it. I cannot trust in any god but Aelilea— not Aecton, not Perabron, and not even the mighty gods of Cuzei."

"But she hasn't healed him, has she?"

"When I accomplish my vow she will."

Oluon turned to me; he seemed troubled. "This won't happen, will it? Weren't we taught that the Babblers' gods were false gods?"

"There are differing opinions," I explained. "Naturally, the Babblers do not know the Source, Iáinos, nor the Shaper, Eīledan, nor the Nurturer, Ulōne. Some maintain that their gods are spirits; others that they are demons, sent into the world to deceive;

still others write that they correspond to nothing at all, and that the effects which are ascribed to them are simply due to magic."

This seemed to satisfy Oluon; he turned back to the girl. "How do you know that this goddess of yours has accepted your vow?" he asked. "How do you know if you please her?"

"She speaks to me through those who serve her."

"And what are these? Are they First Spirits, or Powers, or prophets?" Oluon had to ask me for these words.

"They are spirits [*fantit*], but they borrow the bodies of human beings, and speak through them," she said.

"I would like to see this, to see if your gods are as strong as ours."

"There is a godspeaker who lives in a village we shall pass tomorrow," she replied. "I will take you to see her, and you will see how our gods are, and whether they are as strong as yours."

I was doubtful about this; do the prophets not warn us against the gods of the Babblers? Was not Antāu punished by Iáinos, when he consented to drink the elixir of the crone of the cave? But Oluon insisted that there was no danger. He was not going to drink anything, or let them pray for him; and if the gods addressed him he would declare to them, very straightforwardly, that he did not belong to them and that they could not hurt him.

"Besides, what about the destruction of the Eighty Evil Magicians by the Sojourner? How could he had accomplished that, if he hadn't ventured into their fortress, and watched their secret ceremonies?"

"As you will," I said. "But know that I allow it only because of your great stubbornness, and not because I cannot match you epic for epic. May Ulōne protect us."

The sides of the godspeaker's house were built of earth, in a great circle, curving inwards but not meeting; the top was covered with leaves laid over branches. It was so low to the ground that it seemed impossible that one could even sit inside; but in fact the floor inside was hollowed out. One descended as one entered through the tiny opening; it was like crawling down into the center of the earth.

We were in a dark place, lit by flames, which combined garishly with the green light which filtered in through the leaves of the roof. There were about thirty or forty Babblers crowded around us, silent, but somehow agitated; it was like being in a forest before a storm— some power was roiling and troubling them before its onslaught.

The godspeaker appeared. It was a woman, dressed in long robes dyed red, and with many chains draped around her neck, tingling metallically as she moved. She moved round the circle, greeting people, laughing and chatting, like a noble lady entertaining her guests— except that there was nothing noble about her laughter; it was frequent and girlish, entirely unexpected in this dark, smoky place. When she came near to us Ariħmiera indicated us, and said, "Cuzeians." The godspeaker laughed, and dropped to her knee, in a clumsy imitation of the Cuzeian greeting.

Someone started beating a drum; another played a flute. Nothing seemed to happen for quite a while. The light outside faded, making the inside of the godspeaker's house even more dark and ruddy. The pungent smell of incense reached our noses. The godspeaker began dancing in the middle of the room. Her feet moved in time with the drum; her hands fluttered as if following the tones of the flute. The dance, too, lasted a long time; without any pause or relaxation of energy.

But at last she collapsed on the floor, and lay curled up, trembling, and subject to violent spasms of the limbs. "The *fantos* is coming," Ariħmiera whispered to us.

The woman rose; and she was transformed. Her face had become twisted and harsh; her eyes glowered, as she gazed round the room, with a fierceness which would have been impossible for the laughing Babbler woman we had first seen. When she walked she swaggered; and when she talked she had the voice of a man, raucous and arrogant.

"I speak for the goddess," the spirit said through her. "Beware! The goddess is mighty. Who wishes to approach the goddess?"

A man stepped forward, and extended his hands flat before him, in the Caðinorian gesture of submission. We could not hear his request, only the spirit's questions: "Where does this woman live?" "Is that all?" "What will you offer the goddess?"

The man talked for some time; the spirit hovered over him, nodding impatiently. Finally he gave his instructions; this time in a somewhat lowered voice, so that I could not follow well. I gathered that the man needed to obtain a lock of the woman's hair, bury it in the ground wrapped in a cloth, and water it with his own urine. "Then bring me one hen, and two skins of beer," the spirit instructed him. "The goddess will fulfill your request. The goddess is very powerful." The man thanked him, hugging the godspeaker's knees; the spirit waved his hands over him, dismissingly.

I do not know what the goddess had promised— whether the woman's love, or her death, or something else.

So it went. This was not a ceremony of worship; each person who came wanted something from the goddess. The *fantos* did not talk to everyone, but skipped over some, no matter how they waved or beseeched; presumably they would have to come back another time. During all this time the drum played softly, and the smoke of the incense filled the house.

Finally the spirit came up to Oluon. He inspected him, frowning, while Oluon retreated somewhat; and then he spoke, in his creaking voice: "What is it you want?"

"I— I want nothing of the goddess," said Oluon.

"Why is that?"

"I am— I belong to another god."

"You belong to Iáinos," said the spirit. "Why are you in my house?"

Oluon moved his mouth without speaking, and then stuttered, "I wanted to see it."

The spirit stepped back, and looked him up and down. Then he laughed— a deep, malicious laugh. "Very well, man of Iáinos. You who were curious, you will learn more than it was in your mind to learn. Enjoy women and drink beer, Cuzeian, because your days are short. You will be running alone in the night, and your enemy will come to you, and pierce your heart."

"Your gods can't hurt me," said Oluon, defiantly, but nervously.

The spirit laughed again, reared back, and punched Oluon in the face. Oluon toppled back, hitting the wall; Ariňmiera and I steadied him and kept him from falling. There was blood running from Oluon's nose. His eyes were bleary; he looked at the spirit with horror in his eyes.

"Tell me again whether you can be hurt by other gods," said the spirit. "But now that this lesson has been imparted, foolish one, the goddess tells you, for your own benefit, that she has no quarrel with you. It is not she who will pierce your heart."

Abruptly the godspeaker began to shake, and tumbled crazily about the room. Everyone had to duck to avoid being hit. The drum became louder; the flute played once more. A violent shudder passed through the godspeaker's body, from her head down to her feet. And with this, evidently, the spirit left. The godspeaker looked around her. When she saw us she stopped, looking surprised.

"Is he hurt?" she asked, with concern. "What happened? Bring water, someone." And she stepped forward and laid her hand caressingly on Oluon's face— the same small hand which, minutes before, under the control of a spirit, had felled a Cuzeian warrior.

The next day Oluon was subdued, and did not even resume his flirtation with Ariȟmiera.

"Don't believe the godspeaker," I told him. "The Cađinorian gods have no power over us."

"I know that, but that's not what the spirit said," he protested. "It's not the goddess who is going to kill me; it's a man. Eīledan protects us against the gods, but not against men."

"There is nothing Eīledan cannot do, if we walk in Eīledan's ways," I said. "Eīledan isn't bound by the words of a Babbler god."

"Yes, I know," said Oluon; but the rest of the day he remained silent and withdrawn.

11 · NZX̄A · *Lago*

    We traveled four days withAriħmiera, up the Metōre and then the Elimaēta, to the town of Otaures. She began to be concerned that she would not be able to find anyone to hire her for the journey back to Araunicoros, so we left her in Otaures, and hired another boat, which took us three days further upstream, to the very edge of the foothills of the Gaumê.
    Here we found a man who was going north, and had two extra horses, and we rode two days north with him, along the line of the hills, till we came to the next great river of Cēradānar, the Cunemias, which in these parts is quick and powerful, fresh from its descent of the mountains.
    We could find no guide to take us into the Gaumê. It was considered dangerous country. Farms and villages grew fewer; there were bandits, and Munkhâshi, and wild beasts. We bought a donkey to carry our baggage, and began walking.
    The hills grew taller as we traveled on, till the tops were too steep and rocky to farm, and were left wild. For me it was like a homecoming, because this country was very like that around Tefalē Doro. But in my country there is much more habitation; the farms stretch farther up the hills, the forests are farmed for wood and game, and there are good roads. Here men were only precarious visitors, and the land still belonged to Eīledan.
    Oluon stopped abruptly and pointed. I followed his finger, and after a puzzled moment made out a moving figure on the crest of a hillside across from us. It was a mountain cat, running in pursuit of some small animal. We watched it run till it disappeared in the brush.
    Oluon took to carrying his bow as we walked.

    On the second evening we camped in a clearing near the top of a hill, far from any house of men. We were close enough to hear a rushing mountain stream, but not so near that we might be in the path of animals drinking from it. We tied up our donkey, drew water from the stream, made a fire, and cooked our meal.

We were not far from our goal, and perhaps should have practiced our Cadinor; but in this wilderness it gladdened our hearts to speak our own language. Indeed we began to sing together, in the loud, careless voices that are possible only when the nearest ears of men are lests distant.

I emphasize that we had drunk no wine, but only cold mountain water, which was indeed more of a treat. Since leaving Cuzei we had not tasted it.

Oluon seemed to be singing very well. I was surprised, as his usual voice is gravelly, and he wanders off the music; but perhaps the isolation inspired him. We sang from the Songs of Iáinos, songs which celebrated the beauty of creation, which Eīledan accomplished, following the Idea of Iáinos.

The hand of Eīledan is mighty.
It shaped the hills as a potter shapes the pot.
It raised the vault of the sky as a traveler raises a tent.
Eīledan built up the mountains as a man builds a house;
Eīledan smoothed the plains as a woman smoothes a garden.
Listen to Eīledan's voice
in the sound of mighty waters
in thunder and the roar of the lion
who shouts of the terror of Iáinos.
Come into the Glade which is the world and worship.

"You have a bird's voice," exclaimed Oluon, laughing. "I didn't think you had it in you."

"And you as well," I said, a little disconcerted.

We sang from the Lay of Antāu, which Antāu sings to tell of his great love for Isiliē. I don't know how we thought of it, except that we were listening to the stream, and Antāu begins by comparing his Lady, in her splendor and vivacity, to flowing water. Again I was amazed at the beauty of Oluon's voice, and then I was afraid, because I knew he could not sing so well. He could not improvise a descant on the bass in that way, nor sing an arpeggio so quickly as that.

We stopped. "Is that you?" I asked, in a whisper.

"No, O Beretos," replied Oluon.

I felt afraid, and yet strangely excited. I began another song, a song of Ulōne, from the Unending Songs. It is a song which expresses gladness and longing, and it has always had a calming effect on my mind. I listened carefully, and I was sure that I heard no third voice; there was only my voice and Oluon's, but perfected, as if the two of us could suddenly out-sing the finest singers of the Glade of Eleisa.

I stopped before the last line, which is *Love is in the heart of the world,* and so did Oluon; and this time the song continued, in a voice which was strong and resonant and gentle, playing with the melody as the fire plays above the burning log; and I felt that I heard it not with my ears but with my heart.

Then it was over. We could hear the gurgle of the stream; and a breeze blew from the mountains, making us feel as cold and dead as ashes.

Then we perceived something across from us, very near, a black shape against the stars, impenetrable in the darkness, solid as the earth.

"Who are you, O stranger?" I asked, softly. My hand was on the handle of my knife, though I was certain no metal could avail me now.

"Such suspicious words," came the shadow's voice. It was merry, and wild, and deep, and light; it was the Singer's voice now speaking. The words were in Cuêzi.

"What manner of being you are I know not," I said, childishly. "If only it were light, that I could see you!"

"The light is good, but will the eye receive it?"

"I don't understand."

"That is our burden," said the voice. "Who will understand the iliū?"

The shadow came closer and grew very large, and poked at the fire with a stick. The embers brought forth flame, and revealed our visitor: something like a man, but with blunted nose, and large golden eyes, their stare steady and disconcerting. Its skin looked reddish in the firelight; I knew that it would be blue-gray in the sun, and would glisten, for the iliū are equally at home on land and in the sea, and their skin always looks wet. It had no hair, or perhaps its head was covered by a cap. It seemed to be wearing clothes of leather; but its feet were bare, and had no nails.

I trembled in the dark, and drew my cloak about me. I had never before seen an iliū.

The iliū sank back from the fire, becoming again a black shadow as the coals faded. "What brings you sons of Cuzei to the land of Babblers?"

"We are envoys of the King's Council to a Babbler lord," I replied, with an infinite lack of discretion. "I am Beretos and this is Oluon."

"Well met. You may name me Lago. Will you not rise, O Oluon?"

For the first time I noticed that Oluon was face down on the ground. "I'm not afraid," he cried out, in a voice that belied his words. He heaved himself up, and sat staring at the silhouette of the iliū. "I don't know what Oluon can do for you, but I am your servant, O Lago. Only please don't destroy me."

"Don't be foolish," I said. "How could an iliu hurt you? The iliū are good."

At this Lago laughed, and I felt a chill in my heart. If the stars laughed they would laugh like this. I realized how foolish were my words. Were the iliū too good to hurt us? The lion and the torrent and the lightning are also good, and may kill us; the mountains and the desert and the sea are good, but man cannot live in them. Men are too fragile to bear much good.

The iliu asked about our journey, and its purpose, and I answered, speaking briefly, as I would speak to a king. And then I ventured, "You also are traveling, O Lago. What are the courses of the iliū? What is it you seek?"

"I travel to the southern realm of my people," he said. "I am of the age when such a journey is to be made. I will learn much of Eīledan's world before I am done."

"Do you also speak of Eīledan?" I asked, with a thrill. "Is it true you worship the same gods as we?"

"O Man, it is we who taught you the worship of Eīledan," the iliu said, with a laugh. "You have not forgotten your own books, have you?"

"What do you call Eīledan in your language?"

In answer it seemed that Lago began his song again; but it was over in an instant, and I learned that for the iliū, speech is music.

"O Lago, would that I could learn your language," I said, longingly.

"No man can learn Eteodāole."

"It is forbidden?"

"No; we would willingly teach; but your nature prevents it."

"I have heard that a child who knows no human tongue can learn yours."

"It is not so. Even a child is too human."

"But did not Árrasos the father of men speak it?"

"O Beretos, you are a dialectician," laughed the iliu. "So he did; but that was before he learned smallness."

If I believed with the Babblers, that talking to a godspeaker is truly talking to a god, it would seem the utterest waste to ask for favors; I would instead ask for knowledge. Now, seated before an iliu, of a race that was ancient ten thousand years before the first man walked the earth, I was full of questions. Could he not tell me of the wars against the amnigō, when the earth was young? What did the iliū know of the first days of Cuzei, when Lerīmanio encountered the elcari, when Samīrex sought the secrets of the south, and Celōusio defeated the dragon? Was it true that the iliū lived without sin, and that Iáinos talked to them each day as they rose, and once more before they slept? Was it true that they knew the name of every human, and read their thoughts as well? Was it true that a man could lay with an iliu maiden, but would vanish like smoke if he did so? Why did they keep aloof from men? What was their life like under the sea?

I started to ask these questions, in a rush, without stopping for answers, till I was stopped by the laughter of the iliu. "If I tell you all you wish to know, we'll get no sleep tonight. But knowledge is better than information, and if you are willing, I will cause your own eyes to see something of what the iliū see."

I was not sure what he meant by this, but I readily assented.

Immediately he advanced toward me, and I felt alarmed; I had never truly realized before that the iliū are larger than men. He came around the fire and stood in front of me, and placed his hand on my forehead, and the other on my shoulder. His hand felt wet and leathery, both like and unlike human skin.

"What do I do?" I asked, nervously.

"Do nothing," he responded. "It will come."

Nothing seemed to come; I looked around, making out in the darkness the embers of the fire, and Oluon staring fearfully at us, and of course the iliu looming over me. I felt somewhat foolish.

But then I noticed that the clearing was becoming lighter; or, more precisely, that the clearing was as dark as ever, but that my eyes were becoming more sensitive. It was like coming from a well-lit room into the night, and waiting as the eyes adjust. But there were no moons this night, and we had been sitting in the darkness for hours; this was some deeper seeing.

Soon I could see details of grass and leaves, as clearly as if it were day, yet knowing that it was night. I could see the iliu clearly— his golden eyes, focused on mine, his bluish-grey skin. But these were characteristics of all iliū, so far as I knew; now I became conscious of him as an individual, as Lago. His eyes were browner than those of other iliū; his blunt nose was of a particular shape; his skin was darkened somewhat by the sun; he was young, and pleasant of appearance.

When I turned to Oluon I had something of a shock— he was of such a strange brownish color; his skin looked fragile and dry; his ears were protuberant and convoluted; he was small and seemed to be covered with fur, like an animal.

I looked about me, and I felt that I was growing. Indeed I was seeing more and more of the world around me. I was aware of the hill around me; I saw the stream burbling by; I saw the trees— no, not simply trees: beeches, elm, birch, spruce, maple, apple, each so different that it seemed simple carelessness to call them all by one name. I was aware moreover that they were alive, sleeping in the darkness, but growing, preparing for the day. And there were animals, too. Here, of course, was our own donkey; but there was a fox on the hunt, and there a family of rabbits, there an owl flying by, and mice scattered about like dots. I heard the crickets chirping, and underneath this noise, as it were, a buzzing murmur— the sound of a billion insects, pursuing their small and strange ways.

I could still see Oluon and Lago in the clearing, but now it seemed that they were far below me; I was soaring over the hills, darkened by night, but opened like a windowed hall to my curious sight. To my right, like a sleeping giant, was the bulk of the Gaumê; to my left rolling plains, the entirety of Cēradānar, soft and inviting as a bed. I could trace our route, along the wrinkles of the river valleys, back to Araunicoros, which I felt as a little pool of agitation and sadness. For this landscape was populated by men, and I felt their wills and their desires like colored flames— angry yellow, proud blue, despairing gold, beautiful and comforting green— and I saw the patterns they made, moving constellations of authority and poverty, greed and love, injustice and happiness. And I was not divorced from them, but each one, each person, each passion, touched and changed my own spirit.

With every moment the picture grew denser, the complications increased. In the east loomed a shadow, a blind confusion, a tread of heavy sandals; that was Munkhâsh. To the west, splendor and friendship, youth and foolishness— that was Cuzei, in iliu eyes; but I was looking through my own eyes as well, and I felt longing and tenderness wash over me like a thunderstorm. I stood over sleeping Cuzei like a mother over her child; till another jewel caught my eye. It was the land of the iliū, to the north— a little land, smaller than Cuzei, but dancing with joy and power like a waterfall, and looking out upon the sea, which beckoned to me like first love. And my eyes did not stop at the waves, but plunged down into the thick, watery atmosphere, and made out the world that lay under the waves, with its own community of animals and plants, its own nations and histories. And more and more lives crowded upon me, each with its story to tell, each confronting me with a small bright insistence.

For a brief moment I felt myself like the whole world, shot through with souls, clothed with green plants, with rivers as my veins, with mountains as my bones; and yet there was more to come; I had seen only a fraction of Creation; I was poised over an abyss of stars and mysteries. I could take it no longer; I screamed, in earthquakes and volcanoes; I wished to escape, but how could a world hide from itself?

Then I felt myself shrinking, collapsing, in a headlong, rapid fall. I crashed to the bottom, and for a long time was aware only of blackness and a terrible rushing sound. When I became aware of my own body again it ached all over.

Something was pressed to my lips, and I drank— something sweet as honey, but cooling as water.

"Are you well?" came the voice of Lago.

"I think so," I said.

I became aware that I was lying on my back, staring up at the stars, and at Oluon and Lago crouching over me; but I could see them only dimly; my eyes had grown once more small and dull and dark.

"Is that truly how you see?" I gasped. "You are gods!"

"We are iliū," he said, simply. "Understand that what you have seen is art, not nature. I have shown you true things, but their truth is that of visions, not that of geometry books. And now let us sleep, my friends."

In the morning, when we woke, Lago was gone. But he had left breakfast for us— fish from the stream, and waybread, and a bowlful of red berries. Served with cool mountain water, it was a glad feast.

12 · TIOZ≡ · Berak

The people who live in the Gaumê have a reputation for fierceness. We were warned of the bandits who lived in the mountains, whose terrifying war-cries we would hear before we saw them bearing down on us. They would kill us simply for sport; perhaps even leaving our valuables with our bodies. They wore necklaces of human bones, and when they saw a sick man, their reaction was to laugh rather than to cry.

The first mountaineer we saw was a shepherd, thin, dressed in rags, and looking decidedly unwarlike. He looked at us sadly as we passed, and said nothing in response to our greeting. He turned out to be representative of the people of the Gaumê, which is a land of impoverishment even by the standards of the Caḋinorians. Here the houses were meaner, the children thinner and dirtier, the villages lonelier, than in any country we had yet seen. The very crops of the field are stunted in their growth.

These two pictures are not so incompatible as they might appear. In years of drought the Babblers of the mountains do sweep down on the valleys, no doubt howling like demons; and if they scorn gold and silver it is because they are more attracted by food, animals, and tools. Raiding one's neighbors is no evil in Babbler eyes, but wins glory and respect. It does not even prevent more peaceful forms of commerce in better times.

Follow the Taucrēs almost to its source, to where mountains rise and plunge like rams above the laughing water, and become so high and cold that their tops are white with snow, and you will find a hamlet perched on a rushing stream. Take the road which twists up from the valley, and you will soon see, looming above you like a threatening thundercloud, the stronghold of the Babbler baron Berak.

The keep is situated on a spur of the mountain, so that on two sides, the south and east, it is protected by unclimbable cliffs. To the north and west its approaches are passable, but very steep, and dominated by it. The road passes under its nose and continues climbing into the mountains, till it reaches a valley which threads its way through to the other side of the Gaumê— the Taucrēte Pass itself.

The keep itself is very strong, without subtlety. There are no buttresses to simplify its construction, no towers placed to repel attackers. The builders trusted only in brute strength: walls thicker than a man is tall and too high to climb, arranged in a rough circle, an arrowflight in diameter. There are not even slits for arrows; only the ramparts can be manned. A Cuzeian general could reduce it, brick by brick if need be, but it would be a weary task. Surrounding the keep are a number of outbuildings— barns, barracks, servants' shanties. They are not defended; in war they would have to be abandoned.

A single guard manned the main gate, or more precisely a bench just inside the gate, positioned such that any visitor would appear as a black silhouette against the daylight— if the guard was even looking in that direction; he was not. He was staring off into space; we had to hail him two or three times before he noticed us.

"What do you want?" he asked, finally.

"We want to see your master," I said.

"So go in," he said, with annoyance.

Inside the walls are several buildings: stables, storehouses, a temple, all made of dried mud and roofed with straw; a stone barracks; and a wide circular tower, also made of stone. With its thick walls and weathered appearance, it is obviously the oldest part of the keep, if a pile of loose masonry behind it is not the remains of some still earlier structure.

The inner keep was not guarded at all. We passed into a huge, dark room, which encompasses the whole of the first level, and was crowded with stores— sacks of grain, firewood, armor, sausages and hamhocks, dried fish, onions, tools, jars of wine, casks of beer. There were also hammocks, some of which were occupied, and women working at various tasks, and children playing on the floor. The air was thick with the smell of grease, sweat, mold, food, animals, and urine.

A staircase leads up to the next level. This level is divided in half, along the keep's diameter. One side is a dining hall; the other is the kitchen; both rooms share the huge fire in the center of the keep. Another set of stairs leads up to the third floor, which contains the quarters of the important inhabitants of the keep;

the roof is available for defense. There were quite a few men in the dining hall, in groups of two or three— talking, gambling, or sleeping. A few dogs lay lazily before the fire.

It was not hard to discover who was the baron: the big man sitting in a carved chair, feet on the table, drinking beer and arguing loudly with a soldier a little bigger and older than he was.

I was somewhat annoyed by the absence of ceremony. Visiting the Prince of Araunicoros, we had been announced and escorted, and received courteously. Here we were paid no more attention than a glance. Were we supposed simply to walk up to the baron? We did so; there was no reaction; he continued talking and laughing with his companion. If he had even noticed us, he gave no sign.

I felt increasingly foolish; I had about resolved to leave, to find some functionary to ask when we could be received, when I noticed the baron's eyes upon us. He nodded his head impatiently.

"Eīledan bless you," I said, feeling my tongue heavy in my mouth. "I am Beretos, of the House of Etêia Mitano, and I am sent by the King's Council of Cuzei, and by my Lord Zeilisio, as Resident and Ambassador to your dominion."

Berak looked me over. I examined him at the same time. A large man, even larger in the middle, fortyish, red hair, short beard, very large nose, small eyes, a mouth given to frowning. He looked at me, then at Oluon. He traded glances with the old soldier. Finally he spoke or grunted a response: "Huh."

"I believe I was expected," I said. I felt a desire to fill the silence— to justify myself, to get some kind of response— and only just stopped myself.

"Huh," Berak said again. He turned to his companion. "A military man, you know. That's what they said they'd send."

"A soldier," commented the other. "Not one of these." He raised his mug unsteadily to his mouth and drank.

I realized for the first time that both of them were leaden with drink. A further difficulty was their mountain accent, the vowels drawled and twisting; I would hardly seize their meaning if it were not so simple.

"We're trained in the arts of war," I offered.

"Huh," said Berak, unanswerably. "You know the Cuzeian speech?"

"I am of Cuzei, baron."

"You know writing?"

"Of course."

"You can teach them to the women," he decided. "You'll do for that."

"Willingly, baron; but I assure you—"

"Yeah, you're a soldier," said the baron, and laughed mightily. "Tell me, how many men have you killed?"

"None, baron, but among us—"

The baron laughed again. "A one-souled man! They're all godspeakers," he added, to his friend.

"Mieranac take 'em all."

"You're mistaken, baron. If I could demonstrate..."

"They did say you people can be tiresome," sighed the baron. "Fereto or whatever the name was, I don't have time for you right now. You can see I'm busy. Tomorrow morning you can come and teach the women. Now leave me alone and don't give me any shit about it."

There was no point in arguing with such a request. Oluon and I withdrew. We walked all the way back to the village. We could have stayed in the keep, surely— who would have stopped us? — but I wanted to get as far away from the castle as I could, for one more night at least.

I had to fill in some gaps for Oluon, who had not been able to follow much of the conversation.

"Have we killed anyone!" he said, incredulously. "If that's his test, I'll pass it soon enough. I'll start with him."

"The same thought crossed my mind," I assured him.

"What are you going to do, Beretos? We have to improve his defenses, and he doesn't even want to listen to us."

Oluon had a way of stating problems very clearly, and expecting me to solve them.

"I'll think about it," I said.

13 · b△∧⅂b(XZ · *Sofuseca*

When his friend Oromo was captured by the people of the Cloud Kingdom, the Sojourner traveled south to the ice kingdom of the Turicali, and began to raise falcons.

It was tedious work. First of all, a pair of falcons had to be captured, young enough to be trained. It is necessary to capture them in the wild, because the Turicali do not sell their birds. The training itself requires long hours and much care. And once he had trained them to trust him and to return to his hand, it took many months for them to hunt enough airswallows for his purpose.

To rescue Oromo, he needed to rise to the level of the clouds, and for this of course he needed a vehicle which was lighter than air. Smoke is lighter than air, but it is too unsubstantial to ride on. It was the Sojourner's idea to build a boat of the feathers of birds; but most birds do not rise anywhere near to the level of the Cloud Kingdom, and their feathers were useless to him. Only the airswallows, who actually build their nests in the clouds, and never touch land, have feathers of the necessary lightness. Living so high in the air, they are almost as inaccessible as the Cloud Kingdom; but sometimes they fly low enough that the highest-flying of falcons, those of the land of the Turicali, can catch them.

If he was fortunate, his falcons could find one airswallow each day; and with the feathers of the birds they caught he began to build his boat. He tied the boat to his bed, because otherwise it would slowly rise into the sky. After six months it was large enough to carry his weight. He piloted the boat into the sky, came to the Cloud Kingdom, and rescued his friend.

I often thought of the Sojourner, capturing airswallows one at a time, as I began my stay in the castle of Berak. How alone he must have felt, separated from Oromo and all who knew him; and how tedious and foolish the work must have seemed, however necessary it was.

We were invited to sleep in the lower level of the keep, among the onions and the cooks; or in one of the barns, with the boys who cared for the goats and the cows. Undignified though this would be for a Cuzeian Resident, I would have done it, if doing so would have offered more contact with the baron, and thus opportunities to change his opinion of us. However, the baron and his men seemed intent on ignoring us no matter what we did; and since that was so, it was more convenient to sleep in the village, Cihimia, where we were more comfortable. An old man and his wife let us stay with them. In return for this we helped him with his garden and his animals, and gave them some silver.

My official duties were the teaching of Cuêzi to Berak's wife Sintilna, his two daughters Faliles and Sielineca, and Vaôora, the daughter of his *tiedectescrion*, or Master of Troops. Berak had a son also, named Cruvec, but the baron evidently believed that Cuêzi was only for women.

The time of our lessons was an hour a day. In the first weeks that hour seemed to stretch on without end, like an epoch, like an imprisonment. It was good fortune if just ten minutes of this hour could be spent in language instruction; the rest of the time the women wanted to talk.

It should have been a pleasure to talk with them, for they were very curious about Cuzei; but their chief interests seemed to be what clothes were worn there, what domestic comforts the women had, what the marriages were like, and what kind of sexual pleasures were indulged: subjects, for me, of great tedium. When we had exhausted these they wanted to talk about their own lives: their complaints about Berak, the faults and crimes of the rest of the keep's inhabitants, the details of their daily round.

It did not take long to learn the outlines of their lives, especially since these lessons were reinforced with endless repetition. It was evident that Berak was a cruel man, who had never a kind word to spare for the mother of his children, and indeed punished her frequent outbursts of anger with blows and insults. The constant theme of his comments, whether uttered in the marriage bed or in the dining hall among all the household, was the ugliness of his wife, and her likelihood to betray him with the nearest servant lad or soldier. Both of these were complete slanders, as far as I could see. Sintilna was somewhat fat, but this was counted a virtue among the Babblers; and for a Babbler woman she was by no means difficult to look at, though she had a brown spot on her nose, and her face was generally distorted with petulance. As for her virtue, I am convinced that even if she were not afraid of her husband, it would not have entered her head to desire any other man of that household. He however indulged himself openly with the servant girls.

Curiously, it was not these abuses which were the focus of her complaints. What she decried in her husband was his stinginess about giving her things, and his refusal to support her in her various quarrels. I have rarely met a woman so focused on gifts and on privileges. Her first question for me was what gifts I would give her for learning Cuêzi.

Faliles had fifteen years. This was somewhat old for a Babbler girl and the daughter of a baron to remain unmarried, and Berak teased her unmercifully for it, though it was he himself who kept her unmarried, being unsatisfied with any of the offers he had yet received for her. Given the difference in years, she was an exact copy of her mother in attitude and appearance; they were inseparable.

Sielineca had only twelve years, and was very pretty; her father had already received offers for her hand. She was quieter but more intelligent than her sister, and her questions about Cuzei or Araunicoros were more interesting; but she was moody, and on some days would sit the whole hour without speaking a word. And Vaðora had a year less, and was rather childish; it was evident that she was a particular favorite of Sintilna, and had been indulged to the point of license. At least once each lesson she grew bored and made enormous trouble if she was told she couldn't leave. Sintilna would take her on her lap and cajole and baby-talk her back into a good humor.

Of Cuêzi it seemed that they could learn nothing, or I could not teach. I felt an utter failure: Berak thought me unworthy of anything but the teaching of women, and it was becoming evident that I could not do even that.

After about three weeks I pulled myself together. You're acting like Oluon, I told myself, talking nonsense with women. But Oluon would at least take pleasure from it.

When I thought further I realized what the error was in my tutoring. I was allowing the women to speak Caðinor all the hour long; and if I did not take seriously the task of teaching them Cuêzi, how would they do so themselves?

At the next session I told the women that I must henceforth ration my speaking of Caɗinor: I could speak only two hundred words of it per hour.

Faliles laughed. "You're teasing us," she said.

"No, I'm not," I said. *"Āno, duna, dīma."*

They knew the numbers from one to ten, at least. Faliles looked surprised, but she still didn't believe it. "I'll bet I can make you say more than two hundred words in Caɗinor."

"You'll lose. *Bāor, pâtu.* Don't make me waste words. *Sêta, xāeps, yosi, nebu, dêt."*

They wanted to see what would happen when I reached two hundred, of course. I delayed them by making them rehearse the Cuêzi words they knew. *"Rāe ê?* [What is this?]" I would ask, of object after object, answering myself in Cuêzi if they didn't know it. We moved on to where, how many, what color. It wasn't long before I could be speaking nothing but Cuêzi for minutes on end— and they too were speaking mostly Cuêzi, though frequently dipping into Caɗinor: "How do you say floor? Is that right?"

But to keep the game going I would say something in Caɗinor now and then, being careful to count my words each time. They didn't even know the numbers above ten, but they were learning. They learned the pronouns, too, and some of the verbs in present time. We had gone over some of this before, but now I had their attention.

Finally I did reach two hundred. It was perhaps halfway through the hour. "*'Nô' ê* 'but.' *Aēe! Duna sicātu!"*

"Now what happens?" asked Sielineca.

"Nothing," I said, in Cuêzi. "I can only speak Cuêzi now."

"Oh, come on. What are you saying?"

"Cuêzi, Cuêzi, Cuêzi," I said.

I only kept them in class for five minutes longer that day. I annoyed them with very simple sentences, using the words they were supposed to know: with just a little thought they could understand what I was saying. But this day only Faliles managed to catch most of my babbling.

I played the same game for two more weeks. At first they resisted and teased me, and tried to make me speak Caɗinor. But then they started to cooperate with me, and to scold each other for making me use up any of my two hundred words. By the end of the second week I could get to the end of the hour without using up my ration of Caḍinor. They knew the names of all the things in our classroom, the names of many colors and qualities, and a number of verbs, and they could each, very clumsily, write their own names.

Of my students, Vaḍora was almost hopeless; she could hardly be brought to finish a sentence. She would utter a few words, and then cry out, "I don't know it. I don't know it," and refuse to look at me. But as the others passed her by, and began to say things she could not understand, it was as if she awoke from a dream: she asked a flurry of questions, and bothered us for translations, and paid attention to my explanations. Then, satisfied that she was missing nothing, she would grow bored and stupid once more.

The baron's daughters, Faliles and Sielineca, did very well. They had little trouble with sounds or grammatical points, and picked up words after hearing them only once or twice. Of the two, Sielineca learned more quickly, but her speech was always halting, due to her great fear of making mistakes. I think they took to the language as a game; and I tried to maintain their interest by repeating jokes or nonsense in Cuêzi.

Sintilna was wiser: she was never unwilling to speak, or daunted by errors. Though it took her longer to learn a thing than it did her daughters, and though she mangled the sounds, and as often as not forgot how the verbs went, she equaled them in fluency.

There was indeed a hunger for learning in her, which perhaps was a new thing for her as well. It was a wonder to see in a barbarian woman who had lived all her life first in one mountain fortress and then in another, who perhaps had never heard the name of Cuzei before her lord informed her that she was to learn its language. But once our learning had started in earnest, it was she who pressed us forward, preventing the girls from too much foolishness, resisting even Vaḍora's whining.

I asked her why she wanted to learn Cuêzi. "Because it is *lelîyas* [culture]," she said (using the Cuêzi word; there is no way to say it in Caḍinor).

"But why should a Caðinorian woman want *lelîyas?*" I asked.

"Why are you teaching me, if it is not to be given to Caðinorians?" she retorted.

But in the coming weeks it was Faliles who surprised me with her fluency. The sounds came quicker and quicker to her tongue; she picked up words like a dog eating meat; she corrected her mother; her sister complained that she spoke too fast. And yet she seemed to exert herself no more than she ever had in class. It was as if she were learning the language in her sleep.

It was not in her sleep. I was returning from a walk one day when I was hailed by Faliles, who was sitting on the grass on a hill overlooking the village, speaking happily with Oluon, with his hand in hers.

I waved at them and moved on, leaving them to their privacy. I knew from her fluency how long they had been talking, and could guess how much. I reproved myself for not having guessed the truth. Oluon's task was to help train Berak's soldiers; that being for now impossible, his only duties were to help the old couple with the light tasks they asked of us, and to practice swordsmanship and archery with me for several hours each day. Time must have weighed heavily on his hands; and the opportunity to chatter with an agreeable, pretty maiden must have seemed heaven-sent.

I was not so pleased myself. I trusted Oluon not to misbehave himself; the girl was, although a barbarian, the daughter of the local lord, and I was sure that he would treat her with deference. But what if her father, who had no such faith in this unknown outlander, learned of this relationship? When we next spoke, I exhorted Oluon to discretion.

14 · ⵣⵍⵓⵛⴱⴰⵜⵛⵛⵣⴱ · *Aurisôndias*

No Babblers, outside Cayenas and Araunicoros, make or read maps. To go from one place to another or to distinguish one baron's lands from the next's they rely entirely on memory. A people without writing can accomplish prodigious feats of recall. A storyteller I know in Araunicoros can recite a poem of thirty thousand lines; while a plier of boats like Ariñmiera may know every turn of the river and every hidden sandbar for two hundred lests.

Once every three or four years a Babbler lord walks the limits of his domain with each of his neighbors, to make sure it is known. There is rarely a true lapse of memory; but it does happen that a lord will pretend to remember a larger domain than his father held, and then there is war.

It occurred to me that it would be a valuable thing to have a map of Berak's barony, and that the making of it would be a good use of our idleness. I sought out Berak and told him of my intentions.

"What is this thing, a map?" he asked.

"It's a picture," I explained. "It's as if a painter could see like a bird, and draw a picture of your lands from a dozen lests in the air."

"It sounds like foolishness to me," said Berak. "Why should he paint mere land, without any people in it? And how can he see like a bird, being a man?"

For answer I took a fresh sheet of paper (from the stock I had brought from Cuzei, since there is none to be found in Babbler lands), and drew a quick map of Cēradānar: the mountains on either side, the rivers flowing north to the sea, Cuzei in the west, his own barony perched on the mountains in the east, Munkhâsh across the mountains on the right edge of the map. It took him a long time to understand that the lines corresponded to rivers and borders and seacoasts, and when he did he said that the Plain was much bigger than a sheet of paper.

"Of course," I said. "But the lands must be drawn small to fit on the sheet."

Berak laughed. "So you've shrunk all of Cuzei and all the lands of the Caďinorians onto a sheet of paper. That's a form of magic I never knew. Now if I take a pin and poke it through your map, will the people who live there die?"

"No, no. It's only a picture. It's not Cēradānar itself. If I draw a picture of you and poke it with a pin, will you die?"

He looked at me and frowned. "You're only a minor magician," he said. "I don't think you could harm me. But a very strong magician can kill a man that way."

I stared at him with my mouth open. How could one reason with such a people as this?

He was looking at my map of Cēradānar. "It's such a picture as this you want to draw of my lands? You'll fit all of them on a paper, like this?"

"Yes, baron."

"Very well," he smiled. "That's a magic Neictereho doesn't have. It'll be a good thing for our house to own, and then certainly no enemy can draw our Map. Go, make this thing for me."

I left his presence marveling at his simplicity. Still, it would be well if the baron learned that we had skills other than that of teaching reading and writing.

Berak's armorer helped us make the surveyor's tube. The tube was mounted on top of a plate marked off with the sections of a circle, and on top of the tube we welded the floating lodestone I had brought from Cuzei. The tube allows precise sighting by eliminating distractions, while the lodestone has an affinity for the north. This construction was placed on a stand made of wood. All these things I learned from Sūro.

Our first task was to make a rough map, walking round the barony selecting reference points and deciding what features must appear on the final map. For reference points we chose the high point of Berak's keep, which is visible almost everywhere in the barony; the top of the mountain known as Kravcaene-Limura; two other hills, whose heights we indicated with red standards; and the bridge over the Little Demaresc down in the village.

Now we must accurately plot these points on our map. We would walk to each point in turn and measure the angles of all the other reference points visible from it. This must be done very carefully, lest the whole map be skewed. When this was done, I sat down with map, circle, and straightedge, and worked out the locations of each point. One point is plotted, and the angles to the others are drawn. The next point is plotted a certain distance along the appropriate line drawn from the first point, and its angles are drawn, in the correct orientation. If the angles have been recorded correctly, the remaining points can be added in their proper places.

It was now time to add the scale. For this we needed to know the distance on the ground between any two of our points, and this could be obtained by pacing. This is a simple task in the long flat fields along the Isrēica; in Berak's land of hills becoming mountains it is of great difficulty. The line must be broken into short segments, each one measured, and the angle of each with the horizontal determined. This can be done with a trough of water. There are rules of angles which will convert paces on (say) a sixtieth-circle slope into the true flat distance.

Sometimes we gauge distance by shooting arrows, but this is only an approximate technique, and useless for surveying.

We actually paced three distances, in order to improve the accuracy of our map. It is not necessary to pace each of the lines on the map; if the angles are correct the remaining distances can be read directly from the map.

Now we could plot minor features. The method is simple but laborious. We would take the surveyor's tube to the point to be mapped (a curve in the river, a tree marking the edge of a wood, a small hill) and measure the separation from north of any two of our reference points. If the keep is a thirtieth-circle from north, and Kravcaene-Limura a third-circle from north, then we draw on our map a line a thirtieth-circle from south from the keep, and one a third-circle from south from the mountain. Where the lines intersect, there is the tree's location on the map.

This work lasted several weeks, for we had several hundred points to measure and plot. It was pleasant work. We rose early and spent the morning measuring. We took turns at the surveyor's tube, as it wearies the eye. Toward noon we would stop to take our lunch, which was usually bread with cheese and sausage and beer. If we were near the river we drank from it; this high in the mountains the water is clear and cold. Sometimes we could catch fish in the river, or shoot a rabbit. Once we discovered a field of raspberries and filled our stomachs with them. We would work for a short while in the early afternoon before returning to the keep for our practice in swordsmanship.

Only the valley was well inhabited. Most of the barony was wilderness, with only here or there a farmhouse or a forester's hut. In the east the hills led up and up to the sharp peaks of the Gaumê (much higher and rockier than our mountains in Tefalē Doro). There were cliffs and waterfalls and rolling forests and slopes too steep to climb.

We often neglected our surveying to wander, or swim in a mountain stream, or lay back on the meadow looking at the sky. We are different from the Babblers in this way. Any Babbler we saw (and they were few) was there for work: hunting, fishing, gathering wood, looking for herbs. I never met a Babbler who loved these fields of Eīledan for their own sake. The Babblers leave the mountains to animals, demons, and Munkhâshi; even their gods live in regions of cities and tended fields.

In Berak's keep we felt like Samīrex, when he was in bondage to the lord of the Forest King, and must work as a servant, not revealing his true lineage. In the mountains we could at least remove our disguise, if not our exile. We could talk freely in Cuêzi, and of Etêia Mitano; already we longed for it deeply. I hoped the Lady Caumēliye was well, and was not letting Corumayas once again drag the finances of the House into ruin.

Faliles walked with us some days. She was very useful as a guide, providing names of places to add to our map, and names of trees and plants to improve our knowledge of the land. With my eyes trained by Sūro, I was alive to the differences between this land and ours. The soil is brown here rather than black. The forests are mostly pine and fir in the heights, mixed with beech, maple, elders, and elm further down— no cypress or oak, as in Cuêzi. There are no roses, or lilies, or Isiliē's-tears; but there were daisies, and mountain-blooms, and a small pale flower that dotted the meadows and can only be named in Cadinor: *gerisas*. Faliles pointed out to us plants which were useful for medicines, dyes, or clothing.

It was a very different thing surveying along the river valley, where the Babblers live— in Cihīmia, the village opposite the keep, and in several smaller hamlets. Wherever we ventured we were surrounded by a shifting group of children, naked and dirty and fascinated by the strange work being done by these outlanders with papers and poles and a monstrous one-eyed folding contraption.

"What's that? What's that?" the children would ask.

"It's a tool to help make a map."

"What's a map?"

"It's a type of picture. We're making a picture of all the land that belongs to the Baron."

"Let's see."

I would show them our map, and where all the places they knew were on it. A few of them understood it.

Through the children we met the mothers, and through the mothers the fathers; thus we came to know the villagers of the barony. We were not allowed to eat the lunch we had brought; we were given meat and herbs wrapped in bread, and apples, and cider, and if we did not eat enough— enough to be rendered completely immobile— they were offended.

Their hospitality is the more laudable because of their poverty. The soil is not good here, and does not easily bear sustenance for man. By custom they must either farm or hunt; those who farm must leave all the small animals for those who hunt, while all the large animals (deer or bear) are reserved for the baron's household. Either kind of Babbler may keep sheep or goats, however. The baron and the godspeakers also take a large portion of the crop, and have the right to one sheep and one goat a year from each flock. For all these reasons, there is much sickness here, and much hunger.

The girls of the village run naked until their breasts and lower hair appear. They are then sequestered for six months in a special house; they can be attended only by their mother's female relatives, who give her instruction, and teach her how to make clothes. There is a ceremony when a girl comes out of the house. She is now considered a woman, and must cover her loins at all times.

She will be married at the age of thirteen or fourteen, though she will not go to live with her husband and his family till her coming of blood. She may bear a dozen babies over the course of her life; it is not uncommon for just two to reach adulthood. She will teach her daughters from a young age to help her with her chores (which include cooking, weaving, taking care of younger children, gardening, minding the chickens, making cider, and helping her husband in the fields). Her sons will help their father, whose tasks are working the fields, fishing, making weapons, toys, and tools, caring for sheep and goats, brewing beer, and building their house.

In all of Berak's lands there is no man who makes a living through working metal, or leather, or pottery, or through trade. Each family makes what it needs. However, gifts may be exchanged at times of ceremony, and a villager will occasionally walk to a village in the plains to trade goat's milk or eggs or syrup or rabbits for tools or salt or olive oil or other town goods. A fine knife or pot from Araunicoros will find its way all the way to Cihimia, one trade after another.

The men marry at eighteen or nineteen. They must build a house before they are allowed to take a wife. A rich man of the Babblers may take another wife, and may have his slaves to bed as well. However, it is very rare to find a man in Berak's lands with enough substance to afford a second wife, much less slaves (though the keep is of course full of servants).

The villagers' lives are difficult, but they are not without cheer. There are festivals throughout the year, at which processions are mounted and sacrifices of animals made; and there are celebrations for every ceremony— comings of age, marriages, deaths, births of second children. It is considered inauspicious to celebrate the first child's birth, lest demons take notice of it and mark it for death. These are occasions for music and dancing, and almost everyone gets quite drunk. The godspeakers also hold regular sessions, where petitions are received and payments rendered.

I tried to discover what the villagers knew of Cuzei. "It is a very beautiful place, where the gods live," a child told me; what is more strange is that I heard almost the same words from an adult man. Several knew it as a place very far away, whose gods were very strong. Some had heard it was a kingdom; they thought it was probably not so powerful as that of Araunicoros, which has a mighty reputation among the Babblers. I met two or three men who had gone on pilgrimages to see the holy lake Comex which is the home of their gods, and they had met Cuzeians in Araunicoros. Their opinion was not positive: "They are greedy men," one of them told me. "They are rich, but they always want more money, and they look down on us Caðinorians. I did not like to deal with them." Several of the Babblers had heard of the names of Iáinos, Eiledan, or Ulōne, but none knew a single teaching about them.

They know something more of Munkhâsh, because it is so close. Men from there come through the Pass to trade; and sometimes Caðinorians visit their realm. "It is a powerful kingdom," I was told. "Their gods are mighty, and they have strong weapons and many slaves."

I asked if they knew that Munkhâsh had been expanding, and what they would do if they came through the Pass into Cĕradānar. I received several answers: "We will fight and send them back." "They will stay on their own side of the mountains, because their gods are not strong here." "They have never invaded us and they never will." "I have been to Munkhâsh and I think they are good people. They are stronger than your people."

Only one man, a very old man, said that he feared the Munkhâshi: "When I was born the Munkhâshi lived far away, and another people lived in between us and them. They conquered them and made them their slaves. Many people crossed the Pass into our lands to get away from them. Endauron protect us if they should come any further."

"So the people live as slaves in Munkhâsh?" I asked.

"No, that was in the years after the conquest," he said. "Now there are not so many slaves; they live better."

I resolved that I must visit Munkhâsh for myself.

I drew a copy of my map for Berak, and presented it to him, as he sat eating with his men in his dining hall.

"This is your map, is it?" he asked. "I don't understand it."

I showed him his castle, and the village, and Kravcaene-Limura, and the river, and the other places in his barony.

He followed for a few minutes, but seemed displeased. He turned the map over in his hands, looked at it from various angles. Finally he asked, "What is it made out of?"

"Paper, of course," I said. "Maps are always made of paper."

"It will not be strong," he said. "You should have made it of wood or stone. The magic will not live long in this substance. You Cuzeians give flimsy gifts."

I was dismayed— did he not realize the value of paper, how precious was the small stock that I had dragged all the way from Cuzei? But I answered, "If you give me time, perhaps I can make you a map out of wood."

"A gift cannot be given again," he remarked. "What you have done you have done. Here, take it to the godspeaker. It is he who safeguards our talismans and holy things, of whatever worth."

Surely Samīrex in his bondage had more cheer than I, for at least his work pleased his master. In the nights I cried bitterly to Ulōne, asking for comfort; nor do I think there was ever any time when I felt less of Ulōne's presence.

15 · ZCdZ˘⁊ · *Antāu*

It entered Berak's fancy one day to come to his wife's Cuêzi lessons. He came at his wife's side, and from her peeved and helpless expression it seemed likely that his coming grew out of some quarrel.

He on the other hand was in an uproarious mood. "I thought I'd see how it goes among the women. Among the women and Cuzeians, I mean," he added, and laughed so heartily that I wondered if he was drunk.

"Have you come to learn Cuêzi?" I asked, coldly.

"I wanted to hear your singing a bit. My wife is always talking about it. What a beautiful voice he has, she says. Yes, she likes to hear your beautiful voice, and no doubt likes to look at a fancy young Cuzeian, too, don't you, Sintilna? I wonder what you learn here besides Cuêzi."

"Don't talk like a shameless one, my lord," said Sintilna, with dignity. "And you must call me Cammisi here."

"What?" roared Berak. "What is this Cammisi?"

"That's my Cuêzi name. It means yellow."

Berak laughed again; his wife maintained a cool expression, though her face was flushed. "Yellow! A Caðinorian name is no good to learn Cuêzi in. Only a woman would have thought of it. Tell me, master, what color should I be? How about red? What's the Cuêzi for that?"

"*Ruyise.*"

"*Ru-wisi?*" he repeated. "I don't like that. Too soft. What's green?"

"*Berede.*"

"I could have told you that," cried Sintilna. "We learned that weeks ago. That's where Beretos' name comes from."

"Of course it's his name. I don't have to learn any Cuêzi to know that. So what goes on here, besides calling each other with new names?"

"We're learning to read the book of Antāu," said Faliles, proudly.

"And what color is that?" asked Berak, with a chuckle.

During this time I was writing with soft chalk on a wooden board these lines from Antāu's book:

Heedless of harm, the prince spurred on his mount,
Searching the horizon for signs of the giant.
Untroubled was he by fear of the house-high tyrant;
His mind was on his lady of the Castle Forest.
If he should not return, if the giant should kill
He wished only to die worthy of his Lady.

When Berak had heard this, first in my voice, then in the voices of my class, he had to have it repeated slowly, then translated, and then explained. I ended up giving him much of the fifth canto before he understood it, and even then he would not let us continue, but had to offer his commentary.

"This bastard does think with his frond, doesn't he?" said Berak. "Off to fight giants, and all he can think about is this girl. She must be one witch's night in bed, eh?"

"At this point in the epic Antāu hasn't yet won his Lady," I explained. "So they haven't yet slept together."

Sintilna was eager to teach. "That's the Cuêzi doctrine of *coelīras*. It means devotion, treating women according to the way of Eīledan. It's very important to understand it when you're reading the epics."

"It sounds like foolishness to me," said Berak. "But go ahead, tell me what is this way of treating women."

"Every Cuzeian hero has a lady," Sintilna explained. (I had not yet taught them of the Sojourner.) "He does whatever she asks, and undertakes great deeds to prove his love for her. Only a commoner or an evil man treats a woman badly, or touches a woman if she hasn't given permission. In Cuzei the ladies run the Houses, and men write poems for them, and even the farmers come to them for judgment."

I do not think it is a bad description, especially for one born in barbarism and far from Cuzei. But Berak only chuckled.

"It's a land ruled by women, then," he said. "For your own sake, Beretos, I'll tell you, you're not going to get into their beds treating them like that. They'll just laugh at you, and what've you got for all your pains? Nothing. I'll let you in on a secret. You have to be a man. Do you see a bear writing poems to a female bear? No, he just straddles her and uses his frond. That's how we do it, and as a result we don't have any problem with women. When you learn that you'll be as manly as we are."

Such was Berak's talk, not only in front of his wife, but before his daughters.

We got through little Cuêzi, this day. I kept hoping that he would tire of the class, and spoke as much Cuêzi as I could, to bore him into leaving; but still he stayed, laughing and uttering barbarities and mocking his wife, and asking for translations of every word that was spoken.

I left the class in a foul humor, and as I stroke angrily through the dark halls of Berak's keep, with its rough stone walls, which were blackened from smoke, and never completely dry, I thought of the Lord Zeilisio's bright white House on the river, smiling with pillars and pools and statues; and when I emerged into the daylight, I gazed upon the shacks and the mud surrounding the keep, remembering the gardens outside Zeilisio's House, and the terraces sweeping down to the river, and I could not prevent tears from coming to my eyes.

"O Eīledan, why do you treat with me so?" I cried. "I am in exile, like a disgraced man; I am in prison, like a criminal. Every word this man speaks is brutality; he can see nothing in an epic less vile than himself, and he will not allow me to accomplish my mission... Why is your service so hard, and such an unrelieved weariness? How can such futility be service to you? And Ulōne, where is your strength, and where is your wisdom? I know I am full of weakness, but I've come here out of duty and love of Iáinos. It's very hard of you to allow these things to be."

I tried to remind myself of those who had suffered much worse than I. I was not suffering physically; prophets had been torn apart by the sinful, or murdered by kings; there were poor men who were starving, or weak from disease, or oppressed by cruel tyrannies. But this pious thought was no comfort, but only an added bitterness. It is said that an unhappy man hates the thought of another's joy; but neither does he rejoice in the suffering of any other innocent. If there are martyrs and poor in this world, so much the worse for this world. All these evils cry out to Iáinos; why does Iáinos not answer? *How fatherly, O Lady, is such a father?*

That of course is the verse from the book of Antāu, and it now led me to think of that story, and of all the feats done by the hero, and of the wonders he witnessed, giants and talking beasts and ships that moved of themselves, and the magician who called up an army of men without heads, and how Antāu, almost overwhelmed, hit upon the idea of retreating over a river, so that the sightless army followed him and drowned. He did all this to please his Lady's father, the lord of the Castle Forest, a tyrant who kept his daughter imprisoned in a room, and imposed half a hundred tasks on Antāu, hoping one of them would kill this importunate and penniless suitor.

And even that hero's great heart could not prevent a complaint to his Lady, on one of the occasions he was permitted to see her: how fatherly is such a father? Now here would be a doubled trap for such as Berak; for even if he could be brought to understand the evil done Isilië by her father— he would be more likely to emulate it— how could he begin to understand the Lady's deep and simple reply? *Yet I love him, for he is my father. For my sake, Antāu, do these things, and win me.*

Such beauty of heart, to love one unworthy of love; I am not capable of it myself, though perhaps my Lady Caumēliye is (but of course her father is no tyrant, but is as kind as she is). Of course Antāu executes all the tasks which are set for him, and it avails him nothing. The old king never intended him to have his daughter— he has betrothed her to Antāu's enemy Bodâyo instead. Now Antāu must rescue Isilië from the castle, and then defeat Bodâyo, who comes after her; and only when his enemy is dead can Antāu and Isilië spend the night at last in each other's arms. And then comes the passage which invariably brings tears to my eyes, when Antāu, having won his Lady, draws from their hiding place kingly robes, and reveals that in his own country he is a prince. And even the old father warms in our eyes as he prattles so proudly and foolishly at their wedding feast; and there is the delicious moment when the poet abandons the heroic meter, and describes the father's jig in the rhythm of a country dance, and how Antāu and his wedded Lady laugh.

I had walked far from the castle, and was now among the mountains, which are like the laughter of Eīledan, and reduce to a rag the foolishness of men. The air was cool here. I climbed up a boulder the size of houses, which looked over a meadow dotted with tiny mountain flowers. A hawk flew overhead; I wondered what mice or rabbits or birds were her prey. The only sounds were the whisper of wind, and the rustle of grass on the meadow, and, far off, the persistent call of a bird.

Truly men are capable of clouding Eīledan's world with miseries. But truly also to wander Eīledan's world makes those miseries small. The Babblers are wrong to put their gods in houses. The spirit that made the world cannot fit in them; that is why in Cuzei we worship out of doors.

Ulōne does sometimes give us peace. When I came down from the mountains, it was not myself but Sintilna whom I pitied. Where could she go, to whom could she appeal, to escape the life she led?

16 · Ū ̤X˥Ā̄Cbb(XZ̧ · *Xēcuvisseca*

It was from my youngest and dullest charge, Vaḓora, that I learned that her father Tentesinas was planning a scouting foray on the other side of the Taucrēte Pass. I waylaid the commander, the *tiedectescrion,* as he and some of his men were leaving the great hall after dinner, and told him that I must accompany this expedition.

"What for, to teach us Cuêzi?" asked the troopmaster. "This is a matter for soldiers, not for women and book readers."

"In Cuzei I am known as a swordsman," I replied, with dignity.

"In Cuzei many things pass for soldiers," he said. His companions laughed much at this weak joke, and before I could say more he was gone. I heard the jest from Berak the next day.

Oluon and I had endured many such encounters with Berak's men. I was a figure of fun for them; sometimes they would laugh just to see me, as if there was amusement in my very figure. They would call me names— book-lover, woman, hen, soft-cock, one-souled man— or make foolish jokes in loud voices as I passed.

Hatred can make us burn with anger even over absurdities. What shame is it to love books? What dishonor is it to be compared to women, whose virtues have always been the inspiration for heroes? But these mockeries made me as angry as a tomcat.

The Wise Sentences teach us to ignore such persecution: *None but a fool allows a fool to bait him.* I often doubted this teaching: was not my quietness in the face of their contempt simply mistaken for weakness?

But I think Oluon suffered more. He was not tainted by an association with books and women; but he did not speak Caḓinor well, and because of this he had a reputation for stupidity. When he tried to talk to the soldiers they imitated his mistakes and hesitations, and pretended not to understand what he was saying— tactics which enraged Oluon and made it even more difficult for him to get out his words.

Ironically the Babblers never practiced their military skills, unless the frequent fistfights among themselves or their hunts with Berak counted as training; while Oluon and I practiced our swordsmanship for two or more hours each afternoon. Usually we did this in the village (and as a result our reputation among the villagers was as formidable men), but one day we were practicing the Dance of Swords in the castle courtyard.

Abruptly we heard laughter. Tentesinas and two of his men were watching us. The Dance of Swords is delicate and precise; it is not calculated to earn the respect of a barbarian warrior. The youngest soldier— a boy really, the son of one of Berak's cousins— was imitating us, or at least prancing and bobbing in some way that was intended to be an imitation of us; it was enough to reduce his companions to helpless laughter.

Oluon disengaged, strode over to the boy, and grabbed him by the hair. "You— you— no more of that, if you want— if you know what's good for you," he stammered. The boy stuck his tongue out at him.

The second soldier was Dolbas, a huge man with small pig-like eyes, and the satisfied, stupid smile of a mean-minded man. "You'll notice," he remarked to Tentesinas, "how the Cuzeian threatens Burodoroî, who's half his size. I guess he thinks he could *almost* beat him in a fight."

"If he *could* fight," added Tentesinas.

Oluon pushed Burodoroî away, and turned to glare at Dolbas. I walked up to the two Babblers and looked them over, as a peasant examines pigs for sale.

"It's the book lover," Dolbas informed his chief.

"It's the book lover," I said, coolly. "Do you like our fighting, Babbler?"

I don't think I had ever called a Cadinorian that to his face.

"That was fighting?" asked Tentesinas, in mock surprise. "I thought it was dancing."

"In Cuzei it passes for fighting," said Dolbas, and glanced at his commander to make certain of his smile.

"You wouldn't pass for a fighter in Cuzei," I told him. "But you're big. If you were a little smarter you'd pass for a horse."

"He wants a fight," Tentesinas remarked.

"He's going to get a fight. I'm not going to let him talk to me that way."

Suiting deeds to words, he reared back to ready a punch for me. He had forgotten that I was carrying a sword; I reminded him, by holding it up in front of his face.

"You may be stupid enough to fight me fists against sword, but I wouldn't enjoy it," I said. "You can borrow Oluon's."

"I'll use my own sword," he growled.

"No, if you run away now you might not come back," I said. This was a completely unfair charge— unwillingness to begin a fight is not a Babbler vice— but I knew it would keep him there. Besides, he wouldn't have believed my real reason for wanting him to use Oluon's sword— that there was no sport in a contest of steel against bronze.

Dolbas reluctantly accepted the sword which Oluon held out to him. He adjusted his grip and slashed the air a few times; it was obviously lighter and shorter than anything he was used to. "This is a woman's weapon," he complained.

"It's good enough for fighting women, then," said Tentesinas, with logic. I fought down a response to this; it was time now to concentrate on the bout I had provoked. Tentesinas, Oluon, and the boy stepped back; Dolbas and I faced each other at about three paces distance. I prayed the prayer to Ulōne.

"What are you waiting for?" cried the commander. In response Dolbas charged me, swinging his sword with both hands. I had time to consider an immediate thrust to his belly, decided against it, and parried his blow easily; the air rang with this first meeting of metal, and then with many more.

We felt out each other's guard for a few strokes; then I relaxed, and he grew alert. He was a powerful man, and his blows would be disabling if they had touched me. He swung ponderously, used no doubt to mow down his enemies without thinking, depending on his strength for success and on his reach for defense; nor had he any variation in attack. I dodged or parried a few blows, then took the offensive. His defenses were clumsy, but prevented, for the moment, any decisive stroke. He rallied and swung at my neck; I ducked under the blade. He stepped forward and swung again. I saw my moment: I twisted my sword under his as it descended; his sword flew into the air and fell to the ground behind me. Dolbas cried out; I had slashed his hand. To end the exhibition I brought the flat down hard on his head. He fell to his knees and stayed there, staring stupidly at me, one hand holding his head. The bout had lasted about four minutes.

"You should be glad, Babbler, that I had no thought of killing you," I told him. "You have a natural strength, but you don't know how to use it. I wasn't in any more danger than I would be in bed. You know how to parry a sidestroke, but you don't know any of the defense positions— if I wanted to I could easily have slashed your belly open."

There was blood on my sword; I wiped it on the weeds growing at my feet. Tentesinas stared at me, frowning. He was also a big man, though not as big as Dolbas; but he was older, and sterner, and had much more thought about him. I wondered if he would challenge me next.

"Well fought, Cuzeian," he said, at last. "You have bested the strongest of my men. Yet you have no appearance of strength."

"Strength is nothing without skill and speed, *tiedectescrion*. Dolbas will best me in three months, if you give me the training of him. I was not sent to you as a teacher of women, but to build your strength as men of war."

Tentesinas considered this. "Sit with my men tonight in Berak's hall," he said, and then turned to make his way to the barracks.

Dolbas got up, unsteadily, and looked at us with confusion in his eyes. I let him collect himself, to think what he had to say.

"I— I think— I think I had you figured wrong," he said, slowly.

I nodded. "Now you know better. Are you angry?"

"No," he said, with surprise.

"Good. Go, we will talk with you also at dinner."

He nodded, then moved off quickly to rejoin his commander. The boy, Burodoroî, was still watching us; but when I looked at him he looked away, shamefacedly, and ran off.

Oluon and I sat down and laughed. We laughed for a long time, not so much at the discomfiture of the soldiers, but from relief. It was as if a long night was ended, or a drought had broken. We put away our weapons and mounted into the hills, walking, racing each other, swimming in the streams, and talking like warlords of battles and sieges and combat.

17 • T̄OΔbC̄ΛlαZb • *Brosiveyas*

"Ho there, Aiđoravos!" I cry. "Let's see some more life in you."

"Yes, lord," says the Babbler, and proceeds to wave his sword with somewhat more vigor, if no more precision.

"You're not going to stand up to the Munkhâshi with sleepy little strokes like that."

"Yes, lord."

"Do you want the demons coming through the Pass, into your houses?"

"No, lord."

"All right. Thank you, Aiđoravos. Troops, line up. Even up the line. Is that a straight line? Do you have eyes in your head? Now once around the keep, just to keep your blood moving. Come on, you laggards! Neictetes, Cambodouro, you're not too fat to run."

That's a typical drill session: me yelling, them yes-lording and no-lording, and marching about like sleepwalkers.

Naturally I formed the impression that they were slackers with only the appearance of being soldiers— that a real army would tear them up. Then I saw them in action, defending the keep against another mountain warlord (Aduredasco, who in times of peace trades with Berak; but this year his wheat failed, and he went raiding). They fight like animals. Ululating like demons, they fall upon the enemy, slashing and darting. They will gladly fight till they die, and they seem to ignore pain.

It is no wonder that they are donkeys in drill. They don't believe in it; they don't believe it's war. For them war is raids and invasions. Their aim is to close quickly with the enemy and best a likely opponent in single combat— winning glory, their opponent's weapons, and rewards from their liege if they win, an honorable death on a funeral pyre if they lose.

The Cuzeian concept of an army as a trained body defeating an opposing force through the execution of a single strategy is alien to them. This was worrying to me, for I knew from my talks in Eleisa with Sauōros that the Munkhâshi are well able to fight as an army: if the Munkhâshi ever won their way through the Pass, their advance through the Cadinorian lands would be rapid.

Again, even after I had won their trust, and had been training them for months, I found it almost impossible to get them to practice their archery; this also they do not consider as belonging to war. They are tolerable shots, but they use the bow only for hunting— as a weapon of war, they think it cowardly and degrading. The Babblers eschew any sort of trickery or strategy on the battlefield. The forces line up across from each other, in a leisurely way, spend some time insulting each other, and then rush across the intervening space to grapple. Under such conditions, indeed, an exchange of arrows would only delay the single combats in which alone glory is won.

They will use the bow when besieging a town or a keep, if its defenders will not come out for a battle— more out of frustration than for any tactical object. Unless they are very desperate, or the spoils to be won are very great, they have little patience for sieges. There is no glory in an enemy dying of hunger.

For all their talk of glory, however, their battles are likely to be short: no longer than is necessary for each soldier to find and fight one foe. If one side has suffered a majority of the casualties, it generally retreats; nor do the victors follow— they remain on the field of battle, collecting trophies. In a serious war the troops may engage several more times, till the outcome seems decisive, or one of the opposing commanders is killed. In a raid there is rarely a second engagement. The raiders are usually the victors, since they are generally more numerous. In the battle at Berak's gate, however, we defeated the raiders. I had already been training the men for several weeks, and they were able to defeat almost twice their number of Aduredasco's men.

Our victory did not prevent Aduredasco from raiding the village, for a simple reason: he had raided it before calling on us. Stealing food and animals, despoiling women, and stealing children for use as slaves, come as naturally as breathing to the Cadinorian soldier. These activities are only footnotes in their tales of war, and yet they are the real purpose of the raids. (A true war of conquest is rare among the Babblers; this will also bode ill in case the Munkhâshi come.) The purpose of the battle was not to protect the village or punish the raid, but to protect the keep from itself being ravaged.

A defeated raider is expected to release his adult captives, which Aduredasco did. It would not have been a very serious crime if he had not— one more reason for Berak to raid Aduredasco a few years hence, perhaps. It would be a different story if the captives belonged to the keep, of course— if they were soldiers or kinsmen of Berak. In that case honor would not be satisfied till the captives were returned.

The night of our victory Berak kissed me in front of all his household, and gave me presents— two cows, an amphora of good lowland wine, and a gold bracelet— and called me his son. Oluon also received gifts, not only because he had assisted in the training of the troops, but because he had killed a man— a kinsman of Aduredasco. Oluon was no longer a one-souled man: the dead man's soul was now his as well.

I was never able to change the Babblers' conception of war, or to reduce their cruelty to the innocent. My troops would have been immediately overwhelmed in a confrontation with any Cuzeian general. But I was able to greatly improve their strength and their swordsmanship, and through tireless insistence I gave them some idea of following a plan and obeying orders. I hoped it would be enough to fight Munkhâshi.

It became convenient, after we had been given the training of Berak's troops, for us to move from the village to the castle, where we were given rooms in the commander's house, next to the barracks. From here it was possible to learn how the life of the castle worked.

Berak is an independent *calenorion* or baron, responsible to no man outside his small domain. The Cađinorians have no laws of princes, nor any supreme king. There are customs, as for instance that strangers have right to a night's lodging, or that when brothers war their wives must not be violated; but customs can be broken, and ultimately a Babbler baron's security and power depend only on his own character, and the sort of relationships he has built with his neighbors.

Between his two neighbors Ceoresarȟ and Neictereho there is a fundamental difference: Ceoresarȟ is a kinsman, Neictereho is not. Certain reciprocities hold between Berak and Ceoresarȟ: gifts are exchanged; the two lords may hunt in each others' domains; they are expected to help each other if invasion threatens.

There are limits to the claims of blood; wars within clans are common enough. Berak and Ceoresarȟ are not likely to go to war, but I do not think Berak cares much for his cousin's company. Ceoresarȟ is older, and from childhood has made him the butt of jokes.

Neictereho is an old man, very proud and domineering, with a larger domain than Berak's— perhaps half the size of Etêia Mitano, though with no more than an eighth of the population. Berak's son Cruvec is betrothed to one of Neictereho's daughters. They will marry when Cruvec has some more years; when I left the keep he had eleven, and his bride nine.

When I write the boy's name I have to stop myself from writing Crummâ [sand], which Sielineca named him as soon as she learned the word. It fit him, as his hair was the color of sand, and he was a placid, incurious boy. Occasionally Sintilna would bring him to the Cuêzi lessons, where he learned nothing; now that we were training the men he would sometimes come to watch. Occasionally he would take a wooden rod and challenge the men to a bout, but he was only interested so long as they let him win. Mostly we saw him running around with the other children of the keep. The only education he needed, in Berak's eyes, was in war, and he was too young for that.

Within the household life there are strictly speaking no classes, only individuals. From a Cuzeian point of view, for instance, we would say, "Ancael, Raenca, and Corondas are servants, while Seresos is a soldier." This is not how the Babblers talk; they would say, "Ancael cleans the stables, Raenca is one of the cook's helpers; Corondas works for Sintilna's chief maidservant Seneinda, mostly carrying the heavy things; and Seresos is under the *tiedectescrion*." One asks not "What is his station?" but "Who is he under?"

There is thus no division into Lords, Upper Servants, Servants, and Villagers, as at Etêia Mitano; but there are definite distinctions of rank. The greatest privilege is that of living on the third level of the old keep, and this is restricted to Berak and his kin, Aiđodoroî the old godspeaker, the *domorion* (master of the house, something like a steward), and Seneinda. Excepting this group it is the soldiers, of all those in Berak's domain, who live best, and these indeed have Berak's greatest affection. The *tiedectescrion* lives in a stone house next to the barracks where his men are housed. Outside of war the soldiers have no real duties, except the enforcement of Berak's will, and if there is any complaint against them Berak will take their side. Many of them have taken servants from the castle as wives; if they had not I do not think any woman in the keep would walk safe.

The household servants are worked very hard, but are consoled by their elevation over the mere peasantry who live in the villages; and of course in bad times all who live in the keep eat well, even if the villagers who grow their food are starving. There are also a few slaves in the keep; one of them, a foreign girl captured in a raid against the different-tongued Babblers to the southeast, has become a particular favorite of Berak's; he has made her his personal handmaiden, and she has borne a son by him. Her name is Hānu. However, as a slave she retains a certain inferior status, and she is required to do whatever Sintilna asks of her. Sintilna hates her, and makes her life as difficult as she can.

I once found Hānu cleaning clothes in the courtyard. The lounging and careless manner of her work, and the savage scowl on her face, told that this was unwonted work for her. I ventured to ask if she was following the orders of Sintilna.

"She am goat and witch," replied the girl, in her broken Caḋinor. "I ask the gods' pestilence to her."

"What happened?" I asked.

"There am no happened. She tell me to make the clothes clean. She am cruel woman, but I am just slave, I am under to obey. Stranger, you know magic?"

"I'm not a magician."

"I see you draw things. You draw me a curse, no? A curse on cruel woman?"

"It's not magic that I draw, it's writing. It's completely harmless."

Hānu's expression became crafty. "Lord Berak like me very much," she confided. "I say what and he give it me. I get you things if you help me."

"I really don't know any magic," I said, with some annoyance. "But perhaps I can help you another way. I know Sintilna; I will ask her to treat you better."

For answer she spat on the ground and turned back to her clothes, making a great show of ignoring me. I confess that I rose in anger and walked away. Offered compassion, she could only demand sorcerous help in the pursuit of her own grievances; surely this is the sign of a foolish and violent spirit.

I did ask Sintilna about her. "A worthless, treacherous snake!" exclaimed Sintilna. "Berak should have her drowned in the river, before her tricks and insolence and her loose ass cause any more trouble in this house. But she has her claws wrapped around him, and he can't listen to a word against her." When she had calmed down a bit I asked her for what transgression she was being punished; it turned out that Sintilna had found her lounging in her own bed, as if she were Berak's wife and not his slave. In addition to the work she had imposed on her, she had had her whipped.

In the face of such emotion it did not seem the right time to intercede on the girl's behalf. I marveled at the defiance and ambition in the heart of this girl held as a slave among strangers so far from her home, but I did not expend much more thought on what seemed a mere side incident.

18 · bᴎZGIXZ · *Sulādeca*

It was a glad moment when we clambered to the top of the Hill of Brothers, forgetting our cares and our forebodings, to glimpse for the first time in almost four years the fields of Cuzei. Before us lay nothing more than a vista of vineyards and orchards, with the East Road winding into the distance, and a simple inn half a lest farther on; but even this rude scene spoke eloquently to us of the virtues of civilization: prosperous Houses, paved roads, comfortable lodgings for the traveler.

The authors of the epics must themselves have traveled, to have so carefully captured the joys of homecoming— the coming of Antāu to his own lands, with the Lady Isiliē riding at his side; Celōusio's proud return to his father's house, bearing aloft the head of the dragon— although my own homeward journey was not triumphant; it was more like that of Samīrex, whose heart was heavy with the burial of his brother in the desert.

We were met with long stares in Masāntie, and we did not immediately realize why. We— I and the traders accompanying me— looked like Babblers: sun-darkened, thin, long-haired, dressed in crude, travel-stained Babbler tunics and boots made of fur. I think the townspeople were startled to hear Cuêzi coming from our mouths. We hired swift messengers to ride to Eleisa to see whether the Lord Zeilisio was there or at Etêia Mitano, and while awaiting word from them took the opportunity to rest, and cleanse ourselves, and fit ourselves with new attire proper for Cuzeians.

The word came back that Zeilisio was not in Eleisa. We rode straight west, therefore, reaching the Isrēica thirty lests from Norunayas. We sailed with a cargo boat upriver to the city, and thence to Etêia Mitano.

It was a strange thing to glide along the mighty river and know every curve and every House, almost every tree, when I had seen none of them for four years, except in dreams. And indeed, this voyage seemed but another dream, its very calm and banality revealing its unreality; had I not dreamed many times before of returning to my Lady's House? At any moment, as had happened so many mornings, would I not awake to the sound of scrawny mountain cocks, or Berak's lean ugly dogs barking, or the shrill curses of women gathering water for washing clothes? Or perhaps it would be Oluon come to shake me awake into some new crisis involving Tentesinas, or Sintilna, or Ganacom.

There was more reality to my arrival at Etêia Mitano, because it was raining. It never rains in dreams. The boat pulled up to the dock; I leapt ashore, and promptly slipped on the watery wooden surface, landing with a jar on my rear. There was nothing dreamlike about that, nor about the soaking I received as I ran up the long flights of stairs to the House.

I was recognized by a maidservant, who went to fetch the head butler, who exclaimed over me and hugged me and said he would immediately find Corumayas; both of them disappeared before I had a chance to protest.

"O Beretos! What glad issue from such a stormy day!" cried the old steward, rushing forward to embrace me, and stopping short when he saw the state of my clothes.

"It's good to see you, Corumayas," I said.

"I'll tell the Lady immediately," he said, officiously.

"No you won't. I need to change these clothes; and if you please, have a boy bring a pot of warmed wine to my room."

"Yes, yes, of course, only... I suppose you will want your old room?"

Corumayas has a trick of expressing, without a trace of overt anger or resentment, how infinitely your presence has added to the burden of his duties. It was I whose countenance darkened; why had the old lizard taken over my room anyway? Still, I supposed that it could not be left untenanted for years, and the matter could be pursued later. "Eventually," I said, "but for now, take me anywhere I can get myself ready, and show me where you've stored what was in my room."

"Yes, come with me. I'll put you in— no, now that I think of it, not there... Just turn about and follow me, I'll put you in one of the guest rooms."

He led me upstairs to one of the guest rooms, close to Zeilisio's own chambers; but then he remembered that it was unsuitable, because Feroicolê would be visiting in two weeks, and he always stayed in that room. All this time, of course, I was dripping on the floor, and my tunic was sticking like noodles to my back. I suggested that traces of my presence could be erased from the room in the next two weeks, but that I needed to change clothes now. He rapidly rehearsed a number of other objections as I walked into the room, dropped my bags on the floor, and started to remove my tunic. I asked him where were my clothes.

"Yes, of course, your clothes. Let me see... where *could* I have... Let me check one or two places. It won't take a minute." He darted out of the room.

"Corumayas!"

He reappeared, surprise written all over his face.

"We'll find them later. I beg of you, Corumayas, have the fire lit in this room, and the wine brought, and borrow something to wear from someone my size. And before you do anything at all, bring me a towel."

"Yes, of course," he said.

I removed the rest of my clothes, and placed them by the fireplace where the fire wasn't roaring, and wondered how Lord Feroicolê enjoyed his stays here. But of course he would come bringing his own servants, and he was probably never in his life cold and wet.

I waited long enough to regret not following Corumayas, to ensure that my orders were accomplished. No towel came; but finally a boy appeared carrying logs and kindling. He stared at me curiously, shivering nakedly in front of the empty hearth.

"I think you're new to the House," I remarked.

"My name is Cênno," he said. "I remember you, O Beretos; we used to bring our grain to you, and you were with Lady Caumēliye when she came to our house when the plague took Grandma. I'm working in the House now. My father says that the House hasn't been run so well since you've been gone; Corumayas never knows anything. Will you be the steward again now?"

Fortunately he was not of those who cannot work as they talk; while he prattled he got the fire going.

"I will serve as the Lord Zeilisio asks me," I said, to answer his question. "Now, would you run and find me a towel, and a pot of warmed wine, and then ask Corumayas where are my clothes? Go on, run!"

The Lady Caumēliye arrived before my clothes did, but after the towel and the wine. My heart lifted to see her, lovely in black curls and red lips, wearing a long, simple robe, the color of the sky. I fell on one knee before her, and kissed her hand.

"Don't act like a courtier," she said, tenderly. "Stand up, my traveler among Babblers, and embrace me."

We embraced, and then kissed. "You're as lovely as you ever were in my dreams, O Lady," I told her.

She smiled at me; but when I looked into her eyes I saw sadness there, and I almost burst into tears.

"Come tell me your story," she said.

For the remainder of the day, and all the next, we were almost never apart. We had meals brought to my room, since it continued raining, and talked far into the night. She wanted to hear the entire story of my adventures, from beginning to end; she also had endless questions about the Babblers and how they lived, and what it was like to be so far from Cuzei. She was particularly interested to learn how the peasants in the Babbler lands live, and in my meeting with Lago the iliu.

"How I envy you, O Beretos," she said. "Sūro my father's Master of Scouts has met an iliu, but I never have. I've always wanted to." She laughed. "I've always wanted to spy on one, to see if it committed any sins. I still wonder about that teaching of our old Knower."

"I used to think the same thing, but now that I've met one I don't think I'd want to. It'd be like eavesdropping on a friend, to see if he would say words against me."

"Yes, of course; and besides, what if the iliū decided to spy on you or me? How horrible!"

"They surely wouldn't find anything to complain of in your behavior," I said. "As for mine, I shudder."

"You are supposed to serve me, not to worship," she said, laughing again. "Believe me, I am no iliu. But tell me more about the vision which he granted you."

"I don't think it was a vision," I said. "I mean, I've never had a vision, but I think a vision would be like a dream. This was like utter reality— it made ordinary living seem dreamlike. But I think I'm repeating myself; I would rather hear what has happened at Etêia Mitano."

Her face saddened. "The House is well enough, though not so well that we don't need you home once again! I watch over Corumayas as well as I can, but of course there are the peasants to look after, and Vissánavos and Isiliē..."

"I can't believe how much she's grown," I said (we had had a pleasant and noisy lunch that day with the children). "I could hardly recognize her... of course, she was only a baby when I left. But, my Lady, there's some sadness in you; if it's not in the House, where is it?"

"In Eleisa, where else?" she replied. "The air there is pestilent with intrigue; I fear the coming of some great blow... I worry about Zeilisio; he's getting thinner, and his hair is as grey as ash."

"I hope my story doesn't add to his burdens."

"It will distract him, at least," she said.

Zeilisio returned the next day but one— on horseback, pursued by armed men. He leaped off his horse as soon as he reached the courtyard, and began barking orders; in less than a minute half a dozen armed men had gathered to his side, ready to receive his pursuers, and the Master of Arms was on his way with more. I myself arrived, sword in hand, in time to see three riders galloping toward the house. Just before entering the courtyard, perceiving the arrows trained on them, they reined in, shouted something incomprehensible, turned their horses, and galloped off.

"Shall we pursue, O Lord?" said the Master of Arms. "Your fastest horses can be saddled in a moment; these bandits will not be able to escape us."

"No, better to stick around here, in case they come back with reinforcements," said Zeilisio, still breathing hard from his ride.

"As you wish, Lord," said the Master of Arms, with obvious disappointment. "It's a bold bandit that ventures along the Isrēica Road, in the heart of Cuzei. Where did you find them?"

"Oh, they're not bandits," said Zeilisio. "They're King's men."

"Eīledan!" I uttered. "What were they after you for?"

"They wanted to arrest me, of course. They can't do it here, of course, and really they aren't even allowed to pursue me onto my lands; but they were hoping to catch me before I could get to the House."

"And claim they'd caught you on open land," I exclaimed, with sudden understanding; Zeilisio nodded.

"But, Lord, what is the charge? Why are they after you?" asked the Master of Arms.

And it was a momentous and disturbing answer that the Lord, calm and solemn, made:

"Atheism."

19 · 𝈀𝈁𝈂𝈃𝈄𝈅𝈆 · *Munxenu*

You leave Berak's keep behind and scramble down its steep approaches. You soon reach the bottom of the valley, with the Demaresc running swiftly past; if you follow it down this familiar road you will come to the village. Instead you head up the valley, following a little-used trail which inches its way back up into the mountains. The sides of the valley rise into mountains: the Kravcaene-Limura on your left, Vehendanda to your right. The trail climbs rapidly, so that after only half an hour's walk you can look back to see Berak's keep far below you, already small.

A bend in the trail, and Berak's castle and all the land of Babblers is lost to view. You climb higher and higher, but you have the impression that your effort will be in vain: the great round mass called Totaure, the Handmaiden, looms before you to block further progress. In an hour you are at its foot, and see that the trail winds back and forth up its side.

"My grandfather told tales of Totaure alive with men, swarming down upon us," remarks Tentesinas.

"Munkhâshi?" you ask.

"No, Moȟnaru," he answers. "Those are the people who live on the other side of the mountains. We used to raid them sometimes, and they us, but not as often, because they aren't a manly people."

"And your grandfather saw one of their raids here?"

"It was an invasion. They even had their animals and women with them. They were fleeing the Munkhâshi."

"Did you let them settle among you?"

"We fought them back," he says, simply. "We wanted no sons made from the seed of Moȟnaru men. We did take the women of the men we killed, but the rest we sent back."

In his mind these two statements did not conflict; the Caďinorians consider that the virtues of a man are inherited from the father only.

You will now want to turn your attention back to the road, because the ascent of Totaure is difficult: a single misstep and you will plunge down the slope, not stopping, perhaps, till you crash down upon the rocks below, where the bones of the Moȟnaru who perished here can still be seen.

You are panting by the time you reach the summit; but you are not hot; the air about you is thin and cold, and blowing strongly. You look around: the top of Totaure is but the floor of a new valley, which climbs and narrows ahead of you, disappearing into the teeth of the Gaumê. You shrug, adjust your pack, and march on with your companions.

Farther on you take a trail up the side of the valley. You have left the trees below you; only shrubs and weeds grow on these cold slopes. The unobstructed wind now screeches and whistles down at you; you turn your face away, and bundle your cloak closer about you. Toward the top of the hillside you see flakes of snow blowing past, though it is the middle of summer. In winter the Gaumê cannot be crossed at all.

The valley below you grows ever deeper, the opposite wall looms closer, till you are walking above an abyss. Still you climb. Snow is now blowing past your ears. At least the valley shelters you somewhat from the wind. But this protection does not last; the trail climbs at last to the top of the cliff, leaving you exposed to the full fury of the wind.

You look around: you are on a narrow grassy plain, surrounded by mountains on all sides. The mountains are rocky, unclimbable; their tops are covered with snow. This is the top of the world, silent except for the shrill whistle of the wind, and the occasional deep rumble of an avalanche.

Tentesinas points eastward. A slice of sunlight breaches the ring of mountains at one point, like a gap in a giant's smile. This is the Taucrēte Pass.

You make your way toward it, battling the wind which blows from the land of demons. The land begins to rise; soon not even grass will grow, and you are walking on bare rock. Snow has accumulated in the hollows. It is best to skirt these; one may easily slip on hidden ice, or be buried in unsuspected drifts.

Finally you enter the Pass itself. It rides like a saddle between two mountains, which are called the Pillars of Endauron. It is wide enough in most places for ten men to walk abreast; here and there mighty spurs of rock, buttresses of Endauron's Pillars, narrow the path down to a pace or two.

The Pass is like a street for giants; it humbles a man, and yet lifts his spirits. Even the Babblers look about them, marveling at the peaks that bear the name of their god. As for you, you feel that Eīledan is near— not hidden, as in the lands of men, but rejoicing in naked majesty and power.

The Pass widens as you go east, and the far side broadens into a long, deep valley. The level floor disintegrates into a fan of loose rock; walking on it you unleash innumerable landslides. About halfway down you turn to the right, climbing up till you reach a rocky trail, which leads down and down. You come once more to grass and weeds, and then to shrubs and dwarfish, misshapen trees, and the snow stops, and the wind is not so strong.

You are in Munkhâsh.

By the time we were walking among trees, it was dark, and Tentesinas and I decided to stop for the night. He ordered the men to ready our camp, and he and I got into a fight over whether to start a fire.

It seemed to me the height of folly, newly entered into an enemy land, ignorant of the position of outposts and the habits of patrols, to advertise our presence in any way. To the commander this kind of caution was simply incomprehensible. There is little difference in the Caĉinorian mind between scouting and raiding; how can your enemy learn to fear you if you hide yourself, instead of stalking boldly into his lands?

In this case I have to admit that I was outsmarted, though not because of the strength of Tentesinas' arguments. Indeed, he seemed to rehearse his objections with less fervor than usual, and let me explain at length the need for secrecy and discretion, occasionally nodding with understanding as I made some particularly striking point. I was beginning to think that I would prevail, and was congratulating myself on my diplomacy, when I smelled smoke from the camp, which we had wandered away from in the course of our dispute. The men had lit a fire in our absence.

"Well, if there are eyes to see, they have already seen," I remarked. "Tentesinas, you old coyote, if we're attacked in our sleep tonight don't think I'll bother to defend you."

"A warm fire is a good thing on a cold night," he replied.

The next morning I pointed out to Tentesinas, with indignation, a structure in the hills overlooking our camp: a fortress. We were not so far into the woods that the light from our fire would have been invisible from its windows.

"Look closer, brother," said the commander.

I did, as we passed by it, and saw that the fortress was abandoned. Indeed, it was collapsing into ruin. Its roofs were missing; a tower had fallen; and green weeds spilled out of the windows.

"It's a castle of the Moňnaru," he explained. "You see that it faces west, toward the Pass, towards our lands. But the danger came from the east, from the demons, and it couldn't stand against them."

"I'd like to see it closer, to see how strong it is," I said.

"It's not worth a detour," said Tentesinas, contemptuously. "Berac's is stronger. And ours is very strong in the direction of the demons."

We marched further into Munkhâsh, always eastward and downward. The country is not unlike Berac's, though it is drier, and the high mountains last longer.

We saw another fortress on the second day. This one was alive, and we climbed the hillside opposite it to pass it by, instead of walking past it on the road. It was also made by the Moňnaru, but it had been extended and improved by the Munkhâshi: its lower walls strengthened, earthenworks dug round, a tower replaced, the main gate reworked to allow defenders to fire at an approaching force of men. It was not hard to see from even this little evidence that the Munkhâshi were far the betters of the Caðinorians in the art of fortification.

Toward evening we came to a village. Tentesinas, Oluon and I scouted it out, leaving the rest of the men outside the village— we all wore the commander's idea of Moňnaru peasant dress, but I did not want a dozen amateur Moňnaru wandering the town before we knew what Munkhâshi soldiery was about.

I was as eager to see my first Munkhâshi settlement as a boy on his first hunt. My first impression was that it was not much different from a Babbler village. The houses were of mixed stone and earth, thatched with grass. They were larger than

Babbler houses, but this was because they were more crowded, three or four families living in each. Each house we passed was a commotion of voices, squalling babies, smells of cooking and of animals.

We came into the center of town, and stopped to gawk. Before us, rising far above our heads, and ominously black in the gathering darkness, was a great stone pyramid. On the face of the pyramid was a face drawn in fire: slanted eyes, animal nostrils, a fierce and gaping mouth— the temple's door and windows.

Stepping closer, we could make out carvings on the wall: a battle; a storm with lightning thrown by animal gods in the heavens; a procession of figures bowing down before a trio of shapes like erect, crested crocodiles. I shuddered: these were representations of the amnigō, the demons who dwell in the swamps of the Nameless River.

Behind us was another stone building, a massive square with towers and narrow, barred windows: obviously a garrison. Two guards in leather armor, spears held high, stood at the door, and watched our movements. We turned into a side street, therefore, and continued our examination from the shadows. We could see a number of men through the windows in the garrison; I was sure of six, and assumed that another six or eight must be out of sight or sleeping. I could make out bows and spears and crossbows, as well as barrels of food or oil, ladders, chains, saddles (so there must be horses near as well), ropes, armor.

Oluon pulled my sleeve and pointed. Next to the temple was a smaller building, made of stone, a larger and finer version of the villagers' houses. A wooden silhouette of a goat, the sign of the chief god of the Moňnaru, stood guard above the door. It was only recognizable by its shape, for it was charred black by fire; stains of smoke rose also from the doors and windows of the temple, and one wall was caved in.

No guide could have made clearer the history of this town. It had been built by the Moňnaru, a people much like the Caðinorians, who lived there still; but the Munkhâshi had come and occupied the town, adding it to their empire, bringing in their own gods, and burning out those of the villagers.

When we returned to our camp, we found that our men had captured a peasant. I was angry at their indiscretion, till they explained that he had stumbled on the camp, and that they had detained him so that he would not tell anyone in the village about us.

"Well, what are we going to do with him?" I asked, testily.

Dolbas passed his hand across his throat.

"No, that won't be necessary," said Tentesinas, before I could say anything. "We'll let him go once we're gone. For now let's see what he can tell us."

"Oh, we already interrogated him," said Neictetes. "His name is Dōbno and he traps and cuts wood. He don't have nothing worth taking. He lives with his wife's family and don't even have a sword. I don't think he's hiding anything; you can see how poor he's dressed."

"Thank you, Neictetes," I said. "However, I may be able to think of a few questions more. Who knows his speech?"

Strictly speaking no one did, for he was a Moȟnaru, who have their own language. But he knew some of the Munkhâshi tongue, as did Neictetes and Tentesinas; some communication was therefore possible.

Dōbno was a bulky man, but small, with grayish skin, blue eyes and brown hair, very like the men of Agimbār. He had only straggling strands for a beard; Tentesinas said that the Moȟnaru could never grow more than this, and that was why they were an unmanly race and had been conquered by the Munkhâshi.

He did not seem to be afraid of us, and showed no reluctance to answer our questions. Neictetes said that this was because they had given him food; before that he had been very frightened.

"How many soldiers are there in the village?" asked Tentesinas.

"Fourteen or fifteen. Sometimes there are more, from Nokhdak on the river."

"Why so many? Are you a rebellious people?"

"Rebellion is punished by death," said Dōbno, simply. "They are here to rule us, and to defend the Empire in case the men over the mountains come to invade us."

"Why would we want to do that?"

"The men over the mountains are barbarians and very poor, so they would like to steal our land, because we are rich," explained Dōbno, who had evidently not grasped that he was speaking to the very men he had been taught to fear.

He could not tell us how many soldiers were in Nokhdak, besides "many." He had been to the city only once, as a boy, for some great gathering at the pyramid. The *Monxayo* (such was his word) were not allowed to leave their native towns except when summoned.

"Not even to trade things?" asked Neictetes.

"The Munkhâshi bring us whatever we need," replied Dōbno. Evidently the Munkhâshi are not only the rulers and soldiers of the Moñnaru, but their traders and priests.

I had Tentesinas ask what he knew about the amnigō. The word for them in the Munkhâshi tongue is *gotalh*, which means 'master.'

"I have never seen a master, but they are very wise and fearsome," said Dōbno. "They can touch a man, and he will die. They can live in the water without drowning; they can walk for forty days without eating. They are the masters of the empire."

"Who is worshipped in the temple? Ecaîas?"

As could be expected, the name of the demon meant nothing to him. "The lower worships the higher," was his answer. "We bow down before the Munkhâshi. If a master is there, both of us bow down before him. If Gelalh is there, men cannot live; but the masters can, and bow down."

"Do you not remember your old gods, then?" asked Tentesinas.

"Even to name the old gods is punished by death."

Our prisoner rattled off even such a statement as this like a boy reciting his lessons, without evident emotion or resentment. It was a performance which might have been repeated before an audience of amnigō without the least doubt being cast on his subservient loyalty.

As remarkable, and as disturbing, was the fact that he never asked a single question of us. I have never met a man so amiable, and yet so incurious. He did not even ask what would become of him.

Through Tentesinas, I asked him if the Munkhâshi intended to conquer their neighbors.

"It is the destiny of Gelalh to conquer the whole world," he replied.

This statement caused some stir among the Cađinorians. "When is this going to happen?" asked Neictetes.

"I don't know. It is the destiny of the Empire to grow. We *Monxayo* are now the lowest people in the Empire, and servants to all; but when the Empire grows larger we will become lords."

I marveled: in a few words Dōbno had revealed the entire strategy of the demons. Their empire was not, as Ximāuro had maintained back in Eleisa, based on fear; it was built on ambition. A new people is conquered; and it is reconciled to its conquest and its slave status by the prospect of mastery over the next people to be conquered.

There is no room for doubt in the conclusion. I will reverse the dictum of Ximāuro: the threat from Munkhâsh is not one of gods, but of armies. By its very nature Munkhâsh cannot desist from its advance, lest its prophecies be proved false, and its slaves turn on their masters. When it feels itself ready, Munkhâsh will invade Cēradānar. May Ulōne give us strength on that day.

20 · ᴛᴀᴜ̄ɕᴢx · *Nokhdak*

In the morning we released Dōbno. We did not think it likely he would rush off to tell the Munkhâshi about us; and in case he did, we laid broad hints that we were on our way home. Once he was well gone we broke camp and headed toward the city of Nokhdak.

The march required the remainder of the day and a portion of the next, as the city lies more than thirty lests from the Pass— a distance which brought us to repent leaving our horses in the barony. But horses would have been difficult to lead across the Pass, and made us conspicuous in Munkhâsh; and of course if there were a battle they would be useless, without chariots.

Most of the journey lies along a large river, whose name is Ardênbalo. There is a good road running along the river, but as we came close to the city we scorned it, for fear of meeting a company of soldiers with a strength greater than our own. And indeed we saw soldiers aplenty on the road; we ran past them on the heights, despite my men's eagerness to run down and engage them in battle.

Leaving the men hidden in a nearby farmhouse, Tentesinas and I ventured into the city.

Nokhdak, which has not even the size of Araunicoros, surely holds no high rank among the cities of Munkhâsh; but to reach a larger city would require weeks of travel. Sauōros has traveled to Korkâsh, which is one hundred fifty lests from the Pass.

It is mostly Moňnaru who live in the city, in houses of earth or wood. However, there are also many Munkhâshi, who have large houses of stone, and are clearly of greater estate. It appears that the Munkhâshi of the town have the privilege of accosting any Moňnaru and compelling them to do them services; more than once we saw passing Moňnaru hailed in this way, and forced to carry loads, or given clothes to wash, or buckets to fill.

Almost all the Moňnaru we saw were poor: peasants, craftsmen, men carrying loads or cleaning up after animals. The Munkhâshi themselves were more varied: soldiers in leather armor; priests or rich men in sumptuous silk or alligator hide; robed men with the scowl and quick step of administrators; and even a few poor men, looking just a little better off than the Moȟnaru

There was something amiss in our costumes or deportment; we were attracting stares. After some study of the men in the street, I said, "We don't have the aspect of slaves. Look more humble and downcast."

"Then they will call us over to do work," pointed out Tentesinas.

The solution occurred to both of us at once. We turned into an alley and waited; after an interval a Munkhâshi came toward us. I waved and smiled at him as he passed; he glared at me, outraged by this presumption. Tentesinas felled him with a powerful blow to the back of his neck.

His clothes consisted of cotton trousers (tight and uncomfortable), a silk shirt, a green and blue length of cloth which lay over the chest and back, and a leather mask. The outfit was too small for Tentesinas, so I became the *munxesilo*. We considered what to do with the man in a loincloth laying at our feet. Tentesinas was of the opinion he should be killed; I refused to countenance this. We ended up leaving him tied up in a back corner.

"I thought you were in favor of discretion above all things," remarked the commander.

"Not at the cost of killing a man for his clothes," I replied. "Now quiet down and bow those shoulders; you're a slave, not a warlord."

The trick worked beautifully; a Munkhâshi leading a Moȟnaru through the streets was not even worth a second glance.

We came to the center of town, which is dominated by large stone buildings— fortresses or palaces. The palaces are adorned with carved friezes, depicting scenes of war, obscure mythological scenes, or arrays of amnigō and other fantastic creatures.

The Munkhâshi, like the Babblers, do not know the art of writing. However, at the riverfront, we saw a man inspecting boxes as they were unloaded from a boat, and placing painted beads in a tablet of clay. Afterward he sprinkled the tablet with sand, applied another layer of clay to the top, and pressed it down. He then peeled off the top layer and handed it to the boat's captain, who placed it in a box and carried it away with him. This is obviously a form of bookkeeping, with a neat solution to the problem of ensuring that records match, and alterations be visible.

Though many thousands of souls must live in it, Nokhdak is as free of markets and shops as a village. No doubt the Moȟnaru supply their own needs, or barter among themselves, like the Caḓinorians of remote areas, while the occupiers simply take what they want.

We saw dozens of soldiers, including a company of fifty men executing drills in the street, where it would most impress the Moȟnaru. It had its alarming effect on me as well; apart from my work with Tentesinas' men, there is no group of soldiers within two hundred lests of Munkhâsh which knows the meaning of drill and discipline.

From almost anywhere in the city we could see the pyramid of the temple of Gelalh. Abruptly we came to the edge of the main square and it was almost on top of us, rising above the trees and the palaces, like a small mountain; and it was alive with movement.

There was a mass of people in the square, Moȟnaru and Munkhâshi; and rows of priests and dancers on three levels of the pyramid. Above them yellow banners flapped in the breeze, and smoke rose from the fires within the temple. And there was music, a clanging, angry music on horns and drums and flutes, accompanied by wailing voices.

The priests were dressed in all colors, and some of them were wearing huge masks in the shapes of animals' heads— eagles, sharks, lizards, snakes, and crocodiles— or amnigō. The dresses of the dancing women were also of garish colors, red, blue, gold, purple; their skirts seemed to be made of ribbons. Bright stones on their chests twinkled in the sun; yellow banners attached to their wrists swirled with their dance.

The music increased in intensity— the wails grew louder, the crashes of wood and metal more insistent— and the priests of the middle tier of the pyramid moved back, clearing a space in the middle. Two priests, their faces masked, dressed all in red and black, appeared from the depths of the temple, dragging between them a child, perhaps ten years old, dressed in yellow robes. His head was shaved, and his arms were tied behind him.

The priests made long prayers; incomprehensible operations were performed with a burning torch, and mud, and a grass fan. Finally the child's robe was removed. Without it he looked utterly small and helpless.

One of the priests raised his hands: all at once there was utter silence. All eyes were fastened on the boy on the temple. We were close enough to see the terror in his eyes. All in one terrible moment the boy cried out, making some jumbled plea; the priest raised high his knife, and then plunged it into the boy's chest.

Only then, standing as if paralyzed, did we realize what the boy had said; he had cried out, in Caðinor, "Endauron, save me!"

Tentesinas made no more pretense of being a slave. He grabbed at his pack, where our bows were, and tossed me mine. By the time I had strung it, he had loosed his arrow. It flew too low, and only clattered against the stone; but mine went true. The priest fell dead from the steps of the pyramid. Eïledan guides the arrows of the Cuzeians.

The crowd buzzed with fear and wonder. Immediately in front of us were only Moȟnaru, but our shooting had not grown unnoticed; a group of soldiers several paces away had seen us, and now came after us. We ran for our lives.

Our pursuers were delayed by the crowd, so there was at first a good space between us. We turned the first corner we came to, and dashed through a door into a Munkhâshi mansion, and out the other side, and thought we had got away; but there were more soldiers in the street, and closer. A spear struck earth a pace from my feet; an arrow struck Tentesinas in the back— and fell off harmlessly, deflected by something in his pack.

We ran down one street after another, sometimes closer, sometimes farther from our enemies, at every moment fearing an arrow, or a trap, or a soldier on horseback. We bounded over walls and through alleyways to lose our pursuers, but we did not lose them, or gained new ones. A commotion of noise followed close behind, so that it seemed the whole city was after us.

Finally— there it was, the edge of the city, and the house in which we had left our fellows! There was Oluon, on watch! "Prepare to fight!" I yelled out to him, in Cuêzi. And as we reached the house our company was alive, lining up arrows. Oluon tossed me my sword, and we turned to face our attackers.

There were about a dozen men closing the gap, but more would soon join them. Already our arrows were in the air; two of the Munkhâshi fell at once, and one of our men, Tailariñ, was down, with an arrow in his side. That distracted me; I looked up to see a huge soldier looming over me, sword arm raised. Before I could think, Tentesinas had cut him down. I fenced with the one in back of him, got the upper hand, then chopped his head off. Dolbas and Aiðoravos, curse them, had hopped wildly in the midst of the enemy, yelling, as if they were seeking glory on a Babbler battlefield. I couldn't see Tentesinas. I almost lost an arm, as a wiry little brute, offering guttural curses, slashed down with a short sword. I parried, then slashed at his legs; he jumped nimbly over the sword, and I pierced his side on the backstroke. When I looked up there were no more enemies left.

We had come off very well. Ullinas, who was Dolbas' brother, had fallen with a spear through his shoulder blades; but Tailariñ's arrow wound was not fatal. Two men had sword cuts. The Caðinorians were already exchanging swords with the dead, out of a custom of using the arms of a slain enemy, and because the Munkhâshi swords were better than their own.

"Fools, do you think that's all there are?" cried Tentesinas. "Away, before the next batch comes!"

"What about Ullinas?" cried Dolbas.

"Mieranac take you! So grab him, two of you, and run, you bitches!"

The farmhouse was not far from a woods; we ran for the trees, the ox-like Dolbas carrying his brother's corpse on his back. We did not quite make it before more soldiers arrived, and rushed after us across the fields. There were only half a dozen of them; four of them we killed with arrows; Dolbas and Neictetes killed the other two. More soldiers could now be seen pouring from the city; but we now had time to reach the woods.

With that the battle was won. The new troops had not quite seen where we disappeared to; by the time they found the bodies of their comrades, we were a quarter of a lest away, watching them through the cover of the trees. We did not have to move any farther away than that. There were quite a few soldiers, for a time, examining that stretch of woods; but after about an hour they seemed to have decided they had lost us, and returned to the city.

We laughed, and boasted, and embraced each other, and consoled Dolbas, who was crying like a baby over the loss of his brother. Tentesinas embraced me, and pounded my shoulders.

"Now you are no longer a one-souled man," he told me.

21 · X̄ZTZX̄ΔЛ · *Ganacom*

I had never been more glad to see the old stone of Berak's keep; and when Tentesinas and I climbed upstairs to make our report, I almost looked forward to seeing the baron's beefy face and thin red hair. Surely we had a story for him now.

We found him relaxing at his favorite table, as if he had not moved since first I saw him; he sat with a beer and a visitor, one I did not recognize, though he was evidently at ease with the baron.

"We are returned from the land of demons," said Tentesinas, grandly. "It pleased Mieranac for Ullinas to die in battle; but we more than took our vengeance on the Munkhâshi. Beretos alone slew four of them."

Berak circled my arm with his fingers, and turned to his companion, as if showing off a horse: "He doesn't look it, but he doesn't have a bad arm. He's been helping Tentesinas with the boys."

"Lord, we have much to speak of," said the commander. "Though we bested the Munkhâshi, they have powerful and warlike gods, and we must be ready for raids and invasions from the Pass."

"Not any more," said Berak, with deep self-satisfaction. "Isn't that right, Ganacom?"

The stranger smiled; I considered him more closely. He could have been an uncle to Berak, so like was he to the baron in shape and attitude; he even had the same expression, a mixture of pride and sloth; but his eyes, deep black, were sharper than Berak's. I felt immediately that he was not a man to trust.

"While you've been out raiding and sleeping on the grass just to learn a few nothings about our neighbors, I've learned all that and more as easy as a fart," Berak informed us. "Kind of funny, isn't it, Ganacom? Hope you don't mind the killing."

"It is nothing," said the stranger. His accent haunted me; it was familiar, but I could not immediately place it.

"Not to me," said Tentesinas, crossly. "Don't speak in riddles; what are you talking about?"

The baron indicated his new friend with a beery wave. "This is Ganacom. He'll be our Munkhâshi Resident."

"You are not serious, baron!" I exclaimed. "A resident from Munkhâsh? You don't know what these people are like! You're opening your house to demons!"

"Ganacom is a regular man," said Berak. "He's told me all about Munkhâsh; there's nothing to be afraid of. Women's tales, that's what you've been hearing."

Tentesinas looked on his master with rage in his eyes. "I'm not afraid of anything," he said, with fists clenched, "but in the company of those who give their gods Cadinorian children to eat, I'll say no more." He walked out; I thought of following him, but I stayed put, out of curiosity and annoyance.

"He'll come around," said Berak, unperturbed. "My *tiedectescrion*, and son of my father's *tiedectescrion*. A regular man. And this fish here is our Cuzeian Resident. You'll get to be good friends."

"I'm not so sure. We are enemies, after all," I remarked.

The Munkhâshi laughed, and raised his beer in my direction. "Have a drink with us, Cuzeian. There's no enemies among people who drink beer together."

"Another time," I said. I left the baron and his new friend; I felt that if I stayed a minute longer I would no longer be able to control my actions.

In the next few days it seemed as if we could do nothing and go nowhere without falling under the eyes of the Munkhâshi Resident. He came to watch the men training under my direction; Oluon and I met him walking in the village; there he was fingering the swords in the armory, or talking to the old godspeaker; he even stopped in during my lessons in Cuêzi. Tentesinas remarked upon the same thing— "You can't get away from the devil!"

None of these perambulations caused him to miss a meal with Berak; and late at night or in the middle of the afternoon he could be seen drinking one beer after another with the baron in his dining hall. I wondered if it was by luck or by design that the Munkhâshi had sent Berak a man with such a stomach.

How I wished then for the counsel of Zeilisio! I felt defeated already, that a *munxesilo* was welcomed into the castle of Berak.

It was after all my mission to bolster this barbarian lordling against the land of demons. It should have been straightforward, after our expedition into Munkhâsh; rude and small-minded as he was, Berak should have been able to see the evil and the danger of the Empire across the mountains, and steeled himself to resist their inevitable incursion.

But here Ganacom had already worked corruption. We had misinterpreted what we had seen in Munkhâsh, Berak told us. The Moȟnaru were happy and prosperous under the rule of the Empire. They blessed the powerful gods of the amnigō, who had brought them out of poverty and strife. The killing we had seen was not a sacrifice, but the execution of a criminal. The boy had not spoken Caδinor— how could he have spoken Caδinor, in the middle of Munkhâsh? We had been so full of distrust that we had heard familiar words in speech we could not understand. If we had seen many soldiers, it was only because we were near the borders of Munkhâsh; and because of the necessity to keep order.

"How could you expect to understand what you see, looking around corners and talking to woodcutters?" asked Berak. "Ask Ganacom instead, and he'll explain it all to you in plain Caδinor."

Fortunately Tentesinas was not moved. "If I close my eyes I can hear that boy cry out again," he told me. "And I don't need any of this snake Ganacom's interpretations to know what it was I saw with my own eyes, and heard with my ears."

Things were not as bad as they seemed, I decided. Tentesinas was solid, and so were most of his men. Berak might trust Ganacom, because they had drunk beer together; but for the men who had come with us into Munkhâsh, had fought Munkhâshi soldiers, and burned their brother's body on Munkhâshi soil, beer was not enough to buy their hearts.

I had another ally, too, in Sintilna. She took an immediate dislike to Ganacom. "That man," she called him, and blamed him for everything from her husband's sheltering of that lazy outland bitch Hānu to his not finding a husband for her daughter. I do not think she made anything of Ganacom being from Munkhâsh; it was enough to win her disdain that he was close to her husband.

I began to feel somewhat more cheerful. Had I not suffered much worse in the days of my dishonor, when I had nothing to do but teach Cuêzi to the women? The presence of a lone Munkhâshi in the keep was troubling, but I was not without resources and friends; and if he now had the ear of Berak, none can predict Eiledan's paths. Berak had changed favorites before, and Ganacom might go as easily as he had come.

22 · ⊂ꟾꓥC⊺ XZ₅C⊂ΔƆȦ · *Nūmiū cazinorō*

    Trusting in the forbearance of Ulōne, I will say something of the beliefs of the Caḓinorians; or at least those of the mountains, because not all the Caḓinorians believe the same, or even have the same gods. In the mountains, for instance, I never heard mention of Aelilea and Aecton, who are the chief gods worshipped in Araunicoros.

    The gods known in Berak's parts are many; indeed, it would be impossible to list them all, because there are many minor gods known in only one village or two, or who look after just one craft, or one lordly family. A Babbler normally offers devotion chiefly to only one or two gods; however, he will offer occasional gifts and prayers to several others, both to avoid giving offense, and to receive as many benefits as he can. When times are bad, or he is disappointed with his chief god, he will court others; and if they satisfy him he will switch his allegiance.

    Almost all of the Babblers offer some devotion to Endauron, the lord of the heavens, because he is very powerful; but few choose him as their chief god. Iscira, mistress of the light, is considered to be his consort. Sintilna is devoted to her. Mieranac, the patron of sword and bow, is particularly favored by the soldiers, including Tentesinas, as well as by those who hunt. The earth goddess Kravcaena is said to be the favorite of farmers and fishermen; the god of craft, Necȇruon, of those who work with their hands. The goddess of love, Veharies, receives the particular devotion of those who are seeking a mate or an assignation; but those who are seeking a child call on Iscira or Kravcaena.

    There are also times of the year in which devotion to one god or another is appropriate. The blessings of Kravcaena are implored in the spring, at the time of planting. It is Endauron, however, who receives the credit for the harvest, since he presides over the year's major festival, the Autumn Harvest. Mieranac has a feast day in midsummer, and Veharies has one in midwinter—"because it's dark and there's nothing to do outside of screwing," say the Babblers, who are never delicate.

The public festivals, as well as all of the rites and celebrations within the keep— marriages, second births, deaths, raids, visits from other lords— come under the direction of Aiôdoroî and the three lesser godspeakers in Berak's employ. They are also entitled to collect the portion of the peasant's produce which belongs to the gods— one sixth of that which remains after the baron has extracted his own share. Some of this bounty is returned to the people in the form of the feasts that accompany the great seasonal celebrations; some serves for the support of the castle godspeakers; the rest is simply added to the castle's stores.

One might live long in Berak's house without suspecting that the beliefs and practices of the people outside the keep constitute virtually a separate religion, which has nothing in common with the official one save the names of its chief gods.

To the villagers Endauron and the other gods are as remote as the sun and the stars— too lofty for human beings, even godspeakers, to address. When they seek divine gifts or favor, or offer thanks for services received, they address intermediary spirits, called *fantit,* who can be consulted when they possess the bodies of the village godspeakers. Some *fantit* are the spirits of the dead, or of animals; others seem to be powerful spiritual beings, intermediate between gods and men. They may grant services out of their own power, or by addressing the gods on the petitioner's behalf. The fierce male spirit who punched Oluon in the nose was a *fantos.*

Whereas Aiôdoroî and his assistants inherit their positions, and are exclusively male, the peasants' godspeakers may be of any lineage, and of either sex. The defective, who are unsuited for any other task, often follow this path: one of the godspeakers in Cihimia is blind. Others are chosen by the gods, in mysterious ways. A man, till then a simple farmer, was seeking the services of another godspeaker when he himself was knocked to the floor, and his body occupied by a *fantos,* for which he henceforth served as godspeaker. Another woman killed her own two children and abandoned her husband to live alone in a hovel in the hills; she became a very feared and powerful godspeaker, sought out when curses of death or sickness needed to be made or removed.

A godspeaker holds court at intervals, where any may come and seek the aid of the *fantos,* once it has manifested itself. Generally the petition must be accompanied by gifts, and further gifts are required when a baby is born, or a charm or curse or cure proves effective. I know a man who lay dying, breathing in gasps, until he was brought before a godspeaker; at that point he recovered, and sat up calling loudly for beer. There was another man who had scorned the advances of a young woman; she asked a very strong *fantos* to place a curse on him, and he died within the week.

So far as I could see the village and castle godspeakers coexist peacefully, having nothing to do with one another. The village godspeakers play no part in the seasonal festivals, even those whose patron god is the same served by their own *fantos*; nor would anyone in the castle dream of consulting them on any matter.

I must mention one more element in the religious life of the villagers: the *gesit* or household gods. A *ges* is a small, crudely modeled ceramic human or animal figure, which is hung from the roof of a dwelling, or even inserted into the wall, and occasionally fed with ashes, blood, or beer, in return for which sustenance it confers protection and prosperity. The people are very clear, when asked, that the ceramic form is not simply the home or body of some *fantos* or spirit, but is itself the *ges*. A family makes its own *ges*, since one made by another will protect only the maker's family. The *ges* may be preserved for generations, and carried from house to house. If it does not perform its duty— if, for instance, the family is visited by sickness, or if the garden does not produce well, the *ges* is punished, by being deprived of food or by being buried. I know a man whose wife died, and who in a fit of anger smashed his *ges* to pieces. He was very angry, he explained, because his wife was a very hard worker, and the *ges* had done him a very grave injury by not preserving her.

It will be seen that there is almost nothing in the Caḓinorian religion, in either castle or village, of worship. Adoration is offered to the gods at their festivals, but this is a matter of duty and not love. The peasants bow their heads to Berak, too, but they are not expected to love or praise him. If a Babbler expresses thanks to a god, or to a *fantos*, it is in return for services rendered— never for the gift of life, or for the beauty and bounty of Eīledan's world.

There is some sense of law in the cult of Endauron, who enjoins obedience, usefulness, and benevolence to his people. Evildoers are said to be punished after death. (As for the fate of the rest of mankind, there seems to be a difference of opinion between castle and village. In the village death is described as rest or sleep— presumably an attraction after their hard life on earth. The castle-dwellers seem to have a more active afterlife in mind.) However, custom rather than divine mandate is the usual justification for the rules of social life; and there is no particular idea that the gods are beings of great goodness— only of great power.

Aidodoroî is a white-haired old man, who moves slowly, and must be attended at all times by one of his acolytes, who carries things for him, opens doors, and helps him up stairs. His frailty only enhances his power in the keep, since such longevity is rare among the Babblers and is seen as a sign of divine favor. It also means that he was chief godspeaker in the keep since before Berak was born; he therefore has no fear of Berak and is the only man in the castle who dares to reprimand him or tell him what to do. He also has a fierce temper, and berates one who has crossed him till he is red in the face.

I incurred this treatment not long after I arrived in the barony, because I had not paid my respects to Endauron as a guest should, by offering him a gift, such as a bird, or wine, or a bronze bracelet. When I explained that a worshipper of Iáinos may offer gifts to no other god he was only further incensed. He began to complain to Berak about me, and made threats to have me expelled from the house. Eventually, realizing that I was making an implacable enemy, I offered a gift of six skins of wine and a leather saddlebag (both bought in Araunicoros) not to Endauron but to him personally, and this he accepted.

After Aduredasco's raid he became almost friendly to me, and sometimes asked me about my gods, and in return told me stories of the Cadinorian gods. Once he offered to make devotions to Iáinos and Eīledan, and even sacrifice a goat to them, in gratitude for their help in preserving the keep from ravage.

"Both Iáinos and Eīledan are very jealous, and can only be served by their own Knowers," I told him.

I expected him to be offended, but he only nodded. "They are powerful gods, as you are a powerful people," he said, in his cracking voice. "It is also a strong god who can help one of his people so far from his own land."

"We are far from Cuzei, but not far from Eīledan, since Eīledan created the whole world," I said.

"Well, a strong god in any case," said the godspeaker, with polite skepticism. "But if he will not have my goat, it will go to Endauron instead." And as I did not object, he went his way.

I will repeat here the story told in the castle of the creation of the world; or rather the stories, for different accounts are given at different times. At the spring festival the story is told that the earth is the body of the goddess Kravcaena, and brings forth plants and fruits because of her copulation with Endauron, the god of the heavens. This liaison is somewhat irregular, because Endauron's wife is Iscira; both night, dominated by the two brighter moons (which represent Iscira's breasts), and winter (the snow comes from the moons and shares their color) are Iscira's punishments upon Kravcaena for her husband's infidelity. Another story is told at the Autumn Harvest: Endauron created the earth in the form of a bowl for drinking wine, as a present for his wife; but she dropped it, and it broke. The clay of the bowl became plains; the mountains are the handles; and the seas and rivers are the wine.

Yet another story is told to explain the creation of men and the other intelligent Kinds. Each Kind was created by Endauron (or, sometimes, Necteruon) from a different substance. Man was made from clay, which is why he must still gain his sustenance from the soil. The elcari were made from stone; and they still live in the mountains, and make their homes in the solid rock. The farther elcari, however, were made from thorns, which is why they are hostile to the nearer elcari and to all other Kinds. The iliū were made from water, and the amnigō from the slime of the swamps where they still dwell. The Babblers believe that the forests are inhabited by a small, sly folk called *pinset*, which were made from wood; and that the deserts are inhabited by giants, made from iron. It is remarkable that the Babblers, who have forgotten their making by Eīledan so many ages ago, remember something of the giants.

It will be seen that the Cadinorian stories have nothing of the beauty and wisdom of the Count of Years, which was revealed to us by the iliū, who themselves received it from Iáinos.

The people of the village also tell stories. They are generally about heroes with magical powers, or about animals, or *fantit*; many of them explain, along the way, how things came to be as they are. For instance, there are many stories about a mythical hero called Rabbit, admired as a trickster and a joker, and indeed often the victim of his own tricks. It is said that he originally had a long and beautiful tail, of which he was extremely vain, so much so that he organized a contest among all the animals, to be won by the animal with the biggest tail. His only serious rival was the pheasant, whose tail was large and many-colored; and to ensure his victory he schemed to cut off the pheasant's tail. There was a log in the woods under which a small creature could just wiggle through; he instructed his associates, the dog and the bear, to wait by the log one night for the pheasant to come by. As soon as it was under the log, the bear was to jump on the log, trapping the bird, and the dog would bite off its tail. Rabbit ran off to chase the pheasant toward the log. As he was looking for the pheasant, a wolf appeared and marked Rabbit for his dinner. Running blindly away from the wolf, Rabbit ducked under the log, where the bear trapped him, and the dog bit off his tail, leaving only a white fluffy stump. From that day to this rabbits have all had a short stubby tail instead of a long and beautiful one, and of course they have become the enemies of dogs and bears.

23 · TZOCZ7 · *Bardāu*

I was in my room reading, once again, the epic of Samīrex, when I was interrupted by loud knocking. When I answered, a boy from the keep entered and said, "There's one who wants you in the castle."

"Who is it?" I asked.

"I don't know. Someone from far away."

I made my way quickly to the keep, full of curiosity. A place does not have to be more than ten lests away from Berak's lands to be called "far away"; still, this was surely an unusual event.

Waiting for me in the dining hall, with an unknown and wicked-looking Babbler guide at his side, was a man whose attire was unmistakably Cuzeian and even fashionable, though now showing the effects of three hundred lests' travel.

"You are Beretos?" he asked, rudely, but in Cuêzi.

"I am, and I wonder who it is I have the pleasure of greeting, so far from the homeland," I replied.

"I am named Bardāu of Masāntie, and have been sent by Lord Feroicolê."

"Ah. With what purpose, O Bardāu?"

"To see how you are doing."

"Very well, you'll see all that there is to see. But tell me, how does it go with Lord Feroicolê? Is he well, he and his Lady?"

"They are well; but let's talk of all that later. First, you'll cause some refreshment to be brought, and have rooms prepared for me."

Neither the rooms nor the refreshment could be easily provided to Bardāu's satisfaction. He immediately rejected the suggestion that another bed be laid out in my room. By displacing one of Tentesinas's lieutenants a room could be found for him in the barracks, but this pleased him no better. "I don't think it appropriate to be housed in a barracks," he explained. "The very word. *Barracks*. No, have rooms found for me in the castle."

Any Cuzeian House, of course, maintains rooms for important visitors, into which category Bardāu evidently placed himself; and indeed it would be a great insult to house such a visitor in a mere outbuilding. Berak's keep does not work like this. Berak receives a lordly visitor, usually a relative, no more than once a year, and these are content to pile into the family quarters on the third level of the inner keep. Even a Babbler lord expects no better accommodation than a clean straw pallet laid with furs and placed next to his host's.

I talked to the *domorion*— Bardāu spoke not a word of Caĉinor— and he suggested that Bardāu sleep with the servants on the ground floor; a suggestion that I did not even relay to our Cuzeian visitor. I asked the *domorion* to see what he could do about placing him on the third floor. I considered asking Bardāu for his credentials; what rank or privilege entitled him to grander accommodations than those of the Cuzeian Resident?

I had stew, bread, and wine brought while the *domorion* made his arrangements. He ate ravenously enough; but he was, as he freely confessed, disappointed. He had thought that Cuzeian food would be the appropriate choice to honor a visitor from that land on his first night in the castle, after a long and tiring journey. I noted that my custom was to eat whatever was put before me, and that the castle cooks did not know how to prepare so much as an egg in the Cuzeian fashion; nor were the ingredients and spices needed for Cuzeian cuisine available a lest closer than Araunicoros.

"And you and your servant— Olbaun, was it?"

"Oluon," I supplied.

"Yes. You or Oluon have not some acquaintance with the skills of the kitchen, perhaps?"

"It was not seen fit to send us with cooks or the skills of cooks," I said.

"Pity."

The *domorion* returned, with a smile on his face: Aiĉodoroî had offered to share his chamber with Bardāu. I complimented the house-master; given Bardāu's insistence on staying in the keep, this was the most comfortable and least crowded accommodations which could be found. I explained the offer to Bardāu. He obviously disdained the notion of sharing a room, but reluctantly accepted when I emphasized that no alternative was available.

"Tell me again who is this old man who will be sharing my room?"

"Aiđodoroî, the chief godspeaker. You'll be sharing *his* room," I clarified.

"Azodoros. He's the chief what?"

"Godspeaker. Something like a Knower."

"Well, I suppose it can't be helped. Is he at least clean?"

I asked after news from Eleisa, which he was very willing to give; the time passed pleasantly enough, and we were still talking when Oluon, coming into the hall with Faliles, discovered us. I introduced our visitor.

"Ah, this is your servant," said Bardāu.

"We are both servants of the Lord Zeilisio," I interposed.

"What House are you from?" asked Oluon.

"I've been sent by the Lord Feroicolê."

"Have you brought us any mail?"

"Certainly not. I'm not a porter of letters."

There was a pause after this revelation; and then Faliles asked, in good Cuêzi, "From what city of Cuzei do you come, O Bardāu?"

He looked at her, and then asked me, "She speaks Cuêzi?"

"As you can hear."

"I am from Masāntie," he told her, speaking very loudly and slowly. "What is your name?"

"Faliles. Is your city near Eleisa? Beretos has told us many times about Eleisa. It is a very beautiful city, isn't it?"

"You are a very pretty girl, and Beretos has taught you well," Bardāu said, in the tone people who do not like children use when speaking to children. When he turned back to us it was a dismissal.

"How goes Aēti Fulauto?" pursued Oluon. "Is there news of Feroicolê, or of Lady Alaldillê?"

"Oh, the two of them are well, and the whole House," he said. "We may talk of them later."

He spoke uncomfortably, as if something held his tongue. "I think our visitor is surely tired from his journey, and needs rest," I suggested.

When Berak returned for dinner— he had been out hunting deer— we sent a servant to bring Bardāu back to the dining hall for the evening meal. We were somewhat surprised when the boy returned unaccompanied.

"He doesn't seem to understand. I used gestures," he reported, demonstrating them— very obvious beckonings and pantomiming of food— "but he only spoke your tongue back at me, and would not come. He doesn't have a weak head, does he?"

"I'm sure there's another explanation," I said, though I confess that the boy's theory had its attractions. I sent Oluon, who fetched our guest with no difficulty, and brought him to meet Berak, who was sitting, as he normally did at dinner, with Ganacom.

Bardāu said, "I bring greetings from the King and Council of Cuzei, O Berak. Peace to you and may Iáinos bring prosperity to your House and protection from the demons."

This had to be translated, in two or three pieces.

"This is a friend of yours?" Berak asked me. "I tell you truthfully, he looks as unpromising as you did when you came here; but at least you spoke in a way a man could hear. Does he have some tricks to teach us? Will he help protect us from Ganacom's friends, here?"

"You're a joker, Berak," said Ganacom. "Surely even Beretos will agree that Ganacom's friends are no danger to anyone."

"If Ganacom's friends are like Ganacom, they are a serious threat to the castle's beer casks," I replied. Ganacom raised his glass to me and drank.

"What are they saying, O Beretos?"

"Ah, Berak was reminiscing over my first days here; and he wants to know if you have any soldierly skills."

"Ulōne damn me, no. Tell him I'm a diplomat."

There is no such word in Caðinor; but I attempted to comply: "He's no soldier, but what we call a speaker between lords; he's trained to talk to one Lord on behalf of another, and arrange trade or avoid conflict."

I knew about what Berak would say to this, and he said it: "Without being able to pick up a sword? Imagine sending creatures like that to do your talking for you, Ganacom."

"Unbelievable."

"What are they *saying?*"

"'Unbelievable,'" I translated, without thinking.

"What? What do they mean by that?"

"Ah, they're simply marveling at the sophistication of Cuzeian culture," I offered. "They have a simple culture, in which conflict is more often settled by force of arms than by diplomacy."

"Yes, a very primitive culture," Bardāu agreed.

Neither he nor Berak had any further words for each other, so we retired. Bardāu seemed to be highly satisfied with his reception. I expected him to be put off by the lack of ceremony, but he dismissed my concerns.

"We're in the domain of a different people," he reminded me. "A very primitive culture, as you said. Informal. Manly. Looked at in the right way, it's almost a relief, after serving so many years in dusty old Eleisa. One becomes so tired of pretentiousness."

The first sight that met my eyes the next day was Bardāu, sitting at the foot of my bed, reading my books. He glanced over at me and nodded.

"I was about to wake you up," he informed me. "It was Ecaîas's work finding you here. Come with me back to the castle and help me get some breakfast. I tried to get the *domāuro*— whatever he is— to help me, but he was as dull as a cow. I thought you were teaching them Cuêzi here."

"Not the *domorion,*" I said, smiling at the thought. "Faliles or Sielineca could have helped you. Or Oluon."

"You should have sent one of them for me. Hmm. This is your room? I certainly can't report that you're living in luxury."

After more than a year I had come to feel comfortable in this room. Though even a peasant in our own land would be ashamed to have them in his house, the rude stone walls, the bed laid with furs, the simple table and bench were at least mine, and familiar. Still, there is nothing for making one's possessions seem shabby and shameful like a stranger's obvious disdain. While I dressed and washed myself, Bardāu picked up one thing after another— copies of epics; my notes on the Caɖinor language; sword and bow; the bracelet given me by Berak; a clay wine-flagon— without one of them seeming to excite the least interest or diversion. He looked out the window, at the keep, with Vehendanda looming behind, but the view occupied his mind for only an instant.

I led Bardāu over to the keep and found him some hot porridge and weak beer. This breakfast was not to his liking; it was his custom to eat an orange in the morning, or perhaps a melon. Neither, of course, grows in the Gaumê.

"One does wonder if barbarism is simply lack of intelligence," he remarked. "How difficult would it be to bring them here by river?"

There were several answers to this, such as that the Taucrēs is not navigable in the Gaumê, that Babblers were not accustomed to such trade, that Berak's people did not know what an orange was and, having little taste for novelty, would not eat one if they did. I began to try to explain these things, but Bardāu preferred to pursue his own chain of thought. "Obviously these people have need of what a civilized nation has to offer. But of course trade is only possible where a people can fulfill some need of ours. Perhaps you've discovered something?"

"I haven't thought about it much. We're exceedingly far from Cuzei."

"It's a demon's walk all right. But isn't there something they have here that'd be valuable back home?"

"I don't know. Perhaps some medicinal herbs."

"So the Babbler lands are, in terms of trade, virtually worthless?"

"Not all the Babbler lands. We do trade with the kingdoms along the Cayenas. But the eastern regions are too poor to support much trade, I think."

Bardāu's attitude became confidential. "You don't have to be afraid of me, O Beretos. I come from Feroicolê, after all. I'm sure you've found something. You can't exploit it yourself, can you? You need an agent. Someone to work the other end in Cuzei."

"I've never been much of a trader," I said, a little stiffly.

"That's just what I'm saying. Listen, I know exactly the position you're in. You don't have help. No backing. Just you and this Oluon here— Ulōne damn me, a soldier. You need men you can trust, men with experience, men who speak your language. You need men back home who know what needs to be done, and who'll look out for your interests."

I began to feel that I had wandered into a maze of misunderstanding, and wondered how to get out. Where had Feroicolê found this man? "I really don't know that there's anything worth trading, here," I said, with a shrug. "And even if there were, we're two hundred lests even from Araunicoros. It seems impossible."

Something seemed to occur to Bardāu. "You are from Tefalē Doro, aren't you?"

"Yes."

"In the mountains?"

"Yes, that's right, not far from Aure Árrasex."

"And here you are in the mountains," he said, almost in a whisper. "Tell me, is it silver? Or copper? Don't worry; I can hold a confidence. And what's more, I have connections with the western Houses myself. I could even find some elcari for the work."

Venality and ingratiation vied for control of his face; I wanted to box his ears. Instead I said, "You must excuse me, O Bardāu; it is time for the Babblers' arms training. You can come along if you wish."

Bardāu was not interested in watching the training, nor in attending the lessons in Cuêzi. Oluon offered to translate, should he wish to speak with the baron or the commander, but this offer was also declined. I do not know how he spent most of his time, although it is obvious how he spent some of it. I returned to my room later in the day to find all my papers disarranged, and even the bed and my clothes out of place. An attempt had obviously been made to hide the search; but one who spends much time with his books and scrolls knows when they have been moved.

If I really had written down the location of silver mines he would have found them. None of my papers were hidden. One becomes careless, living among people who cannot read or write.

I did not talk with Bardāu again until dinner. I expected him to press the subject of trade; but he seemed to have another thing on his mind. He looked somber and nervous, as if he had seen something he didn't like; but he did not at first talk about it.

It was Oluon who noticed that he was not eating the beef in his stew. "They don't cook like back home, do they?" he asked, suppressing a laugh.

"Of course not, but it's not that," said Bardāu. He moved the pieces of beef around in his bowl with his spoon for awhile, then said, "The old man you've put me with, he's their, mm, magician?"

"Godspeaker."

"I saw him today killing a cow."

He looked at us significantly.

"You haven't seen cows killed before?" asked Oluon.

"No. I mean of course I have, but that's not it. I mean— why's it the old man? Something with their gods, isn't it?"

"Of course it is," said Oluon. "It's a sacrifice. You feed the gods first when you eat an important animal, like a cow. Of course, lucky for us, the gods turn out to have a taste for blood and intestines, and leave the better parts to us."

"Then this meat has been sacrificed to demons?"

"If you believe that explanation of the Babbler gods," I said.

"You should have told me this last night," he told me, accusingly. "And you, why do you eat it?"

"If we didn't eat meat that was sacrificed to Babbler gods, we wouldn't eat red meat at all outside of Cuzei," I said, calmly. "What do you think Cuzeians do in Araunicoros, or Cayenas?"

"Does that make it right? I'm a religious man, one who does not accept corrupt practices simply because others do."

"You are saying that we are not faithful to Eīledan, O Bardāu?"

"No, but... I say nothing against you, but I don't believe it's right."

"We are protected by Ulōne," I pointed out. "Animals for food were apportioned by Eīledan as nourishment for man, and so for us this beef is a gift from Eīledan, no matter what words have been said over it by Babbler godspeakers. You may not be used to traveling outside our land, O Bardāu. This has been the statement of the Knowers of the Glade in Eleisa for as long as Cuzeians have had need to leave their borders."

Bardāu mulled this over; he didn't look like he accepted it, and he did not begin eating his meat, but he knew that he had no response. But he was not a man to give up an argument easily.

"Some men may travel too much," he said. "Those who live among pagans may begin to become accustomed to pagan ways. Someone less used to foreign ways, such as myself, may perhaps see them in the same way they are seen in the eyes of Iáinos."

"And how is that?"

"They're offensive, of course," he said. "Denying Iáinos, sacrificing to demons, living like savages— well, evil lived with is evil unseen; but these horrors are new to my eyes. This is not how Iáinos intended men to live; and were not these Babblers made by Eīledan like all men?"

"Ah, you wish us to bring Iáinos to them," I said, with sudden understanding.

"Precisely. Indeed, this very purpose was spoken of in Eleisa, before your journey began."

"Nor have we neglected it," I said. "Frequently in my teaching of Cuêzi we take our text from the holy books, or discuss the nature of Iáinos. And I have freely spoken, to Berak, to the commander, even to the godspeakers, of Iáinos as the source of Cuzei's strength."

"Faliles, the baron's daughter, asks about Iáinos all the time," offered Oluon. "She's virtually given up the Babbler gods."

"Yes, yes, but why are you not offering worship to Iáinos here? Why do you not put an end to these sacrifices?"

I attempted to retain my courtesy. "We have been concentrating on our military mission."

"You should apply some imagination to your diplomacy," Bardāu informed us. "No doubt you'll tell me the Babblers don't care for Iáinos, but they're interested in Cuzeian arms. It's the easiest thing in the world, then. Teach only those who consent to offer worship to Iáinos."

Bardāu held to this notion in the face of all attempts at education. I said that the Babblers were glad enough of our training, but would forego it without regret if it required the abandonment of their gods. He was sure that this was untrue, though he had not exchanged a word with any one of Berak's men. I said that the Taucrēte Pass was too important to be jeopardized by games-playing. He took offense at the characterization of his pious suggestion as a game. I said two men hundreds of lests from Cuzei would not be likely to succeed in bringing Iáinos to the Caðinorians, when greater numbers of Cuzeians had failed in Araunicoros or Cayenas. He asserted that his own simple faith was not so easily discouraged.

Some men stay in Cuzei too much. No one can be against teaching the worship of Iáinos to the Babblers! But for some reason some men insist on emptying their brains when they speak of the things of Iáinos. On what other matter would a man take ignorance and inexperience to be virtue? In what other area of life is a refusal to engage one's common wit admired as sincere and simple faith?

A Lord does not suffer thoughtless counsel because of the loyalty of the adviser. It is just the opposite: the loyal adviser takes care to speak with all the wisdom he can muster. Should it not be the same, and indeed more so, when we serve Iáinos? Not only love and respect, but knowledge and wisdom, must be offered to Iáinos.

We could not convince Bardāu; perhaps just as annoyingly, we could not make him mad. The longer the conversation lasted, the greater became his benevolence, his tolerance, his pity for the weakness of our faith.

The next day he announced that he was leaving. The same Babbler who had guided him to Berak's castle had reappeared, and Bardāu had him given a good meal while he readied himself to depart.

The prospect seemed to have roused good spirits in him. "It's a terrible thing to leave the two of you here at the end of the earth," he said, cheerfully. "Making a demon's rush back to Cuzei, downstream this time. I won't miss dirt trails and straw beds and bedbugs, that I can tell you."

"It was you who wanted to sleep in the keep," I said, with a laugh. "There's no bugs in my bed."

"You should have said so. But Ulōne damn me, I'm so content to be heading for home that I don't hold it against you."

Oluon came upon us talking, and learned of our guest's departure. He looked flustered. "Ulōne! I haven't finished my letter. When do you leave? Can you hold a quarter of an hour?"

"No more than that," said Bardāu. "Now I must finish my packing. Please have some wayfarer's meals packed for us."

He stalked off; I turned to Oluon. "And what are you sending with our visitor, O Oluon? Letters for some women friends, I suppose?"

"No, no, for my parents. And you? Aren't you sending a letter to Lord Zeilisio, or Lady Caumēliye?"

"No. Oluon, I think I should read your letter before you give it to this Bardāu."

"Of course, if you want," he said, with surprise. "Is there something wrong? Don't you trust him? Why, because of that jabber about Iáinos?"

"There's something uneasy in my mind about that, but I'm not sure what it is," I confessed. "But what's stuck in my ear is what he said when we asked about Feroicolê and Alaldillê. Do you remember?"

"He said the two of them were doing well."

"Yes. The two of them, and the House. Doesn't that sound odd to you?"

Oluon thought a moment. "No."

"Doesn't it sound like he thinks Feroicolê and Lady Alaldillê are married?"

"Well, yes, but who could possibly think that?" protested Oluon. "Alaldillê is old enough to be his mother."

"So you think he must have meant something else?"

"I don't know, Beretos.'"

"You're a lot of help, Oluon. Go write your letter. And let me see it before you give it to Bardāu."

I read his letter carefully— which did not take long; in its entirety it read something like this:

Dear Mother and old Dad. Here I am in the land of Babblers with Beretos who is good to me. We are teatching these Babbilers how to fight in case the daemons come here and we have been into Munxas and fought some men I am fine however. There is good beer here Dad. I ask Ulōne's blessing on you everyday. I wd. write more but the mans alredy leaving. Wth embrcs frm Yr lovg son Oluon.

There was nothing in this letter more worrisome than a few misspellings. The report to fear, if there was one, was Bardāu's own. What message did he carry? And on whose ears it would fall?

For some days after Lord Zeilisio's return to Etêia Mitano there was no great sense of menace in the air. Zeilisio bathed in the river, and enjoyed fine meals, and sat for long hours listening to my story, with grave and careful attention, asking many questions, as if his own situation were of no import at all. Indeed, when I pressed him to tell of his problems he bade me not to speak of it. "There'll be time for that," he said.

At Lady Caumēliye's request I occupied myself with the affairs of the House— going over the books of accounts, uncovering errors, resolving disputes with the peasants. It wasn't so bad as before I came to Etêia Mitano, because Caumēliye had watched over Corumayas, and made him keep records and remember most of his duties. But there were plenty of records to bring up to date, and mistakes to correct, and inspections to be made. I also reclaimed my old room, near to Lady Caumēliye's.

Feroicolê arrived, along with Sauōros of Eleisa, and we sat down with them, and Caumēliye, and the Master of Arms, to hear the words of Zeilisio and offer him counsel.

"O Feroicolê, I am honored that you've come so far for my sake; you are a precious friend and a true ally," said Zeilisio. "And you also, O Sauōros; I will be pleased indeed to hear your counsel."

"*When duty and friendship coincide, there is no sense of burden*, as the Wise Sentences say, O Zeilisio," responded Feroicolê.

I had never heard the two of them talking like that to each other; this was another sign, if any were needed, of the gravity of the situation.

"O Beretos, it's good to see you," said Sauōros. "I want to hear everything about your journey. I hear you're no longer a one-souled man."

I smiled; Sauōros was one of the few men in Cuzei who understood this expression. "You'll hear all about it, Sauōros. But first we must consider Lord Zeilisio's predicament, which I wish someone would explain to me."

"I think I can give a quick summary," said Feroicolê. "That is, if you have no objection, Zeilisio?"

"Have at it."

"Well, it has to be understood with reference to the situation with Inibē, of course," Feroicolê began. "As you can well imagine, the charge is just a pretext. Completely laughable. Of course, they came up with it as a diversion from Gintūro, where they were caught like a pig in the kitchen. Anyone could see through it, but of course it's caused us any amount of trouble. It's the sort of thing they're *likely* to say, of course; even a Babbler baby would know to discount anything they say on the subject. They said the same kind of things about the old Lord, Xamenāu, although that was before your time, of course. The problem is that *some* people do find it plausible. No one who really knows Zeilisio, to be sure, but Eleisa is a place where everyone thinks they know you because they've run into you at a dinner, or because they've known your father, or because your Lady knows their sister, and so there's been a terrible flurry of rumors about the festival, and about your own trip, Beretos, and if you want to see how they can twist something, the matter of Murgêde's son. Completely wrongheaded, but when there's talk of Iáinos some people feel they can't be against it. It's maddening. But also very serious, a very serious thing."

Feroicolê has never been able to tell a connected story in his life.

"Thank you, Feroicolê," said Zeilisio. "Perhaps I can fill in a few details. It began with one of their own Knowers, a brainless goat of a man named Gintūro, who lacked the virtue to keep his hands off the Glade offerings, and the intelligence to be discreet about it. One does begin to ask questions when a Knower buys a mansion from a Lord, and dresses his servants in livery. He said it was a gift from his friends; but we found boxes in his cellars still marked with the seal of the Glade. Dyes, wool, linen, silver."

"How horrible!" I exclaimed.

"It gets worse," commented the Master of Arms, grimly.

"We didn't immediately expose the man," continued Zeilisio. "Instead, we approached Murgêde and suggested that repentance was in order. Well, it was like a game of knights-and-kings. They denied it. They kept to the story of gifts. We showed them the boxes; they denied that they came from Gintūro's house. This was in private, mind you. This is what I've never understood. I understand lying in public; at least there's cunning behind it. But when we know the truth and he knows the truth, what's the gain in it?"

"Lies come quicker to their tongues than truth," shrugged Feroicolê.

"Then they offered us a share in the proceeds," said Zeilisio. "Not that they put it so frankly, of course. I believe the offer was for Gintūro to make a certain donation to the Glade in Norunayas. Well, I bypassed that chance at riches. I think that offended them. We wanted Gintūro to renounce his position; he wouldn't hear of it. So we brought a public accusation, and the game went on. They denied it; we presented our evidence; they planted some Glade boxes in my own cellars in Eleisa..."

"Ulōne!" I said.

"Well, to make a long story short, we won that round. Gintūro is out, and owes triple his ill gains to the Glade. And we tried, honestly we tried, to keep from crowing. But truly I don't understand the idiots. We approached them in discretion, we didn't try to cause them any trouble they didn't richly deserve. What did they gain by denying everything and refusing to talk?"

"They don't understand an honest man," suggested Caumēliye. "If the situation were reversed, they would have tried to profit from it as much as they could. If you couldn't be bought, they assumed you had something even more malicious in mind."

I have always wondered how Caumēliye, who is herself as innocent as a cloud, can have such insight into the souls of iniquitous men.

"Lord, I'm as far from understanding the charges against you as at the beginning," I protested. "I'd think all this would have enhanced your reputation, not led to charges against you."

"Stopping to give Inibē the time of day, much less fighting with him, is enough to soil one's name," countered Zeilisio. "No, we didn't look as good as you might think. True, it was their man who was caught with the goods, but they'd managed to suggest that it was simply a political persecution, and there was that foolishness about boxes in my cellar."

"No one could possibly be taken in by that trick," said Feroicolê.

"Of course it was an obvious plant," said Sauōros. "The problem is, a lot of people could begin to think that the boxes in Gintūro's cellar were a plant, too."

"Exactly," said Zeilisio. "The next move we misread at first. They started a big campaign for piety and holiness in Eleisa. They wanted more Glade observances, more readings from the Songs of Iáinos at Council, public instruction in the Way of Knowing, that sort of thing. We thought it was just a bald-faced attempt to wrap themselves in Iáinos after the fiasco with Gintūro, and also a reversion to form— they've always been the Gladey-ladey faction."

"As if you can *teach* holiness," said Caumēliye. "Didn't they ever read that duty leads no one a step closer to Iáinos?"

"Even in that campaign of theirs there was a lot of criticism of Zeilisio," said Sauōros. "Especially when he didn't attend the Festival of Making."

"Seen it before," explained Zeilisio.

"But they really went over the top over Murgīllede," said Feroicolê. "Almost can see why. It must have seemed like you were against them in everything."

"I am."

"Who's Murgīllede? Oh, I remember— Murgêde's son," I said.

"Right. He's the frog with the loudest croak in their public piety campaign," said Zeilisio. "They wanted to put him on the Council for it, and I opposed it, of course."

"We all did," said Feroicolê. "Most of us, I mean. Completely shameless, Murgêde already being on, and painting the boy as a prophet."

"When he's a parrot," finished Zeilisio. "But yes, looking at it out of their own little reptilian eyes, it must have been like the last chicken going to the fox. If reptiles kept chickens, I mean. That was only a month ago; they raised the charges just last week. I'd be before the Council right now if I hadn't discovered some pressing business back here— or if my Master of Arms had been sleeping."

The Master of Arms beamed.

"Iáinos Onnamêto persecute these idiots!" I cried. "What are you going to do now?"

"We were hoping you'd tell us," said Zeilisio. "No ideas? If not, it's back to Munkhâsh with you."

Feroicolê showed me a copy of the document describing the charges against Zeilisio, what are called the statements of basis:

TO ALL WHO FEAR IÁINOS BE THERE FAVOR.

> Under the grace of our Lord King Bisbazuo son of Lovimanis, be it known to the Houses and Cities of Cuzei that a predication of ATHEISM and DESPISING OF RELIGION is made against ZEILISIO son of Xamenāu, Lord of the House of Etêia Mitano and member of the King's Council; who
>
> Has disdained the gravity and long custom of public worship of Iáinos, thus harming public morality and dishonoring his own Lordship.
>
> Has on many occasions, and before many witnesses which will be produced, shown disrespect for Iáinos, for Knowers of Eīledan, and for the traditional practices of Cuzei taught to us by Lerīmanio and deriving from Ulōne.
>
> Has persecuted, slandered, and disrespected the Knower of Eīledan Gintūro, causing him the loss of his office, and burglarizing his home.
>
> Has stood in opposition to the movement of awakening now by Ulōne's grace arising in our land, cast scorn upon its leaders before the Council, and opposed the work of Iáinos with legal and procedural trickery.
>
> The matter to be decided in full Council in Eleisa before the Lord our King, by the compassion of Ulōne, in the power of Eīledan, under the law of Iáinos.
>
> In Eleisa, in the 641st year after Calēsias.

These, of course, were only the public charges; others could be brought out before the Council.

We spent some time discussing Zeilisio's options. For a Lord, only treason and the murder of a noble are as grave a charge as atheism; these are the only crimes for which a Lord can lose his title (and if the King wills, even his life).

For the moment the case could not be heard, because Zeilisio was not in Eleisa, and the King's men have not the right to arrest a Lord in his own House. If he would not come to Eleisa, however, and had refused three times to respond to an orderly summons, the Council had the right to consider and even decide the case without him.

It was Feroicolê's recommendation (and Alaldillê's) that the deliberation be allowed to proceed in this way; he himself would occupy himself with Zeilisio's defense.

On hearing this, Zeilisio said that to answer the charges through another, even one so gifted in rhetoric as Feroicolê, would be to give himself up for lost— it would be taken as an admission of guilt, or as arrogant disdain for the Council; fatal in either case. He intended to return to Eleisa, and defend himself in person at the deliberation.

Feroicolê said he was being an ass, and there was some heated discussion. Feroicolê's words were unconsidered, as usual, but his concern was well-grounded. In Eleisa, for a charge of this nature, the Council had the right to order Zeilisio detained, for as long as it took for it to reach a decision— and there is no law to impel the Council ever to finish a deliberation, should it choose to delay it. Feroicolê, though quite sure that the Council would never find Zeilisio guilty, was convinced it would vote to place him in detention. I pointed this out as a contradiction, and Feroicolê and I also exchanged some angry words. Feroicolê seemed to believe that I was doubting his judgment, but I was not; I was attempting to gauge Zeilisio's support within the Council.

We ended up considering each member of the Council in turn— forty in all— or thirty-nine without Zeilisio, who of course had no vote in his own deliberation. This discussion took quite some time, and required careful interpretation and shrewd judgment, and even so foundered on the fact that so many members were still unreadable, undecided, or quick to change their minds. We ended up with a count of 14 Lords certainly and 3 probably on Inibē's side, 10 certainly and 5 probably on ours, and 7 unpredictable.

The Master of Arms wondered if there was any way to counter-attack. Inibē and Murgêde were surely violating every law of justice and community— why not charge *them* with atheism?

"Atheism won't work," said Zeilisio. "They're certainly not atheists. Hypocrites, certainly, and vile smells in the nostril of Iáinos, but that's not actionable."

"There are penalties for bringing false charges, however," pointed out Sauōros.

"It doesn't help us now," said Feroicolê. "The charges have to be proved false first. But don't think we won't stick them with it when we've won."

"Iáinos willing," said Caumēliye.

The options were few and unattractive, and agreement slowly came on the course of action to pursue. There was no reason, except vainglory, for Zeilisio to travel to Eleisa now, and risk the uselessness and indignity of detention. On the other hand, he would not hear of allowing the deliberation to proceed without him; and though we did not like to think it, we had to agree that it was too great a risk also to appoint someone to speak for him. The best course was for Zeilisio to stay at Etêia Mitano till the deliberation began, and only then to appear in Eleisa.

"It's not going to be pleasant," said Zeilisio, blankly, looking around at all of us. "It's all stupid foolishness, and what's so insufferable about these people is that they can never admit their damned mistakes. They have to chew on it and pursue it and twist it into an injury and cover it up with aggression. Why couldn't they just have sent Gintūro to the demons, and be done with it? But just for Ulône's sake, and just to answer foolishness with truth, I'll answer them back, and keep answering, even if I have to do it from a jail cell."

Caumēliye put her arms around him. "Oh, well spoken, my Lord," she said.

Zeilisio looked at her, surprised. "Thank you, Caumēliye. And thank you, all of you, for your support. You are the best friends under Eīledan's sun. And now let's have some supper, and find something more cheerful to talk about, such as the demons of Munkhâsh. Sauōros and Feroicolê haven't heard your story, O Beretos."

25 · T̄OC X̄ZCZXΔЛIŪ · *Bri Ganacomex*

The conversation I record here lives vividly in my memory, and even in my nightmares; and yet I cannot truly say whether it truly happened, or if I dreamt it. The unreality resides in the feverish intensity rather than the vagueness of the experience, and in the lack of context: I cannot remember how the conversation began, or what preceded it or followed. The setting was the castle: we talked walking, through courtyards, barracks, servants' quarters, kitchens, halls, the baron's chamber; and every room was deserted, silent; even those rooms which ordinarily bustled with life were abandoned, motionless, and dead. This solitude is certainly dreamlike, and yet it may not have been a dream; once or twice a year a great outdoors festival is held in honor of Endauron, and almost everyone who lives in the castle attends it.

My companion was Ganacom.

—Tell me honestly, Beretos (he said). Why has your country sent you here? It cannot be of any importance to great Cuzei, so far away, to teach its language to the primitives of this tiny barony. Trade wouldn't be profitable: there's nothing here worth taking back to the Isrēica. Nor is Berak of any use as a military ally.

—You've seen with your own eyes how we occupy our time. We're training the commander's troops.

—Of course, but to what end? Perhaps you're planning on invading the Empire?

—You're not crazy, are you, Ganacom? Invade Munkhâsh, with this puny little force, against thousands of men, and for all I know demons, on the other side of the Gaumê? Invasions are your kind of game. Our only purpose is to help Berak defend himself.

—And yet when I met you, you were freshly returned from a raid against our lands, and boasting of the numbers of Munkhâshi you had killed. Is that your idea of defense?

—Very well, Ganacom, you wished for the truth, and you shall have it. Cuzei doesn't trust your Empire. It doesn't have any reason to. Fifty years ago Munkhâsh was a hundred lests to the east of the Gaumê; before that, even farther away. The safety of

Cēradānar is our responsibility. It's our task to defend the Caḓinorians and keep you from invading. We crossed the mountains to gather information— to better understand the danger. We didn't intend to kill anyone, but after seeing how your people treat the Moȟnaru, and seeing one of your priests kill a Caḓinorian boy, I can't say I regret what we did.

—Beretos, you sadden me. It doesn't surprise me that these barbarians misunderstand the Empire; the ignorant bastards don't know any better. But a traveled man like yourself, from a powerful country, should have a subtler understanding.

—What is there to understand? Are you going to tell me that you aren't invading innocent peoples, and killing Caḓinorians?

—Beretos, fifty years ago, when Munkhâsh was at a distance you approved of, there were no Cuzeian soldiers on the edge of the Gaumê, making claims to protect all of Cēradānar for Cuzei and making raids into Nokhdak; and not so long before that, there was no principality in Araunicoros, organized along Cuzeian lines and bound by oaths to the Cuzeian King. I would say that you are making up for the error of the iliū.

—What error? The iliū never stray from Iáinos!

—But even in your teachings, they may make mistakes, no? As they refuse to rule men directly, they aimed to create a great human empire along the Cayenas. Their mistake was to trust you Cuzeians, who quarreled and came to war among yourselves, leaving the river to the Babblers, and building their state far to the west, on the Isrēica. Now you are attempting to correct that mistake, building an empire over all of Cēradānar.

—That's absurd. You're crazy. Cuzei doesn't have any interest in building an empire. Araunicoros and the other states are allies, nothing more, who have freely associated themselves with us. And our presence here, and the Munkhâshi killed on our expedition, are both reactions to the provocations of your own Empire.

—Really? So you'd say that my understanding of your country is insufficient?

—Exactly.

—That things aren't quite as they seem, if I looked closer?

—Of course!

—Well, that may be, Beretos. But aren't you smart enough to ask the same questions about your notions of Munkhâsh? Don't you think you just might be mistaken about us?

—That you're really not an empire, and are full of loving-kindness? I don't think so.

—I didn't say that, did I? Why don't you give me a chance to explain?

—All right, if there is anything to be explained, explain it.

—I will do so. Of course we're an Empire, and proud of it, just as you are rightfully proud of your own strong state. Why we expanded into the valley of the Ardênbalo is a long story, which perhaps I'll tell another time; for now let's just say that it was a combination of things. It's the destiny of the Empire ever to increase in glory and strength. But in this case there were also requests from some of the Moňnaru chieftains to accede to the Empire, and I won't disguise the fact that we were concerned about the power of your country. We wanted to reach the Gaumê, the natural border between our realms, before you did, and take the Moňnaru into our Empire before you could take them into yours.

—Well, that's quite a favor you've done for the Moňnaru. It's certainly glory for them, being slaves for Munkhâshi.

—Use your brain, Beretos. Should I criticize you because these barbarians of Berak's live in miserable huts rather than fine Cuzeian cities, and worship a gaggle of petty gods, and spend most of their time beating each other over their thick heads? The Moňnaru are new to the Empire. Already they're better off than they were before— filthy, wretched, half-savages they were, not even as advanced as your Caḋinorians. Did you know that they abandoned their parents in old age, so as not to have to support them? Did you know they engaged in endless wars, and passed their women among each other, and killed their daughters in times of drought or war? We've stopped those things. And in time they'll be as prosperous and proud as the rest of the Empire. Just a few centuries ago my own people, the people of the Dakêsh, weren't much better off.

—Yes, I know how your Empire works. The Moňnaru can move up as soon as you conquer some more people. A clever system; but you can't blame your neighbors for mistrusting you.

—You must give us more credit than that. I don't ask you to trust in our goodness— that's not the issue. But at least look realistically at our situation, and whether we're as dangerous to you as you think. We will expand the Empire, of course, as Gelalh ordains; but we don't have any taste for making trouble for ourselves. Why would we want to invade Cēradānar, and almost certainly get into a long and difficult war with a strong and well-armed nation? There are plenty of barbarians to conquer. We haven't brought all the Moňnaru into our Empire; and elsewhere, far to the east, there are other peoples to occupy ourselves with.

—How fortunate. And when do you plan to get around to us?

—Beretos, there's no need to assume such a hostile attitude. I've been trying to explain that we have just as much reason to distrust you and your nation as you have mine. Why is Cuzei making a military mission here, and raiding our cities, when we've sent no one but traders and diplomats into Cēradānar? But I bring up these things only to show how easily misunderstandings can occur. In truth there's no need for us to be enemies.

—No?

—No, why should we be? Why not be partners instead?

I stared open-mouthed at the Munkhâshi for some time, and then sputtered:

—What are you talking about?

—It only stands to reason. Let's divide up the uncivilized peoples between us, and rule them together. Can't you see the enormous benefits? Each of us turns his worst enemy into a friend and a support, and can freely exploit the riches of the lesser peoples. Our nations have much in common, Beretos.

—Much in common? I don't believe that.

Ulōne protect me from the danger of even writing the words of Ganacom's reply; but it must be done, for my account to be complete.

—Are we not both advanced nations, surrounded by barbarians? Are our fields not richer, our cities stronger, our armies braver, our knowledge deeper, than any of our neighbors, and worthy of comparison only to each other? Are we not both believers in true gods, as against the pagan perversities of the barbarians? Are we not both tutored by greater races, the lords of the earlier ages of Almea— you by the sea-swimmers, ourselves by the masters?

—Ganacom, it's true that we are both powerful nations; but surely in every other respect we're as different as summer and winter! You make slaves of your conquered peoples; in our lands we outlaw slavery. Your Empire is a ladder of absolute obedience; our Lords are equals, and our people have rights even Kings must respect. Above all, Iáinos is the opposite of Ecaîas, whose House is wholly evil!

—What would summer be without winter, or rain without sun, or male without female? Because we are different from you, must you call us evil? We don't say that your god is evil— only that you're mistaken in understanding the divine nature. What, Beretos, is God?

—Iáinos is God. Iáinos is the Idea and the Power; Eīledan is the Creator and the Shaper; Ulōne is the Lover and the spirit within.

—We do not have all these names; we only say Gelalh— the Six Gods are only faces he wears. What we say about him (for we are not afraid to say that Gelalh is male) is not perhaps so very different from you. But I believe we concentrate on the essentials, what is most important about him, which is that he is God, and we are not. That is, he is all power, and power is the measure of God. He who has the greater power is closer to Gelalh. The stronger is above the weaker, the intelligent man above the fool, the man of energy above the lazy, the adult above the child, the male above the female, the master above the servant. All life is the struggle of greater against lesser; and it is in defeating the lesser, and ruling him wisely, that the greater shows his greatness.

—This is nothing like our beliefs.

—It is the core of your beliefs— or at least of your actions. Didn't you just tell me about the Power of Iáinos? Do you not dominate Cēradānar as the sun dominates the sky, because of the superiority of your people and your God to the Babblers? Could it possibly be any other way? You would not have the barbarians, lazy, ignorant, and filthy, like this Berak, ruling over you! Wouldn't such a situation be intolerable, absurd, an offense against God? The lesser peoples themselves are better off under your guidance— as the Moĥnaru are under ours— as my own people are under the masters. Isn't this how the world around us works, the nonhuman world you Cuzeians make so much of? The deer and the rabbit are masters of grain and leaf; the eagle is master of the rabbit, the lion of the deer.

—As Iáinos says, *Power is made to work for love.* Where is the place in your world for love, Ganacom, or compassion, or justice? Without compassion, power is only tyranny and domination. Why should we model ourselves after the lion? The lion is a murderer.

—Do you think there's no love in our hearts, Beretos? We are not monsters. Where the world is well-ordered, when strength and merit rules, love can take its place. When lesser men rule, there is war and corruption and want, and the finer sentiments are too weak to live.

—Your words are pretty, Ganacom, but I don't trust you. All your words and all your eloquence cannot outweigh in my mind the cry of the Cadinorian boy on the temple steps, before he was killed by the priest of your Gelalh. Between us and the people who can do such a thing there is a gulf which cannot be bridged.

Ganacom was silent for a minute, and when he spoke again his voice was a little colder, and tinged with anger and disdain.

—One Cadinorian boy. A criminal or a spy, no doubt— perhaps a common thief, or an escaped servant. Did you think of that? Did you investigate or ask questions, or simply turn to violence? And because of this one moment's outburst, the voice of a barbarian who is nothing to you, whose story you do not know, you will forget all you know of statecraft, and betray the best interests of your country? I expected more of you, Beretos.

If we spoke more words I do not remember them.

In the speeches spiders make to flies, their webs are beds. I have seen Munkhâsh, and I did not fly into Ganacom's web. But Berak had ears for his words.

O my countrymen, you will easily reject Ganacom's vile insinuations. If there is a reason I have written down these terrible words, it is to ask you to consider how the comparison of Cuzeian with Munkhâshi sits in the eyes of a Berak, or of a Prince of Araunicoros or Dācuas. By our actions, by our words, by the sort of men we send them, do we make the difference between us clear? Is it so obvious, not only in our own eyes but in theirs, that we believe in something besides the Munkhâshi subjugation of the lesser to the greater?

The visit of Bardāu came when we had lived nearly two years in Berak's barony; and the sending away of Faliles, when we were there three years and a season.

We continued our training of the commander's troops. By the end of our stay I believe my men could have met an equal number of Cuzeian men at arms on equal terms. Their grasp of tactics was hazy (being so divorced from their own ways of war), and they lacked community and grace; but on the other hand they had no other duties but war, which can be said of only a few men in a Cuzeian army. Their discipline had greatly improved under my tutelage; they acquired some rude facility for drill, though never a taste for it, and could execute at least a rudimentary plan of battle, so that their ferocity could prove an advantage, rather than a dangerous liability, in the hands of a skillful general.

The lessons in Cuêzi continued also. We went through the entire book of Antāu, and then through that of Samīrex, and the Unending Songs, and parts of the Ten Prophets. Both Faliles and Sielineca achieved a remarkable fluency in our language, and even used to speak it to each other when they didn't want servants or their father to understand; and Sintilna learned to speak well enough, though she never lost her heavy accent, and her hand remained a childish scrawl. Vaḋora's study however came to nothing. There comes a point when a language begins to come naturally from the tongue, and one can concentrate on what is being said rather than on the language itself; she never reached it. She was not stupid, but the work didn't interest her, and in the end she abandoned it.

For a brief period we had Cruvec in the class: Tentesinas had impressed upon him that he should learn Cuêzi. He learned the alphabet, but once he discovered that there was far more to learning a language than that, he stopped. In any case, at this point it was impossible to teach both the girls and a beginner at the same time.

I never succeeded in achieving any great friendship with Berak. He never had more than a few words for me; never sought my company; never seemed glad to see me. I would have done better if I were more fond of strong drink. He does little besides drink with one old soldier or another, eat, and pursue the servant girls. Each year he is slightly larger than the year before.

His only real diversion is hunting. Oluon and I once accompanied his party, but we did not find it great sport. I was used to Lord Tancī's hunts— on foot, three or four men only, under the direction of Sūro the Master of Scouts, relying on skill, stealth, and knowledge to bring home one's deer or boar. Berak takes twenty or thirty men with him, and enough beer and wine to swim in. They blunder over the hills and fields on horseback, and let dogs do the tracking for them. They come home drunk as ducks, and seldom finish a hunt without a stray arrow hitting a dog, or a peasant, or one of their own number.

If I have said little of the relations between Oluon and Faliles, it is the mirror of my own inattention. In our first year among the Babblers I heard much about her, for he had many questions about the language and about Babbler customs; and naturally he had none other in which to confide his hopes and frustrations.

For awhile it seemed that their friendship had waned. I no longer saw them together, and more than once I saw Oluon deep in conversation with some maiden of the castle, or more likely one from the village; and once, coming unexpectedly to his room, I found one of the serving maids in his arms.

I thought nothing of it; this was the Oluon of Etêia Mitano I knew. More than once Zeilisio has had to give gifts and privileges to some village family, that they might not press a claim of matrimony against Oluon. Zeilisio always said that he had expectations of a crop of fine swordsmen in the next generation, which was his way of saying that Oluon's value in his guard was of more import than his transgressions. My Lady Caumēliye was less forgiving.

Later still he was back with Faliles, as I understood when she once again began to accompany us on our walks in the mountains. She had now seventeen years, and looked very well: long black hair, flowing almost to her waist; a girlish face, bright-eyed, intelligent, and ready to laughter; long, thin limbs, sometimes awkward, usually graceful. And Oluon found favor in her sight:

she and Oluon played like children together, and held hands, and laid back in one another's laps, with the happiness of new lovers.

I felt a foreshadowing sorrow for them both, for Faliles must soon be given to the baron or godspeaker or rich man who would marry her; I knew that this day was delayed only because Berak still hoped for a better match or a better price than he had yet been offered. From comments of Sintilna's, however, I came to understand that the girl also was resisting—this would not stop Berak, but it did make him proceed cautiously.

There was indeed an engagement proclaimed, with an old baron whose lands, situated thirty lests away, were several times the size of Berak's. I believe he was some sort of distant relation. He came with all his retinue to dine, exchange gifts, and meet his bride, and left the next morning, furious with rage, repudiating the arrangement. I heard different reasons for this: Tentesinas and the other men of the keep said that Berak had sent him away with insults, because the bride-price he offered was disdainfully low; while Sintilna and the women maintained that the old man had been offended by the paltriness of the gifts and festivities he had received.

Oluon gave me what he said was the true story: Faliles was unwilling to marry such a man, old, ugly, and brutal, and had conspired to prevent the wedding. She had been rude to the baron at dinner, and tricked one of the cook's men to serve wine that had gone bad, and hinted to one of the baron's men that she was being married to someone from so far away because no local lord wanted her.

There was some talk of war over the broken arrangement; I believe Berak even went hunting for allies among the local barons, but nothing came of it. The mountain barons would have been willing enough to relieve the old lord of some of his wealth; but he was too far away, and would be too well defended.

This incident worried me, for likely it would not have happened but for Faliles' love for Oluon. I became angry with him. "What do you intend with this girl?" I asked him. "You don't intend to marry her, do you— a barefoot Babbler girl with a Babbler lordling for a father?"

"No, no," he said, very quickly. "Nothing like that. You know me, Beretos."

"I do know you, that's why I'm talking to you. Do you think Zeilisio is going to come to redeem you, if you get her— no, I don't even want to think about it."

"It's only a friendship," he protested. "I mean, I like her a lot, and if she was a Cuzeian girl, or even a Little Sister, then... but she's not, I know that. There's nothing to it. But while we're here, so far from Cuzei..."

"It's not just that," I interrupted, angrily. "Are you even thinking of what we're doing here? What if Berak blames us for the failed engagement? What words could Ganacom be pouring in his ear on the subject? For that matter, what would it look like to Inibē and the idiots back home?"

"Yes, you're right, Beretos," he said, sadly, disarmingly. "I've been very foolish. I wouldn't do anything to hurt you, or Lord Zeilisio. Really, Beretos, I don't know how to argue with you; you make me see things very clearly. I have to watch myself, and think more about Iáinos..."

And he went on like that for quite a time. I detest talk like that, and he knows it. He counts on it to make me tire of talking to him. After a time I realized that he was saying nothing specific, and I said, "You see that you're acting foolishly, then?"

"Oh yes, O Beretos. I am a weak person..."

"So you won't see her any more?"

"Please, no, that would be too hard," he said, without the slightest change of tone. "She is really a pleasant girl. Surely there's no harm in spending some time with her now and then. Of course I'll talk to her about her engagement; I understand that she's got to be married off. But until then..."

Let the reader judge which of us is more of a fool; I let his promises and expressions of regret persuade me, and dropped the subject.

What worried me more than Oluon was the increasing influence of Ganacom. I was shocked one day to learn that the castle godspeaker, old Aiđodoroî, had begun making devotions to Gelalh.

A little enquiry revealed an distressingly simple story. The idea was Aiđodoroî's own; he simply offered to make a sacrifice to Gelalh, as he had offered one to Iáinos, and Ganacom accepted.

Gelalh is not a very jealous god, outside his own lands. Tentesinas, who didn't much care for Aiđodoroî, suggested that the godspeaker was seeking influence with Berak. Berak was not very interested in the Cađinorian gods, and took no part in the ceremonies of the cult, except as demanded by tradition; perhaps the godspeaker had that idea that if Ganacom had his ear, he must go through Ganacom's god to treat with Berak. He might even have the idea, according to the commander, that Sielineca might be married to his son, his successor. If such was his scheme, it was a failure; Berak did not even attend the ceremonies honoring Gelalh.

I was moved to protest to Berak concerning Aiđodoroî's activities. "This should not be. Berak, Munkhâsh is the enemy of your people. You should not allow your godspeaker to bow to the gods of your enemies."

"You take these things far too seriously," he informed me. "Listen. Whenever a lord's defeated in war, whenever there's a drought, or a prince dies, or his wife bears another man's son, do you think he hasn't had his godspeaker praying and sacrificing? And it doesn't do him a shit of good. If it mattered what godspeakers do, we'd remember great godspeakers, not great lords. Ha! Think of that! We'd remember mighty prayers, and not battles. No, put it out of your mind."

"Don't you know what kind of god he is, this Gelalh? Don't you know that Cađinorian children are sacrificed to him in Munkhâsh?"

"Yes, yes. He eats children like they were berries. I know what it is, you know. You don't have to pretend that you're concerned for our children. It's just that you're a Cuzeian and you don't like the Munkhâshi gods."

"Ask your commander, then. He feels the same way I do. He's been in Munkhâsh."

"Oh, he has a bedbug in his tunic, all right. The two of you tire me out with all this shit about Munkhâsh. Look at Ganacom; he's not a bad fellow."

No words could persuade him.

I spoke to Aiđodoroî also, to no greater effect. He could not be brought to understand the difference between Gelalh and his own gods. If Gelalh was known to eat Cađinorian boys, that was all the more reason to sacrifice to him, and propitiate him; he would learn to see the Cadinorians more favorably, and such a powerful god would be a good friend. And, like Berak, he was certain that Tentesinas and I exaggerated the Munkhâshi threat. Ganacom's poison had done its work here as well.

Aidodorot̂ sacrificed a goat or a pig to Gelalh once a month or so; when he did, we did not eat of it. A Babbler god is one thing; Ecaîas is another— Ecaîas is real.

27 · ⱭꞮⲦdŌẒXẔⲦẔÃẒb · *Duntrâcanavas*

All of my readers will have heard something of the deliberation upon Lord Zeilisio, and I will say nothing of the public controversies on the subject in the weeks preceding the meeting of the council— that febrile mix of excitement, and rumor, and suspicion, and morbidity, which attends the troubles of great men. I will tell instead of the deliberation itself, about which much less has been said, and much of that inaccurate.

I must say something, however, of the great disappointment that awaited us on our arrival in Eleisa— the defection of Lord Ximāuro. The old Lord was completely under the sway of Murgīllede and his campaign for religious revival. He would not even meet with Zeilisio. It was not seemly, he explained, for the devotee of Iáinos to countenance even the appearance of impiety.

"Eīledan strike him, does he *believe* what the idiots are saying?" I asked Feroicolê, who had relayed this message.

"He says that's not the point; it's a matter of keeping the name of Iáinos pure. I said it *was* the point, by Ulōne, but I couldn't budge him. When it comes to Iáinos that old goat has always been as bull-headed as a donkey."

Zeilisio had nothing to say, not even a joke, when we told him the news. This alone was enough to tell that it affected him deeply.

I spent some time in the Mansion of Learning, among the tomes of history and law, reading stories of other deliberations on religious matters. One of the librarians, a friend of mine named Lanêdos, helped me; he had read much on the deliberations against Lords. He likes reading about them because he hates Lords; he likes to say that when Cuzei abolished slaves it should have abolished Lords as well; that Lords were as arrogant as cats, and no more intelligent, but no good at catching mice. But despite these strange opinions he is an educated man and a very agreeable companion. I do not know why he dislikes Lords in this way; he serves no Lord himself, and Lords have no privileges above beggars in the Mansion.

"Look through these," he told me, loading me with an armful of scrolls and books. "Those all deal with the Sworn Cabal, more than a century ago. Some of the Caballists were tried for atheism— all successfully. Let's see, what else is there? Ulidallê, of course. He was burned alive."

"That's cheerful," I said.

"Look him up," he said, tossing me another book. "He deserved it."

We found about two dozen cases in all. Serious charges against Lords are rare enough, except in the early days of Cuzei, and in hard times since then; and charges of atheism are very rare indeed. Rarer still is an acquittal. We found only three, and none of them were very propitious for our cause. Dīnsācio of Norunayas was cleared of all suspicion when he began prophesying before the very Lords in Council, revealing their innermost secrets and making known Iáinos' wrath to them. The other two were dismissed when their accusers died before the deliberation could start.

"It's clear enough what you have to do," said Lanêdos. "Kill them off— Inibē, Murgêde, and his snake of a son. Believe me, the world will be better off."

More typical were the Caballists, a conspiracy of Lords who had attempted to win the King's chair with a campaign of murder; they succeeded in killing King Melebrexos and all his family, but were observed by a servant hiding high up on a ledge. Or Tīcio of Utâtos Crinuē, who had slept with his own daughter, thrown Knowers out of his lands, and cursed Iáinos in the Glade of Eleisa. Or the Lady Usēye, who had led the persecution of the prophet Araunixue.

I remarked that past Councils had been slow to bring charges of atheism against a Lord; and that in most of the accounts we had read the charges had seemed justified.

"That's how it is with deliberations against Lords," said Lanêdos. "The laws of Iáinos, if not those of the King, apply to them no less than us; but to be forced to answer for anything, they virtually have to cut a virgin in two in the Glade. Not that they apply justice so leniently among their subjects, of course. Some Stewards have been put to death by their Lords for so much as using a personal pronoun to refer to Iáinos."

"I suppose you'll be satisfied if Zeilisio suffers the same fate," I said, bitterly.

"Oh, no, you wrong me, O Beretos," he replied. "I couldn't be fonder of Zeilisio. He's amusing and decent and it's Inibē and his biting spiders who should be facing deliberations. Anyone can see that this is a new political ploy. A serious charge of atheism has almost always been successful— but it's never been as blatantly political as this. If they succeed, we'll see the same trick used again and again. If that happens, fear for Cuzei."

It was about three months before all the Lords of the Council had assembled in Eleisa, other business before the Council had been decided, and the Lords were ready for Zeilisio's deliberation. During this time Zeilisio was free (though barred from the Council), but naturally subdued. He had no stomach for the plays, dinner parties, and intrigues which were normally his avocations in Eleisa; he spent his time instead with close friends, or his children, or at the Mansion of Learning.

The deliberation began in the morning after Glade worship, with the utmost of solemnity. The Lords were dressed in formal robes, all in white linen. They stood behind their chairs as the King entered, dressed in his finest attire, all red and blue and black and gold, with the Staff of Calēsias in one hand, and the Belt of Lēivio round his hips; he was assisted by a young man and woman. Knowers came in, and asked for the presence of Iáinos and Ulōne, and showed the Cloth of Cuzei.

Zeilisio was brought in, naked to the waist, and led to a place opposite the Council's long half-circle table. The law allowed him to rest on a stool, if he felt "weakened or feeble", but he did not. He stood facing his accusers.

In the spectators' benches, I put my arm around the Lady Caumēliye, because she was crying.

The King opened the deliberation; I could not hear his words, but I knew about what they must be: the Council of Cuzei meets in sadness to hear an accusation against a sovereign Lord of the land; every question will be asked to determine the truth or falsity of the charge; may Ulōne guide us to the execution of true justice. The King was then led out; he was too weak to sit through an entire morning of deliberations. Narrisio, the Ruler of the Council, would preside in his absence.

If the King were in his prime, surely this deliberation would never have occurred. The Wise Sentences say truly: *Drought, banditry, and injustice wait for the reign of a weak king.*

A Lord being charged has the opportunity to have the first word, because the litany of complaints from his accusers might otherwise precipitate the Council to a rash and unjust decision. However, this right is not as effective as it might be, because the Lord does not have the benefit of hearing the accusations as they will be made, and is thus somewhat in the dark as to the charges that will be placed against him. Lord Zeilisio's initial remarks were as follows.

"O King, fellow Lords of the Council, guests, people of Cuzei; the blessings of Ulōne be on you.

"O Lords and Ladies, it has never been in my nature to have patience with defenses and apologies. The offering of excuses, the obvious and suspicious self-interest, the playing at humility or virtue by men who obviously don't possess these gifts by nature and can't act either— none of this is to my taste. That is why I leave most judgments on my own lands to my wife.

"Now that I myself am subject to judgment, my feelings have not changed. I don't find pleadings on my behalf any more interesting than those offered for others. And I am convinced that they are not necessary. Those of you who are my friends do not need my assurance in words that I indeed love Iáinos and Eīledan. Who could be convinced by the words of a man facing the perils of judgment, if they were not already convinced by the deeds of the free man? And as for my accusers, I do not think they brought these charges because they think them true, and so they will not be touched by demonstrations that they are false.

"O Lords, in the next days you are going to hear many words, many details and much foolishness— questions of who was in what cellar, of the virtue of Gintūro the very rich Knower, of whether such and such words were said at this dinner or that. It will sound very much like any other deliberation you have judged, and the aim of it will be to keep your minds as far as possible from dwelling on what you are being asked to do.

"First of all, of course, you are being asked to judge a man for despising of religion. This is a serious charge, for of course I completely agree that a Lord of Cuzei must be a servant of Eīledan. I wish that all of you could do as my steward Beretos has done, and examine in the Mansion of Learning the stories of those others who have faced the same charge, and see if the present circumstances are truly those which would have led our fathers to begin such a deliberation. But there is a second question which is before you, and which is much more important.

"O Lords and Ladies, by means of this deliberation you will decide how the Lords of Cuzei shall walk. You will decide what sort of public life we will have; you will decide if the ways we have inherited from our fathers shall be respected, or if we should proceed on a new and dangerous path.

"Have you ever seen a man and a woman quarreling, and it comes into the man's head to hit the woman? Have you ever seen two men fighting, giving and receiving blows, when one of them brings forth a dagger, and stabs his opponent in the stomach?

"Do not be deceived by the words you will hear from Inibē and others, which will be full of piety and let us honor tradition and we must not tolerate this and that. Behind the fine words is the suggestion to conduct public life in a new way. You are being asked to place a sword on the table of the Council.

"And do not think that men behave better when they fight with swords rather than fists. A boxing match is as full of strategy and skill as a swordfight, for those who care for those entertainments; and has the advantage that the physician need not be summoned quite so often.

"The dissensions and discussions we have in the Council are not always edifying; I will be the first to admit it. But they have never before led to false charges of atheism. Perhaps even my opponents regret the terrible step they have taken, though they do not know how to unmake it. But you, my Lords and Ladies, can undo this wrong, and keep us from adding this new and dangerous arrow to our quivers.

"O Council, you are here to decide my fate; but also your own. Inibē and Murgêde wish to set themselves up as judges, not only over myself, but over all of you. In their vision it is not Iáinos who is our Judge, but other men, with all their passions and imperfections. In their vision it is not the pure and loving heart which pleases Iáinos, but the observance of ritual and the subscription to public campaigns. In their vision it is not the inner voice of Ulōne which guides us, nor the drive to grasp the Design in the mind of Iáinos; it is the threat of prison, and the voices of men in Council.

"When you hear the fine words of my accusers, remember the threat that lies behind them. And judge well, O Lords and Ladies of Cuzei. It is the way we shall live in Cuzei you are deciding, and the way we shall worship Iáinos."

It was Inibē himself who gave the accusation. While Zeilisio was talking, Inibē's face had turned entirely red; when he stood up, it looked as if he had been boiled.

"O King, O Lords of the Council, it is difficult for a man of Eīledan to hear such malice, such prevarication. You have heard the deceptive words of one of the cleverest rhetors of Cuzei. Now hear the truth.

"It is no new way that Inibē of Alaldas advocates to you. It is the old way, the way of Iáinos. Zeilisio would urge you to shrink from your duty to uphold the law of Iáinos. The traditions of Cuzei. I urge you only to do your duty, the duty that has always been yours as Lords.

"I urge you also to reject the insulting suggestion that anything motivates my own behavior besides the love of justice. Or will you take a man suffering deliberation on serious charges before the Council as a judge of character and of motives?

"Let us make no mistake; the charges are serious. Atheism. Despising of religion. Honest men quake even at the naming of these evils. Nor would we lightly make such a serious charge. Let us examine our evidence."

Inibē then proceeded to outline the charges. I do not have the patience to write down all his words; and also it would be a needless repetition: Inibē's party made many copies of his speech, and distributed them throughout Eleisa that evening, and copies have not been lacking in Cuzei to this day.

Most of the charges we already knew from the statements of basis. First, there was Zeilisio's shunning of the Festival of Making and other public worship, which in Inibē's opinion was in itself proof of atheism. If a man loves Iáinos, he should not be ashamed to worship Iáinos in the Glade with his fellow Cuzeians.

Second, he had treated Iáinos, the Knowers of Eīledan, and the rituals and commandments of religion with jesting, disrespect, and contempt. Inibē confessed that he did not understand how a man with such a record of sin could be so shameless as to boast before the Council of a "pure and loving heart." Who can treat a Knower, or the sacred and holy institution of religion itself, with anything but respectful gravity?

Third, he had engaged in a hypocritical campaign of slander and vilification against the worthy Knower Gintūro, being so malicious as to see abuses and theft in the gifts offered by grateful worshippers to the Knower who had helped them. What sort of man besides an atheist could choose as his enemy a man whose profession it was to know Eīledan?

Fourth, he had opposed the Movement of Awakening which Ulōne had caused to blossom in Cuzei. He had opposed seating its leader Murgīllede on the Council, and cast public aspersion on the Movement and its leaders. What was the Movement, but a wind that quickened the ardor of men for Iáinos? Who could oppose a greater devotion to prayer, abstinence from wine and the sexual act two days a week, the enforcement of laws against adultery, gluttony, and bad language, the destruction of immoral plays and books, finally, an increase in the levy for the Glade, and thus in the comfort of those who were dedicated to the service of God, the edification of their fellows, and the education of children? Who but an atheist?

The last charges Inibē made were new.

"The next sin Zeilisio has already confessed, indeed vaunted before you. It is the inordinate power of his wife, which usurps his own; we will show that she, and not he, is the judge and master in his House, that she is the mirror and perhaps the source of his godless politicking. An ambitious and disdainful woman. This disrespect for the place which Iáinos has decreed for women should be offensive to every man of Eīledan, and it troubles me very deeply.

"Finally we must not let the policies and practices which Zeilisio has advocated in this Council escape notice. The mission which this Council entrusted to his House four years ago, which recently ended so shamefully— you have heard the public reports. But I will reveal now before you that we are not dependent for information solely on servants of Zeilisio. A man of my House visited the castle of Babblers to which this mission was sent, and observed all that there was to see.

"Was it not the charge of this Council that the Babblers be given the word of Eīledan? Was it not stated that Beretos of Tefalē Doro would serve not only as Resident, teacher, military ambassador, but as a Knower, and educate the Babblers, worshippers of idols and demons and despairing in the darkness of untruth, in the Way of our people?

"O Lords, there was no education of the Babblers. No giving of the word of Eīledan. The Babblers are as beset by idols as the day Beretos left this city. Indeed, a priest of these false gods was the chief confidant of the baron of that place, and every day there was served at his table meat sacrificed to false gods, and this man Beretos and his servant ate of it.

"But a servant is only the reflection of his master. Where impiety sits at the head of the table, can the children love Eīledan? We can have no doubt that the conduct of this mission among the Babblers was according to the dictates of Zeilisio, and perfectly reflects his impiety, his despising of the traditions of Cuzei.

"O Lords, such shamelessness must not escape the justice of this Council."

28 · ᴀɴ⅂ᴀᴄ ʌᴢɴᴄɴιdᴀ · *Oluon Falile-to*

The news reached us, through a man who traveled through the mountains bringing town goods to trade with the mountaineers, that a band of Caĉinorians had begun a raiding expedition not far from Berak's lands. There was some surprise in this; the previous year had yielded good harvests, and the local baronies had no lack of food; nor had we heard from any visitor or neighbor of any feuds or grievances likely to impel one of the local barons to war. But it is not impossible, only unusual, for Babblers to go to war for no evident reason; and a raiding party is not much of a war anyway, by our standards.

If anything, Tentesinas and the men were excited by the news, and hoped that the raiders would draw near. They had not fought a good battle since our expedition to Munkhâsh, and were growing bored with nothing but military exercises and the occasional suppression of a peasant brawl to test their skills. For my part, I was not anxious; I knew that Berak's men were better swordsmen and bowmen than any Babblers within a hundred lests or more. I was training them to stand up to Munkhâshi; Babbler raiders would be nothing to them.

The only person who seemed worried, amusingly enough, was Ganacom. I heard him asking Berak about the raiders, and about the strength of his defenses; and he came once more to watch our training, as if to reassure himself. I almost felt sorry for him; alone among barbarians, having to trust forces more primitive than any he knew against the mountaineers' ululating bandits.

Oluon suggested that we wake him up late at night by screaming outside his window, and firing arrows at his walls. He'd do it, he said, if he could figure out how to be inside the room at the same time, so as to observe Ganacom's reaction.

To walk in the mountains, with their thin air and small proud plants, was our escape from the cramped stuffy world of Berak's keep. Faliles often came with us, both to be with Oluon and to get away from her mother. She and Sintilna were beginning to quarrel frequently; it was starting to make our Cuêzi classes difficult.

We climbed into the mountains one warm day not long after we had heard the news of the raiding force. We climbed high enough to shiver with the cold, and see snowflakes swirling about our heads; then we descended into a remote valley, and walked till we were hot and tired. We sat by a rushing brook and ate a lunch of fruit, sausages, wine, and flatbread baked with cheese in the Cuzeian style, which Faliles had learned to make, and we talked to each other in Cuêzi, which Faliles could now speak with a wonderful fluency.

There was a place where the stream, thick with spring rains and melting snow, crossed a meadow, and widened into a slow and lazy pond. The pond, heated by the sun, was just warm enough to swim in, except for the stream's main channel, which ran deep and clear down one side of the pond.

We took off our clothes and swam in the pond. The pond was not made for serious swimming; it was not deep enough, or large enough, and there were grasses on the bottom that brushed against us, and impeded us; but we amused ourselves paddling around, and splashing water on each other, and trying to force each other into the cold waters of the main channel.

We came out of the water, and Oluon and Faliles fell to chasing each other round the meadow, in order to dry off— a project which succeeded so well that they made themselves hot again, and dipped back into the water to cool off.

It was a pleasure to watch Faliles, on land or in the water, with her careless, energetic movements, her muscular limbs, her young thin body, her ready smile and long black hair. In the last years she had grown from a girl into a beautiful young woman. She lacked the graceful self-presence and the compassionate, intelligent eyes of Lady Caumēliye, but she shared with her one trait: she looked happy and alive in the open air, as if she belonged there.

I lay back on the grass above the pond, and Oluon and Faliles lay in each others' arms, talking and caressing. The day seemed to stop; the sun beat down on us, making me warm and sleepy. There was nothing to do anywhere in the world, except lay back and feel the sun on my closed eyelids, and the grass beneath my back, and the breeze brushing against my skin, and listen to the birds, and the wind in the trees, and the voices of Oluon and Faliles farther down on the grassy bank.

I was awakened by a noise somewhere above me; and looked up to see at the top of the hill, half-concealed behind a rock, staring back down at me, the face of Hānu, Berak's handmaiden from the keep. In my state of relaxation I made little of it; I waved at her, inviting her to join us. But her face disappeared, and there were noises as if she had run off.

I got up and walked over to Oluon and Faliles, and asked if they had seen Hānu.

"No, we were busy," said Oluon, laughing.

But Faliles looked thoughtful. "I don't like it that she was here," she said.

"What's wrong?" I asked.

"I don't know. I don't trust her."

"You just don't like her," suggested Oluon. "I don't blame you. I don't think that creature knows how to smile."

"She's always talking with my father, and there's always intrigues, and she does things against my mother, and then they're both at each other's throats. I really hate it. What was she doing out here anyway? She must have followed us."

"Perhaps we should be getting back," I said.

Berak found me in my room, reading the epics, a few hours after we returned. His face was red, his movements uncertain—the effect of wine, I thought, until I heard his first words:

"The penalty for what your servant has done is death."

"What? What are you talking about? Oluon?" I asked, in confusion.

"Who do you think?"

"What about him? What's he done?"

"Don't play games with me, Cuzeian," Berak exclaimed, slapping his palm on the desk in front of me. "You were there as well, weren't you?"

"I was where?"

"Up in the mountains. Don't play the idiot, you son of a bastard! You're not going to deny that this great hog of a servant of yours was screwing my daughter, are you?"

I gaped at him like a fish for a moment, before answering, "Ulōne darken me! Of course he wasn't. We were swimming."

"Yes, that's right, if swimming means screwing," said Berak. "Look, my servant Hānu was there, and she saw the two of them, naked as plucked chickens, and what they were doing together wasn't swimming."

"They were in each other's arms, but they weren't making love," I said.

"Naked?"

"Yes. I told you—"

"Look, Cuzeian, is this servant of yours a whole man?"

"A whole man? What do you mean?"

"I mean, has he got his shells?"

Berak was asking if Oluon had been castrated. He had not been, I assured him.

"You tire me, Cuzeian," said Berak. "The man's got the shells Mieranac gave him, he's got a naked girl between his legs, and he's not screwing her?"

"They were just caressing, baron."

"You're really going to pretend that he never screwed the girl?"

"I don't know," I said, with more honesty than intelligence; but I was flustered, and felt bound, in the face of this terrible misunderstanding, to stick to the truth. "I hope not; he promised me he wouldn't, and he should know better."

"I've never met a man with more of an ability to wander with words," remarked Berak. "If you simply called Hānu a liar I'd know what you're about; as it is I can't get any sense out of you. I think you're just trying to confuse me. It's very simple, Cuzeian; your servant is screwing my daughter, and what are we going to do about it? What do you think I'm going to get for her now? He's spoiled her; he's robbed me. Aiđodoroî and Ganacom are all for killing him, and I am a thumb-span away from doing it; but Sintilna doesn't want it."

"That's nice of her," I said.

"She wants him unshelled."

I was beginning to see the seriousness of the diplomatic situation. My anger burned against Oluon— what could keep that man from thinking with his penis?— but also against Hānu, and against the obscene imaginations of these Babblers. Must they see lovemaking whenever a man and a woman are alone together? At the same time I felt the ground uncertain under my feet; through filthy-mindedness and malice Hānu had seen lovemaking in an embrace, but I had no assurance that Oluon and Falies had not been making love at other times, in other places.

Berak sat down on the bed, and looked at me. He looked a little calmer now; he looked tired and annoyed rather than angry. I could well imagine the conversation he had just endured with Sintilna, who for once would tell him her full mind without fear.

"I'll tell you something," he said. "When I was a young man I was sent to live at an uncle's castle, and I was like your man Oluon. Talk to all the girls, kiss them, see what you can get. I would have got the baron's daughter, but she didn't like me; I slept with her cousin instead. So it's not like I don't understand him. Or you, for that matter. Hānu says you were naked too. Maybe you've been screwing Falies too, eh?"

"No, baron," I said. "I was—"

"I know, you were swimming. What's it matter? Like I say, I can't blame you— I wish she weren't my own daughter myself sometimes. But you lose that game, you take your punishment. You pay up. So what are we going to do?"

This was clear enough; Berak's daughter could no longer be married off to an important baron, or bring a large bride-price. Her value had declined, and Berak expected me to make up for it.

I asked what he had in mind. His first thought was that I should pay her full value, and marry her myself. She could not marry Oluon, who was in Caðinorian eyes only a servant, and a foreign one at that; but it would be acceptable, and even honorable, for her to marry a Cuzeian ambassador. I declined the offer. It is always my instinct to turn down the first terms proposed in a negotiation; but I am not sure that this would not have been the best solution— better, certainly, than what actually transpired. In the eyes of the Caðinorians she would have been mine; but when we returned to Cuzei I would have made Oluon marry her.

Ultimately I agreed to pay what was, in effect, the difference between the bride-price she would have received as a virgin, and the price which would be received if she married a baron's brother or younger son, her current prospects. It amounted to five horses, several casks of wine, two boxes of spices, a spool of Cuzeian linen, and a box of silver ornaments.

Obviously I had none of these things at hand; I had to send Oluon to Otaures to have them brought to the mountains. It seemed wisest to send him immediately; Sintilna was still talking about having him "unshelled," and the godspeaker and others were calling for his punishment as well; tempers might cool in the weeks the journey would take.

He bid a sad farewell to Faliles. He was not allowed to be alone with her (and indeed, she was virtually sequestered in the keep), and her parents would not even let them embrace; but they whispered words to each other in Cuêzi, and both of them cried, before Oluon set off down the road to the village, and Faliles was ushered back upstairs by Seneinda, the chief maid.

No one in the castle doubted Hānu's story, not even Sintilna, who was Hānu's enemy. Indeed, it was soon told that Hānu had seen the two of them making love on many occasions, that the three of us had slept together on our walks in the mountains, that Oluon had made love to the soldiers' wives... I do not want to repeat some of the other details which were related. In the end it comes down to the ways of the Babblers; for among them, if a woman shows her body to any man but her husband it is as much as to sleep with him. Indeed, a Caĉinorian woman must be careful where she takes a bath, because it is she who is blamed if a man sees her and lies with her.

I have asked a few Caĉinorians about the behavior of Ariȟmiera, who swam with us after taking us up the river in her boat; they invariably interpret her behavior as an acceptance of Oluon's seduction. But Oluon paid for his ignorance of Babbler ways; he slept alone that night!

Two things particularly galled me. One was that the Babblers of the castle were right, but for the wrong reasons. Hānu was lying; she had not seen Oluon and Faliles making love. But when I asked, Oluon admitted to me that they were indeed lovers. He swore by Ulōne and Eīledan, however, that he had not taken her maidenhood; she had previously lain with a servant boy, and also with one of the soldiers. So it was not Oluon who had robbed Berak; but we could hardly make the fact known; the two boys would certainly be killed, and their blood would be on our hands.

The second was the more serious: the treatment of Faliles. She was vilified by the entire household, from her father down to the stupidest kitchen-boy; kept a virtual prisoner by her mother and Seneinda; and beaten by her father.

"This is a difficult people to love," said my Lady Caumēliye, when I told her of these things.

When Oluon returned, several weeks later, bearing some of the gifts which were due Berak, and having arranged for delivery of the rest, Faliles was already gone. Berak had found a husband for her— the nephew of a baron from along the Taucrēs, almost fifty lests distant.

It could be worse, Faliles told me. She had met the man a few years ago; he was not too old, or too brutal; they could probably manage to live together.

"And there's one thing at least," she said, on the day she was to leave. "I'll never have to spend another night in this castle."

"Faliles, I owe you a lifetime of apologies," I said. "What have we done to you, coming here?"

"You've awakened me," she replied, softly. "I'll never forget you, or Oluon. Speak to him of my love. And may Iáinos smile on both of you."

I had not realized before this moment how much I would miss Faliles. While she lived in the keep I think I saw her as simply a Babbler girl, a pleasant acquaintance amid my exile; it was only as she was leaving forever that I recognized her as a lively, beautiful, and good-hearted young woman, and besides Oluon and myself the only fluent speaker of Cuêzi for a hundred lests in any direction.

29 • ΛZT̄ĮCZb X̄ZCZX⊥ЛIŪ • *Fabēias Ganacomex*

There were no more Cuêzi lessons; Sintilna had turned distant with me, and seemingly with the rest of the castle as well; I think that the departure of Falíles left her in a deep depression. Berak spent his time hunting, or with his mistresses, or drinking with his soldiers or with Ganacom. It would have been a repetition of my first months in the baron's lands, if it were not for Tentesinas, whose friendship and trust remained firm.

The more I knew of the commander, the more I found to admire. He had not seemed a promising companion, at first: a barbarian, simple in his tastes and habits, rude in his expressions, a stranger to Iáinos, unacquainted with *lelïyas*. But he was a courageous man and an excellent commander of men, and of a decency and loyalty that many Cuzeians would do well to imitate.

There were suggestions at this time (and not only from Ganacom) that Oluon and I be sent away, or at least barred from training the baron's troops. It was Tentesinas who shouted down the cries of the moment, and insisted that we stay, and continue instructing his men.

It was he also who informed me of the next move of the Munkhâshi. He burst into my room one night, red as an apple, and exclaimed, "Mieranac take me!"

"What is it?" I asked.

"Mieranac damn him to the caverns of hell, and damn me for an idiot while he's at it," he replied.

"Who?"

"Who do you think? That slinking snake out of Munkhâsh. I've only found out about it from Berak. He wants my *opinion* of it. Mieranac take me!"

"Calm down and explain yourself. I don't know what you're talking about," I complained.

"It's simple enough. The viper is offering a troop of Munkhâshi soldiers to defend him against the raiders in the area."

"Iáinos! What did he say?"

"He should have thrown him off the cliff of Kravcaene-Limura, but no, he's *thinking* about it," said Tentesinas, spitting with disgust. "He asked my opinion, and I gave it to him, with pepper on it. 'Baron, what happened to your brains?' I said. I said, 'Are these not the enemies of our people? Are they not hated by Endauron and Mieranac? Did I not see with my own eyes their priests preparing to sacrifice Cadinorian children to the misshapen demons they worship? Are you senile before your time, has the Munkhâshi come to lead your brains about like a shepherdess her sheep, that you would ask these devils into your keep to defend against raiders? Raiders! When your own army is the strongest and boldest in six days' travel! It's we who should be raiding; you could be a great man in these mountains.'"

He spoke with emotion and anger, repeating precisely his speech and his gestures before the baron; it is how the Babblers tell a story.

"'Mieranac damn me, Berak,'" he continued, "'but there will be no Munkhâshi army in this keep while I have breath in me.'"

"And what did he say to that?"

He imitated Berak's drawl: "'They aren't as bad as you think.' It's what he says whenever I talk about the Munkhâshi. What kind of spell does that cockroach of a Munkhâshi put on him? He doesn't look like a wizard; but then you didn't look like a soldier."

"He doesn't seem to use any potion but alcohol to gain his way into Berak's heart," I said. "But obviously there's more in his own brain than barley. Very likely there's a band of Munkhâshi troops ready and waiting to come at his bidding. But Berak hasn't decided to do this thing, has he? And in any case, what can we do about it?"

"He's *thinking*," Tentesinas repeated, grimly. "My words scared him, by Mieranac! You talk to him too. As for me, I will go see the godspeaker. He listens to Ganacom too much himself, Mieranac take him; but maybe I can spill some sense into him."

At the best of times I would not have looked forward to speaking with Berak; and now that I was in disrepute it seemed even less likely of success; I wondered if the best way to hinder Ganacom's proposal would be for me to support it myself.

Nonetheless I steeled myself to talk to him. I found the baron in consultation with his gardener, talking about brewing;

for it was that official's responsibility to gather the barley and brew the castle's beer.

I knew better than to ask him to send the gardener away; he would simply look at me as if I were mad. The Babblers do not care who listens to what they have to say; they rarely have secrets from one another, and never pause to think in advance of the effect of their words.

"Baron, if you please," I said, "I have been speaking with the commander about the proposal of Ganacom, which strikes us both as ill-advised in the extreme..."

"Now why, why, why doesn't that surprise me one shit?" commented Berak. "I knew what you'd say about Ganacom's honor guard without asking you, and Tentesinas as well, which hasn't stopped either of you from telling me all about it. Naturally."

"Yes, of course, but it's not simply the Munkhâshi," I said, attempting to change tactics. "It's the imprudence of allowing *any* army, any soldiery you don't intimately know and trust, into your keep. It's the height of incaution and imprudence. No prince would be so foolish as to allow such a thing."

"Are you calling me a fool, Beretos?"

"If you let these Munkhâshi into your castle, then yes, you will be a fool," I said, recklessly.

Berak laughed. "Well, we have different thoughts on the Munkhâshi, you and I. Ganacom isn't a bad type, is he? Really it's an expression of esteem on the part of the Empire. Just ten men, well-trained, and under my orders, not Ganacom's. It doesn't sound so bad, does it?"

"Baron, don't even think about it. The demons didn't advance to the very edge of your realm by holding their neighbors in esteem. They're conquerors; but they'd be as glad to conquer with a trick as with sword and bow."

"I like to hear you talk," said Berak. "Always so serious. Don't they ever laugh in Cuzei? Do they have beer there? Eh, Aecredurris, what do you think of that? Do they have beer in Cuzei?"

"If they do, it isn't as rich as ours," offered the gardener.

"Certainly we have beer; and wine and ale and cider as well," I said. "But if we could return to this scheme of Ganacom's..."

Berak slapped me on the back. "Ruthless. Well, son, I surrender. You boys don't have to worry. I won't have the honor guard."

"How's that?" I said, in stupefaction.

"I may not be a Cuzeian, but I don't have milk in my veins," explained Berak. "As it happens I think the same as you. Ganacom's all right, but I don't need ten more of him, and soldiers at that. So don't worry yourself any more."

I felt a bit dazed, uncertain what to think. "I'm certainly glad to hear it," I babbled. "You're making the right decision. Tentesinas will be happy as well..."

Berak looked at me as if he couldn't understand why I was still there and still talking. He turned ostentatiously back to the gardener. "Now, if we could get back to important matters, Aecredurris. What I want to know is when the next batch of malt will be ready. The kitchen tells me we're low, and it'd be a disaster if we ran out."

I went in search of Tentesinas, feeling some relief, but also worry. It seemed to me that Ganacom was not one to sink into repose when he met with a defeat.

Till now Zeilisio had been allowed to remain in his house in Eleisa, although a King's guard was stationed in the Garden House, to keep him from escaping the country or plotting mischief. (The guard was a young man named Boulo, and was as dull as a stone. He spent most of his time in the kitchen, cadging food from the cook, and rolling dice. He had years ago, he explained to us, set one hand gaming against the other; it was now the case that his left hand owed three hundred bottles of wine to his right hand, and four goats.)

Once the opening arguments had been given, however, the accusers asked the Council to have Zeilisio detained. When Zeilisio had come to Eleisa of his own free will to be examined, it could not be maintained that he was likely to wish to escape justice; but it was unseemly for one accused of such a serious crime to stroll the streets of the capital like an honest man.

The Council agreed, by a tally of 23 to 14, with two Lords absent. This was the first tally in the deliberation, and a dispiriting one.

The Ruler of the Council, Narrisio, therefore gave the order that Zeilisio be detained for the duration of his deliberation in the Red Garrison, the barracks belonging to the Council, and instructed his household to bring furniture and provisions there for his maintenance.

The Lady Caumēliye stood up, and asked to address the Council.

"What is it, O Lady?" asked the Ruler.

Caumēliye advanced through the ranks of the spectators— we had arrived late this morning, and were seated near the back— till she reached the edge of the platform which bore the Council table, and stood there, tall and firm, not very far from her husband. All the room considered her curiously. I saw that her hands, which she held behind her back, were trembling.

She spoke, in a soft, firm voice: "O Lords and Ladies of the Council, you must take me also to be detained with my husband."

There was silence for a moment; and then a confusion of murmurs— surprise, bewilderment, disapproval.

"Go sit down, O Lady Caumēliye," Narrisio told her. "There is no requirement that the wife of a Lord under deliberation be detained as well."

"Yes, Lady, it is neither law nor tradition," offered Ximāuro, who had joined in the vote to detain Zeilisio.

"Nonetheless I insist on it," said Caumēliye, with assurance. "If you choose to persecute my husband, you persecute me too. Among us a marriage is not only an alliance, but a union. That's what it says in the Book of Instructions. My place is with my Lord."

"This is completely irregular," complained Murgêde.

Zeilisio said something to her, which I could not quite hear; she shook her head slowly in reply, and looked back at the Council.

Several Lords were protesting: "It isn't right." "What is she doing?" "Lady, sit down!" "Diversion!"

Alaldillê's high, old voice cut over them all, and silenced them. "Stop it, all of you. Caumēliye, dear, don't be a fool. You're kind, but you don't know what you're doing. What do you think you're going to accomplish?"

"You're not the one under accusation," said another Lord.

"She certainly is, if you listen to Inibē," countered Feroicolê.

"You should be thinking of your family," said Murgêde.

"It is you who are dividing my family," replied Lady Caumēliye. "It is you, who pretend to be concerned with the things of Iáinos, who are dividing father from son, and friend from friend, and speaking lies of the best man in Cuzei. You may accuse my husband of anything you please, but wherever he goes I will go, and share his fate."

There was another pause; and then Alaldillê said, "But what of your children?"

"I will ask the Council to have them with us," she answered. "The warriors of Iáinos on the Council will not divide a mother from her children, will they?"

"Really, Caumēliye," said the Ruler of the Council, in that patronizing tone which persuades no woman, and Caumēliye least of all, "you don't know what you're asking for. Your husband will be kept in a barracks, not a house— bare stone walls, insects on the floor, a bucket of water for a bath, no fire for the night. It's no place for a lady. And the detention regimen is strict, although I suppose some accommodations could be made for a woman— waking at dawn; no eating and washing done except with permission from the custodians; no clothing but a cloth. Once you think about it you'll see what a foolish idea it is. Now please sit down and don't impede us any further."

For answer Caumēliye reached up and undid the clasp at her shoulder. Her gown fell away, revealing her naked, but for a rude skirt about her hips, much like the one worn by her husband. She took off her sandals, and walked barefoot over to Zeilisio, and put one hand on his shoulder.

"I have thought about it, and I insist," she said.

In the face of such determination, the Council capitulated, with a certain ill grace. It ordered that Caumēliye accompany her husband in detention, and be subject "to the same treatment and the same privations, without concession to her sex."

I looked round at the Lords as the pronouncement was made. Zeilisio's friends and supporters seemed embarrassed; those who were neutral or uncertain looked angry, or amused, or resigned. Murgêde and others of his faction wore a puzzled triumph, as if they had received an unexpected victory; I wondered if they had had some idea of proposing Caumēliye's imprisonment themselves. Inibē glared with disgust at Zeilisio, as if this were only one more perverse and atheistical outrage to be laid to his charge.

Caumēliye was not allowed to stay before the Council, but was escorted immediately to the Red Garrison. I was allowed to go with her; as we walked she gave me instructions for the house and for the children, and asked for some specific things to be brought to the Garrison.

We approached the Garrison— a square, crenellated block rebuking the fountains of Eleisa; it had never looked taller, or darker, or colder. "This is no place for a Lady, O Caumēliye," I said, sadly.

"Do you mean it's a place for a Lord?" she replied. "Don't say such foolish things."

"I'm sorry, my Lady. I was only thinking of how hard it will be for you."

"You're some comfort, Beretos! Now, beloved, take some of these guards to our house and have the children brought here. Tell them they're coming to be with their mother and father. Oh, Ulōne, I don't have any doubt they'll be filthy. Guards, will you let them be bathed before they come?"

"They'll get dirty enough inside, O Lady," said the King's Man she had addressed.

"Yes, I know, but they should at least start out clean. If you please, O Guard; I don't think it's against your orders."

The guard shrugged. "It doesn't matter to me."

"Thank you so much. Make sure they get clean, Beretos, and don't dally. Now Ulōne be with you, my Beretos. Don't look so sad; you depress me."

"I can't help it, Lady. Ulōne be with you."

She kissed me, and accompanied by King's Men, disappeared through the doors of the Garrison.

Only Lords had the right to visit the Red Garrison— we had to deliver provisions for Cauměliye and Zeilisio to the guards at the gate— so I never saw the conditions of their imprisonment. But Cauměliye was allowed to write letters, and wrote this to me a week or two later, describing what had happened to her.

My loyal and cherished Beretos,

May Ulōne give you comfort and peace. I have never felt closer to Ulōne than here. It is true and good comfort, what was told to us by the Knower at Tefalē Doro, that the less we are encumbered by riches and luxuries, the closer can Ulōne approach to us. But in ordinary times, we don't listen to such words!

The food which you and Corumayas sent was given to us. I do not think that the servants steal any of it, because we give some of it to them. We do not require that much food anyway. I do miss the fresh things which we would be eating in the Garden House here in Eleisa, or at Etêia Mitano— milk and fresh greens and new-caught fish and soft cheese; but of course all that would spoil here.

You will be thinking that we are suffering in a dungeon, like Antāu suffering in the caves of the Half-height King; but it is nothing like that. We have a room to ourselves, and our own benches and chairs. They would not let us have a bed; they said it was too big. It does not make much sense, but it is detention after all and you cannot argue with them. So we sleep on straw pallets, covered with blankets, and huddled up together, because it becomes very cold at night.

There are not any windows, but I think we must be on the top floor. We can hear noises below us at night, and to the right and left, but nothing above. Really, they are very noisy here! They all have heavy shoes, and never seem to talk to one another except by shouting.

There are not many insects, just cockroaches and spiders. Well, there are fleas, too. That is one advantage of not having many clothes; they have fewer places to hide. They really only bother us at night. Sometimes they really persecute us; and of course it is impossible to hunt for them in the dark. Even during the day they are not easy to find; they hide in the seams of the blankets.

Vissánavos and Isiliē are being very brave; I am quite proud of them. Vissánavos says that he would like to talk to the Council, to tell them that his father is not a bad man; and if they do not listen he would kill them all! Isiliē does not really understand why we are here. She is too young to understand how evil men can be. But they do not complain, although they miss the servants and their House. But we play games with them and tell them stories.

I have to report that they like Zeilisio's stories best. I cannot blame them, because they have never had him so much to themselves before. He tells them the plots of plays, and stories from history. They do not always understand, but he is very patient to explain things.

At times they have to leave him alone, because he must think what he will say before his accusers. You might think that it was at these times that his imprisonment and disgrace would weigh most heavily on him; but it is not so. He says that it is like knights-and-kings. It is late at night, when the children are sleeping, that loneliness and doubt plague him. He prays to Iáinos, and sits for hours, as if waiting. At first he wanted to be alone during these times, but now he lets me lay on his lap, and takes my hand in his.

It is not all quiet, of course. In the mornings Zeilisio is brought before the Council. During the rest of the day guards may come in at any time to bring food or wine, or empty the bucket of waste, or march us to the courtyard and back for exercise, or simply stand about watching us. A Knower comes every day for an hour, for instruction and prayer. If we ever become atheists it will be because of his dullness. He speaks in a monotone, and says nothing that ten thousand Knowers have not said before him. Sometimes Lords come to visit— Narrisio, for instance, comes to ask questions; while Feroicolê comes to talk with Zeilisio about the deliberation, and Alaldillê simply to talk, and to offer comfort.

I wish you could be here, Beretos, to read the epics to me. Now I know how it was for the Maiden in the tower, when she was abducted by the wizard. I maintain myself well, Beretos, content to be at the side of my husband, who is as brave and as noble as Samīrex, and my children; and I trust in the way of Iáinos. But I confess also that there is not a day in which I do not cry over the evils that are visited on us, and those that our enemies plan for us— men who have deadened their hearts and lost shame, and convinced themselves that their evilest impulses are pleasing to Eīledan.

I must stop now, because I have to write also to my father. All my love to you, my Beretīllos. I will write to you again if they let me.

I kiss you. Your friend, Caumēliye.

31 · lūçōZaítixz · *Exdrayêneca*

I was having a nightmare, a nightmare of persecution. Evil men pursued me through the halls of the keep (but a Keep vastly enlarged, and having some of the features of the House at Etêia Mitano). I looked for friends— I talked to Tentesinas, and spied the Lady Caumēliye from a distance— but staying with them I would endanger them, and I had to move on. I found myself with Berak, asking for his assistance. He seemed skeptical, and I tried to explain that it was in his own interest. "I've never met a man with more of an ability to wander with words," he replied. "And besides that, Cuzeian, you're the fox. I'm sorry, but that's the way it is." And the next moment he was chasing me, across the hills, crashing through the streams, with his friends and dogs.

I called upon Eīledan to save me. I hid myself in a deserted house, and waited for the hunters to pass; but then Ganacom was beside me, laughing. "Do you really think Eīledan can help you?" he asked. "Look, I've trapped your god here in this cage." I looked up, and saw Eīledan, a tiny figure imprisoned in a little stone cell— a sad humiliation for the maker of worlds.

"If Eīledan is there, it must be the end of the world," I said to Ganacom. Ganacom was no longer there; but it did seem to be the end of the world— at the end the evil will be burned with fire, and it was indeed becoming hotter and hotter. The hunters were surely expecting me to run from the house into their hands; but I had a plan to evade them. I saw Bardāu eating at a table, and asked him to come with me. He refused; he wanted to keep on eating. "If you stay here you'll be as cooked as your meat," I said, reasonably; but he wouldn't listen. I tried to pull him from his chair, but he held onto the table, and tried to hit me. "It's the first good food I've had since I left Cuzei," he said.

I abandoned him, and ran down the stairs to the cellar, where there was a river in which I could make my escape, swimming. I plunged into the water, which was already warm and sticky from the heat (but refreshing compared to the air). I swam along, but soon came to fear that it was too late: the water was going to boil, and kill me as surely as my enemies would. I scrambled out of the water, into tall weeds which wrapped me up and clung to me; it was heavy going. Was it still the end of the world? If it was, the moons would be falling from the sky. There was an enormous crash, so loud that I woke from the dream.

Or was I awake? It was still terribly hot, and I was still wet, as from the river. And there seemed to be things happening in the room— strong smells, roiling shapes. With the moons fallen, it was terribly dark...

I struggled to move, broke free of my blankets, which were wrapped tight around me— no wonder I had dreamed of clinging plants— and tried to sit up. The heat increased enormously, and I sank back down, now wide awake. Something was wrong— heat— *fire*. The house was on fire.

My first thought— before clothes, or arms, or saving myself, or Oluon— was my books. I must save my books and scrolls! Almost leapt to my desk, feeling in the dark for my papers. They were already hot, but untouched as yet by flame. I gathered them together, and wrapped them in a blanket from the bed. Now what?

Look around! What was on fire? Nothing yet, as far as I could see— no flame— though there was plenty of smoke. The fire must be in another room.

The light increased; it was coming from the window. I peered out, and recoiled in horror: the back of the barracks was on fire. Apparently the straw roof had just caught fire, and the fire was coming this way. There were shouts, cries, tramps of feet, a horse's whinny. Some of the soldiers must have already awakened, and run from the building; there was a confusion of noise outside. Were the others asleep? And what of Oluon, of Tentesinas?

I quickly slipped on clothes, took my parcel of books, and headed out the door, crawling on hands on knees to save myself from the smoke and heat, stumbling against things on the floor— a pair of sandals, a large stone— where had that come from? (For the first time I understood why the Sojourner, when he was battling with the Fire Spirits, crouched low to the ground and aimed his sword at their ankles. I had always thought that the story was allegorical; that it told how the mighty are undone by the troubles they ignore at their feet.)

Oluon's chamber was next to mine; I crawled in and found him asleep, helpless as a baby. I shook him violently. "Stop that," he said, almost at once— he was never a heavy sleeper. "I'm awake. What is it?"

"The barracks are on fire, you big lout," I said.

"Ulōne save us!"

"Stay down!" I shouted, as he was about to try to stand. "Grab some clothes and follow me. Got to get out of here."

A horrible sight met us in the hallway: the upper hall of the barracks, where half the men slept, was now bright with fire. Two men brushed past us, scuttling away from the flames.

"Get out, get out," they said.

"Is anyone left inside?" I asked.

"Nobody. Last ones out," they panted.

They crawled past us; I went toward the barracks hall, trying not to look at the flames— the wooden beams of the roof seemed to be on fire now, and the straw bedding. I reached the door, looked briefly inside, prayed to Ulōne that no one was left inside, and shut it with a crash.

"Oh, that's better," said Oluon.

"Not for long," I said. "Let's find Tentesinas."

We made our way to his room, but he was not in it. We checked the room next to his, that of the chief of arms; it was empty.

There was a tremendous crash from the barracks hall. No doubt the rafters were giving way. The roofing above us was already smoking like soup; if we waited much longer we'd be burned alive.

"Here he is!" cried Oluon. "He's in your room."

"That's right," said Tentesinas, just behind him. "Looking for you. Your gods have protected you."

"So far," I said,

"Take this," said the commander, handing me something long and flat. My sword.

"What's this for?"

"You think this is just a fire?" asked Tentesinas. "You'll need your sword and your prayers. It's a raid."

We stumbled to the stairs, and made our way downstairs. Downstairs, it was cooler, and not even smoky; we had not even realized, until we reached the clear lower air, how much the smoke had been making our eyes itch. We could even stand up again.

I immediately walked over to the door to the lower barracks hall. It was already closed, but when I placed my hand on it I felt strong heat.

"There's fire inside there," I said, heading for the front door. "We don't have long, let's go."

"Hold," said Tentesinas, who was already at the door. "And what if their swordsmen are on the outside of the door, ready to cut us down as we come out?"

"How do you know there's anybody out there?" asked Oluon.

"Saw them from the window. There's a big fight out there. Obviously some of the boys got out; they're fighting now. But someone was trying to burn us up as we slept. Fortunately Mieranac took care of me; he woke me, and wouldn't let me be burned by fire."

"Instead he'll let us be cut up by swordsmen," I said. "What are we going to do? That's the only door on this side of the building."

"The only door, but not the only exit," said Tentesinas. "Our forefathers who built these buildings had foresight; they built a tunnel to the keep for just this turning of fate."

"Wonderful!" I said. "Where's the entrance, then?"

"Just inside the barracks hall."

I wandered back to the door; it was hotter than ever. "Very foresightful."

Oluon looked at the front door. "I'd rather take my chances with the swordsmen."

"Don't be a fool," said Tentesinas. "The barracks isn't completely on fire yet, and the entrance is only about twenty paces away, just inside the inner storeroom."

"Isn't completely on fire," I repeated. "They can write that by our names in the Memory of the Dead. Well, it's not quite certain death; let's go."

We crouched down. Tentesinas placed his hand on the door's handle, and immediately pulled it away, with an oath. I took the cloth from my bundle of books, and offered it to him.

"What in Mieranac's caves is that?" he asked.

"My books."

"You're bringing your *books* along?"

"Of course."

Tentesinas snorted and shook his head, and turned his attention back to the door. He wrapped his hand with the cloth and pulled on the handle. The door opened; thick black smoke poured into the room, almost blinding us. We dropped even closer to the floor.

There was no time to lose. A naive reader might have supposed that it was no great danger to be trapped in a stone building during a fire; stone does not burn. But the barracks had a thatched roof, and wooden supporting beams, and straw beds, clothes, furniture, and ropes, and firewood, and wooden arrows; the stone walls would survive, but not any human beings left inside.

We scrambled forward as fast as we could. Most of the straw beds were ablaze, and as we scuttled forward the fire leapt to the bed next to us, which lit up like a torch. The ceiling was invisible, hidden by smoke; the end of the room was a sheet of flame. We made our way to the door of the storeroom; Tentesinas, his hand still wrapped in cloth, opened it.

Fortunately, the fire had not yet reached the contents of the storeroom, which contained casks of wine, clothes, furs, swords, helmets, harnesses, a huge bellows. We had to move some of these things to reveal the door to the underground passageway.

"Fire's going to come in here," said Oluon. "Let's shut the door."

"No, we need the light," said Tentesinas. There was a clink on the floor. "Shit! I dropped the key."

"Ulōne take you!" I cried out. "Where did you drop it?"

"If I knew that, I'd have it. Damn, damn. Why don't they keep this room clean, so you can find something in it? Give me some light; the goddamn barracks is on fire and there's no goddamn light."

We all felt on the floor for the key.

"Here it is," I said; it had bounced toward me.

He busied himself with the door. Smoke filled the storeroom; a burning spear tumbled inside, and almost set a pile of harnesses on fire. The trapdoor was stuck. Tentesinas and I pulled at it; then all three of us. We couldn't rise up far, and could hardly keep our eyes open, because of the smoke. We all swore, to various gods.

Finally it opened, revealing wooden stairs. We clambered down, closing the trapdoor after us; it was immediately dark as pitch.

"We need a torch," I said.

"No we don't," said Tentesinas. "I know this tunnel like it was my wife's face. And we don't have time."

I thought this was foolish, but I had no wish to climb back in the storeroom. So we felt our way forward, after Tentesinas. I had expected a stone corridor, nicely cut and big enough to walk in; but the passageway was simply cut through the earth and clay, and was barely tall enough to crawl through. We kept calling out to each other, to keep track of where we were in the dark. I was following after Tentesinas, and felt that I was forever touching his feet, forever waiting for him to move, and trying to avoid kicking Oluon, who was just behind me.

The bottom of the tunnel was wet; the top brushed our hair; we would be a terrible sight, if we could be seen. We crawled in unearthly silence, hearing nothing from the burning barracks behind us, feeling no more heat and smoke, but rather cold, and the musty smell of the earth.

"Are there spiders down here?" asked Oluon, helpfully.

Once or twice I felt a moment of utter panic— I felt trapped, needing to move my limbs as I needed to breathe, and unable to. I stopped, closed my eyes (not that I could see anything with them open), and breathed deeply until I could recover myself.

After an eternity the clay gave way to wood beneath our hands, the space opened out, and we felt the first steps of the stairs leading upward to the keep.

"A terrible thought just occurred to me," I said. "You didn't happen to unlock the other side before coming to bed tonight, did you? Because if you didn't..."

"This side isn't locked. Passageway's for escaping the castle," said Tentesinas. "Of course, they may have put a big washtub on top of the door, or something. They do that every couple of days— I'm always having to clear it off."

We struggled up the stairs— or rather, Tentesinas climbed to the top, and I climbed partway up. I heard him pushing on the door, and swearing.

I felt that I preferred my nightmare. Better the moons falling from the sky than to be trapped underground, the only exit to the outside world a burning building.

But then there was a wooden creak and a clatter of something spinning away, and the door opened, and there was again light and noise. We bustled out of the passageway: we were in the ground floor of the keep, amid the laundry and sausages.

We rushed out of the keep, and saw the barracks, blazing merrily, and men fighting in the firelight. There were some of our men nearby, looking for horses. We rounded them up and tried to get an idea of where the raiders were. Some were between the barracks and the castle, we learned; others were on the far side of the barracks, by the main gate.

And where were our men? Here and there, it seemed, and in disarray. As the commander had suspected, a number of the men had been slaughtered as they sought to escape from the burning barracks; some had perished inside. Others had escaped, and were wandering around, dazed, or looking for weapons; others were fighting back.

"We need to find as many of the men as possible, and get them together," I said. "We can still beat them. If they resorted to fire, it's because they're afraid of us."

"All right, let's try to regroup here," said Tentesinas. "We can get inside the castle if we need to. Aiđoravos, Zolbareň, go find as many of ours as you can. Don't get into fights; just get the men to fall back here."

The men moved off, each in a different direction. "You might as well help them, Oluon," I said.

"Right," he said. "Ulōne be with you."

He started off, sword in hand, heading for the sounds of fighting. He had not gone far when there was a loud crack from the barracks; we all turned to look, and saw the last of the roof cave in, in a shower of sparks. I looked back at Oluon just in time to see the arrow penetrate his chest; it was silhouetted for a moment against the firelight, a thin, finned, deadly line, before he fell slowly, almost gracefully, to the ground.

32 · T̄OC ZX˧OCdZ̧O(Ū · *Bri Acūritārex*

When the Lady Alaldillê invited me to dinner, I supposed that she and her guests were interested in my stay among the Babblers. However, their questions were of a quite different nature:

"How does Lady Caumēliye fare in detention?"
"What caused her to do such a thing?"
"Is she suffering much?"
"She won't stay there for the whole deliberation, will she?"
"What will she do if Zeilisio is judged guilty?"

This was my first inkling of the effect of Caumēliye's sacrifice on the public of Eleisa. There was no doubt that she had caused a sensation, first among the women, and then among the men. Some thought her noble, others thought her foolish; but everyone was fascinated by her ordeal, and wanted to know as much as possible about it.

There was no immediate effect on the deliberation itself, of course— it was Zeilisio and not Caumēliye who was being judged, after all— but the commotion was nonetheless a setback for the party of the idiots. For their plans to succeed, the worthy of Eleisa should be discussing the crimes and outrages of Zeilisio, and not the sufferings of his wife. And from "This is a terrible thing for her, poor dear," it is no great step to "This is a terrible thing for them." And inevitably the image of the defiant and scornful atheist supported by his ambitious virago of a wife, which Inibē's party wished to inculcate, was softened and undermined by the picture of Caumēliye, in prisoner's cloth, her loyal hand on the shoulder of the accused. And many were led to wonder, no doubt, if the sort of villain pictured by the accusers could inspire such devotion in a woman.

Significantly, Ruitei, the daughter of Inibē, was among those invited to Alaldillê's dinner; and she was as curious and as sympathetic as any of the other women. I imagined that she may have returned to subject Inibē to a painful quarter of an hour.

During one day of the deliberation against Zeilisio, I was summoned to appear before the Council— in principle, to answer questions; in fact, largely to hear the speculations and fantasies of Inibē and Murgêde. I stood before the circle of Lords, not far from Zeilisio, and endured the assault.

"We have heard from Bardāu," Murgêde would say, "of the pagan practices in which the Cuzeian Resident, the emissary of this Council, indulged himself, at the orders of Zeilisio. No meat was prepared or eaten in that land, except it had been sacrificed to demonic powers, the same which have ever opposed Iáinos since the creation of the world. Did the Resident, Beretos of Zeilisio's house, abstain from these meals, still smoking with the corruption of devils? No, O Lords and Ladies of the Council; he ate willingly. Is it not so, O Beretos?"

"Of course not, O Murgêde."

"You deny that you ate of this meat?"

"I deny that I ate anything at the orders of Zeilisio, or did anything that any Cuzeian Resident among Babblers is not allowed to do, according to the opinion of the Knowers of Eleisa."

"But you do not deny that you ate meat in the land of Babblers?"

"No; but then your own man in Araunicoros, Ambrisio—"

"A simple yes or no will be enough, Beretos. Did you eat meat in the land of Babblers?"

"Yes, as with—"

"It is as I said, Lords and Ladies," said Murgêde, triumphantly.

It was a wearisome day.

Another exchange, which perhaps went somewhat less as Murgêde would have wished, was as follows.

"The duplicity and mendaciousness of Lord Zeilisio knows no bounds," Murgêde began. "In order to tempt the alertness of men's minds away from the purity Iáinos requires of us, he has ever sought to conjure up various foreign phantasms and dangers. It was the nefarious achievement of this Zeilisio to cause a military mission to be made almost to the ends of Almea, three hundred lests distant. Even that might be excused, if the Resident had exerted himself to bring to the primitive peoples of those climes the light of Iáinos; but instead he engaged himself to offer military drills, and to teach the Dance of Swords to savages. But

Lords and Ladies of the Council, you have heard from the lips of Bardāu how empty are the threats with which Zeilisio has so often attempted to frighten and distract this Council. No country could be more quiet, more at peace; their very castles are piles of decaying stone, and not even a single Munkhâshi footstep, much less the tread of invading demons, is heard there. Can you deny it, Beretos?"

"You are lying or misinformed, O Murgêde," I said.

There were some whispers at my audacity. Murgêde approached me with a cold smile. "Do you still hold to these stories of your master? This man certainly has a hold on his retainers. And yet Bardāu encountered not a single Munkhâshi among the Babblers; do you deny it?"

"Of course I do," I said. "He might have had the eyes of a dead man, for all he saw looking around him. Your man Bardāu was as close to a Munkhâshi, in the very castle of Berak, as I am to you."

"But how is this? How could he see a Munkhâshi and not know it?"

"What do you expect, when you send a man to the Gaumê who cannot even speak the language of its people? If you had been present to hear the account I gave to the Council on my return, you would have learned that Munkhâsh too had a Resident at the court of Berak."

"A Munkhâshi Resident? I am sure I would have heard of such a thing from Bardāu," said Murgêde, a little uncertainly.

"Where is Bardāu? Let us ask him," I said, turning around to look for the man.

I spotted him on the spectators' benches, and stood forward to wave to him. "Bardāu! O Bardāu! Come and let us settle the truth of this."

"It is the place of Beretos to answer questions, not to call witnesses," complained Murgêde.

"We are here to learn the truth, not to stand on procedure," said Narrisio, quietly. "Let Bardāu approach the Council."

Murgêde fumed, but Bardāu came up and stood facing the Council. He avoided my gaze.

"Now, Bardāu, will you affirm once again before the Council, that you met no Munkhâshi in the Babbler castle?"

"Willingly, O Murgêde—" he began; but I interrupted:

"Think well, O Bardāu! Do not lie in the presence of Eīledan. Can you truly say that you can identify every man you met among the Babblers, when you spoke not a word of their language?"

"I— well, of course I can't say that. But I would have heard—"

"How would you have heard, since you don't speak the language?"

"Well, that is so," he conceded. "Still, such a thing as a Munkhâshi Resident— I don't know how I could miss something like that."

"Do you remember the baron, Bardāu?"

"Of course."

"Could you describe him?"

"Hmm, let's see. A big man, fairly old, bald—"

"Not at all. He has all his hair, except for a spot on the top of his head."

"Did he? Perhaps he did. Always drinking. A— a beard, if I'm not—"

"That's right. And who was with him, when you met him?"

"Oh, I don't know. Some other men."

"This is the man who could not have missed anything there was to see in Berak's house," I remarked. "There was a man sitting next to Berak. Do you remember him? Can you describe him?"

"Eīledan, that was two years ago. I think I remember someone. Yes, he was definitely talking to someone. Another big man, right?"

"Yes. Go on."

"Ulōne take me, I don't remember any more. Black hair."

"Gray."

"Oh, that's right. Yes, I can picture him. He was drinking too."

"Congratulations, Bardāu. You've described the Munkhâshi Resident to the court of Berak."

There were more murmurs, of surprise or consternation. "I don't see how that can be—" said Murgêde. "A Munkhâshi, after all..."

"What do you expect a Munkhâshi to look like?" I shot back. "Do you think he has horns, or claws?"

"Certainly not," he snapped, recovering himself. "But leaving that aside— even if there were this one Munkhâshi in this Babbler castle— you cannot deny that there was no military presence, no threat which would justify the rhetoric of Zeilisio before the Council."

"Once more, you are lying or misinformed," I said.

"You are very insolent," said Murgêde.

"Your spies are not very diligent, O Murgêde," I informed him. "Bardāu was in Berak's keep for two days; what do you expect him to see? He was not there when the Munkhâshi came across the mountains to make war upon Berak's castle. No, O Lords and Ladies, the footsteps of Munkhâshi men at arms have been heard in Berak's lands; and it is likely that they can be heard there today."

There was more consternation among the Council and the spectators. I had spoken of these things before, but only Zeilisio's allies and a few other interested Lords had bothered to hear my report; and Bardāu, as we have seen, was no very astute observer. It was the first time, therefore, that Inibē's party, as well as many others, had heard about soldiers of Munkhâsh setting foot in Cēradānar.

I had to explain these things for some time, as one member of the Council after another asked questions; and it was some time before Murgêde was able to regain control of the interrogation, and proceed again to his attack.

"Well done, Beretos," Zeilisio whispered to me. "That's spilled some salt in their custard."

33 · ιῡ⊓ÇZb · *Exbuîas*

"Munkhâshi," Tentesinas commented, as we ran over to the fallen Oluon. He was right: the Caðinorians relied on swords, not bows, for their raids.

Oluon was not dead, but he was gravely wounded, the arrow stuck deep in his right breast. He was breathing with obvious difficulty, and though his mouth worked when he saw us, he could say nothing.

"Don't try," I told him. "Rest, you can't do anything."

He shook his head, agitated; I laid my hand on his brow. "By Iáinos, we will avenge you," I said.

"Leave another to look after him," Tentesinas told me, sharply. "I have need of you, if we're not all to end up like him."

It was cruel, but there was a terrible necessity to his words. I waved over one of our men, and sent him for wine. But before rejoining Tentesinas I removed the arrow. It was not easy, and when Oluon cried out I thought I had killed him. But I thought it would only do him more harm while it was still inside him, and I did not trust the Caðinorians to remove it with any skill.

A battle considered at leisure, discussed over maps, is a problem to be solved; in the event it is a calamity to be suffered, and mitigated if possible by intuitive leaps.

Picture our situation: under assault, in dead of night, by an unknown enemy, who has already come into the walls of our stronghold and set one or more buildings afire; the strength and numbers of our own men hardly known; one of our best warriors already fallen; the light from the fires dim and erratic; the air rent and the mind stupefied by shouts, screams, footsteps, clatter of swords, hooves of horses. In the next moment the battle, or your own life, may be lost: quick, quick, what are your orders?

Pages and pages are written on the great battles of Cuzei— from Dunōmeyū and Cantiego and Rêstirōpas onward— on the decisions of generals, on the tactics of commanders— pages which must make a general laugh, if he comes to remember them in the midst of a battle. If I were writing such an account I would say something like this: Cognizant that the enemy had penetrated into the confines of the castle grounds, and had occupied positions enveloping our allies' dormitive emplacements, and pursuant to a strategy of destruction of the enemy along with opportunistic harassment of the escapees, the commanders of our forces settled on a tactic of division, with as its goal the separation of the better-trained and equipped Munkhâshi forces from their Cadinorian allies, and the concentration of friendly forces upon the latter.

In fact, as I caught up with Tentesinas, he said, "I've got a mind to rush at them, by Mieranac. They're on us like dogs on a rat and I'm sick of it."

"Charge them? Where?"

"Right in their bellies. Toward the barracks."

"They're Munkhâshi, you can't fight like that, they'll kill us all. Go where they don't expect it. Flank them; drive toward the gate. There's bound to be more on the other side."

"Fine. At least it's doing something."

By this time we had gathered together perhaps a dozen of our men. Tentesinas and I led them toward the main gate, keeping the Munkhâshi to our right. As I reflect back on it I remain convinced of the foolishness of Tentesinas's idea— there must have been twenty Munkhâshi or more between the barracks and the inner tower, and in better shape to fight than we were. However, my own course now seems hardly less rash. For all I knew, a force of Munkhâshi twice the size of the first lay waiting at the gate.

In fact only a few men were at the gate. There was some fighting to its left, in the big storehouse— some Munkhâshi were trying to set it afire, as we learned later. To our right, between the barracks and the outer wall of the keep, was a motley number of Babblers, here and there tangling with those of our men who had escaped the burning barracks.

With fearsome yells— the war-cries of the mountain men I had once been warned against— our men rushed to the attack. The Babblers were discomfited. Setting buildings on fire in dead of night is not the Babbler way of battle, but at least it was relatively safe work, and offered some sport. Being themselves victims of surprise was more unwelcome; and with our numbers magnified by night and noise and fear, it must have been almost intolerable. The first Babblers we came across were all lucklessly cut down, and many of the rest ran from us.

As it happened a troop of six or eight of our men, led by Dolbas, had earlier escaped from the barracks, and made a stand not far from the stables; so that fleeing from us, the raiders ran straight into the swords of Dolbas's men. They turned to engage us, then, and there was another round of fights, which once again we had the best of. I saw Tentesinas kill two men, one right after the other, and wheel himself around to face a third. But these successive defeats were too much for the raiders; they scurried to escape. They made for the gate, and we hurried them on with threats and laughter.

Our victory did not come without price: one of our men, Zolbareň, had been run through the heart with a sword; and Dolbas too, the stout, bold, slow soldier I had once engaged in a duel, lay dying in the mud. Tentesinas bent over him as I had bent over Oluon, hearing his last words, and crying like a baby.

By now most of those who had made it out of the barracks had found us, so that we were now two dozen or so— enough, we judged, to meet the Munkhâshi.

"Maybe they've moved," Tentesinas suggested. "Where do you suppose they are?"

"Setting fire to the temple, maybe," I said.

"Or the castle," said Aiđoravos.

"Mieranac!" said Tentesinas. "They could be murdering the baron in his sleep, while we stand here talking."

"From here there's only two ways we can go anyway," I pointed out. "Around the stables, or back toward the gate. Maybe we should head that way, and make sure the Cadinorians are gone."

"But the Munkhâshi saw us go that way, and they may expect us to come back from there. Let's go the other way."

"All right, let's go."

We circled round the stables, and paused before coming to the field that separates the barracks from the tower, while the building still hid us from the view. We saw some soldiers milling about, looking at the last dying flames from the barracks. Most of the Munkhâshi still seemed to be here. We had the men spread out into a line, and advance quietly, in hopes of surprising them.

The first man we came upon was Ganacom.

We saw him when we were almost upon him, for he was dressed in black. He turned and saw us, and gaped in surprise, an expression replaced quickly with one of assumed excitement.

"Tentesinas, Beretos, how good it is to see you," he exclaimed. "Do you see what these raiders have done? Quick, save us!"

"You're a lying dog," said Tentesinas, advancing on him with sword drawn. "Let's see what you're made of, you lizard, by Mieranac! To your sword!"

Ganacom did raise his sword, but backed away slowly. "It's a mistake," he said. He glanced behind him at the Munkhâshi, seemed to hesitate, looked again at Tentesinas, opened his mouth to shout: "*Tiedectescrion!* I pledge my *honor!*"

He still backed away, hoping no doubt for the success of this one last deception, trusting that the Munkhâshi behind him would come to his rescue; but Tentesinas, waiting no longer, leapt toward him, his sword falling like fate. Ganacom barely managed to parry; and then they were both fighting furiously, and the night was loud with the clank of iron on iron— Ganacom's own sword, and the sword Tentesinas had brought back from Munkhâsh as a trophy.

The Munkhâshi did not move, nor did our own men; all watched this single combat, hardly breathing. Ganacom was no great swordsman, but for some minutes he held his own, parrying Tentesinas's strokes and jabbing when he could at his opponent's head or stomach. Tentesinas attacked in fury, aiming stroke after stroke at his hated enemy. If he survives, I told myself, I have to teach him to guard himself better, and vary his strokes.

Ganacom was forced back; Tentesinas followed. They almost stumbled against the first of the Munkhâshi troops, and this was surely Ganacom's last hope and chance; but I advanced along with them, sword ready, and was ready to fall upon the nearest Munkhâshi if he moved toward them. But he did not; he moved out of their way, letting the combat take its course. Ganacom at one point glanced angrily at him and spoke some words in his own language— a curse, judging from the tone and the man's disdainful reaction.

Tentesinas reached his man with a cut to the face, and this seemed to stir Ganacom to a new level of activity; he swung wildly at the Caðinorian, wearing an expression of animal desperation. He managed to force Tentesinas to step back, and even wounded him, reaching his side with a stroke the commander could not entirely deflect. But he paused after this slight victory, indulging the fatal temptation it is the entire purpose of the Dance of Swords to overmaster, and Tentesinas reached under his sword and cut him grievously in the stomach. Ganacom parried the next stroke, weakly, but not the one after that: Tentesinas's sword cleaved his shoulder, almost severing his arm.

He collapsed, not quite dead; but Tentesinas disdained to administer the final blow. "This man's soul I don't want," he said. "Take him and throw him in the barracks. Add some wood if you need to. Let him die in his own fire."

Now we faced the Munkhâshi; but these did not stay to fight us. Cautiously and slowly, but without panic, they abandoned the field and headed toward the gate. A few of them made moves toward their own dead, to collect them or their gear; but we hastened them on, and did not let them stop. They sidled warily through the gate; one of them, presumably their leader, stopped there a moment, looking back at us, at the smoldering ruins of the barracks, at the high Babbler tower. But he had no message for us; he turned and rejoined his men, and the troop of them clambered down to the road and thence up into the mountains, back to the Taucrēte Pass, back to Munkhâsh.

34 • ÇOZNZÇIXZ • *Dralādeca*

We spent some time finding and numbering the dead. They came to fifteen, out of the baron's forty-one men— an unusual and demoralizing figure for a Babbler war. The survivors cried and consoled each other with plans for revenge. Their relatives in the castle and the village were sent for, and soon the night air was filled with their wailings, and the sound of the preparations for their funeral pyres.

Six Munkhâshi and more than a dozen of the Babbler raiders also lay dead in the mud. Berak's men recognized a few of the Babbler faces. "Worthless men and renegades," said Aiðoravos. Most likely the band belonged to no baron, but had come together to seek their fortunes in plunder, before accepting Ganacom's invitation to raid Berak, in concert with the Munkhâshi. Some of the rewards for their collusion were visible on their bodies: new Munkhâshi shoes, better than any made in the Gaumê, metal ornaments, and skins of sweet wine, a Munkhâshi delicacy.

It was no doubt Ganacom himself who opened the door to the raiders; the two guards who were posted at the main gate would have readily opened it at the command of the baron's close confidant. The invaders tied up both guards, although one managed to escape later.

It would have been the Munkhâshi who started the fire. The Babbler raiders helped cut down the escapees; but their chief role was as the dragons in the story Ganacom was spinning for Berak. If only you had listened, he would have said, and accepted the Munkhâshi honor guard which I urged upon you. Perhaps your commander and the Cuzeians would be alive today, instead of perishing so tragically in the fire. Would he not even now reconsider?...

Berak had stayed in the tower during the raid, and was now asleep. I suspect Ganacom had made him drink even more than usual. But finally the sound of activity in the tower awakened him— hurried searches for funeral wrappings and kindling, the preparation of meals, the sobbing of kin. He came down to see what was wrong, and listened in shock to the events of the night, and looked over the field of battle in the twilight of dawn.

"You're sure they were Munkhâshi?" he asked, more than once.

"Come see for yourself," said Tentesinas, and led him to the dead Munkhâshi.

Berak looked them over. "They could be Moňnaru," he said. "Or some people we don't know. Where's Ganacom? He will tell us."

"Ganacom is dead."

The baron's eyes widened; his mouth worked in horror. "They killed Ganacom?"

"*I* killed Ganacom."

The baron stared at the commander. "No. It can't be. You, Tentesinas?"

Following Tentesinas's orders, the body of Ganacom had been carried into the barracks, dropped on a smoldering bed, and covered with burning straw. He was not a pleasant sight. Most of his clothing was burned away, except for his belt and shoes, and the thicker cloth at the ends of his sleeves; his skin was charred or red, and completely burnt away in spots; his expression was monstrous.

Berak stared at him for a long time, silently. Then he turned to Tentesinas and said, "Say how it happened."

"We found him with the raiders," said Tentesinas. "He spoke to them in their own language. It was his own scheme, obviously, the cursed of gods. He intended to burn us as we slept. When we came upon him, he tried to get his soldiers to attack us, so I fought him and killed him."

Berak rushed at him with fury in his face, and began to hit him in the chest. "You traitor! Murderer! You're lying!"

He reached for his neck to choke him; but Tentesinas took hold of his hands and held them away from him, till the baron, red as a child in a tantrum, relented.

Abruptly Berak stalked out of the barracks; we followed.

"You don't understand," he muttered, walking back and forth, agitated and confused. "He woke me up... Ganacom. Carrying my boy, Cruvec... placed him in my arms, told me to keep him safe. Then went off to fight the raiders."

"A ruse," I said, without thinking; the commander nodded. It was obvious, but the notion only reignited Berak's rage.

"You liars! You both hated him, and now where is he to give his own words to gainsay you?"

"Ask any of your men," I said. "Ask those who accompanied us across the Pass if these men they fought were not Munkhâshi."

"It's you who killed him!" he shouted, turning on me. "This is all your doing, Cuzeian. Before you came here there were no raids and no fifteen dead men and no backtalk from my own commander. You will leave at once, you and your servant." He shook his fist at me. "Let this be the last I see of you."

He started to walk away. "Baron, you're not thinking clearly," said Tentesinas, paternally; but Berak ignored him.

Tentesinas did not follow; he came back to me and put his arm around my shoulders. "The *fantit* have taken his reason away, because of his great pain," he said. "But it will come back, and he will forget his evil words. I will speak to him. Now come, we have much to do."

For the third or fourth time I went to see how Oluon was doing. He lay in a servant's bed on the first floor of the keep; one of the kitchen maids was watching over him. He was not well. He grimaced with every breath, due to the pain of the wound in his chest; he alternated between fever and chills, except when he became weak and cold. At those times we thought him near death.

There was not much that could be done for him, except to try to keep him warm, and give him wine to drink, when he could take it.

When he saw me come in again, he looked at me mournfully, and managed to speak:

"I'm sorry, Beretos..."

The effort made him cough, and we rushed to him to hold him. Each cough was obviously a torment to him.

"Please don't try to talk," I said. "My brave Oluon, it is I who bear guilt before Iáinos; I should have foreseen... no! Don't talk, you'll hurt yourself!"

"Speak of other things," suggested the servant girl. I looked at her; I think Oluon had known her very well at one time. I nodded.

"Oluon, my brother, try to rest, so you'll get better. You will get well, by Ulōne."

"No," he whispered.

"Hush," I said. "And don't be a fool."

"Pierced... heart... She was right."

"What? ... No, don't say it again, let me think."

Oluon was pointing, jabbing his finger at the wall. What was he talking about? The wall? What was on that wall... no, beyond the wall. The town? The west?

"Ulōne!" I said. "The godspeaker on the Elimaēta. By Eīledan, Oluon, don't take that seriously."

But I spoke more firmly than I felt, and I knew that Oluon wholly despaired. A god had predicted that his heart would be pierced, and he believed that his time had come.

The day was long with funerals, and black with the smoke of the fires which brought the Babbler dead to meet their gods.

The barracks were unlivable; the soldiers had to be moved into the castle; the servants moved into storehouses, or into tents in the castle grounds. It seemed best not to move Oluon, and I stayed at his side, and took what sleep I could.

The *fantit* did not restore Berak's reason: he continued to insist that we leave the castle. Tentesinas thought that he might change his mind tomorrow. He did not; instead he berated the commander because we had not departed.

"They can't move yet; Oluon is gravely wounded," Tentesinas told the baron. "Walking or even being carried on a horse may mean his death."

"So much the better," said Berak.

Tentesinas spat on the floor. "I've served you since I was a boy, and my father served your father, and by Mieranac, never in fifty years have you been such a fool."

"Shut your mouth. I'll hear none of your disloyalties."

"I am a man and not a slave, and will name foolishness when I see it," said Tentesinas.

But none of Tentesinas's words, whether angry reprimands or warm entreaties, could move the baron. Tentesinas advised us to stay in the village for some days; so we moved to the house of the old couple with whom we had stayed when we first came to Berak's lands.

210 · IN THE LAND OF BABBLERS

We stayed there two weeks, during which Oluon's condition improved somewhat; he came to be able to sit up, and then stand, and he could talk again without coughing. But he had received some sickness with the wound— it may be that the Munkhâshi arrows are poisoned— and often had chills, and even hallucinations, in which enemies pursued him, and godspeakers prophesied against him, and Ganacom's laughter echoed without end.

Then Tentesinas came to us, and told us that Berak had not recovered his mind, and indeed spoke of nothing but revenge against us. Tentesinas had told him that we were gone, but he did not believe him, and was speaking of sending his soldiers throughout his lands, to find us and have us killed.

"The *fantit* have taken him," he said, pointing at the earth, as the Caðinorians do when talking about turns of fate. "He cries every day about Ganacom; but today he told me he had spoken to Ganacom, and that he'd be eating dinner with him tonight... And Sintilna says that he's convinced she knows where you are, that she talks to you through the window in Cuêzi, and he threatens to beat her if she doesn't tell."

"I see how it is," I said, sadly. "It's best that we go from here."

"It may be the best for you, but I think things will never be right here any more," lamented Tentesinas. "Little brother, my heart is broken for you. I wish it were you and not Berak whom I served."

I never learned what to do when big, burly Caðinorians cried; it is not how soldiers behave in Cuzei.

35 · X̄CCdꞮOA · *Gintūro*

Gintūro was fetched before the Council, and depicted as the great victim of Zeilisio's machinations. He sat on a chair near the Council's table, well-dressed, plump and pleasant-looking; as Inibē thundered forth his accusations he listened with a cheerful expression, as if he expected soon to be served dinner. When he was asked questions he answered loyally and happily, often making little jokes— taunts against Zeilisio and his allies— careless abuse, without wit, such as is amusing only to partisans.

Zeilisio once told me that it was not the leaders of the idiots but men like Gintūro that he feared— men not only without vision, but unconscious of their lack, and therefore without hope of change.

It was granted to Zeilisio to speak with Gintūro.

He began by looking over the Knower, in silence— the balding head, the cheerful face, the rich red robes. "You are well dressed today, O Gintūro," was his comment.

"Not nearly as well as you; your outfit becomes you," said Gintūro, with a smirk.

Zeilisio looked down at the cloth he wore round his waist; and seeing no key there to Gintūro's words, continued: "As a Knower, you must be familiar with the Praise of Poverty, I would think?"

"Certainly. The readings for the months of deep winter come from its wisdom, O Zeilisio."

"Perhaps you can quote from it for us?"

"Quote from it? Certainly, certainly, although I can't imagine why it would interest you." He laughed. "I will recite from the seventh canto, which is said on the longest day of the year."

He stood, to show his respect for the words, and chanted, richly and well, in the way of Knowers.

To be rich in Iáinos
Empty your hands.
Wealth casts sleep into the eyes,
so that Iáinos cannot be seen.

*A rich man has a rich man for a friend,
but a poor man sups with Eīledan.*

*If you wish to know Iáinos
you begin in ignorance.
The one who shouts out answers
also shouts down Ulōne.
As he has no questions, he will hear no answers.
Listen to the sage
who knows he knows nothing.*

"Very good," said Zeilisio. "*Wealth casts sleep into the eyes.* Beautiful words, aren't they? Do you think they're true?"

"Every word of Iáinos is true, for *us* at least."

"It's a pleasure to talk to a pious man," remarked Zeilisio. "Still, they are difficult words, don't you think, especially for a rich man such as yourself?"

"Ah, you're paradoxical," said Gintūro, with a laugh. "Paradoxical!"

"Actually, the words of the book are as clear as could be; it's the behavior of Knowers that creates paradoxes. Don't you agree, Gintūro? For instance, in the fourth canto, we read that riches buy no favor with Iáinos— *With the mountains as crowns, Iáinos scorns the glories of lords, and sends his words to the wandering sage.* That seems clear enough, doesn't it? How can a Knower be a rich man?"

"Were you addressing me?"

"I believe I was, now that I think of it," said Zeilisio. "How can a Knower be a rich man?"

"It's extremely annoying," remarked Gintūro. "Everyone reads those passages and japes at Knowers because of them. What they don't realize is that they're metaphorical."

"Metaphorical?"

"That's right."

"Hmm. Yet I believe Araunixue warned us against this very interpretation. *The clear sense of the holy books is always to be preferred to the subtle and the difficult. Distrust every word which removes the mystery of Iáinos; and every word which shrouds the simplicity of right and wrong.*"

"Just so. Just so. However, the prophet Araunixue was herself being metaphorical."

"Do you think so? Perhaps you could tell us what is the metaphorical meaning behind the Praise of Poverty; or behind the Book of the Ram, which speaks so eloquently of the humble and simple life— the life Araunixue herself lived, as we know."

"Certainly, I am always glad to instruct— even *you*, Zeilisio. The riches in the Praises are the riches of the spirit, of course."

Zeilisio waited a moment, perhaps expecting a fuller explanation, and then commented, mildly, "But is not the book the Praises of *poverty*, not riches? Are the riches of the spirit to be scorned, then?"

"Only by such as you," laughed Gintūro.

"Then your explanation makes no sense, doesn't it?"

"Excuse me?"

"You say the book's riches are those of the spirit, and that these are not to be scorned. But the book is praising poverty, not riches. *Wealth casts sleep into the eyes*, remember?"

"Yes, but that's— well, it's metaphorical."

Gintūro spoke a bit hesitantly now, as if suspecting that there were better answers he could make, but not entirely sure where they could be found.

"You're familiar with the four books of Numisidiē, of course," continued Zeilisio.

"Certainly," said Gintūro, happily.

"Oh, forgive me," said Zeilisio, raising his hands as if in perplexity. "The three books of Numisidiē, that is; she only wrote that many. You are familiar with her words describing the Knowers she had the pleasure to encounter?"

"I can't say that I have it readily in memory," admitted Gintūro.

"But you'd say that it perfectly captures the essence of the Knowers of Eleisa?"

Gintūro hesitated; then said, dismissingly, "As she was a very wise woman, a glory of the holy books, it is necessarily full of her wisdom."

"You would urge us to give it our full trust, then."

"Yes, certainly."

"That is my recommendation as well," noted Zeilisio. "I will recite some of it, simply so that we may savor the pleasure of hearing that wisdom. *Never was a flock of pigeons so self-important, so absurd, and so contentious as the pack of Knowers in this city of Eleisa. There would be reason to praise Iáinos greatly if the plague took them, both for the relief from their molestations, and for the restoration of dignity to the name of Iáinos.*"

At the recitation of this familiar passage almost the entire chamber burst into laughter.

Much later I mentioned to Zeilisio that his interrogation of Gintūro had greatly surprised many, and that he had acquired the reputation of a scholar of divinity, who must pore for hours every day over the holy books. He laughed.

"Every day! I think I read them once every five years; but I have a good memory. And I have read some of the commentaries, which not many of that crowd has done; and I've read the philosophers, including all the ones they disapprove of. It's not so hard to impress an audience of Lords as a scholar. Real Knowers would have had me in a minute."

Not content with the deliberation against Zeilisio, the idiots had also launched a new campaign: Murgīllede's awakening movement was proposing the banning of that impious institution, the house of plays.

There is generally an uproar once a year or so about some particularly scurrilous satire which is playing in Eleisa, and there are demands that the play be banned by the King's Reader. Those who are offended by satire, not to mention those who are its targets, never seem to learn that threatening a ban is the surest way to ensure that all Eleisa will rush to see the play. There are sometimes calls to ban plays "without serious or pious content", but of course most plays are a mixture of seriousness, poetry, and comedy, so that this stricture would be virtually without effect.

There was at this very time a play satirizing the awakening movement itself— a very successful work called the Heroes of Virtue, which portrayed a trio of Knowers who come to a House and impose on it a strict regimen of holiness, while they themselves indulge every sin. The three were obviously images of Inibē, Murgêde, and Murgīllede, though of course no one had ever seen any of these three come drunk into a Glade or attempt to seduce a Lord's wife, as was represented in the play. However, Murgīllede and his allies never made mention of this play, and denied that it was the cause of their campaign.

It was their complaint that it was not any individual play, but the theater in general, which was a corruption and a snare for the people of Eīledan. Their charges were, first, that virtually every play contained statements of dubious piety, or even outright immorality, as well as attacks on the dignity of respectable men; second, that the theater was a frivolity which took men and women away from the practice of domestic virtue and public worship, which should be their sole occupations; third, that actors were forced to assume the characters of evil and immoral persons, which was bound to corrupt their spirit; fourth, that plays related falsehoods and inventions, which were forbidden by Iáinos' laws; and finally, that Eleisa in the days of our forefathers had no such corrupting entertainments.

If Lord Zeilisio had not been in detention, he would surely have withered this campaign at its root with mockery; for only Zeilisio would have the courage and honesty to defend the plays as diversions, gladly permitted by Iáinos, who does not despise the laughter of men. He would also have pressed the matter of Gintūro; were the idiots not assailing the corruption of the stage in order to distract men's minds from the greater immorality and impiety of their own Knowers? Were they not, after all, very like the Heroes of Virtue, with their double faces?

But without Zeilisio, those who opposed Murgīllede felt compelled to answer his complaints on their own terms— pointing out how the plays glorified Iáinos, how they taught history, the epics, and the lives of heroes and saints; while even the wholly invented stories imparted worthy lessons and fortified virtue. These arguments are no doubt true; but they could easily play into the hands of the awakeners. Already misguided mediators were offering counter-proposals, such as that the King's Reader, or a council of Lords and Knowers, should strike out offensive passages, leaving that which was edifying; or that villains and immoral persons should not be represented on the stage, but their actions described only.

Murgīllede resisted these ideas, insisting that only a total prohibition could be satisfying to Iáinos (whose opinions he now seemed to interpret without even the need of reflection). I feared, however, that the awakeners had taken such an extreme position only to renounce it and accept this compromise; that control rather than abolition of the theater was their true goal.

The deliberation was drawing to a close; the members of the Council must now debate among themselves, and come to a decision on the charges against Zeilisio; and if he were found guilty, to decide on his penalty: whether he should lose his Lordship, whether he should be put to death.

Even with a reward on his head, Oluon was unable to walk for more than a few minutes at a time, and that would leave him exhausted. Tentesinas therefore gave us a donkey from the keep for him to ride on. It would be missed at the keep— Berak is not so rich that he does not know every animal within his walls— but Tentesinas said that he would tell Berak that it had been killed by a stray arrow during the battle.

He helped me lift Oluon to the donkey's back, and gave us food for our journey, which we also loaded onto the animal. I also took a pack, and Tentesinas joked with Oluon, calling him a lazy dog for not carrying one himself.

He insisted on walking with us to the edge of Berak's lands.

"You don't have to," I said. "I have my sword; and it's hard to believe any of the men would kill me, when I've been training them for three years."

"With some beer in their bellies, there's a few of them who'd forget all that for the reward Berak's promising. And I couldn't live with myself if you were struck down where I could have protected you. So don't argue."

We left Cihimia and walked slowly, at the pace of the donkey, along the valley of the Little Demaresc. It was early autumn, and here in the mountains the trees were beginning to change color, and the air was cool. The riding seemed to be painful for Oluon, though he said nothing, and suppressed his groans. His only hope was to get safely to the Elimaēta, which was several days away at this pace; from there we could hire a boat to take us to Araunicoros, where we hoped he might regain his health.

After a little more than an hour we came to the place where the Little Demaresc meets the Greater, which is the western boundary of Berak's lands. Stones have been dropped here to make a ford. In the spring the river is nonetheless uncrossable except by swimming; but now in the fall it ran low enough that we could make our way across easily enough.

Wet and cold, we made our farewells to Tentesinas. At the last minute, impulsively, he suggested that we exchange swords.

"We're not dead yet," I pointed out.

"It's for brotherhood, you fool," he said. "It's an honor among us. But if you don't want it..."

"No, no, I appreciate it very much," I said.

Almost anywhere in the Babbler lands, a Cuzeian who accepts a Caðinorian sword for his own receives the worst of the deal. This was the case here; my steel sword was stronger and better balanced than his; but at least his sword, of polished iron, was better than that of most Babblers; he had taken it from one of the Munkhâshi we had defeated. But I was glad for Tentesinas to have my sword, and to have his own as a remembrance of him.

We embraced, and he embraced Oluon on his donkey, and headed back across the Greater Demaresc to the baron's castle, while we began climbing up the side of the valley (for the Demaresc would not take us on our way; it drains into the Taucrēs).

At the top I looked back to see Berak's lands for the last time. The castle and Cihimia were too far away to see; but there were fields and hills that I knew, and behind them Kravcaene-Limura and the teeth of the Gaumê. On one hill there still waved one of the flags Oluon and I had planted when we surveyed the barony to make Berak's map. Behind were the mountains of the Gaumê. I thought I saw the gap that marked the Taucrēte Pass, now an open door to the land of Munkhâsh.

We continued on.

By the end of the first day, Oluon was feverish. His body and head were hot, though sometimes he shook and shivered. I had to walk next to him, with my arm on his shoulder, or he would have fallen off the donkey. We stopped in a small village, where we were gladly given food and beds. We were also offered the services of the thin, bent old crone who was the local god-speaker. I contemplated polite ways to refuse the sacrifices or rituals she might recommend; but she only inspected Oluon briefly, shook her head compassionately, and told me to be ready for the departure of his *fantos*. She gave him some odorous herbal tea, which she said would ease his pains.

He felt better after resting, and we talked. I told Oluon that I would leave him here, and search for help further on. He would hear none of it, and I confess that I had no heart to argue with him. It was unlikely I could find any help for him closer than

Araunicoros— not even a wagon to ease his journey, since we were still in the mountains, where a wagon was as useless as a boat. It would perhaps have been wisest to stay with him in the village, but Oluon insisted on traveling. He said that traveling might kill him, but at least he would be moving toward home; staying in the mountains he would surely die.

With a heavy heart, then, I loaded him on the donkey the next morning, and we trudged on.

There was no village nearby when dusk came, and I did not think Oluon could take more travel that day; so we stopped to camp on the hillside above the road. There was a stream nearby, so that we had fresh water to drink, instead of beer. I made a fire and cooked some bacon and onions which Tentesinas had given us; and there were apple trees nearby with tart, ripe apples. Oluon ate what he could, and then lay back on the ground, breathing heavily.

"Beretos, I want you to tell my parents something," he said.

"You can tell them yourself," I insisted, fearfully.

"Tell them I'm sorry," he continued. "I wanted to care for them in their old age, and I wanted to marry and have grandchildren to show them. I don't understand it. I was always with girls, but I never ended up married. It was the one thing they wanted... I always thought I'd have more time."

I wanted to contradict him, but knew that it would reassure neither of us. "I'll tell them," I said.

"Drink some wine for me with Lāuros and Eyagas. They were my best friends— besides you, I mean, Beretos. Will you do that?"

"Of course, Oluon," I said.

There was a silence, and then he said, reflecting, "What bothers me is how stupid it was. We escape from a burning building, and I get shot by an arrow. I didn't even get to poke a sword at them— me, the Cuzeian warrior. Stupid, stupid. But at least I rid Almea of some of them, back when we were in Munkhâsh."

There was a longer silence. I tried to think what to say to Oluon, and could think of nothing that seemed worthy. Foolish scruple; if it were my last night on Almea I would rather hear banalities from my friends than silence.

"Are there any more apples?" asked Oluon.

"No," I said looking around. "I mean, not here. I can get you some more."

"That's all right. Actually I don't like apples that much, although these are pretty good. I'd rather have an orange."

"You and Bardāu," I said.

He laughed, painfully. "Yes, I'd like an orange or two right now! And a fish dinner— a *xuzāu* right from the river."

"Oranges don't go very well with *xuzāu*," I said.

Oluon laughed heartily; indeed, it seemed he couldn't stop laughing. "Oranges, fish, and ices," he said, and began laughing again.

"You're going to hurt yourself," I said, worried.

"I feel fine," said Oluon. "I needed a good laugh... Listen, the woods are laughing with me."

I listened a moment. There was something that sounded like wind, or running water, I thought. "It's the brook," I said. At this Oluon burst into even more hilarity. I laughed myself, simply because of his own merriment, and felt the same thing Oluon had felt: there was someone else with us in the woods, laughing along with us, or at us.

"What is it?" I asked, thinking of Caðinorians and Munkhâshi. "Who's there?"

The laughter burst out again— not from Oluon this time, but from some other voice. It was laughter and it was music, high and low, merry and grave, an infinite distance away and right beside us. It was not a human sound.

"In Ulōne's name, what is it?" I whispered, more to myself than to the chattering twilight.

"It's taken you long enough to remember Ulōne," said the musical voice, and laughed again.

"It's the voice of Lago," said Oluon, with joy and fear in his voice.

I looked around, but saw no one. "Come join us, O Lago," I said.

The iliu laughed. "Never offer invitations to iliū, my friends. We do not come when you call! But when we last met in this place, you were singing, and tonight you sing no songs. Why is that?"

"We have no heart for singing, Lago," I replied. "Oluon is gravely ill."

"There are songs for that as well," said Lago. "But perhaps we will not need them. Come, my starfish, we have need of you. See, my friends, I am not alone tonight."

And now I saw him, and indeed he was not alone. There was another iliu standing by him. Like a doe in a forest glade, it seemed poised for flight; but now they both came forward.

"Beretos and Oluon of Cuzei, I present to you my bride," said Lago.

I rose to my feet, almost knocking my dinner plate into the fire; Oluon also sat up straight, with difficulty. Lago's bride came into the firelight, and we looked upon her with awe. It was not possible to think of anything else. She was darker than her mate; in the last light of day, a deep blue, the color of the sea. She was almost as large as Lago— which meant that she was bigger than me, bigger even than Oluon; as strong and wild and free as a lion. She was naked to the waist; and her breasts, small but as perfectly formed as a statue's, were crowned in purple. Around her waist she wore some sort of leather skirt; her feet were bare, and were the least human part of her; their soles were thick and ribbed, and her toes had no nails. Her eyes were large and golden, and full of curiosity and power; her hair was short and stiff, and rusty red in color.

She spoke, in a high voice, like a flute; we could not understand a word she said, although it seemed not to be the iliu language. Lago laughed, and spoke to her for a few minutes.

"She has not learned Cuêzi," he told us. "But do not think that she knows nothing of humans; she spoke to you in a language called Qaraumcán, which belongs to another nation which has listened to the iliū, and she knows how to heal human bodies. Oluon, are you willing for her to treat you?"

"I cannot refuse you, O Lago," said Oluon, fearfully.

"It may hurt."

"All the same, my Lord."

"Mournfully agreed to!" laughed Lago. "Go ahead, my sea star!"

The iliu woman knelt beside Oluon, and felt his forehead, held his head between her hands, felt his heart and his hands. He was shaking, and kept his eyes closed shut.

"Oluon," she said, and it was like the voice of the sea. He opened his eyes and looked at her with surprise. His trembling died down, and, responding to her touch, he laid down on his back.

She undid his cloak and examined his wound with her fingers, and then she tasted it with her tongue. Now she probed the wound with her fingers, and Oluon cried out. I winced in sympathy. I noticed that she used her other hand to caress his brow.

She worked for quite some time, patiently, skillfully. She had some sort of pouch at her waist, from which she drew some sort of herbs; some she applied to the wound, others she had Oluon chew and swallow. At one point she leaned over and spit into the wound. Finally she rested for some time with her hands on Oluon's chest and eyes. When she stood up Oluon was sleeping deeply.

She spoke to Lago in her language, and Lago interpreted for me. "His body will complete the process my bride has started, but he needs much rest— a few weeks. And during this time he must eat only the freshest of foods, nothing that has begun to spoil."

"I understand. I thank you, Lago. And I most humbly thank you, O Lady," I added, kneeling before her. "What is her name, O Lago?"

He laughed again, and sang me the melody which was her name. "In Qaraumcán she is called Fon-atcê-siumé," he added. "It means, the healer from the sea at morning."

"It's a very nice name, and very appropriate, except that it's evening," I said, with a laugh.

"Your name is Beretos, but you are not green," he said.

Lago wanted to hear of my sojourn among the Babblers; so I told him my story, and answered his questions. Oluon snored peacefully; and Fon-atcê-siumé laid herself on the grass next to Lago, as naturally and gracefully as a cat, and fell asleep as we talked.

"These are grave events you tell me of," said Lago, when I had done. "Let us hope Ulōne makes us ready for whatever comes of them."

"Do you think they're grave?" I asked. "They mostly seemed foolish to me, and full of the stupidity and banality of everyday things."

"Really, Beretos?"

"Well, of course it's important; it's all as serious as we always said, back in Cuzei. But it wasn't serious to live through, only annoying. Or rather it just seemed like ordinary life, except for the things that turned out to be important, and those turned out to be mostly foolish, or maybe heartbreaking."

Lago said nothing, and I was afraid that I was babbling. "O Lago, can you tell me why things are this way?" I asked him.

He laughed. "You humans! Your questions are such as to fall apart when we look at them."

"I'm sorry, Lago," I said. "What I want to know is, are these things not important to Iáinos? And if they are, why doesn't Iáinos help us more?"

"More than what?"

"More than we're helped now."

"This question is not much firmer," remarked the iliu. "Why is Iáinos not more than Iáinos is?"

I thought a moment before trying again. "It seems that Iáinos leaves us on our own too much. I know Ulōne is with us, but most of the time Ulōne is invisible. Why must Iáinos work invisibly?"

"Well asked, O Beretos," said Lago. "I will tell you a story to answer it— my own story. There came a time when I wished to have a bride. It is done this way among the iliū of my lineage: I walked far to the south, into the wild. It was on my way that we met for the first time, Beretos. I learned to overmaster isolation, and danger, and pain; I crossed mountains, and deserts, and forests, and knew summer and winter; I met men and elcari and wild animals, and learned much of Eīledan's world. You will remember that we are a people of the sea; this country is stranger to us than it is to you.

"On the other end of this continent, on the southern sea, there is another place of habitation for my people. Your holy books remember it; they call it Asicondār. I arrived there, and I searched for my bride.

"I found her in the first month; but of course I could not simply bring her back. I had to win her. I had to devote myself to her, and learn to love her, and surpass others who also wished to be her companion. At the same time I had to wait for her love, to see if she would choose to live with me. Our women are not like yours; they cannot be taken by force! It took me a year to travel to her land, and it took more than a year for us to choose each other.

"And now I am taking her back to my people; and all that I endured and enjoyed alone we now face together.

"It is not the only way iliū can come to live together, but it is a good way. We become very precious to each other because of it." He looked down at his sleeping bride as he said this, and caressed her back.

"But what if we had come together as your people do, by the arrangement of our parents? What if my parents had simply presented her to me, as they would have given me a trout? How much would we value each other, when we had gone through nothing to win each other?"

I thought about this for a long time; but I was still not satisfied. "I think I understand. Iáinos won't simply give us things either. But is it not one thing to find a mate, and another to find war and peace among nations?"

"No, it is the same thing," said Lago.

"I don't understand how that can be," I complained. "A nation is more important than one person, isn't it?"

"That is another question which comes apart," he noted. "What can an iliu say to it, except that a soul is an entire world, and a nation is a world of souls?"

I thought a bit more, and then said, "O Lago, tell me one thing. Your parents will not give you a bride, but they will help you if you ask, won't they? Could not Iáinos at least help us as much as a mother does, or a Lord?"

"In every wise word and deed Ulōne acts," Lago reminded me. "But before you ask me another of your breakable questions, I will tell you another story. This is not a story of true things; I am inventing it. There was a human who lived in the mountains. One day he went out to hunt rabbits for his dinner. He was a poor man, who did not own even a bow; he trapped rabbits with bent sticks.

"But there were no rabbits that day, so he wandered farther afield, into unfamiliar hills and valleys. And as he was walking down a sleep slope he slipped and fell, and fell into a cavern. He was trapped in the cavern, for there was no way out; to return as he had come he would have had to fly. Then he heard a growling sound: there was a black bear in the cave with him!

"He hid from the bear, but it had caught his scent, and came after him. He was driven into a dark recess in the cave, and the bear trundled after him, intent on having man-flesh for dinner. But then the man reached into his quiver and drew out an arrow, and shot it straight into the heart of the bear. He was saved!"

"Hold, O Lago," I said. "I thought you said he had no bow."

"It's so; but I reconsidered, and let him have a bow. Why should I let a man die, even in a story? Now that the bear was dead, the man climbed out of the cave—"

"But there was no exit to the cave!"

"Ah, yes, I didn't tell you. There was a rockfall, and an entrance was opened. So he walked out of the cave, and shot rabbits for his dinner; and he came home to his castle, and his servants took off his sandals, and he rested while his meal was cooked."

"He was a poor man! You can't change the story like that," I protested. "It's not a story at all; it's an absurdity!"

Lago laughed. "You don't like my story? And yet is this not the sort of story you want Iáinos to tell?"

"Do you mean that you compare the world to a story Iáinos is telling?" I asked, trying to understand.

"Almea *is* a story," said Lago. "Iáinos is the Storyteller; Eïledan is the Writer; Ulōne is the Reader."

A fear gripped me. "Are we only puppets then, in the story? For created things have no life of their own, but only do their author's bidding."

"The stories of the iliū have life to them. You of all men should know that, O Beretos! Have you forgotten the story I told you when you first came this way? Will we not find as much life and more, in the stories Iáinos tells?"

"That was a story?"

For answer he only laughed.

"I hope at least the story of Iáinos is not a tragedy," I said.

"Why do you humans insist on making Creation one thing?" he complained. "It is not a tragedy; but it contains tragedies; it is not happy, or beautiful, or instructive, although it contains joyful and beautiful and instructive things. It is nothing smaller than it is. And don't ask me again why it is the way it is!"

"I won't; but I have one more question," I said. I wanted to ask about something Ganacom said.

"No you don't!" said Lago. "I have already given you two answers, and Fon-atcê-siumé has healed your brother. Now, don't hang your head, only rest yourself."

He came over to me and laid his hand on my forehead. I had not realized how full of anxiety and excitement and tiredness I was; now I felt peaceful, and was soon asleep.

In the morning they were gone. Oluon was calm and rested. He had not recovered his strength, but his fever was past. We made ourselves ready and continued our journey home.

37 · ꓯCƂCꞆ⌂ꓕZb · *Mizidomas*

 I arrived at the Red Garrison, with Feroicolê, at dawn. Even then there were others waiting, and as the hours passed, more and more came to wait and watch. Before two hours had passed there was a great crowd round the garrison, as if all Eleisa wished to see this day— nobles and commoners, warriors, Knowers, actors, scholars, and servants.
 As the day stretched on, long past the appointed time, some people drifted away; but others filtered in. Vendors came selling food; some Little Cuzeian girls performed their dances and asked for alms; a group of Knowers from a holy community knelt down on the ground and prayed.
 I tried to talk with Feroicolê, and later with Alaldillê and others who had come to wait with us, but it was difficult to talk; our minds were on the Garrison, and our eyes stole constantly to its closed black doors. I envied a young scholar who had come with a scroll, and sat reading it, looking up only when some change in the noises of the crowds suggested that something was happening.
 The sun was well past her zenith when the doors finally parted. A troop of King's Men came out and lined themselves up on either side of the door, clearing a space, with some difficulty. Two Knowers came out, surveyed the crowd, and returned into the building; a little later more King's Men appeared, to enlarge the open space in front of the doors.
 The crowd shuffled up close to the line of King's Men, pressing against each other uncomfortably. People tried to slip in front of us; we begged them, in the name of Ulōne, to stay back. I was next to Alaldillê; she was wearing an enormous hat to protect her face from the sun, and it was constantly knocking against my ears. We stood thus, without the possibility of resting or exercising our limbs, for another eternal stretch of time. What were they doing inside?
 Finally, there was a great cheer. Every voice cried out, as Zeilisio and Caumēliye came out of the Garrison, accompanied by four more King's Men, and the two Knowers. They looked pale

and tired, and shaded their eyes from the unaccustomed sun. The Lady Caumēliye wore a simple robe, and walked barefoot; her hair, though combed, was dull; her eyes seemed years older. Zeilisio wore a beard, and his hair was noticeably more gray. He held Lady Caumēliye's hand, while she carried little Isiliē. Vissánavos walked proudly beside them.

They looked around at the crowd, and almost past by us, though we were waving like madmen. The guards let us through, and we embraced with great joy. The crowd roared.

"Congratulations, by Iáinos!" said Feroicolê. "I hope you will come immediately to my House. Everything is prepared for you, and I've invited a little handful of people who'd like to see you."

"Feroicolê, you old fool," said Alaldillê. "Can't you see they're falling down on their feet? They'll want to rest on their first day out of detention. You're welcome to come with me, my dears, while your own place is put in order."

"Everything is in order in the Garden House, my Lord," I said.

"But I have a hundred and fifty people at my House waiting to see you," protested Feroicolê.

"Is that your handful?" asked Zeilisio. "Tell you what, they can wait till tonight, don't you think? We thank you all, but we want nothing but baths and peace within our own walls for some hours. Beretos, have someone pick up our things from the Garrison, and then find us a boat, would you?"

"Of course," I said, and sent off two of the servants we had brought with us to execute these tasks.

"Oh, Caumēliye, love, forgive me," said Alaldillê. "You're suffering from the sun. Take my hat."

"Thank you, Alaldillê," said Caumēliye, placing the huge hat on her head, and immediately taking Zeilisio's hand again.

"Can we expect you at sunset, perhaps, brother?" asked Feroicolê.

"Certainly," said Zeilisio. "Expect us then; but we'll actually show up some hours later, if anyone is still around."

All day long the servants had been heating water— and reheating it, as the wait stretched on; so that Caumēliye and Zeilisio could immediately bathe themselves, which was their first desire when we arrived home. The children did not care about baths; they wanted to eat, and they were sent with their tutor to the table. Alaldillê accompanied Caumēliye to her bath, and I accompanied Zeilisio.

"Iáinos! You look like you've had the measles," I said, as Zeilisio removed his tunic.

"Flea bites, mostly," he replied. "A few spiders. You should see Caumēliye; they seemed to find her tastier."

"Oh, poor Caumēliye," I said.

"Yes, she's suffered much," said Zeilisio, with an unexpected tenderness. "You know, before the deliberation... I was married to her, but I never knew her. She has a very deep heart, Caumelīlle..."

"I've always known it, Lord."

Zeilisio lowered himself into the hot water. "Ah, wonderful," he said, relaxing. "Even the stones are warm. In the Garrison we got a bucket of cold water once a week. But I suppose that's nothing to you, you who bathe in mountain streams."

"Streams are much nicer than buckets," I said.

"They're still too cold."

We talked about the end of the deliberation. The final arguments had been long, not so much because the Council found it difficult to agree, but because virtually each Lord and Lady had an extended and impassioned speech to offer. The final result was nonetheless surprisingly one-sided: 11 Lords supporting Inibē, 28 against. Some even of Inibē's own faction had deserted him.

"It was Murgīllede's scheme to close down the theaters," maintained Zeilisio. "No one wants to be against a religious revival; but woe to him who stands between Eleisa and its entertainment!"

There was something to this theory; but I prefer to think that the Lords had simply seen through Inibē's and Murgêde's pious verbiage, and understood that it was power and not Iáinos to which their hearts inclined. Zeilisio's defense had also had its effect— his warnings about the danger of political persecutions; his humiliation of Gintūro the false Knower. And even my testimony had awakened the reason of some: when Munkhâshi men of arms had crossed the Gaumê, Inibē's depiction of Munkhâsh as a phantasm spuriously manipulated by Zeilisio could be believed by no one.

Perhaps outweighing all of these, however, was the Lady Caumēliye's decision to accompany her husband into detention. The graveness of the idiots' error was soon apparent, for their charges against Caumēliye herself now rang false, and sympathy for Caumēliye and her children was widespread in the city. And inevitably it was asked how a man as depraved as the idiots claimed Zeilisio to be could awaken such devotion and sacrifice in his wife.

Of course, Zeilisio said that he didn't understand that himself.

Zeilisio did not seem to want to go to Feroicolê's dinner; he said he wanted to go to bed for about twenty hours, and suggested that I go to the dinner pretending to be him. He would supply me with a scroll of witticisms to read at choice moments. However, once we were at Feroicolê's House — eating good food, soothed by music and fountains, encircled by a good fraction of Feroicolê's handful, hanging on his every word— he seemed to enjoy himself, telling his story and joking about the idiots.

Caumēliye is not so content to talk about herself, and she was very tired; she answered the questions of the guests with courtesy, but with few words. It seemed that this night she could no wrong, however; I heard others speaking of her great modesty and grace.

Feroicolê and many others wished to proceed immediately to the persecution of Inibē and Murgêde. Zeilisio had the right to ask that penalties be applied to them for bringing false charges, and there was some discussion of the possibilities. Many felt that the Council would agree to place them in prison for an period equivalent to the time of Zeilisio's detention; others suggested that Zeilisio seek confiscation of part of their Houses, or physical castigation.

"Hasn't this ordeal taught you anything more than that?" asked Caumēliye, irritably. "Do we need more revenge and intrigue?"

"We're talking of the punishment your persecutors so richly deserve, not of revenge," explained Feroicolê.

"You more than anyone should understand the justice of that," said Alaldillê's son.

"I more than anyone understand the futility of it," said Caumēliye.

"I am truly baffled," said Feroicolê. "What is it you're saying?"

"Yes, what do you mean, dearest?" asked Alaldillê. "Take a deep breath and tell us; and the rest of you keep quiet."

"I mean that after spending more than eight weeks in prison, I don't want anyone else to suffer the same thing, not even Inibē and Murgêde. Doesn't anyone understand that? Zeilisio, do you want that? To do to your idiots what they did to you?"

"But that's only fair," protested Feroicolê.

"You're not Zeilisio," Alaldillê reminded him.

We all looked at Zeilisio; he thought for a few moments, and then sighed. "I have to confess that the thought of doing just that was what kept me going, sometimes," he said. "Inibē and Murgêde in a cell together, wondering what's going to happen to them, whether death or public whipping or the loss of their land... They should know what it's like."

"Don't you think they're wondering that right now?" asked Caumēliye.

"I suppose they are," said Zeilisio, with a laugh. "Yes, I'd be worried, if I were them!"

"But it goes beyond that," she insisted. "Don't you listen to your own words? What is the Cuzei you wish to build? Is it one in which one Lord sends another to prison, and then in his turn the accused does the same? It is yours to decide, O my friends. If it were up to Inibē and his company, we know how they would choose; but it is not. The Lords and Ladies of Cuzei had ears to listen to you, O Zeilisio; they have indeed chosen not to place a sword on the table of the Council. Will you now pick it up again? Is that what you wish? Is that what Ulōne puts in your heart?"

There was a long silence; and then Feroicolê said, "Not *exactly*, O Lady Caumēliye."

"Not exactly, you old toad?" exclaimed Alaldillê. "Not at all. Caumēliye is completely right."

"I think so too," said Zeilisio, a little regretfully perhaps. "Let's put aside thoughts of revenge, and concentrate on intrigue."

The conversation did not end there; there were some who still maintained that if the Council laid damages on the idiots, it would not be merely vindictive; Caumēliye disagreed. Others suggested that Inibē and Murgêde should be reprimanded by the King, and publicly apologize to Zeilisio. Caumēliye did not object to the reprimand, but thought that a show of repentance was pointless from those who certainly felt no sorrow.

After some time Zeilisio looked over at his wife and said, "My Lady, your eyes are seeking sleep, and come to think of it so are mine. Perhaps you could find some beds for us, Feroicolê? We're used to piles of straw with fleas, of course, but don't put yourself out; anything will do."

The next day the Lady Caumēliye complained of headache and weakness, and kept to her bed. For several days she suffered, and could not eat anything but soup. Finally Zeilisio decided that I should take her home to Etêia Mitano. I could see she had great joy in this conception, but she said that she would miss Zeilisio, and only consented to go when he agreed to follow her in a few days.

And indeed once she was in her own House she began to recover. She busied herself preparing the House for Zeilisio's return, and speaking to the peasants who came to see her for counsel or judgment, and worrying over her children. She kept thinking that something was wrong with them, although so far as I could see detention had had no effect on them at all. They found their accustomed playmates and tumbled about Etêia Mitano as happily as Caumēliye and I had once roamed the hills of Tefalē Doro.

"I think it was the party," she told me, as we sat together on the topmost balcony of the House, looking out over the slow-flowing Isrēica. "It was too much for me, after being in prison."

"How so, my Lady?" I asked.

"So many people, such rich food, such noise."

"It must be a great contrast."

"It's not a contrast, it's a different world," she insisted. "Do you know what detention is like? It's not even that it's so bad; I know that we were treated well, because we were Lords. But the simplicity, the darkness, the lack of so many things... You come to appreciate little things. The taste of bread— sometimes they gave us fresh bread, and it was like being at Eīledan's table. After that, seeing the sauces and lobsters and mushrooms and desserts piled on Feroicolê's table, I actually felt ill in my stomach. I shouldn't feel that way; those are all good things too, but that's how it is. Or to hear beautiful music, and watch the dancers, and the silk hangings on the walls, all at once... in prison there was so little to look at. The carvings on the chairs that they let us bring in— I think I memorized the patterns, tracing them with my fingers.

Never seeing the sun; they only let us exercise early in the day, when nothing could be seen from the courtyard but blue sky; and yet what a beautiful blue it was, as rich as Feroicolê's hangings. If we wanted music we had to sing. Zeilisio doesn't have a voice for singing, but I loved to hear him; he was so merry. And then to see all these things at Feroicolê's... I would have liked to see one thing at a time, I think, one thing each day."

"I think I understand," I said. "It's different and more pleasant for a traveler; you regain the comforts of Cuzei slowly. Araunicoros seems like the height of civilization after you've been in the Gaumê, and then Dācuas is grander yet, and then you come to Cuzei..."

She laughed. "You shame me, Beretos! We lived far better in the Red Garrison than you did in your barracks in the mountains. At least our guards spoke Cuêzi, and we could have visitors!"

"I didn't mean to compare my privations with yours, O Caumēliye. I think you've suffered much more than I."

"I don't know about that. And what of Oluon? Have you heard anything of him?"

"Not since the letter you've already seen, from a week ago," I said. "He's well enough to travel; in fact, I hope he's left Araunicoros by now."

"It must have been very hard to come home alone," commented Caumēliye. "That was our great consolation, Beretos, and the one I never expected. I think Zeilisio and I spoke more words to each other in our weeks in prison than in the last many years here in Etêia Mitano. There is something to be said for prison, you see! My children were there, Zeilisio, and Ulōne..."

"And yet you didn't want to confer those same benefits on Inibē and Murgêde."

"No, Beretos, you can't put other people in prison to improve them," she said, laughing.

"I suppose not."

We watched the river for awhile. A bird landed on the edge of the balcony, and then darted down to where some bread crumbs had fallen. It picked them up one by one, keeping a wary eye cocked at us, and on guard for cats.

"Do you know, I was retelling the epics for Zeilisio?" said Caumēliye.

"Really? Did he like that? He always told me he couldn't understand why I kept re-reading the epics, when I already know the story."

"He said he liked them," she said. "We were simply telling each other whatever stories we knew. He told me stories from history, and told me plays he'd seen and I hadn't. I hope we'll continue to do that. I wonder when he's coming back. When do you think, Beretos? He said he'd come in a few days; but we came by boat, and he'll come by horse; it shouldn't be long, should it?"

"You never used to complain about Zeilisio's absence," I commented. "You used to say that my *coelīras* was enough for you."

"Beretos, you're jealous," she said, putting her hand on mine.

"I'm not jealous."

She was smiling at me, and I thought of pulling my hand away. She pulled me to her, put her arms around me, and kissed me.

"Don't make faces at me," she said. "I love you, Beretos, and your devotion is precious to me."

"Thank you, my Lady. My heart is yours. But things won't be the same again, will they?"

"If anything has changed, it's not that I love you less, but that my love for Zeilisio has grown. You will not object to that, will you? After all, Isiliē too loved her husband!"

"I'm glad for you," I said, sadly.

"But not for yourself? I think I have to find you a wife!"

"There isn't another woman like you," I lamented.

"If there were, I wouldn't let you marry her," she countered. "A wife wants to be loved, not worshipped! It's a pity you didn't marry that Faliles when you had the chance. Maybe you should go back to the Gaumê to bring back her sister!"

"Oh, no, by Ulōne," I said.

I cannot close without some words about Munkhâsh, the enemy of Cuzei.

After Zeilisio's deliberation there was much alarm over Munkhâsh, but since then it has died down somewhat. This must not be. I hope my readers will learn from this book how serious is the threat of Munkhâsh, especially now that the barrier of the Gaumê no longer stands before them.

Nor can we be content to treat the Babblers as we always have. We cannot continue to send them foolish and prideful Residents, who know nothing about their lives and speak no Caðinor. We cannot assume that they will naturally ally themselves with us against the Munkhâshi. It is in the course of nature that younger brothers love and respect their elders; but if the older brothers are disdainful and dissipated, the younger will learn not love but hatred and rejection.

If we can win their trust, we will be strong enough to face the Munkhâshi. For make no mistake, it is not Knowers, but diplomats and soldiers and travelers who can teach us about Munkhâsh. We need not frighten ourselves with stories of the demons, nor console ourselves with the misconception that the demons are spiritual enemies, which Iáinos will fight for us. The Munkhâshi are men— dangerous men, who would take Cēradānar from us if they could; but men and not demons, and no more difficult to understand than other men.

It was Zeilisio who made me understand this point. When he heard my story, he bade me think about the noise that awakened me in the barracks, and the stone that I found on the floor. Who had thrown that stone? My window faced the tower; and it was the Munkhâshi who stood between the barracks and the inner keep.

Following Ganacom's orders, the Munkhâshi were content to set the barracks on fire; but it did not please them, or some one of them, simply to broil their enemies like lobsters in their beds, and one of them flung the stone to awaken us.

Even among our enemies there is, now and then, a movement of Ulōne.

If the stories of the Sojourner have such richness, one reason is that, like life, they never come to a firm end, with all questions answered. The Sojourner moves on; but sometimes he returns, and finds his friends older; the princess he rescued learning to rule, the lovers he brought together busy with children. The villains he defeated sometimes rise again, and he must confront them once more; or sometimes they have reflected and followed the good path, while the wise king has become corrupted.

And again, the epics of Samīrex or Antāu end in merriment and repose; while each of the cantos of the Sojourner end with a movement: he rides for many days and comes to a new place, where he meets a prince or a woodcutter or a thief or a woman in tears; one whose story is told in the next canto.

My story, like the Sojourner's, refuses to end neatly. Inibē is defeated and takes no role in Council, but Murgêde has mounted a new intrigue, with a new ally; my Lady pursues her purpose of finding me a wife; and strange tales are heard in another Babbler land.

But, as it is said in the book of the Sojourner, these are things to be spoken of at another time.

Commentary

The work
This book is a translation of the ancient Cuzeian work called by its author

ū˥˩ı̆bCXoZ˛CZ˛bʌZ˛bZ˛ıŪıÇ˥CdoZ˛XC⊤˥oZ˛ıbZ˛Ū˥Cd˥C(CC(ʌZ˛¦

which is transliterated *Xuêsicranas fâsaex eduntrâcinu rāe sā xūntu Neni-Nemaē,* and translated 'A defense before the judges of my conduct which was in the land of Babblers.' Beretos began his journey eastward in Z.E. 287, during the reign of king Bisbazuo.

Beretos returned from the lands of the barbarians eager to explain his role in the events at Berak's keep, to a nation seeking someone to blame. Under Cuzeian law he was responsible only to Zeilisio, who was not interested in punishing him, and indeed resisted pressure (from the 'idiots') to do so. With time, and as the Munkhâshi tarried, this pressure abated, but Beretos felt himself dishonored, and wrote the *Xuêsicranas* to explain the loss of the Pass, and to warn his countrymen both of the new strategic situation, and of the results of their barbarian policy.

It seems to have achieved its immediate object, for we see Beretos' name appear later in public life. He seems to have undertaken another embassy among the Cad̂inorians, and one to the kingdom of Agimbār.

More importantly, the Cuzeians were awakened to the threat of Munkhâsh— especially after the Esocadi dynasty was replaced in 327 by the more active Mitano. Its first kings, Aētaonelo and Nūmiruiddâ, sent military expeditions into the east of Cēradānar. Either because these deterred the Munkhâshi, or because the latter were not ready, there was no invasion for more than a century. We do not have specific information on the fate of Berak— the closest we have is a general's remark from Z.E. 342 that "the Taucrēte holds".

But by the 400s these exercises had ceased, and Cuzei was embroiled in a dynastic dispute, resulting in the fall of the Mitano kings. In 440, the Munkhâshi invaded in force, occupying half of

Cēradānar and sending an army to besiege Eleisa. To expel the Munkhâshi from Cēradānar was the fight of the next half millennium, and the one which forged a great empire— which however would not be that of the Cuzeians but of the Caðinorians. Modern Verdurians descend from the Caðinorians, and call the plain of Cēradānar *Eretald.*

Beretos' work has outlived the practical politics which engendered it, and even the epic events to which it was the prelude. For one thing it served as a travelogue: Beretos was not the first Cuzeian to have traveled from one end of Cēradānar to the other, but he was the first to write about it. Beretos has also long been admired for the simplicity and purity of his Cuêzi, the result no doubt of his long study of the classics and his relative distance from the fads and fashions of the capital. The contention of some, that a lad from the mountains of Tefalē Doro would be incapable of such a style, and that the book is instead the work of Zeilisio, should be rejected as aristophilic nonsense.
　　The book is also a valuable glimpse into the nature of Munkhâsh. Beretos was the first writer to clearly explain the ethnic strategy of the *amnigō:* reconciling newly conquered peoples to their role by assuring them that they would dominate later conquests.
　　Copyists were not above improving a work, and many later manuscripts are edited in line with the greater pietism of later centuries. Beretos becomes far more religious and references to the 'idiots' are toned down; the chapters on pagan gods are often omitted. Three chapters called the "Prayers of Beretos" had great popularity in the Silver Age. This edition removes all the later insertions and alterations.
　　I have, however, switched Beretos' chapters 3 and 4, to follow temporal order. The later interleaving of chapters set in the Gaumê and in Cuzei is kept, as being integral to his storytelling. Some scholars suggest that he began writing the book at the keep, and had reached this point in the story at his return, at which point the urgent events of Zeilisio's persecution clamored to be recorded.
　　In imperial times, Beretos' depiction of the Caðinorians rankled, and the book was never translated into Caðinor. The

240 · IN THE LAND OF BABBLERS

Verdurians do not share their hangups, and in modern times the *Xuêsicranas* has emerged as one of the most important of our documents on classical Cuzei— an invaluable source not only on the nature of the early Cađinorians, but on how the Houses and Councils of Cuzei, so often romanticized in more conventional sources, really worked.

The best modern edition of the *Xuêsicranas* is printed by the Scholars' Circle of Avéla, edited by Nađanél Ložey (*Soa conđayeca Beretei*, Z.E. 3452). My translation is mainly from Ložey's text, but follows the readings in other versions where the sense reads better, or where Ložey in my opinion has been taken in by a traditional error.

The usual caveats of Almean scholarship apply. Almea is a different planet, with distinct flora and fauna. It would be tedious and distracting to use native words for these— to explain that a *eîca*, a member of a bipedal, mammalian, intelligent species, rode on top of a *tīble*, a large, fast herbivore. I have preferred to write that a man was riding a horse. For fear of overwhelming the reader, I have even omitted the picturesque details, such as that the ears of the *tīble* hang down rather than point up, or that the male *tīblē* are too fierce to ride.

Beretos, naturally, approximated foreign words to Cuêzi. In most cases I have spelled Cađinor and Munkhâshi words according to the usual transliterations of those languages in Almean scholarship— e.g. *Cađinor, Berak, Munkhâsh, Gelalh* for his *Cazinoro, Berac, Munxeas, Gellâx*. However, to preserve the Cuzeian flavor of the work, I've used Cuêzi terms such as *amnigō, Gaumê, Isrēica, Cēradānar, Araunicoros* in place of the more modern, Verdurian-based *ktuvoks, Ctelm, Eärdur, Eretald, Aránicer*.

On Cuzei

Beretos' work is itself sufficient introduction to classical Cuzei. However, some notes on its history may be of interest.

The earliest histories of the iliū, echoed in the Cuzeian *Count of Years*, tell of the creation of Almea and of the Four Thinking Kinds by Eīledan, followed by eight great wars between the iliū and amnigō. It was during these wars that the amnigō living in the Lācatosūelo swamps were expelled, and joined their brethren far to the east. Some of the wars seem to have been fought with high technology; details are hard to come by since we cannot read the iliū sources. The iliū maintained that humans (*eicē*) were created in the course of these wars, and were corrupted by the greatest of the demons, Ecaîas.

The wars had been over for thousands of years before the first men, the Metailō, appeared in the great plain of Cēradānar. In the course of time they established the first organized states in Cēradānar, around Z.E. -1150. In form their kingdoms were confederacies of barons, with an elected king. The Metailō had little stomach for war, and responded to catastrophe, such as an invasion by a rival kingdom or a failed counter-invasion, by beheading their own king and suing for peace— habits that would soon stand them in very ill stead.

By this time the realm of Munkhâsh had already been organized by the amnigō. The earthly historian must not too quickly accept the judgments of the men of Almea on this event— that it was enslavement, achieved by trickery. The human tribes co-opted by the amnigō were neolithic in culture; in return for their submission they received agriculture, domesticated animals, metals, peace and order, and empire over their neighbors. It may not have seemed a bad bargain.

Around Z.E. -350, seven hundred years before our story starts, Cēradānar was invaded by the Cuzeians and Cađinorians. The Cuzeians were divided into four lineages, those of Inibē, Voricêlias, Lēivio, and Calēsias. They quickly conquered the center of the plain, the valley of the Cayenas. They cannily exploited the divisions of the Metailō; and where that didn't suffice their superior weapons (of bronze, at that time) and stricter organization did. The Metailō were absorbed into the new kingdoms of the conquerors, or retreated to the north or east (the latter are known as the Moňnaru).

This is the time in which the Cuzeian epics were set: a time of many kings, frequent war, and many novelties (cities, stringed instruments, wine, oranges, olives, sailing ships, the sea, all were new to the Cuzeians). The epics were written several centuries later, of course, and retrofitted later notions of chivalry and orthodoxy into the heroic age.

The four lords' agreement was to divide their conquests equally between them, and the spoils were indeed divided, but Inibē managed to retain sole political control. It was partly to escape this that the other lineages conquered the valley of the Isrēica, where Calēsias founded Eleisa and the sons of Lēivio founded Aure Árrasex.

The *Count of Years* relates, as a dire warning, how the lineage of Inibē became ever more prideful, defied the Knowers of Eīledan, and fell into atheism. His sons turned to civil war, and his kingdom was lost to the Cađinorians and Little Cuzeians. (The latter were simply Cuzeians who remained largely pastoral, and outside Cuzei's organized network of Houses.) It's a minor irony that the leader of the pietist faction in Beretos' time is named after the founder of this renegade dynasty; but the first Inibē was also a renowned fighter and hero. The loss of the Cayenas is attributed by Ganacom in chapter 25 to the failure of the iliū in guiding the *eîcē*.

The state of Cuzei was established by the dynastic union of the heirs of Calēsias and Lēivio, in -250; our earliest records date from a bit earlier than this. The Cuzeians claimed to have learned writing from the iliū. Their script bears no resemblance to that of the iliū, but that is of little import; a script suitable for recording iliu speech would be of little use for human language. It's likely the idea rather than the specifics of writing was borrowed.

The *Count of Years* tells of the beginnings of the friendship between the Cuzeians and the iliū, which is reported to have occurred before the conquest of Cēradānar, spearheaded by the prince Lerīmanio. (The Cuzeians, already worshippers of Iáinos, paid no attention to the Metailo gods— unlike the Cađinorians, who apparently took over Metailo religion as they took over Metailo forms of government; the gods of Araunicoros are said to be those of the Metailō renamed.) According to the book, the iliū chose the Cuzeians for friendship because only they responded to their offer to teach men about Iáinos; the other races of men were already too attached to their own gods.

Acknowledgments

Many thanks to those who read earlier drafts and offered invaluable feedback: Jeffrey Henning, Clarke Stone, Chris Livingston, Lore Sjöberg, Mathieu Richir, John Cowan, Sally Burr, Cherie Campbell, Michael Kitchin, and my wife Lida.

The cover illustration is by Edwin Perales.

More information

Information about Cuzei has grown far too large for appendices, and I've made it available as a separate book— *The Book of Cuzei*. This book contains:

- a grammar and lexicon of Cuêzi, including part of chapter 2 of this book in the original Cuêzi
- a description of Cuzeian theism
- the text of the *Count of Years*, giving the Cuzeian account of creation, the origins of the Thinking Kinds, the wars of the iliu and amnigō, and the rise of Cuzei
- a pietist letter, *The Shame of Etêia Mitano,* attacking Beretos and Zeilisio
- a Silver Age play, *The Munkhâshi,* a satiric account of a Munkhâshi lord visiting Cuzei
- A selection of Caðinorian descriptions of late Cuzei

In addition, the *Historical Atlas of Almea* is available as a full color printed book, covering 30,000 years of Almean history, including that of Cēradānar.

Most of this material is also available for free on my website:
www.zompist.com

Also of interest on the site are grammars of Caðinor and Munkhâsh, a discussion of Caðinorian religion, and a short description of life in the heart of Munkhâsh.

More chronicles of Almea are planned...

—*Mark Rosenfelder, August 2014*

Glossary

Most Cuêzi and Cađinor words used in the text are explained on first reference, but the definitions are repeated here for convenience. In addition I have translated a number of personal and place names. The chapter titles are translated in the next section.

For more information, see the online Cuêzi and Cađinor grammars, or the *Book of Cuzei*.

Cuêzi

Plurals generally have lengthened vowels: *amnigo, amnigō; iliu, iliū; eîca, eîcē*. But nouns ending in a consonant form their plural in -*i*: *elcár, elcari; ecivas, ecivi*.

Agimbār: name of a Metailo state in the north of Cēradānar; Verdurian Ažimbea. From *Agibna*, the name of the Metailo sea goddess.
alaldillê: starlike, from *alaldas* 'star'.
Amnās: a follower of Ecaîas in his rebellion against Iáinos; he is blamed for most of the evil in the world, including the creation of the *amnigō*.
amnigo: 'child of Amnās': the inhuman species who rule the empire of Munkhâsh; also called *ktuvoks*.
ando: an honorific used in formal address: e.g. *ande Beretos!* 'O Beretos!'
Antāu: 'unity'; the name of an epic hero, the lover of Isiliē. His story is summarized in chapter 15.
Araunicoros: port of eagles; the name is Cuêzi, not Cađinor. A city and princedom in southern Cēradānar, modern *Aránicer*.
Araunixue: 'eagle eye'; the name of a (female) prophet. Cuzeian prophets and Knowers could be of either sex.
Árrasos: the name of the first created human, husband of Denūra, claimed as the founder of Aure Árrasex.
Ataiggār: 'place of life', the planet Almea.
Aure Árrasex 'House of Árrasos'; the name of the second-largest city in Cuzei, after Eleisa, and once the seat of the duchy of Tevarē.
bardāu: communion, intimacy, brotherly love; from *bardu* 'brother'. *Bardāu* and *dêrias* 'creation, art' were the two central virtues of Cuzeian philosophy.
Beretos: a man's name, from *berede* 'green'.
Bisbazuo: the King in the time of *Babblers*, from 'without deceit'.
Calēsiōre: name of the dynasty which unified the kingdom of Cuzei. The dynasty is named for Calēsias, the founder and first ruler of Eleisa.
cammisi: yellow.
Caumēliye: sweetheart, from *cāuma* 'hearth' + *mēliye* 'girl'.

Cayenas: name of the chief river of Cēradānar and of a Babbler state along it. The people of this state spoke a variant of Caḍinor called Kahinisa; like 'Caḍinas', this word can be traced back to proto-Central *Ekaduns.

Celōusio: 'swordsman', name of an epic hero, illegitimate son of the duke of Tevarē, the only hero named in the *Count of Years*. Fought dragons and warrior women; one of the latter came with him, and married his unheroic brother Pûntio.

Cēradānar: the Cuêzi name for the fertile plain (Verdurian *Eretald*) between the western and the eastern mountains; from *cēr* 'center' + *adānar* 'plain'.

coelīras: devotion, especially to women; from *coêli* 'like, be fond of'.

Cuêzaye: Cuzei. 'Cuzei' is the Verdurian form of the word, which is conventionally used in Almean studies.

Cuêzi: the Cuêzi language.

Dācuas: name of a Caḍinorian state along the Cayenas.

Ecaîas: name of a mighty *einalandāua* who revolted against Iáinos, brought evil into the world, and corrupted the elcari and humankind.

eîca: name of the most populous Thinking Kind of Almea; here translated man or human. The word is feminine in form. A male is a *pumas*; a female, a *moêli*.

Eīledan: the Shaper or Creative Force in Cuzeian theology, who creates and maintains the material world according to the eternal conception and law of Iáinos.

Einalandāuē: from *eine* 'first' + *landāua* 'reasoning being'.

elcár: name of a man-like species dwelling in the mountains. Smaller but stronger than men, the elcari undertake all the mining and goldworking on Almea. The name in their own language means 'makers'.

Eleisa: name of the capital of Cuzei, founded by Calēsias in Z.E. -350; the Cuzeians reckoned their years from this event.

Etêia Mitano: flower of the south.

Feroicolê: 'cold-lover' (i.e. 'hardy, resistant').

Gaumê: name of the mountains forming the eastern border of Cēradānar; Caḍinor *Cîelm*; both words are apparently borrowed from a Metailo word meaning 'iron'.

Iáinos: the Eternal Idea in Cuzeian theology, who conceives of the timeless and faultless spiritual creation which is translated into time and matter by Eīledan. Sometimes called *Iáinos Onnamêto* 'Iáinos, lord of all'.

iliu: a species distantly related to man, and adapted for life on the continental shelf, dwelling also on land near the sea. The iliū and amnigō fought great wars thousands of years in the past, before the arrival of men. The iliū taught the Cuzeians their religion and their alphabet.

Inibē: one of the four great dukes who invaded Cēradānar— a great conqueror but remembered for his pride and his refusal to share power. Namesake of the leader of the pietists in Beretos' day.

Isiliē: an epic heroine, lover of Antāu.

Isrēica: name of the great river flowing through Cuzei.

Lago: This word seems to have no meaning in Cuêzi or Caḍinor.

lelîyas: art, culture, civilization— what distinguishes the Cuzeians from the barbarians. Related to *lerê* 'see, perceive, understand'.
Lerīmanio: founder of Cuzeian theism; his name means 'powerful in seeing'.
lestas: a unit of distance, about two kilometers or 1.2 miles; anglicized as 'lest'.
Metailo: the people who occupied all of Cēradānar before the Cuzeian invasion, and still occupied the northern coast, from *Metayu,* one of their kingdoms.
munxesilo: Munkhâshi.
murgêde: stony.
namo: Lord, one of the hereditary nobles of Cuzei. The feminine form is *namiēi* 'Lady.' In earlier years Lords had to be warriors, but by Beretos' time about half of the Houses allowed female inheritance.
narrûos: the title of the hereditary monarch of Cuzei (here translated King). In Cuzeian thought the title could only be used for the monarch of an entire ethnic group (*sodeyas*); if the *sodeyas* was divided its leaders were *yaviciū* 'dukes'.
oluon: buttress.
roccâ: epic; from *rōci* 'relate'. The epics, reduced to writing between Z.E. -100 and 50, are among the oldest Cuêzi literature we have; but they are set during the invasion of Cēradānar which began around Z.E. -375. As such they are full of anachronisms, such as the attribution of *coelīras* and mature Cuzeian theology to the time of the invasion.
Samīrex: name of an epic hero ('son of brightness'), a prince of Cuzei. When his Lady falls sick, he goes voyaging in the south of the world for the Well of Light whose waters will cure her. When he drinks from it himself he is punished by losing his memory and wandering for five years. When he returns to Cuzei his Lady's House has been usurped by wood goblins, whom he must defeat before he can apply the cure.
sindas: city; that is, a settlement large enough to be outside the jurisdiction of all Houses.
sodeyas: lineage, from *sodâ* 'bequeath'. An ethnic group, such as the Cuzeians, descended from one of the sons of Árrasos. In Cuzeian thought, a *sodeyas* should be united and ruled by a *narrûos*.
sūro: owl.
Taucrēs: name of the third major river of Cēradānar, besides the Isrēica and the Cayenas. Where the river emerges from the Gaumê is the Taucrēte Pass, one of the few practical ways across the mountains into Munkhâsh.
Tefalē Doro: mountain hollow.
Ulōne: the Divine Response in Cuêzi theology. The divine creation produces not only matter but divinity; Ulōne is the divine spark in nature and in the souls of the Thinking Kinds, responding in love to the Idea of Iáinos and the Forming of Eīledan. Feminine in gender, and often in symbolology.
Vissánavos: from *vissanavas* 'knowledge', from *vissê* 'know'.
xuêsicranas: defense, apology; from *xuêsi* 'remove' + *cranas* 'shame'.
xuzāu: a type of freshwater fish.
Zeilisio: A man's name, from *zeili* 'lively'.

Cadinor

Cadinor is a sister language of Cuêzi, both deriving from proto-Eastern. The resemblance was noted in ancient times (see chapter 10), but attributed to imitation.

Aecton: name of the chief god worshipped in Araunicoros.
Aelilea: name of the chief goddess worshipped in Araunicoros.
aidoclitus: godspeaker, priest; from *aidos* 'god' + *clitec* 'formally address'.
Alameia: the world (the planet Almea); from *ales* 'earthly' + *meis* 'water': that is, 'the earth and seas'.
Arihmiera: from *arih* 'dominant' + *miera* 'fire'.
berak: glory, renown.
Cadinor: name of the Cadinorian language; ultimately from proto-Central *Ekaduns* '(people of the) river fork', the name of a Cadinorian tribe along the middle Cayenas.
calenorion: baron, lord of a fortress; from *calenos* 'fortress, keep'.
cruvec: 'shielding', from *cruva* 'shield'.
Ctesifos: the name of a village along the Cayenas; the future capital of the Cadinorian Empire; modern Žésifo.
domorion: steward (literally, master of the house).
Endauron: chief of the gods among the central Cadinorians; the only god name that can be traced back to proto-Eastern— cognate to *(Eīl)edan*.
Eraudor: the Cadinor name of the Isrēica, Verdurian *Eärdur*.
faliles: white.
fantos (plural *fantit*): spirit, soul; especially one of the powerful spirits (demigods or departed human souls) which inhabit godspeakers and intervene in mortal affairs.
Gardom: 'sense' + 'stone'.
ges (plural *gesit*): household idol; source of the word *žes* 'home' in Verdurian.
Iscira: name of the chief goddess among the central Cadinorians.
Kravcaene-Limura: Kravcaena's Breast. Kravcaena is the goddess of agriculture.
Mieranac: god of fire (*miera*) and war.
Mohnaru: name of the tribes east of the Gaumê— remnants of the peoples occupying Cēradānar before the Cuzeian-Cadinorian invasion.
murina: a small boat.
Seraea: the Cadinor name for the Taucrēs.
Sielineca: 'graceful daughter'
Sintilna: name of a bright yellow flower found in the mountains.
Spetela: the Cadinor name for the middle Cayenas and the Metōre, Verdurian *Svetla*.
tentesinas: 'weaver'.
tiedectescrion: captain of troops; literally, master of forty (*tiedect*) men.
vadora: delicacy, grace.

Other languages

Almea: Verdurian form of Caðinor *Alameia*.
Eteodāole: the name of the iliu language, meaning unknown.
Fon-atcê-siumé: a Qarau name: 'hearer from the morning sea'.
Ganacom: probably Munkhâshi *gankrino* 'heart-man'.
Gelalh: the Munkhâshi name for their chief god, from *gel* 'holy, frightening'.
gotalh: 'master': Munkhâshi name for the amnigō, normally called ktuvoks in Almean studies.
Hānu: a Moňnaru name, possibly meaning 'ivy'.
Korkâsh: 'proud spider', name of a major city in western Munkhâsh as well as one of the Six Gods
Munkhâsh: Munkhâshi name for the great empire of the amnigō: 'strong rich (land)'. Cuêzi, *Munxeas*; Caðinor, *Munȟas*.
Nokhdak: 'western pillar'
Qaraumcán: A language of men, a continent away from Cēradānar. Beretos writes *Corāuncê*, which clearly points to the people who call themselves Qaraus; another nation, though never a civilized one, which was greatly influenced by the iliū.
Scóndoro: the main river in the plain east of the Gaumê, from *shkono* 'earth magic'.
Z.E.: Verdurian *zon erei*, Caðinor *zonnos aerei*, 'year of the south'; the reckoning of dates from the founding of Ctesifos, in general use in Almean studies. The mission of Beretos to the Caðinorians began in Z.E. 287, or 637 in Cuzeian reckoning.

Notes

1 • *Baezāuco* • *In the beginning*

In the beginning (p. 1)— The entire *Count of Years* is available in the *Book of Cuzei*, and on my website. Beretos cites the beginning in the southern version, which is what would have been read in Tefalē Doro and Etêia Mitano.

The Sojourner, was the hero of the greatest of the Cuzeian epics, and according to some an avatar of Eīledan. Cuêzi *Enōtivas*, from *nōtive* 'to stay', literally to spend one night (*nōtu*).

House (1)— *aure*, literally the mansion or palace of a Cuzeian noble; by extension, the noble's property or domain.

2 • *Tefalē Doro* • *Mountain Hollow*

Babblers (3)— Beretos uses *neni-nemi* 'Babbler' (the name is imitative) for any non-Cuzeians. These in particular were Somoyi-Meťelyi nomads.

Steward— *enatēras*, from *natēre* 'oversee, run', itself from *na* 'over' + *tēre* 'watch over' (cf. *etēras* 'shepherd'). The Master of Arms is the *enatēras sonurdaē*; *sonurdas* = 'things provided, weapons', from *sonure* 'provide', ultimately from *nure* 'give suck'

Glade (3)— *lusi*, consecrated ground, generally a meadow or clearing, though the main Glade of Eleisa was a building. Also used to refer to the Knowers associated with it.

Knowers (*evissi*) were those dedicated to knowing Eīledan and offering spiritual guidance to other Cuzeians.

marriage (4)— this was a *barīdeca*; the walk symbolized the blessings of Ulōne upon the couple.

servant (4)— *ecivas*, used loosely for anyone in the House who wasn't actually a peasant (*mēsigo* 'child of the fields'), and more precisely for those who were bound to the house, as opposed to *mâsiō* 'stewards' or 'upper servants', who are legally free, but serve a particular House out of loyalty.

Peasants were tied to a particular House. However, a peasant could run away to another House, or even to a City; he would have little or no legal protection there, but his children would belong to the new jurisdiction.

Master of Arms (5)— *enatēras sonurdaē*; *sonurdas* = 'things provided, weapons', from *sonure* 'provide'.

amnigō (7)— an ancient and warlike species dwelling in swamps, the overlords of the empire of Munkhâsh. The name means 'child of Amnās', the demon who created them. In Verdurian, *ktuvok*.

trolls— *edāumiri*, an evil species created in mythic times by the demon Amnās.

250 · IN THE LAND OF BABBLERS

warrior Lady (7)— Xetīsiē was an *eguendei*, one of a legendary race of warrior women. Celōusio at first fights with her, then brings her back to Cuzei, where she falls in love with Pûntio.

The Giants (*bārumemaniciū* 'mountain powers') and Ogres (*gauminiū*, from *Gaumê*) appear in the Count of Years as the first-created species, one good, one evil. Both were destroyed in the iliu-amnigo wars, though they were frequently revived in adventure stories.

3 • *Zeilisio*

chief steward (10)— literally, first of the *mâsiō*. Zeilisio undoubtedly inherited this headache from his parents.

medium of exchange (12)— Markets are a technology. Cuzei invented coins and the market economy in northern Ereláe, but as this section suggests, the Houses were often run by a web of traditional mutual duties. Note that a unit of account was mostly virtual: the transactions between House and peasants, or between the peasants, were only rarely mediated with actual coins.

4 • *Caumēliye*

Little Cuzeians (16)— *bardīllū* 'little brothers', nomadic Karazi tribes related to the Cuzeians, specifically Lovitrui and Nimoicū. Merchants were a necesssary but despised class, and it was just as well if the job was done by near-barbarians.

clinging to the altar (19)— The Glade was holy ground, and no violence was permitted there. There was no obligation to succor the criminal, but at least it gave some time for passions to calm.

5 • *Neni-nemā* • *Babblers*

Ctesifos (23)— This is actually one of the earliest references to the future Imperial capital. It had been controlled for centuries by the Scadrorion clan; in 462 Erbelaica finally kicked them out.

Any stranger (24)— Still a proverb in modern Verdurian. Possibly a matter of relative prosperity: a foreigner in Cuzei was almost certainly poor, and possibly up to no good.

6 • *Araunicoros*

free men (29)— Beretos calls himself *cipatoro* 'generous, noble', what we might call 'persons of quality'. In an aristocratic society the opposite of 'free' is 'servile, calculating, ungenerous'. Merchants and mercenaries are *bisnamociū*, without Lords, but they are not *cipatorō*.

The idiots (32)— In history we refer to them as the pietists, as opposed to the privatists. Knowers taught that all must pursue *yēvīras* 'righteousness', but not all were called to *nēreyas* 'holiness'. The pietists however believed that Cuzei must be a 'holy nation', and coerced into it if necessary.

7 • *Mētudomas* • *Assignment*

Dance of Swords (33)— the *Brissâ cêleē*, a 2nd century manual of swordsmanship. The Cuzeians had developed a terminology and graphical notation for swordfighting that allowed a fight to be re-created with great precision.

8 • Āetīlle • Litte lake

king (41)— this is king Bisbazuo, already in his seventies. The last four kings of the Esocadi dynasty were called *pitui* 'the weak ones'.

Council of Cuzei— Acūritār Cuêzayeē, consisting of the King and the forty most prominent Lords and Ladies (cf. *curi* 'talk'). In theory each Lord was sovereign, and Cuzei was a confederacy; but in the course of its 1500-year history, as civilization grew more complex and Cuzei fought with Munkhâsh, the central government became stronger and stronger.

Lerīmanio (44)— the Cuzeian prince who, even before the invasion of Cēradānar, brought knowledge of Iáinos, Eīledan and Ulōne from the iliū. Along the way he blessed the future site of Eleisa.

9 • Eleisa

Eīnalandāuē (48)— an order of spiritual beings created by Eīledan to people the heavens. Ecaîas was one of these; he rebelled and was punished by being bound deep within Almea. His lieutenant Amnās, considered more sinful than his master, became the chief antagonist of Iáinos; the *amnigō* are said to be his creations.

Ximāuro is recapitulating the *Count of Years*. It's unlikely that any Cuzeians visited Munkhâsh before it expanded to the Gaumê; the news of its formation probably came through the iliū.

snake skin (52)— Biologically the amnigō are mammals, but their own classification, and thus that of the Munkhâshi, is that they are reptiles; mammals are considered ugly and weak. Thus the aesthetic valuation of the non-mammalian. See the pictures of Munkhâshi clothing on my website.

10 • Oluon

Caḑinor (53)— Beretos must have had a good ear; his approximations are a good match for classical Caḑinor. He generally wrote ⸲b ꞔb ts dz for t̂ d̂, wrote Ū for both h and ḣ, and wrote ϰϰ cc for k. The Caḑinor t̂ d̂ derive historically from t d, and some scholars have suggested that they were actually affricates at this time. He adds tone marks to some vowels, sometimes correlating with stress (e.g. Ctēsifos)— hearing, so to speak, with a Cuzeian ear.

Fantit (58)— Beretos is one of our major sources on the popular side of Caḑinorian religion. During the reconquest, religion was closely controlled by the state, and these unauthorized godspeakers disappeared.

11 • Lago

Lago (65)— Curiously, a sprite named Lago (not an iliu) is worshipped in Caḑinorian paganism. Did Lago amuse himself with visitations on Caḑinorians?

12 • Berak

baron (72)— Beretos uses the Caḑinor term *calenorion* (rather than, say, *namo* 'lord').

13 • Sofuseca • Teaching

Turicali (73)— The Turicali are legendary, but the nomads of the Barbarian Plain, to the south of Cēradānar, do raise and train falcons.

14 • Aurisôndias • Mapmaking

ceremony (84)— Verdurian pagan girls still undergo this coming-of-age ceremony, the *redel*. The period of sequestration is just two days in modern times. Boys have one too, the *nacuyát*. Boys are expected to survive an ordeal (one something like a hunt, scarification, or a drug trip; today more likely to be a fast or an athletic feat); girls to create handicrafts.

15 • Antāu

coelīras (89)— the respectful submission owed to women, part of the tradition of romantic adultery among the Lords, a natural development when marriages were arranged. Berac's judgment should not be taken as fact: to the misogynist, having to treat women as equals feels like oppression.

16 • Xēcuvisseca • Demonstration

lighter and shorter (95)— The Caḑinorian sword (*belaca*), even in Imperial times, was long and heavy, and in these times was made of iron. Beretos' sword is far sharper, and its lightness makes him nimble. In modern times the belaca has given way to the light curved *carḑë*, borrowed from the nomads.

defense positions (96)— Dolbas's response must have been "what positions?" They had all been documented and named in Cuzeian swordfighting manuals. In later times, Caḑinorian officers learned Cuêzi in order to train their men.

17 • Brosiveyas • Training

laws of princes (100)— Cuzeian rulers were expected to follow the precepts of the *Teaching of Kings*, which included restrictions on warfare against other Cuzeians. One might cynically point out that there was no enforcement mechanism; on the other hand, it has some effect if the holy books define when one is being a tyrant.

Lords, Upper Servants, Servants, Villagers (101)— Beretos writes *namō, mâsiō, ecivi, mēsigō-to*. 'Upper servant' is my attempt to indicate that the *mâsiō* were higher in class yet grouped with the servants.

different-tongued (102)— the Moȟnaru, the natives of Sarnáe, east of the Gaumê. At the time of *Babblers* Munkhâsh had not conquered all of the southwest.

18 • Sulādeca • Return

atheism (109)— *bisnūmias* 'godlessness', atheism, or rebellion against Iáinos. Atheism had very different connotations for the Cuzeians. Cuzei was the most advanced nation among humans, and the source of its power was believed to be its belief in Iáinos, which moreover was imparted by the iliū. In the *Count of Years*, the middle portion of Cēradānar was lost by its Cuzeian lords because of its *bisnūmias*.

19 • Munxenu • Into Munkhâsh

grayish skin (115)— Terrestrial humans have two types of melanin, one dark brown, one orangeish. Almean humans have a third type, cyanomelanin, bluish in color. The iliū have only this type, which is why their skin is blue. The Munkhâshi, Moňnaru, and Metailō have a fair amount of cyanomelanin and thus have an unearthly brownish-gray color.

20 • Nokhdak

free of markets (120)— The Munkhâshi had a command economy: individual estates specialized in one good or another, which are distributed in a wide area. Within an estate, individuals might be given a specialization by the elders.

21 • Ganacom

Ganacom— It's clear from Beretos' account that Munkhâshi wandered Cēradānar at least as far as Araunicoros, as traders. Most would have passed through Berac's barony, which is how Tentesinas learned some of their language. Evidently some were spies, or reported back to their leaders, thus the canny attempt to use a Resident to undermine the keep from within.

22 • Nūmiū cazinorō • Caḋinorian gods

gods (128)— The gods of the mountains are those of the middle Cayenas, the future Caḋinas, suggesting that the pattern of settlement was from the west. Missing are Caloteion (the Sun), Fidora (night), Oronteion (wisdom), Escis (art), Boḋnehais (war), and Agireis (the sea). Agireis was (for obvious reasons) a northern deity, and probably Fidora as well. Boḋnehais and Escis were later creations. How Caloteion and Oronteion got lost is unknown.

offered to make devotions (131)— As was regularly done in the states along the Cayenas, despite Cuzeian discouragement. The practice died out by the 800s, when Cuzei was no longer perceived as powerful.

Kinds (132)— *landāuē*, from *lanê* 'think'. The 'farther elcari' are better known under the Verdurian name *múrtanî*. The *pinset* are a shy, primitive anthropoid race, Verdurain *icëlanî*.

23 • Bardāu

254 · IN THE LAND OF BABBLERS

speaker between lords (137)— Beretos is making an interpretive translation of *sāemissas*, literally 'between-speaker'. This is his own title, but for non-Cuzeian states the title *esûsêras* 'Resident' was preferred.

no trader (139)— Beretos would rather be a *mēsigo* (peasant) than a trader.

find some elcari (140)— Cuzeians could do their own metallurgy, but mining was generally done by the elcari, who roamed the mountains finding ores and gems, and trading with humans.

24 • Ecūrita • Accusation

put him on the Council (148)— The pietists could find precedents for placing the son of a Lord on the Council, but only in far earlier times when the Council was broader-based and less powerful.

King's Men have not the right (150)— the *Esocadi* dynasty (-65 to 327) was the height of the Council's power— the word means 'regents', as the founder Nalerio was regent for Cueporio, the last descendant of Calēsias. Even in the period of their strength they allowed the Lords great sovereignty, and by Beretos' time they were figureheads. In later times the kings asserted greater power over the Lords.

25 • Bri Ganacomex • With Ganacom

building an empire (153)— This has a very specific meaning in Cuzeian political theory: ruling non-Cuzeians. Cuzei was a *narras*, a kingdom, precisely because it claimed rulership over all Cuzeians. Of course it required only token service from Dācuas and Nayas.

sea-swimmers (155)— representing *tutujno* 'paddlers', the Munkhâshi term for the iliū.

26 • Faliles

Oluon's value (159)— Oluon must have been charming, and there is no hint that he forced himself on anyone. But he must have left a string of angry or creeped-out women in his wake.

27 • Duntrâcanavas • Deliberation

Staff and Belt (166)— symbolizing the duchies of Eleisa and Tevarē which united to form Cuzei. The Cloth of Cuzei was a tapestry depicting the reception of Lerīmanio by the iliū, both precious and holy as it was a gift from the iliū.

Inibē's speech (169)— These copies are lost today. We do have a letter from the pietists concerning Beretos and Zeilisio; see the *Book of Cuzei*.

28 • Oluon Falile-to • Oluon and Faliles

bride-price (176)— as we saw in chapter 4, the custom in Cuzei was a dowry paid by the bride's family. In a little-populated area like the mountains, cultures are more likely to reward fertility, thus paying bride-price instead.

29 • Fabēias Ganacomex • Ganacom's Proposal

30 • *Abrolur* • *Prison*

On Earth too, prison in premodern countries was not always miserable for those who could pay for comforts.

31 • *Exdrayêneca* • *Raid*

parcel of books (190)— I'd grab my Flash drives, wouldn't you? ...In any case, it seems likely that we wouldn't have *Babblers* if Beretos had lost his notes.

32 • *Bri Acūritārex* • *Before the Council*

The Ruler of the Council *Enacadas Acūritārex* was elected by the Council; at this time he was arguably the real ruler of the country.

33 • *Exbuîas* • *Battle*

pages and pages (201)— The military manuals of Beretos' day may have been dry precisely because their writers had little experience in battle. The great classics of strategy were written after 440.

34 • *Dralādeca* • *Consequences*

ruse (208)— Ganacom not only creates an alibi, but removes one more warrior from the battle.

35 • *Gintūro*

King's Reader (214)— the result of an earlier holiness campaign, this official had to approve all plays for performance in Eleisa. Yes, there's an obvious loophole: really salacious material would be seen in Vionosindas.

36 • *Fon-atcê-siumē*

Asicondār (223)— The iliū live on almost the entire continental shelf, avoiding only the vicinity of *amnigo* empires. They maintain land enclaves mostly to create crafts and tools; Lerīmanio met the iliū at Atellār Namoē near Cēradānar. Asicondār is about 4000 km to the southeast.

37 • *Mizidomas* • *Decision*

Caumelīlle (229)— The Cuêzi diminutive was an infixed -*īll*-; note also *Beretīllos* in chapter 30.

38 • *Rêsāu* • *End*

wife (235)— She must have succeeded, as we have a reference in a later document to Beretos' family.

Printed in Dunstable, United Kingdom